TRIUMPH OF THE SUPERBUG AND THE RISE OF THE GOLDEN ERA

Triumph of the Superbug and the Rise of the Golden Era

Sonja H. Lüsch

Columbus, Ohio

Triumph of the Superbug and the Rise of the Golden Era

Published by Gatekeeper Press
2167 Stringtown Rd, Suite 109
Columbus, OH 43123-2989
www.GatekeeperPress.com

Library of Congress Control Number: 2022937255

ISBN (paperback): 9781737491514
eISBN: 9781737491507

Table of Contents

This is a book of fiction and the author is not a medical doctor, therapist or herbalist and makes no guarantees as to the efficacy of the remedies mentioned in the book. All statements of advice listed in the book pertaining to medical advice, mental therapy, herbal remedies and all other advice listed are not a substitute for medical care and are not intended to diagnose, treat, cure or prevent any condition or disease. The reader should consult with a physician or healthcare specialist for personalized medical care.

All suggestions listed in the book pertaining to political systems, banking and business practices, monetary system, warfare, matters of faith and all other practices executed in everyday society are all fictional and the author makes no claims any of them will work. Any view or opinions mentioned in the book are not intended to malign any religion, ethnic group, club, organization, company, individual or anyone or anything.

To Rex and Analisa

Your Strength Comes from Within

Practice Thinking with Your Heart

The Art of Listening Requires Two Ears

PART ONE

—————

THE COLLAPSE

CHAPTER 1

She had just turned thirteen years old and Linnéa slowly walked on the sunlit path in the forest looking for mushrooms. She was a cute, petite girl with light brown hair and a slim figure. The silence in the pine forest was soothing and only a few birds could be heard. The August sun felt like nourishment on her skin and she was in no hurry. The boletes and chanterelles were easy mushrooms to recognize and safe to eat and she avoided all other mushrooms. She also picked the new shoots from the white pine trees. They made good additions to her diet of mostly freeze-dried food and she enjoyed chewing on the tips and also collected some for her tea. When she had filled her basket with mushrooms and pine shoots she turned around and slowly wandered back to her parents' hunting cabin where she lived alone with her cat Kitty. She alone had survived the superbug.

A whole year had passed since she moved into the cabin and what a year it had been. Her family had succumbed to the superbug that had mutated and gained immunity to every drug the doctors used in a desperate attempt to stop the killing spree. Nothing worked. Half the population had died from the bug, but when the electric grid went down in most of the states shortly thereafter, many more died from lack of food, medicine and violence by gangs that quickly formed in the cities. Eventually, the gangs spread to the suburbs. No one knew for sure how many Americans were alive. It was also unknown why the power system failed. Some people hinted it was an act of terrorists, but most likely there was no one alive to maintain the power grid. The few people who had survived fled to the countryside. Society had ceased to exist and there was no government or police force.

Even though Linnéa was still a child, she had a good understanding of the disaster that had ended society in 2035 and her parents had not kept any information from her. On the contrary, they had deliberately informed her and her brother Karl, who was four years older, what may happen to all of them and they had also prepared her and Karl with endless lessons on how to survive in the event she or her brother would be lucky enough to become immune to the killer bug. Only she, Linnéa, had survived and was immune to the superbug. As a family, they had worked out a survival plan and decided that their hunting cabin in Inland Pacific Northwest was the safest place to live if they could reach it without being ambushed along the road. The cabin was well stocked with food and firewood and had a manual pump supplying fresh water. Its location in the forest a mile away from a small country road made it invisible. During this year that she had lived alone in the cabin, no one had found it and she felt rather safe. She always carried her father's Dirty Harry six-shooter in a bag over her shoulder hoping she would never have to use it to kill another human being, but she would shoot a bear or cougar if her life depended on it. Her father had taught her how to control it by using both hands to stabilize the weapon. It was heavy, but she could manage it.

Linnéa had adapted rather well to her solitary life. Even though she was only thirteen years old, the atrocities she had been forced to live through had matured her. The paralyzing torment she had felt when all the members of her family were gone was slowly becoming easier to live with and even though she would never get over her grief fully, she was able to function and her daily routine kept her sanity under control.

She was alone, but not lonely. Kitty, her orange male cat, was good company and two deer, Minnie and Ears, were always around the cabin and she often talked to them. Minnie had a split ear and a scar on her neck, reminders of a close encounter with a cougar. Ears had short ears and when she focused them forward, they resembled two cups. Linnéa's father had taught her how to shoot a deer and she had watched him butcher it, but she hoped she would never have to kill a deer and go through the gruesome details of cutting it up. She had freeze dried foods for several years and the forest around her supplied mushrooms, edible weeds such as dandelion, plantain, lamb's quarters and other plants she sun-dried. Her mother had been a dedicated gardener and herbalist and had taught her what plants to use for food and medicinal use. Linnéa loved plants and her mother had chosen to name her children in honor of the Swedish botanist Karl von Linné and she named her son Karl and her daughter Linnéa. The cabin was surrounded with forest, but there was a small clearing around the cabin with enough sunlight to support a small vegetable garden. A wire fence kept the deer out.

The winters were hard in the northwest corner of Montana and Linnéa had spent one winter already in the cabin. It was a log cabin and quite cozy with two small bedrooms and a large kitchen. A cast iron cookstove supplied heat for the whole cabin. There was enough firewood to last two years and it was well protected with tarps. During warm weather, she cooked her meals using a butane camping stove and her supply of fifty canisters of butane would last her several years. When it was unbearably cold, she stayed indoors and only ventured outside to use the outhouse. How she dreaded going there and she placed sheets of newspaper on the wooden seat to avoid the freezing wood. Her supply of toilet paper was low, so in the summer she used the leaves of mullein instead. They grew all over the forest and she always picked the leaves when she found a plant. The only snow shoveling she felt was necessary was a path to the outhouse and one to the woodpile. Most of her time during the winter was spent keeping the fire alive, cooking and reading. Her parents had been avid readers, so the cabin had a bookcase filled with books she had not read. Candle light was not bright enough for reading, so she could only read during daylight hours and in the evening, there was not much to do but play with Kitty and then go to bed. Besides, she had to ration her use of candles as she did not have an oversupply of them.

******

Linnéa sat outside the cabin enjoying the September sun. She was thinking of the trip she had made from her parents' home outside Spokane, Washington to the cabin in Montana. The distance was about one hundred and seventy miles and she had managed to make the trip in four and a half days riding her bicycle. She did not know how to drive a car and all gas stations were closed anyway. Many people had switched to electric cars, but standard gas engine cars were still around and her parents had used a standard car. With no driving skills, the only choice she had was to use her bicycle. It was relatively new and had several gears, a great help for the long uphill grades she would have to struggle with.

In the fall of 2033 both her parents succumbed to the virus, which started as a severe flu and developed into pneumonia that led to an inflammatory response. She and Karl were not affected by the superbug when their parents died and continued living in their home. It was a struggle for both of them and very dangerous. They had a small supply of canned and freeze-dried foods, but when their tap water stopped, bottled water had to be bartered for silver coins. Karl was exposed to danger from both the superbug and criminals during these outings. Then, in July of 2035, Karl caught the superbug and died shortly thereafter. Linnéa was numb with grief. She thought she would suffocate when she covered his young body with a sheet. Her parents had been properly buried, but Karl died in his bed and there was no one alive she knew of in the area that she could ask for help with Karl's burial. She and Karl had been very close and Karl had been so protective of her. One incident she would never forget was when Karl was only twelve years old and stood up to the neighborhood bully in defense of her. He had placed himself in front of Linnéa and said in a stern voice "you touch her and I'll beat you up". One look at Karl's determined face was enough and the bully mumbled "I was only kidding" and took off as fast as he could. Linnéa was her parents' favorite and still Karl never showed envy of any kind, always flashing his winning smile of generosity. Now he was dead at the young age of sixteen.

Linnéa knew she had no choice but to leave and hope she would survive the trip to the cabin. She packed as much as would fit into three bags that she hung over the back of her bike carefully balancing the weight and strapped them down with Karl's belt. A fourth carrier bag for Kitty was also strapped down so she had two bags on each side of the bike. She placed a cardboard box inside Kitty's bag so he would be able to lie down. A bag of trail mix, a small bag of dried cat food and a few bottles of water would sustain them during the trip. The last thing she packed was fifty silver dollars and ten half-ounce gold coins. Her parents had bought these coins years ago to use for bartering if times turned bad and Karl had used some of the coins in exchange for food. She was grateful to have them and would use them wisely. She wondered if she would ever see her home again, but the thought of seeing her beloved brother's body in a decomposed state would be more than she could endure.

Linnéa knew she had to make the trip during the safety of darkness as travelers often were killed in ambushes on the highways and even country roads were unsafe. As soon as dusk arrived, she said goodbye for the last time to Karl and patted his covered body, grabbed Kitty and without mercy jammed him inside his travel bag, tied it closed and left. She was dressed in dark clothes to be as invisible as possible. For defense, she had a claw hammer strapped to the handlebar with a bungee cord. There was just enough moonlight to enable her to see the road and she did not turn on her headlamp. She would travel east, cross the Idaho Panhandle and then continue to Montana, where the cabin was. No one was out when she left and she did not know whether anyone was alive or if the few survivors in the neighborhood hid in their houses. There was no light in any of the houses. She pedaled all night long with only a few short breaks to rest. The road was familiar and she had traveled to the cabin many times with her parents using the same route. There were many long arduous hills where she had trouble biking much faster than walking speed. She felt driven and reminded herself that she had to cover as much ground as possible each night. No one was on the road. She was in rather good physical shape, but her legs were almost numb from the hard work and she had trouble controlling her fears. Panic attacks plagued her, so she tried to give herself pep talks. No other biker was on the road, but twice she heard car engines in the distance and quickly pulled off the road and hid behind the trees. Kitty had been meowing at first, but soon became quiet as she talked to him in a low voice and reassured him, she was right there. The only incident she encountered the first night was a dead man lying on the road. He had apparently been walking on the road and died there. She only saw him the last minute and stopped a distance away not knowing if it was a trap or not. With her hammer in hand, she slowly approached him and put her headlamp on. She realized he was dead and sighed with relief it was not an ambush.

When the sun came up, she walked the bike into the forest and found a tree with low branches that would protect her and the bike from sight. With Kitty still in his basket, she lay down totally exhausted and fell asleep until the afternoon. She had no appetite, but forced herself to eat a handful of trail mix. Kitty refused both food and water, so she just left him alone. Finally, the sun set and it turned dark and she continued her journey.

She reached the town of Sandpoint very early the next morning and was able to bicycle through the town without anyone stopping her. There were a few people here and there and a couple of cars on the road, but no one paid any attention to her and she pedaled through the town as fast as she could being careful not to look at anyone or draw attention to herself. She trembled with fear that someone would jump her and steal her bike. It was almost daylight and she nervously looked around for a wooded area where she could hide until the next night. A mile outside town, she found a perfect place a distance away from the road and pulled the bike under the low hanging branches of a huge fir tree and crawled in. The branches surrounded her and she was in a little cave. She was hyper ventilating and felt dehydrated and nauseous. Her legs ached and she had occasional leg cramps that she had to shake off to make them stop. Slowly she leaned her back against the trunk of the tree and said a quiet thank you to whoever was listening up there that she had survived her second night on the road. For several hours she rested without moving and tried to breathe slowly. Even though she had not eaten all night, she was not hungry. She forced herself to swallow a few handfuls of her trail mix and washed it down with water. Kitty was alive, but quiet, and she did not dare to open his basket. If he would escape, she would never be able to catch him again. She put water on a tablespoon and pushed the spoon through a small gap in the lid and Kitty did accept several spoons of water, but no cat food.

A feeling of security came over her as she sat silently under the tree and she dozed off for a few hours. She could not see the road from her hiding place and she heard no car from the road all day. It was as if she was alone in the world. Very few people had been walking around in Sandpoint and she understood that the aftermath of both the superbug and the loss of electricity had made survival extremely difficult for most people. The lack of prescription drugs and medical doctors had taken thousands of lives. The two years that she and Karl had lived alone in her parents' home had been hard and filled with anxiety. No services were available and they had used a small butane camping stove for cooking. By the time Karl died, their supply of food was almost gone. Karl caught the superbug when he was bartering with a food vendor a few blocks from their house. They both understood it was risky to be face to face with another person, but they were desperate to find more food, especially canned food.

Their little suburb had not been taken over by gangs yet, but they knew it was only a matter of time until the gangs in Spokane would investigate their area in search of food and women to rape. They had a twelve-gauge shotgun loaded with 00 buckshot for defense and Karl knew how to use the gun. All the doors were reinforced with door jammers so they did not feel the need to be on guard duty. Neither of them ever had a restful sleep, but tossed and turned most of the night.

As soon as nighttime returned, Linnéa took off ignoring the soreness in her legs. She was able to get through the town of Clark Fork, Idaho without seeing anyone and the rest of the trip was hard work with many long uphill grades. Her eyes had adjusted to the dark and she did not wear her head lamp. Several times as she pedaled along, she was hit by panic attacks and felt the adrenalin pumping. Her heart was banging in her chest. She managed to calm herself and continued on. Twice she heard a vehicle in the distance and had just enough time to pull off the road and hide behind a few bushes. Both times the vehicle passed and no one saw her. There were no ambushes on the road and Linnéa gave a prayer of thanks for escaping this dangerous threat.

She spent one more day hiding under a tree and then, finally, started her last night of biking. All was fine until she heard two gunshots. They were loud and she realized that whoever fired them was not too far ahead of her on the road. She quickly jumped off her bike and dragged it off the road and into the trees. Luckily, there were trees close to the road. She stood there in the dark almost numb with fear and just waited for whatever would happen next. Then she heard a car engine and driving past her towards Sandpoint was an old pickup with two men in the front. The moon was up and she clearly saw two men and what appeared to be a motorcycle in the back of the pickup. Everything fell silent and after half an hour she told herself she must take the chance and get back on the road.

She started pedaling and within five minutes she saw a grisly scene. An elderly couple lay dead on the highway with bullet wounds on their heads. They were obviously the victims of the two men on the motorcycle. Several very large stones had been placed across the road and the elderly couple had had no choice but to stop. The two men had dragged them out of the pickup and shot them and then stolen their vehicle. Even though Linnéa was trembling with fear she forced herself to continue biking, barely slowing down all night. Midday, the next day, she finally arrived at the trail leading to the cabin. One more mile and there it was, her sanctuary. She got off her bike with shaking legs and found the key. Her fingers trembled as she opened the door. To her relief, everything was in order and no one had broken into the cabin. She grabbed Kitty's bag and walked inside closing the door behind her. Now she could finally open up Kitty's bag and let him out. Kitty was meowing and hungry. He had refused to eat and had only had a few spoons of water. Remarkably, his cardboard box was dry and not soiled. He eagerly jumped out of his box and started sniffing on everything. This was not his first visit to the cabin and he remembered it. Linnéa felt totally exhausted. Her body ached and she had never been so tired in her whole life. She took the bags off the bike and brought them inside in case it would rain and then locked the door. After she had fed Kitty and showed him his litter box that was still in the wash room, she ate the rest of the trail mix and washed it down with a cup of tea and collapsed in bed. She slept until early evening.

When she woke up, she checked the inventory of the cabin and was relieved to find that the food supply was huge with freeze dried foods, lots of canned food and various dried fruits and vegetables. There was a small supply of cat food also, but Kitty was a good hunter and there was no shortage of mice around the cabin. During the winter, she would share her rations with him. Her father had installed a manual old-fashioned water pump outside the cabin and the supply of water was more than adequate.

CHAPTER 2

It was November 2036 and winter had just arrived. Linnéa was shoveling away the first snow of the season when she sensed a presence. She looked up and saw a man standing a distance away staring at her. He was in his early twenties, sand colored hair and quite handsome looking. She was at first happy to see a live person again, but as she walked over to greet him, she stopped and froze when she saw his cold, blue eyes. They were mean and matched his voice.

"Go inside the cabin!" he ordered Linnéa and she knew there was nothing she could do. Her pistol was hidden in the cabin out of reach. She could not run away; there was nowhere to go and it was already too cold to survive the night outside without a blanket. Shaking with fear she stumbled into the cabin with the man right behind her and when he locked the cabin door, she knew she was in deep trouble. He sized her up and slowly walked over to her.

"Don't shake, you'll make it worse," he said. His voice was unyielding and hard. "Do as I say and don't fight."

Then he grabbed her with hard hands and threw her on her bed, ripped her clothes off and violated her. He pinned her down with his left arm across her chest and Linnéa was gasping for air. She felt she was suffocating and the violence of the act was so overwhelming that she was sure she would not survive. The rape was terribly painful and she was totally unprepared for the cruelty of the act.

"You're suffocating me," she finally managed to whisper. He did not react at first, but after a few seconds he did remove his arm and finally climbed off her. She was paralyzed with fear, hyperventilating and could not move. He violated her several more times until he finally allowed her to leave the bed. Her heart was racing and she felt throbbing pain in her lower body. Somehow, she was able to put on her clothes with trembling hands.

"Make something to eat," he demanded and Linnéa struggled to prepare a package of freeze-dried beef stew and served him.

"You're the only one alive within miles of here," he said after he had finished his meal. "I've been walking for days without seeing anyone and I just found your cabin by accident. I wasn't aware you were here."

"What's your name and where do you come from?" Linnéa whispered, still too shocked to be able to talk in a normal voice.

"I just walked out of prison in Spokane. The electric grid went down and all the doors unlocked. You can call me Jake. "

"Where are you headed?"

"Up north to British Columbia, Canada. More people survived up there."

"What did you do to land you in jail?" Linnéa asked.

"I killed two people. They got what they deserved," Jake replied without remorse in his voice.

Jake got up from the table and reached inside his backpack. He had a set of handcuffs in his hand and directed Linnéa to sit on a chair next to the cookstove. He handcuffed her left ankle to the stove and shoved her night potty over with his foot.

"In case you have to go," he said and lay down on her bed and fell asleep.

As Linnéa sat chained to the stove, her battered body aching, she aged ten years that night. She dreaded what would happen in the morning when he woke up. There was blood in her underwear and she was also terribly hungry and thirsty.

Over the next four days Jake assaulted her every day and at night he handcuffed her to the stove. Each time she was violated she went through the same terror. It was a paralyzing fear so overwhelming that she wished herself dead. She hated him and wanted to kill him. She learned to sleep a couple of hours while being handcuffed, but her fear of him was so immense that she was awake most of the time. During the day she was not handcuffed, but Jake had his eye on her the whole time and escape was impossible.

On the fifth day, Linnéa had to get her father's toolbox out to fix the handle of the manual pump outside the cabin. It had frozen into place and had to be tapped with the hammer so she could raise the handle. The toolbox was left next to the stove and neither of them noticed it. Jake was sleeping on her bed and Linnéa spotted the toolbox. She was trying to reach the hammer, but was an inch short. Using all her willpower she stretched her arm as much as she could and was able to grab on to the hammer and pull it towards her. During the cold nights of winter, Linnéa pulled her bed close to the stove to stay warm and she saw that she was within reach to deliver a fatal blow with the hammer to his head. One hard strike would for sure crack his skull. She lifted her right arm to gain momentum to strike, when she heard from within *NO*. It was that low, whispering voice again, but this time the voice was louder and non-yielding. She often heard it and it was always so low she could barely detect it, but it commanded attention and she had learned to respect it. Then she heard the other voice from within saying *kill the bastard, it's your only chance*. The whispering voice came back saying *it's the wrong choice*. She slowly lowered the hammer and sat down again on her chair. She had made her choice.

Linnéa's parents had been atheists and spiritual beliefs were never discussed, actually they were frowned upon and referred to as voodoo. Linnéa had read several books about reincarnation and even though she was by no means interested in traditional religions, she felt drawn towards mysticism and the possibility that the soul survives death. From within, she often heard the loud voice and the very low voice giving her conflicting advice. The loud voice made sense and she usually agreed with its message, but the low, whispering voice stirred something deep within her and she could not resist it. She just knew it came from goodness showing her the right choices. Her discovery of spiritual things and mysticism was accidental and walking home from school one day, she had walked past someone's garage sale and on one of the tables was a stack of very old books. They were low priced and as she picked up a few of them and saw their titles, she realized they were all dealing with reincarnation and the afterlife. She bought six of them and kept them hidden in the back of her bookcase. She was only eleven years old at the time, but old enough to comprehend the message of the books. Some of the information was too complicated and she had no idea what it meant. Linnéa had an open mind and was curious and found the books fascinating. She did not tell her parents or Karl that she had them and the message they gave touched her soul. She revered the books and had read them several times and each time the meaning became more understandable.

Jake woke up early and walked towards the door to relieve himself outside. As he walked past her, he spotted the hammer in her hand and flinched. He looked at her with surprise and took the hammer out of her hand.

"Why didn't you do it?" he asked. His voice was low and confused.

"You have a soul," she managed to whisper after a minute.

Jake looked at her bewildered and perhaps it was the first time in his life he had encountered true kindness. He stared at her several minutes, maybe thinking about the ordeal he had put her through and how she still had chosen to spare his life. After breakfast, Jake packed his bag, walked to the door and then stopped. He turned around, looked straight into her eyes and said -

"Forgive me, if you can."

Linnéa nodded, unable to speak from all the emotions shaking her inside, but she could see Jake accepted her nod as an act of forgiveness. He walked out and disappeared. She never saw him or heard of him again. What Linnéa did not know was that her gracious act of forgiveness as well as sparing his life had astonished Jake so much that for the first time in his life, he saw himself with an outsider's eye and he did not like what he saw. When he was out of sight of the cabin, he sat down to reflect on what had happened. He started to cry uncontrollably and all the cruelties he had endured most of his life were flashing in front of his eyes, but he also saw all the brutal acts he himself had mercilessly inflicted upon so many innocent people. After he stopped crying, he felt emotionally drained. Slowly he dragged himself up and found his bicycle that was hidden not too far from the road and headed north. His goal was to find an empty house with some food left and stay there until the spring and then continue by bike to Vancouver. What he did not know was that his trip would be full of hardships with starvation, two ambushes when he was beaten severely and robbed of all his belongings except the bike and several snow storms that almost killed him. By the time he finally arrived in Vancouver, he was so weak that he caught a severe flu that turned into pneumonia and he died shortly afterwards.

Several weeks went by and slowly Linnéa's tormented body healed. Emotionally she felt dead. The joy of being alive that had helped her through the death of her family was gone. She felt a vacuum inside. The daily chores took her time and the snow was now a foot deep outside, so she spent most days inside reading with Kitty on her lap. His purring was comforting.

January and February went by and she felt sick. She had always been healthy and was not used to feeling ill. This strange feeling of nausea that plagued her, what was it? Suddenly she knew and the frightening truth hit her hard. She was pregnant.

"No, no, no," she screamed out loud. "I'm only thirteen, I'm a kid, I'm not ready." She sank down on the floor and cried, her fists banging on her belly. Her cycle had recently started so she knew the possibility of becoming pregnant was real.

"I hate you," she screamed to her belly. "Go away, I don't want you."

Emotionally empty, she sat on the floor a long time refusing to accept the idea that a baby was on the way. Her only thought was how to get it out. Should she bang it with a stone? She knew she must kill it. She dragged herself to her bed and lay there staring at the ceiling for hours.

The following weeks she was tormented by thoughts how to kill the baby, but every time she picked up a stone to slam against her belly she stopped. She could not find the strength from within to go through with the killing.

Spring arrived and Linnéa was due in August. Slowly she had accepted that she was going to give birth, but felt no joy and the delivery of the baby scared her to death. The summer was spent sewing baby clothes from towels and cutting up sheets to be used as cloth diapers. She was quite handy and there was a small supply of sewing equipment in the cabin. As she noticed her belly growing, she hated it. Even the first kick by the baby was unwelcome and did not mellow her heart.

The dreaded month of August had arrived and Linnéa was now fourteen years old, a petite girl facing adult responsibilities. Everything was ready for the birth and she had made a baby bed from a cardboard box. She did not know anything about giving birth and she struggled to keep her fears under control. Her belly was not overly big, but she knew that the forthcoming labor and getting the baby out would test her endurance to the limit. She had never endured pain in her young life.

A few days later Linnéa's water broke. Not knowing what it meant, she could only guess it had something to do with the arrival of the baby and mild contractions tormented her all day. She lay on top of her bed with no relief from the pain that had now become more and more intense. The bed was covered with a sheet and underneath she had a cut-up plastic trash bag to make cleanup easier. When nighttime arrived, she understood the baby would probably be born during the night. The contractions were unbearable, sweat was pouring from her forehead and she was squeezing a towel in each hand. Fear was welling over her in waves. She was panting and felt movement of something down below. Her instinct told her to push and she felt something between her legs. In a desperate wish to get it over with, she pushed with all her strength and the last of the baby's body came out. It was early morning and she was now a mother. Never had she experienced such intense physical pain. She slowly raised herself up on her elbow and saw the baby for the first time. It was a boy, waving his little hands around and trying to draw his first breath. Still shaking from the pain, she sat up and gently wrapped a towel around him and pulled him to her chest. She wiped his mouth with a tissue and he was able to draw his first breath. The navel cord was dangling and she cut it with the boiled scissors she had prepared and put gauze around the stump. He was small, but everything appeared normal. His name would be Karl after her brother.

Linnéa lay on the bed with Karl next to her until she felt the afterbirth come out. She had a rough idea what it was. Karl had already nursed a few minutes and when the afterbirth was out, Linnéa managed to get out of bed and wash Karl, diaper him and put his first clothes on. She felt weak and unsure of herself and hoped she would not pass out. She was too tired to cook and just ate a few handfuls of nuts. Gently she put Karl in his cardboard box and when he was asleep, she washed herself and removed the bloody sheet from her bed. Luckily, the plastic cover had protected her bed sheets and no washing was necessary. Exhaustion came over her and she slowly put on a clean pajama, lined her underwear with a towel to catch the blood and lay down in her bed and fell asleep. She slept deeply until early afternoon when Karl woke her up with an ear-splitting sound. He nursed eagerly and she noticed she had milk in both breasts. It was actually colostrum, but Linnéa did not know that. She stayed in bed for three days and only got up briefly to diaper Karl and make a quick freeze-dried meal for herself. On the fourth day she had regained some strength and stayed up most of the day. She was starving and enjoyed a large dinner with a glass of powder milk. Her food supply was not dangerously low, but she knew she had to be careful and not waste anything.

The following weeks were spent learning to be a mother. Linnéa felt no love for Karl and only cared for him as a duty. She could not erase Jake and the repeated assaults from her mind and Karl was the result of the worst cruelties she had ever experienced. When she looked at him, she just saw Jake.

******

Linnéa sat outside the cabin holding Karl. He had just finished nursing and looked up at her intently with his blue eyes. Four weeks had passed since she gave birth and she felt stronger and more content now. She looked at him and then she heard the low voice again *the child is innocent*. The message totally startled her. She felt confused. Was the voice right and she wrong? She had blamed all her suffering on Karl. But Karl had not hurt her, Jake had. Her thoughts were tumbling around in her head. Then she looked down at Karl and noticed how beautiful he was. He had refined features and his little body was well proportioned. She met his gazing eyes and suddenly felt an enormous love for him. He was hers, half of her was in him. She felt the tears coming and let it happen, held him tight and rocked him slowly back and forth. She understood in that moment she was in the process of healing emotionally. It was time to go forward. She would never forget the horror of being violated, but she had to be strong now for Karl. He needed her. Karl would heal her tormented soul.

Kitty was gone. He had taken off on his usual morning hunting trip and never came back. Linnéa kept hoping for weeks he would find his way back, but she finally had to accept the grim truth he had been killed by a predator, probably a coyote. There was barely any wildlife left in the area and both cougars and bears had been hunted almost to extinction by the local hunters. Everyone was looking for meat and the deer and elk population was decimated. Turkeys were nowhere to be seen. Coyotes were still around mostly because they were not hunted for food.

Everywhere Linnéa went she brought Karl along. She carried him in a sling across her chest. Fall had arrived and she was busy sewing winter clothes for him. After Jake left, no one had stopped by at the cabin and she was grateful for that. Her food supply was still adequate, but she was running low on several items and also detergent. Endless washing of Karl's diapers had wiped out half her supply. All she could do was hoping that one of these days society would return to normal and enough people would be alive to restart civilization.

Linnéa was busy picking vegetables in her garden and noticed she had forgotten her basket in the kitchen. Karl was lying in his cardboard box next to the garden and she walked back into the cabin to fetch her basket. When she came out again, she jumped with terror as she saw a coyote with his head inside Karl's cardboard box sniffing at him. She let out a blood-curdling scream so intense that the coyote almost jumped out of his skin and took off like a rocket. She gently picked up Karl and at that moment she felt a love for him that was more intense than any feelings she had ever experienced before.

The winter was hard and long. It seemed every winter was nastier than the previous one and the temperature often fell to fifteen degrees below zero overnight. To stretch her firewood supply, she had collected large twigs and fallen small trees she had cut into firewood. The saw was faster for cutting up logs than her axe and she preferred it. Caring for Karl and doing the chores kept her occupied all winter. Karl was now six months old and becoming more aware of his surroundings. He was able to drag himself across the floor, but he had not started to crawl yet. His vocabulary was restricted to gurgling sounds and "ba-ba". Linnéa had never been around small children and babies, so she was learning from Karl every day. She was fascinated by his development. So far, he had never been sick and she understood their isolation may have saved her from the misery of dealing with a sick child. She worried if he was immune to the superbug, but calmed herself by thinking that both she and Jake were survivors and most likely Karl had inherited their strong immune systems. She was still nursing him, but had introduced little pieces of solid food that he was able to digest with ease.

CHAPTER 3

The spring sun was strong and the snow had melted. Linnéa was working in her garden with Karl safely parked in his cardboard box next to her. That was his playpen and she allowed him to play with her wooden kitchen tools. He loved to bang with the wooden spoon on the floor. She had no toys for him and had to create playthings from the items she had around the house. A noise caught her attention and when she looked up, she saw a man and a woman in their thirties approaching her waving a white flag.

"Don't shoot, we're friends," they shouted.

Linnéa quickly got up and waited for them to come closer. She had her gun in her hand just to be sure. Ever since her encounter with Jake she never hid the gun anymore and it was usually lying next to the granny stove. She always carried it when she left the cabin.

"We're searching for survivors," the man explained. "I'm Joseph Thorpe and this is my wife, Sarah. We've seen smoke coming from this area, but couldn't find your cabin until today. You're really well hidden."

"My name is Linnéa and this is my son Karl," Linnéa said in a low voice. She was afraid, unsure if it was a trap.

"Are you two alone here?"

"Yes."

"We're searching for anyone alive and there are more survivors hidden in the area than we first anticipated. People are too fearful to make contact with anyone. We're hoping to find everyone and start all over again, perhaps in Sandpoint, Idaho. Would you want to join us?"

"Yes, when would you be ready to leave?" Linnéa asked. Her fears subsided as she looked at Joseph and saw his kind eyes. He was pleasant looking with blondish hair and a short beard. His wife Sarah was cute with dark hair and a warm smile.

"In a few weeks. We're looking for skilled people to restart the power grid. There's nothing wrong with the local grid, but the people who managed it are all dead. The infrastructure is undamaged in the Sandpoint area, but the cities are hellholes. Many cities have been burned down and no one can live there because of the gangs. As long as they have food, they stay in the cities. No one knows yet how many people have died in the whole country and the only communication we have is by ham radio. Eventually we will know how many are dead, but we're guessing that half of the American population died from the superbug and when the electric grid failed, millions more died. We haven't heard if the bug spread to other countries or Europe, but it probably did," Joseph said. "I suggest you pack your belongings and we'll pick you up by car in about two weeks. We need a little time to prepare the empty houses in Sandpoint and stock them with food and basic items."

"These houses are empty and no one has claimed ownership, so we feel we have the right to take them over and move families from this area into those houses," Joseph continued. "We need a town with enough houses and undamaged infrastructure to accommodate several hundred people and Sandpoint was the closest town that met the requirements."

"I'll be ready for you in two weeks," Linnéa replied. She was grateful they had not asked about Karl's father and preferred not having to explain.

They said goodbye and left. Linnéa had to sit down on a stump and think about what they had said. Was it true? It probably was true as they had not tried to enter her cabin or take her food supply. There was not much for her to pack and she would just lock up the cabin and use it for weekends in the future, if life would ever return to normal and she would own a car.

A small car came to pick her and Karl up two weeks later, just as Joseph had said. There was a couple already in the car plus the driver. They introduced themselves as Mr. and Mrs. Bauer and the driver was their son. They were in their late forties. Even though they had a house not too far from her cabin they did not know Linnéa or her parents. They explained to her that they could not stay in their house as all their supplies had been used up and they felt the only chance they had for survival was to join the other people in Sandpoint and start over.

Linnéa locked up her cabin and felt mixed emotions. She had lived there almost three years and gone through hell, but also experienced the wonder of giving birth to another human being and grown to love this little baby of hers more than anything in the world. Soon she would be fifteen years old, but emotionally she was much older than her age.

The drive from Montana to Sandpoint was uneventful and Linnéa saw no people anywhere. It was as if the world was dead. Thankfully, the Bauers did not ask where Karl's father was.

They arrived at the town park in Sandpoint and Joseph and Sarah were there with a large group of people. Linnéa climbed out of the car and strapped on her backpack. She held Karl tight to her chest and waited anxiously for Joseph to give instructions. It was apparent he was the leader. Several more cars pulled in and then Joseph got up on a platform and started explaining.

"Welcome to all of you. You're the survivors of the valley between Sandpoint and Paradise, Montana. We couldn't reach anyone south of Paradise as the bridge over Clark Fork River was destroyed by explosives. Luckily the bridge in the town of Clark Fork, Idaho was still undamaged so we could reach Sandpoint. Very few people live in Sandpoint and most houses are empty. We'll move into these houses. There are no gangs in the town and you should be safe. The electricity is down for now, but we're fortunate to have found two engineers who are working on restoring power and that is the first step back to civilization."

"There are very few people living between Bonners Ferry and Coeur d'Alene north/south," Joseph continued. "East/west between Coeur d'Alene and Spokane the population is very sparse. We picked Sandpoint because there are fields here for growing crops and enough empty houses so all of you can live in your own house. No stores are open and gasoline is not available. We do have a few small tanks of gasoline for emergencies only and a few tanks of propane, but the amount is very limited. The dollar has lost all its value, so the only way of paying for goods is by bartering or working in the fields or for the community. Some vendors will accept silver coins as payment. No services of any kind are available. There is a doctor here among you, who has agreed to work for the community. His name is Dr. Schultz. No medicines are available, but the local hospital will open and we hope it will eventually function as normal. For parents with children, we'll try to organize babysitting services so the parents can work and pay for their living expenses. We have a better chance of surviving as a group rather than living apart and in the event that we must defend the town, we have no chance if we don't stick together. There are several trained soldiers among you who will advise us in case gangs show up here in town. As to news, we'll try to print some kind of newsletter and distribute it among you, but we haven't worked out the details yet on how to handle the printing of it."

Joseph looked over the people and continued -

"I understand you're all bewildered and worn out. Many of you haven't eaten for days. Life as you knew it is over, but if we work together, we'll eventually restore a lifestyle that is at least acceptable. I don't want to give you a pep talk and make believe we'll sail through this hardship and it will be a breeze. We'll go through gains and losses; work will have to be done manually and food may be scarce at times. Winters will be very difficult to live through as you must have noticed that each winter seems to be more severe than the previous one. "

"The houses will be offered depending on family size. Each house has been stocked with dried foods to last about a week. We found a warehouse with some foods left and distributed it evenly over the houses we chose to occupy. Some of the houses have a little propane left that can be used for cooking, but some of you will have no cooking facility and have to make do without cooking. If you want, you can make a gravel pit in your backyard and use a live fire for cooking. It works rather well. There is no heat in the houses, but spring is here and it's not that cold anymore overnight."

Linnéa looked around and noticed many people looking stressed and probably regretted leaving their hideouts. She had the same thought herself. Joseph's description of what was ahead sounded harsh, but she reminded herself that her supplies in the cabin would soon run out and Karl needed other children to play with. She braced herself for what Joseph would say next.

"Water for drinking will have to be fetched every day by each household. There are several wells in the area with manual pumps and we believe the supply is adequate for all of us as a start. For washing, we'll take lake water and fill cisterns every day and place them close to the houses you occupy. This water can be used for flushing toilets also. Anyone who wants to is allowed to build an outhouse in their backyard. One of our first tasks will be to grow crops, in particular wheat. There are several fields nearby that are suitable for wheat and we're working on finding seed."

"Whatever trash you have, put it in the dumpster next to the school and we'll take it to the landfill," Joseph added.

He finished his speech and asked if anyone had questions, but all were quiet and seemed to have accepted their fate. Some looked beaten. Joseph had a list of everyone's name and small groups of people were walked to their houses. Joseph and Sarah walked off with a group each and soon returned to show the next group of people their assigned houses.

Some of the people were taken by car to their neighborhood and Linnéa had to travel to her house by car. It was not far away and when she saw the house that had been chosen for her, she was pleasantly surprised. It was small, but well-kept and attractive. She felt relieved and eagerly stepped inside. There were three small bedrooms, two on the second floor and one on the main floor. The kitchen was small, but seemed modern and well equipped. A table and chairs were against the wall and she instantly fell in love with the house. All the furnishings were in place and she found sheets and towels in the closet. The house seemed relatively new and the carpets were in good shape. There were two bathrooms and a small basement for storage. Linnéa felt elated and noticed how clean everything was. She put Karl down on the kitchen floor and opened the pantry to see what was available to eat. Just as Joseph had promised, several rows of cans, dried foods such as cereal, flour, sugar and even some freeze-dried foods were neatly stacked in her pantry. Even six bottles of water were standing next to the cans. She checked the gas stove and, wow, the flame lit right up. She knew she had to be careful not to waste the propane. A strong feeling of gratitude came over her and she felt she would be able to start a new life with Karl in this beautiful little house.

She nursed Karl and put him to sleep on one of the beds. Her first chore would be to wean Karl from nursing, but she had no idea if milk of any kind was available. When she checked the closets, she found both men's and women's clothes, but too big for her. Perhaps she could barter and get something her own size.

******

As the summer passed, everyone worked very hard to prepare for the coming winter. One field of wheat had been sown and it was soon time to harvest the wheat by hand. No combine was available so cutting and threshing must be done manually. Linnéa had been assigned to work in the community kitchen and she did not mind it. Two women had volunteered to be babysitters and they looked after Karl and a few other babies for free. The small community kitchen was a temporary arrangement for people who did not know how to cook, but most people managed their own cooking and everybody had a little vegetable garden in the backyard. Joseph had found a supply of seeds in a hardware store and had distributed a small supply to each household. He was a master at digging up supplies. The food supply was very sparse and even though a team of men were constantly hunting, the wildlife population was almost nonexistent. One moose had been shot over the summer and shared with everyone. There was no livestock anywhere and the only milk available for the children was powder milk and it was in short supply. Some warehouses still had food left, but most of them were located in the cities and anyone entering a city took a big chance. A few underground tanks of gasoline had been found and the men were planning on using this gas for a full-size truck to empty a warehouse that had been located with lots of foods and equipment. Armed guards would accompany the truck. Joseph kept a few guns under lock and key to be used in emergencies. Linnéa was hoping they would succeed so she could get her share. She was always hungry and literally dreamed of food. Karl had finally been weaned from nursing, which had been a big demand on her body.

Linnéa had hired a teenage boy in the neighborhood to bring her both drinking water and lake water every day. His fee was three silver dollars for six months of work. It was well worth it as the weight of the water jugs was too much for Linnéa to deal with. This hardworking teenager used a hand truck to transport the water and had no trouble with the weight at all.

One day in late summer a young man on a bicycle came pedaling over to the community kitchen where Linnéa worked. He looked Scandinavian with dark blond hair.

"My name is Bjorn Nordin and I noticed you people have moved in here. I live a few miles north in Colburn. My mother has a goat, a doe, in full lactation that she is willing to sell for ten silver dollars. I know that's a lot of money, but there are very few goats alive and the doe gives a gallon of milk every day. Would you be interested in buying her?" he asked.

"Yes," Linnéa replied immediately. "How long has the doe been in milk?"

"She just had babies six weeks ago, so she'll be giving milk for another year at least," Bjorn replied. "If you don't know how to milk, I'll show you and I'll bring a few bales of hay to get you started. The doe will graze any field you bring her to, but you have to be careful and protect her from being stolen."

"Can I buy hay from you, enough for several months? I'll store it in my basement."

"Yes, when we bring her, we'll also bring ten bales of mixed grass and clover hay for you. It's last year's hay, but still good. That will be two more silver dollars. Do you have that much money?"

Linnéa assured him she had the money and told him her address.

"My brother Lars and I were lucky to find an antique horse-drawn sickle mower," Bjorn explained. "We also found a rusty old horse-drawn rake we refurbished so we could rake the hay into wind-rows, but we ran into trouble with baling the hay. We ended up having to invent a baler from a wooden box that we move from pile to pile in the field and we load and compress the hay manually. That's why the bales aren't very strong and pop easily. It's a lot of work," Bjorn said with a grin. He looked to be around eighteen, nineteen years old and was muscular from hard work. Linnéa liked his friendly smile.

They agreed he and his brother would deliver the goat and hay that same evening as soon as it turned dark. Everyone felt safer traveling in the dark even though the roads were almost always deserted and cars were seldom seen. Linnéa had a totally fenced in backyard so she knew the goat could not escape and the fencing also protected the doe from being seen. There was a small shed in her yard that could become shelter for the goat. To part with twelve of her silver dollars was a huge expense for Linnéa, but she needed milk for Karl and also for herself and any leftover milk could be bartered with the neighbors. She felt she had no choice but to buy the goat. Listening carefully to Bjorn's explanation about the hay, she realized the goat would have to graze as much as possible during the growing season so the hay would last over the winter.

Bjorn and his brother Lars delivered the goat and hay as promised and they pulled up in a run-down farm truck that labored hard and backfired. The goat and Lars were in the back of the truck and Bjorn was the driver. They had brought a wheelbarrow along and carefully loaded each hay bale in the wheelbarrow and placed them in a corner of her basement. When the hay was unloaded, they lifted the goat out of the truck and walked her into Linnéa's backyard. Bjorn gave her a quick lesson how to milk and tips how to clean her udder before milking. Since no refrigeration was available, they advised her to drink the milk soon after milking.

"Are you babysitting?" Lars asked when he spotted Karl in the backyard.

"He is my son," Linnéa said in a low voice.

Both Lars and Bjorn looked at her with disbelief.

"I was assaulted," Linnéa explained. She felt uneasy, unsure how to answer, so the truth was the only way she could respond.

"Oh God, I'm so sorry to hear that," Bjorn finally said when he had recovered from the surprise. His face showed true compassion. "If I could lay my hands on that bastard, I would hook him up to my plow and work him to death in my fields," he added in an angry voice. Lars nodded in agreement.

She paid them and Bjorn told Linnéa he would stop by in a few weeks in case she had questions for him.

Linnéa patted the white doe and checked her udder. It seemed very full and she had already prepared soap water and a rag for washing her udder. The moon supplied enough light so she could see. The doe wore a collar so she tied her to a garden chair and standing on her knees, she washed her udder and started to milk her. It took a while until she got the knack of it, but she succeeded in emptying the udder. To milk a goat, one had to squeeze the teat, not pump. She had almost a gallon in her bowl and put the precious liquid inside the door to protect it from being knocked over. Then she went back to the doe, untied her and threw her arms around her.

"Gosh, you're beautiful," she said and hugged the doe. She felt so grateful for the milk. "I'm gonna call you Snow-White." In response, the doe turned her head around and licked Linnéa's cheek. A good start to a loving bond between them.

She left the doe alone in the backyard. The yard was totally fenced in and her vegetable garden had a sturdy wire fence around, so the doe was allowed to roam around freely. She started grazing immediately. Linnéa went inside to give Karl the warm milk. She had borrowed a baby bottle from a woman in the neighborhood and filled it. Karl was already used to the bottle and she had given him powdered milk several times. Now she offered him fresh raw milk and he eagerly drank it. She drank a tall glass herself and it was delicious and did not taste 'goaty'. From now on, she would milk Snow-White twice a day and the doe gave close to a gallon daily. The milk was truly needed by both Linnéa and Karl. Linnéa had just turned fifteen years old and was still growing. She was thin and the supply of foods was at times inadequate. The low amount of fat in her diet was a problem, but Snow-White's milk was rich and would give her and Karl the fat they both so badly needed.

Snow-White settled in quickly. Linnéa was only gone three hours every day and she and Karl spent most afternoons with the goat. Karl was crawling around and just learning how to walk a few steps at the time. Snow-White understood he was a baby and would stand immobile when Karl crawled under her belly. At first, Linnéa had panicked when Karl crawled between Snow-White's legs, but her calm nature and patience quickly told Linnéa that she had nothing to fear. Karl grew up with Snow-White and they became best friends. Goats are herd animals, but Snow-White never seemed lonely and her two human friends became her herd.

Before Linnéa left her job, she would quickly cut as much of the wild grass from the adjacent field as she estimated Snow-White would eat for that day and she had still barely touched the hay. Her neighbors were grateful to get all leftover milk and paid with large buckets of grass. It was much more than Snow-White could eat and Linnéa dried this grass in her backyard and saved it in her garden shed for the winter. The goat lived outside in the summer and Linnéa would only open up the shed when the nights turned very cold. In the worst of the winter, she had planned to keep Snow-White in the basement and had prepared a small corner right by the door for her. Newspaper and dried grass protected the goat from the chilly concrete floor. The only problem she had not solved yet was how to supply bedding for the doe such as shavings, but she was hoping Bjorn would help her find something.

Linnéa had asked around if anyone knew about goats and the Bauers had stepped forward. Ten years ago, they had had a small herd of dairy goats and they gave Linnéa invaluable lessons about goat care. They also showed her how to make a pot-in-a-pot refrigerator, or zeer pot, to store the milk in.

"A zeer pot is a simple refrigerator," Mrs. Bauer explained. "It consists of an unglazed, porous terra cotta pot with a smaller pot set inside and a layer of wet sand in between the two pots. As the moisture evaporates from the wet sand, it cools the inner pot. The inner pot can be glazed terra cotta or metal. The distance between the two pots should be about two inches and this space should be filled with sand and watered twice a day. It's best to keep the zeer pot a few inches above the floor to allow air to circulate around the pot. A wet towel over the zeer pot will protect it from warm air and light. Keep the pot out of the sun in a dry location. It works very well."

Once Linnéa understood the principle of the zeer pot, she stored the milk and other perishable foods in the inner pot and became totally dependent on it. She found clean sand down by the lake and kept the zeer pot in her basement standing on two flat stones she found by the lake. She kept a cookie sheet under the zeer pot to catch any water that would drip out as she watered the sand. The milk kept surprisingly cold.

******

Once a week all the people would meet in the high school auditorium and Joseph and other speakers would tell the group all the new things they had learned during the week. Everyone showed up and was eager to find out if food or equipment had been found. Some were able to walk to the high school and others were picked up by car. A small amount of gasoline was still available for the cars. Not a drop was wasted and all the people knew how scarce it was.

"We have located another warehouse stocked with both food and equipment," Joseph started. "All of the food will be distributed evenly between every household. We have also found a ham radio operator with capability to communicate with other hams around the world. He runs his ham radio on battery power that he generates from solar panels. He informed us there are survivors in all countries and in the countries that didn't lose electricity, half the population survived the superbug. How many have died worldwide we don't know, but we're guessing more than half. The virus spread rather quickly to most countries. Our country has been very hard hit, because the grid failed. There's no active government in Washington and no army. Most cities are too dangerous to enter. So far, we're rather safe here and the inmates from the Spokane prison didn't stay in this area. The few people that were living in Sandpoint before we came here have now joined our group and we're about 250 people right now."

"I know you want to hear about food supplies," Joseph continued. "We planted a twenty-acre field this spring with soft white wheat, also called pastry flour, which is used for cakes, cookies and soft breads. That was all the seed we could find and since the wheat field was not fertilized, we may only get thirty bushels per acre, perhaps less, but that may still yield about six hundred bushels of wheat, plus/minus. Not bad. All of us will share the wheat. This fall, we'll plant hard red wheat for bread making on the same field. We've been able to find a small amount of fertilizer that we'll use and we expect the yield to be a little larger. The cutting and threshing of this year's crop, which looks rather good by the way, must be done by hand and all of us have to help out. There's no combine available so we'll use sickles and make small bundles of sheaves. These sheaves will be air dried in the field by arranging the sheaves into stooks. The threshing will be done by banging the sheaves inside a garbage can to remove the wheat kernels. This is hard work and after that the wheat must be separated from the chaff by winnowing. If all of us chip in, the whole project is manageable. We estimate that the harvesting can start in a week. Milling of the flour must be done by each household, but bread can also be made from whole wheat kernels by first sprouting the kernels and then making bread from the sprouted kernels. Then you don't have to mill the flour. For those of you who need tips on how to make bread, we'll supply recipes later on."

"We still have no news if we'll ever get the electricity back. The hams tell us the whole western grid is down and for the time being we have to make do without it. The next problem we face is how to heat our houses this coming winter. Every house we selected for you has a fireplace and some even have two fireplaces, but it will be cold, I'm afraid. There's a small amount of gas available for chain saws and we have three guys who are cutting down trees right now and slicing them up for firewood. You can barter or pay with silver coins to pay for the wood and the firewood will be loaded on a few trucks we have and delivered to your house."

Joseph looked over the people to see how they reacted to what he had just said.

One person stood up and asked -

"Are you, our leader?"

"Only for now," Joseph replied. "We obviously don't need a government for our small community, but if there is a major decision to be made, we'll have to vote on the issue and let the majority rule. Anyone can be the leader who has organizational skills. I became the leader because my wife and I decided to find all survivors in the valley in Montana and then organized the relocation to Sandpoint, but I would very much welcome some help. Anyone is welcome to be part of our little group who act as your leaders. More questions?"

"What do we do if a gang tries to attack us?" someone asked.

"We will not fight. The killing sprees are over. We will invite them to join us," Joseph said in a firm voice. "We are unarmed and will remain so. Throughout history people have believed killing will solve all problems and if you look back at history, wars never resolved anything."

"What do we do if they start shooting at us?"

"'I'll negotiate with them and, hopefully, deter them. That's all we can do, but I feel confident we'll succeed in stopping bloodshed."

Linnéa walked home carrying Karl. She felt uneasy when she thought about what Joseph had said about other people invading them and perhaps even shooting at them. She had left her gun in the cabin and decided not to worry and instead allow Joseph to deal with the matter should it ever occur.

******

Only a few days later the unthinkable happened. Two men from the community were bicycling and saw in the distance a group of people walking towards the town where they lived. One look at this bunch told the story and it was not good news. They bicycled back to the town as fast as they could, found Joseph and told him. He calmly assured them he would deal with the group and took out his large white flag he had made for an occasion such as this. He would face them alone.

Joseph was an intelligent man with a calm disposition, a natural leader, but also a humble man with strong spiritual beliefs. Before the collapse he had worked as a programmer and achieved great success in his career. His organizational skills had helped him both in his former career and in his present life as leader of the community. His greatest sorrow was that he and Sarah, a nurse by occupation, still had no children, but they had not given up hope.

As he now faced the criminal gang in front of him, Joseph felt a chill running down his spine and a wave of fear rolled over him. It took all his mental strength to push the feelings aside and concentrate on approaching them. The gang numbered around thirty and was a mix of men and women and a few half-grown children. What caught his eye was the sight of two small boys in the back, barely old enough to walk. The gang was a mix of riffraff with some apathetic souls mixed in here and there, who had apparently joined them for lack of other options. Most of them carried firearms of different calibers.

Waving his white flag, Joseph slowly walked towards them and stopped about twenty feet away.

"Don't shoot!" he said in a firm voice. We're all unarmed. We're a community of two hundred and fifty people and have no gold or silver, but we have created a community that we think will survive. We are by no means socialists, but right now we have to work together and share our resources in order to survive. The only wealth we have is the value of our abilities and skills. We ask you to lay down your weapons and join our community as valued members. What you have done in the past will remain in the past and if you join us your new life starts now, right here, a new beginning. The population of our country has dwindled and every surviving person is important. You are important, every one of you. If you kill all of us, you'll eventually run out of people to kill. You have no future if you continue on the path, you're on right now. Stop the killing and join us."

The gang members whispered back and forth to each other and seemed positive, but then looked towards their leader for clues. The leader was a tall, skinny man with long dark hair, about thirty years old, but with a hard, unyielding face, not bad looking. There was a young woman next to him who appeared to be his wife and she seemed to be kinder and more willing to listen than the leader. She was plain looking, but Joseph noticed an aura of bright light generating from her body and the light intrigued him. She looked at the leader and quickly said something Joseph could not hear, took his hand and pleaded with her eyes that he should agree. The leader looked at her with obvious affection, laid down his gun and started speaking.

"I am called Quick-Shoot by these gang members, but from now on I prefer my birth name Jeremiah Simms. My wife's name is Ayasha. She is a Cheyenne. We, my wife and I, agree to your terms and will join you and abide by the rules of your community. The rest of the people behind me are free to choose what they want."

Joseph felt great relief as the anxiety finally left him and with a big grin, he stretched out his hand and shook Jeremiah's hand. The two men looked into each other's eyes and both knew this was the end of brutality and the beginning of a normal life. Every single gang member laid down his or her weapon, some whistled in enthusiasm and most of them were all smiles.

"I didn't think anyone would want us," Jeremiah said to Joseph.

"We welcome all of you with open arms," Joseph responded. "Let's all go to the school's auditorium and we'll write down your names, ages and any skills you may have. You will stay overnight in the auditorium and by tomorrow we hope to have each of you assigned to a house here in Sandpoint."

The whole group proceeded to follow Joseph and the weapons were left on the ground. When the group was out of sight, two men from the community arrived with several burlap bags, collected the weapons and tied the bags closed.   They had a row boat nearby at Lake Pend Oreille and started rowing. Half a mile from shore the weapons were dropped overboard and sank quickly.

The newcomers settled in quickly and once they were living in their houses, none of them was a problem. They participated in the harvest of the wheat crop without complaining and several of them had very useful skills. One of them was a barber, a welcome addition to the skilled labor force of the community. Joseph and Sarah took in the two small boys and raised them as their own. Even though they were half starved they were healthy and quickly recovered once they were properly fed. Jeremiah explained that the boys had been sitting on the street abandoned and crying when the group walked through the town. Two of the men had grabbed them and tossed them up on their shoulders and brought them along. Sarah guessed their ages to be two and three years old and they named them Derek and Wesley. They entered their date of birth, using the day they were taken in by Joseph and Sarah, in the official register kept by the local government and entered their ages as two for Wesley and three for Derek. Joseph and Sarah never had any children of their own and they were grateful destiny had rewarded them with two handsome little boys. They looked somewhat similar so most likely they were brothers.

Linnéa also helped bring the wheat in and found it very interesting to learn how to harvest the crop. There was always someone willing to look after Karl for a few hours. More children were needed to make the community grow and Joseph would, in his humble way, remind the people to have more kids. Dr. Schultz was a competent family doctor and eager to help each baby into this world.

CHAPTER 4

Winter arrived and the temperature dropped to below zero. Karl was now one a half years old and walking well. He was able to say a few words and was busy with his toys that occupied him for hours. Several neighbors had dropped off both children's books and toys and Karl was fascinated with them. There was another boy his age in the community, but they lived at the other end of town and not within walking distance, so Karl played mostly with Snow-White, his beloved friend and playmate. Snow-White returned his love and the two were inseparable. She spent the nights in her shed and Bjorn had supplied straw as bedding, so there was no need for her to move into the basement. Her fur protected her and she seemed quite comfortable. She still supplied close to a gallon of milk every day, but Linnéa knew that sooner or later Snow-White would dry up and she would have to breed her to one of Bjorn's bucks. The hay supply was still adequate and all the extra grass Linnéa had dried and saved came in handy in the cold weather. Snow-White had a healthy appetite and ate at least five pounds of hay every day and all vegetable scraps from the kitchen went to her. She loved her water very warm and Linnéa heated it to almost tea warm. Snow-White drank this hot water with utmost delight.

Linnéa heated her house with firewood and she had bought two cords from a vendor at one silver dollar per cord. She still had over thirty silver dollars left in addition to the gold coins, so financially she was in safe harbor. How grateful she was that her parents had saved the coins for bad times. The coins were well hidden under the carpet in her bedroom and invisible.

The school library had opened this winter and Linnéa was an eager member. She devoured book after book and even science books were of great interest to her. History was her favorite subject, but any book teaching a skill was sought after and she kept detailed records in her notebooks about all the various skills she learned from the books. The library was well stocked and had books about almost any subject.

The rumor was out that the Sandpoint community was an ideal and safe place to live and people wandered in now and then, not many, but one or two came walking in every month asking to join them. No one was turned away as long as they agreed to abide by the rules of the community. One day an African American family showed up, husband and wife and a half-grown son. The husband was of dark complexion and strong looking while his wife was small and frail. She had a cute face and gentle eyes. They were shown to Joseph's house and he came out to talk to them. The husband looked anxious.

"I'm Earnie Jefferson and this is my wife Chloe and our son Malik. I am a blacksmith by trade and we ask to join you. We will, of course, honor all the rules you have."

"Welcome, of course you can stay," Joseph responded enthusiastically. He shook Earnie's hand smiling. "We've been looking for a farrier to trim our horses' feet as well as deal with all the other blacksmith work, we have."

"My son Malik works as an apprentice for me and is learning fast. He will soon be able to work independently. My wife is a hairdresser, if you need someone with that skill."

"Definitely, we have a barber for the men, but no hairdresser for the women," Joseph answered.

Over the next few years several African American families joined them and also two Chinese couples without children, Chen and Wenling Kwan and Pengfei and Jun Tsang. The two Chinese couples had walked from Spokane and arrived half-starved and totally exhausted. None of them had been in good shape when they started their walking trip to Sandpoint and it was a wonder, they were still alive. Mr. Tsang was an electrical engineer and Mr. Kwan a marketing director with years of business experience. It turned out they were full of ideas and later became teachers in the school that for now was only in the planning stages. Jun Tsang had been a librarian and Wenling Kwan had owned a flower shop. Jun would later run the library in the town and Wenling opened a store selling used books. After they had regained their strength, they met with Joseph and worked out the details for the school. All four of them had many good suggestions.

The community was stunned. A murder had occurred and the perpetrator had turned himself in. A man in his thirties had strangled another man out of jealousy over a girl. The girl had not committed herself to either of the men and had tried to distance herself from both of them. The murderer, Tom O'Leary, was full of remorse and pleaded with Joseph to allow him to stay. Joseph's usually kind face was stern as he handcuffed O'Leary to the handrail outside his house. He went over to his neighbor and asked him to harness one of the horses to the only sled they had and return right away. It was full winter and very cold outside. O'Leary had winter clothes on, so Joseph did not allow him to go back to his house to pack any of his belongings. Joseph went back inside his house and put two days' worth of food in a bag, put on his jacket, hat and gloves and waited for the horse to arrive. Joseph and his neighbor led O'Leary to the sled and ordered him to climb up on it. He did so without fighting and was handcuffed to the railing of the sled. Joseph took the reins and the neighbor sat in the sled with the prisoner. Joseph put the horse into a trot and traveled west for one hour. He stopped, uncuffed O'Leary and told him to get off. O'Leary was panicky and begging to be forgiven, but to no avail.

"Here is food for two days. Try to walk to Spokane and you may find shelter there. Don't come back to us. You will never be allowed to return," Joseph said.

He quickly hopped up on the sled and the horse took off in a fast trot before O'Leary had a chance to stop him. It was bitter cold and a foot of snow covered the ground making walking very hard. All three of them knew O'Leary's chances of survival were small. This serious crime was the only one that the community had to deal with for several years and in the future only minor incidents occurred. Their little town was very safe and no one feared venturing outside in the dark. Everyone learned about O'Leary's fate and the lesson learned was a good deterrent for anyone tempted to break the rules.

******

Life proceeded in the town and the barber from the gang and Chloe Jefferson opened a little shop together. It soon grew into a profitable business and people would often pay for their haircuts with goods. Some had silver coins of small value that they used as payment, but most of their customers had no choice but to barter. The barber and Chloe did not mind bartering and often came home with enough foods to cook a full dinner. Her husband Earnie had opened a smithy and he and Malik worked hard and had no lack of work. They also were paid by mostly bartering, but occasionally some people paid with silver coins. Earnie was an excellent blacksmith and his skills were very appreciated.

Dr. Schultz had reopened the little hospital in town and Sarah Thorpe had joined him as his nurse. They did not have many patients as people often tried to cure themselves, but just knowing there was a doctor at the hospital was reassuring. There was no dentist available and Sarah had instructed the people how to take care of their teeth by brushing with baking soda and chewing on herbs, especially oregano, to keep bacteria down. Clean ashes worked well as a dentifrice. Since junk food did not exist, the people were rather healthy. Two babies had been born into the community to the delight of the people. The children were the future and every child was welcome.

Linnéa was hoping the school would be up and running by the time Karl was school age. The power grid had still not been repaired, but everyone had become so used to living without electricity that it was no longer a problem.

They got their news from the hams and Sarah Thorpe would write down the messages by hand and circulate the papers from house to house. It was a slow process.

There were no active churches in town and people felt no need for them. People with religious beliefs practiced their faith in the privacy of their homes. Many found answers by looking within. No beliefs were forced on anyone and free will was highly respected.

Out of necessity, the community had started out using socialist ways. Food and resources were shared, but as the town grew and little businesses started, it was abandoned. The currency used was silver. No taxes were collected, but anyone who could afford it donated some of their income to the town government. Every donation was wisely used to acquire equipment and necessities and Joseph posted how the money from every donation was spent in the auditorium. Everyone voted once a year on important decisions with majority rule. The library had a book about the Constitution and Linnéa found it by accident as she was searching for history books. She decided to copy the Constitution and wrote it down by hand. Proudly, she posted it on the wall in the school's auditorium, which was used both as a government office and meeting place for the citizens. Everyone read it and many said they had never read it before. All the people admired the wisdom of the Constitution and at their next voting, everyone agreed to incorporate it into their government rules. People often discussed the Constitution and recognized the importance of it.

Linnéa's love for plants as food and medicine had only increased and she picked the most common plants and made a little bouquet of each plant. She then copied the information about each plant from her books. In the auditorium she found a small table and laid out all her plant bouquets and written notes for people to see. The table was soon full with plants and every two weeks she changed her display. At the end of summer, she had featured about fifty different plants. Her table was so popular that many came with notebooks and copied down the written information as well as the medicinal usage of the plants. The mullein leaves with Linnéa's note as "world's best toilet paper" put a smile on everyone's face.

Joseph had been elected leader with two other people chosen as his assistants, one man and one woman. Joseph accepted to be their leader, but when he addressed the people after the voting result was revealed, he emphasized that he would immediately step down if they found someone else, they preferred to be in charge. The people were grateful for Joseph's guidance and his gentle ways of resolving conflicts and he continued leading them for many years, always with fairness and wisdom.

Not many children were born and Dr. Schultz speculated that the people's diet was too skimpy and too lean. Fats were scarce and the wild game the hunters sold was almost void of fat. Fertility was down and the women had trouble conceiving. Many people went fishing in the lake to help with the food supply, but often came back empty-handed. A few people in the area were breeding pigs to add to the livestock, but so far, the number of pigs was still too small to make a difference. Dr. Schultz knew that later on, when the pigs were offered for sale, the fats from the pigs could easily be rendered into healthy lard and he theorized that this added fat could make the women more fertile. Regardless of if his theory was right or wrong, he knew the diet was entirely too lean and a certain amount of fat was essential for overall health. He was an independent thinker and had never believed the nonsense peddled by the nutritionists that saturated fats contributed to heart disease.

The suicide rate was low, but five suicides had occurred since the community started. One person walked into the lake and drowned himself and the other four had hung themselves. Everyone grieved and thought they had given up too quickly. Their lives were hard and not enough food was available, but most people were grateful to be alive and had strong hopes their situation would improve.

Bjorn, Lars and their parents had become an invaluable food source for the community and they sold egg laying chickens at very affordable prices. Everyone wanted chickens and they were snapped up as soon as they were offered. Linnéa's neighbor had five chickens and bartered eggs for milk. The eggs were a luxury and highly appreciated. The Nordin family also bred dairy goats and sold the babies to eager people on the waiting list. They kept three bucks for breeding services and Snow-White had recently visited with one of the bucks. She was still lactating, but her milk supply was down and Linnéa knew it was time to breed her. She continued milking her until Snow-White gave birth to a healthy baby doe that she gave to a neighbor in exchange for a mule deer. The meat had been dried into jerky and did not need refrigeration. Both she and Karl loved the jerky and the meat was a welcome addition to their skimpy diet. She had heard from the Bauers that there was no need to wean dairy goats from milking and no harm was done by continuing to milk the doe until she gave birth.

Slowly more food was produced, but it would take time until the food supply was adequate. During the winters people sprouted wheat kernels into wheat grass and this supplied fresh greens during the winter as well as a dose of probiotics, which was a natural part of the micro greens.

Meat was scarce and an occasional moose was brought down by the hunters. By agreement, the meat was sold at very low prices to make sure everyone had access to some of it. Fish was sold at the community food store and both fresh caught and dried were available. A team of fishermen went fishing daily to the lake and between them they often managed to catch enough to supply the store in town.

Only sourdough bread was sold as modern yeast was unavailable. People got used to the roughness of this old-fashioned bread and enjoyed it. The food store had a small supply of bread for sale, but willingly taught anyone who was interested how to make their own. They also supplied the sourdough starter for free to anyone who asked for it.

There were now several little shops in town and nothing was expensive. People mostly bartered when shopping, but some of the people used silver coins as payment. A small group of people worked for free just to help out the community. Greed and hoarding of various things were rare and people's mindset was more directed at finding solutions to problems they all faced. The lack of modern amenities and how to live without them in the long run was a constant problem.

Electricity had not been restored. The two engineers had found why the power station went down, but without spare parts they were unable to repair the grid. The hams informed them that most of the power stations around the country had collapsed and ceased to function. Skilled people and lack of spare parts were listed as reason for failure.

People had adapted to living without electricity and many had invented solar cookers they kept in their backyards. They worked well in the summer, but during the winter people cooked in their fireplaces.

Since the town had no churches and no judicial system per se, marriage ceremonies were conducted by having five witnesses attend each marriage and after the couple had said their vows, Joseph would write a marriage license signed by the five attending witnesses. This license was recognized as a legal document by all citizens. Divorce was allowed, but required that both husband and wife agreed to the divorce and if they had children, who would be the caretaker of them.

******

Linnéa was eager to learn how to cook and bake and enjoyed it. One day she walked over to the bakery and asked for a piece of sourdough starter and instructions how to make a loaf of bread. She was given a cup of starter and told to add one and a half cups water, two teaspoons salt and two and a half cups of whole wheat flour. Work the ingredients into a medium thick dough with a wooden spoon about five minutes and then let the dough rise at least twelve hours. Bake in a solar oven until done or in a fireplace in the winter. Linnéa had to ask a neighbor how to grind the wheat kernels and was told that one neighbor had a manual grinder she could borrow or she could just grind the wheat in a mortar and pestle. She had a mortar and pestle in her kitchen and decided to try that option. It was a slow process, but worked better than she had expected. She baked the loaf inside her fireplace by putting the dough in a standard loaf pan, then putting the loaf pan on top of four stones placed inside a cast iron Dutch Oven. She knew she had to lift the bread pan up a little to avoid burning the bread and the stones were just right. She put the lid on the Dutch Oven and placed it next to the burning fire. It was a medium hot fire. A small burning twig was placed on top of the lid to provide heat from above. After thirty minutes she rotated the pan and the bread was done after fifty minutes. It was very good; unlike anything she had ever tasted and she felt proud when she cut it up for her and Karl.

CHAPTER 5

Linnéa was now seventeen years old and quite attractive, her body still slim but with a woman's shape. Several of the young men had tried to date her, but she turned them down with a smile and said she had a three-year-old child to care for and she was not dating. The fact that she had a child did not deter most of them, but a few had backed off immediately. There was only one man who interested her and that was Bjorn. Every time he stopped by to deliver hay or other farm items, he would play with Karl and seemed genuinely fond of him. The two of them would romp around the backyard and Karl was breathless with laughter. The first thing Bjorn always asked about was Karl. A few months earlier when he was visiting, Linnéa had worked up her courage and asked him to stay for dinner, which he accepted right away. They put Karl to bed together and stayed up half the night talking. Their outlook on life was so similar and they ended up telling each other about their childhoods, the way they had lived through the collapse of society and then adjusted to this new, simpler way of life. The whole Nordin family had been immune to the superbug while in Linnéa's family she alone had been immune. Linnéa told Bjorn the painful story of Jake and how she had delivered Karl all alone in the cabin, hated him at first and then slowly grown to love him. She found that his attentive listening and compassion for her ordeal made it possible for her to tell him the whole story without bursting into tears. Even though Bjorn was only twenty-one years old, he was mature from shouldering an adult's responsibilities since he was fifteen years old.

That was the beginning of their courtship and after only two months of dating, Bjorn proposed and Linnéa eagerly said yes. When he hugged her, she felt almost dizzy with happiness. He came down one day with his old car to pick up Linnéa and Karl to meet his parents. They were in their fifties and overjoyed to meet both Linnéa and Karl. Bjorn had told them about Jake and they were very understanding. Lars was present and seemed pleased with the news that Linnéa would soon be his sister-in-law. After a pleasant dinner they all decided the wedding should take place in one month. His parents needed a little time to convert the top floor of their house to living quarters for the new couple. Lars lived in a cabin on the property and his parents would stay on the bottom floor.

Linnéa gave Snow-White to the neighbor and this arrangement worked well as the neighbor had been an almost daily visitor and loved the goat. Joseph was notified that a wedding was in the works and was delighted.

A neighbor walked over to Linnéa with a beautiful dress and after a few minor alterations it looked stunning on her. Everything was ready and the top floor of the Nordin house was painted and comfortably furnished and Linnéa had her few belongings packed already. The whole Nordin family came to pick her up and Bjorn and Lars whistled when they saw how beautiful Linnéa was in her dress. Bjorn was so handsome wearing his father's suit. The Nordins, Lars, Joseph and Sarah signed the marriage license and Joseph pronounced Bjorn and Linnéa husband and wife. Linnéa could not stop a few happy tears from running down her cheeks.

Mrs. Nordin had prepared a feast and after a joyful dinner, the new couple went upstairs to their own place. Karl stayed with Mrs. Nordin and was already attached to her and felt totally at home in the Nordin house.

As they undressed, Linnéa felt a mild panic attack coming over her and Bjorn backed off immediately.

"I can wait, let's just go to bed," he said in a low voice.

Linnéa looked into his loving eyes and as fast as the panic had come over her, it vanished. She put her arms around his neck and whispered into his ear "I am ready, right now".

Their married life was happy and they grew closer all the time. Karl accepted Bjorn as his father and Bjorn adopted Karl as his legal son. Joseph Thorpe signed the papers and filed them with the town legal documents. Joseph and Sarah had never asked who Karl's father was, but they guessed Linnéa had been violated. Linnéa was very fond of her parents-in-law and she and Mrs. Nordin always cooked dinner together. After a while she started calling Bjorn's parents 'mom' and 'pop' and the extended family arrangement worked well. There was so much work to do on the farm and every extra hand was appreciated. Linnéa immersed herself in the farm work eventually learning all there was to know about farming, crops, animals, preserving and cooking. She loved her new life.

******

Two years had passed with no major threat to the community. Joseph had three men working as his scouts and one day one of them came back bicycling at top speed with an anxious look on his face. He threw his bike down and banged on Joseph's door.

"A gang is walking to the town and they look to be the meanest bunch I ever saw, about thirty of them. They're about half an hour from town," he shouted while panting and nervously awaiting Joseph's reply.

"I'll take care of it and thanks for telling me," Joseph replied in his usual calm voice. He thanked the man once again and went inside to prepare himself mentally and grabbed two white flags. He ran a few houses down the road to Jeremiah Simms' house and breathed a sigh of relief when Jeremiah opened the door right away.

"Jeremiah, we may have trouble coming. A gang is fast approaching town and my scout described them as a mean bunch. Will you assist me in talking to them?"

Jeremiah quickly agreed and took the white flag Joseph gave him. Together they walked out to the road leading into town to meet them and they did not have to wait long. They held up their white flags and waited until the group was only twenty feet from them. Joseph spoke first, using his most stern voice.

"Don't shoot. We're unarmed. We welcome all of you to stay with us permanently, but if you choose to do so, you'll have to agree to our rules. We have no guns in town. Whatever crimes you have committed are in the past and we will accept you as one of us if you join us. You'll have to change your ways and live a lawful life and it will be a new beginning for you. If you agree, lay down your guns."

The leader had studied Jeremiah intensely and finally spoke with a hesitating voice.

"Are you Quick-Shoot? *The* famous Quick-Shoot?"

"I sure am and I also ask you to join us. We and the members of my gang joined this community a couple of years ago and none of us has regretted it. There's no future for you out there and eventually you'll starve to death or perhaps you'll be shot by another gang. Life here is good and Ayasha and I are very happy to belong to this town. Will you join us?"

The leader appeared to be thinking over the offer.

"My gang members call me Brass Knuckles, but my real name is Bruno Gutiérrez," he finally said. "Let me talk to my guys." He was a heavily tattooed man in his early thirties with a Mohawk haircut and several scars across his face, probably from knife wounds. Even though his face had chiseled features and radiated cruelty, Joseph sensed that this man could be converted and emerge as a normal man, perhaps with a little help from Jeremiah.

Brass Knuckles talked quietly but very forcefully to his members and gestured vividly with his arms as he spoke. Some of the men looked excited, but several had steely faces and squeezed their firearms.

"I and twenty of my guys will join you, but the remaining ten guys will move on," Brass Knuckles declared. "They will never conform to any rules other than their own. I told them they can leave, but never come back in this direction in the future."

Brass Knuckles put his gun on the ground and the rest of his men did the same. All of them moved forward to join Joseph and Jeremiah forming a circle around them. Joseph proceeded to explain to them the rules of the town, what they hoped to accomplish for the future and that free housing would be allotted to them, two men per house if they were unmarried. Questions and answers were flying back and forth, but finally the group walked back to town and to the auditorium, where they would spend their first night. The rest of the gang members had already left and were out of sight. As usual, two men from the town collected the guns and sank them in the lake far from shore.

When they were alone, Joseph thanked Jeremiah for his help and Jeremiah promised Joseph that he would spend time with Brass Knuckles and his men and try to instill a sense of rightness in them. These men had grown up in the gutter and only knew the law as 'an eye for an eye'. Jeremiah knew of Brass Knuckles, but had not known him personally. As he promised, Jeremiah worked on and off with the gang and they eventually adjusted to a normal life in the town without causing any problems. Most of them married and had families.

******

Linnéa had just delivered a baby girl, her first baby since she married Bjorn. She was nineteen years old and enjoyed life immensely. The love and nurturing Bjorn showered on her made her feel buoyant and full of energy. The birth went well and Dr. Schultz and Sarah Thorpe came to their house to deliver the baby. They named the girl Joy. Bjorn was a proud father and Karl was allowed to hold the baby on his lap. Linnéa and Bjorn were grateful that they had been rewarded with a child and hoped to have at least one more, hopefully two more.

Lars had recently married a local girl, April, and they lived in his cabin on the Nordin property. They had no children yet. Both of them worked on the farm and were part of the extended Nordin family.

Life on the Nordin farm was earthy and without any modern amenities. Even though the work Linnéa had to do was labor intensive and sometimes tested her endurance, she never complained and neither did anyone else of her extended family. Everything was done manually and to keep enough firewood for cooking and heating was a constant struggle. Winters were tremendously cold and they went through several cords of firewood every winter. Fireplaces had to be tended to and cleaned out and Karl was learning to rake the ashes out. A large granny cookstove was used for cooking and baking and it took Linnéa several lessons from Mrs. Nordin to get the knack of using it. To keep the oven at a constant temperature was difficult and, in the beginning, Linnéa's bread was burned to a crisp. She eventually figured out how to tame the oven and got used to it. The kitchen had gravity fed running cold water, totally potable, and the dishes were placed in a very large basin with boiling hot water from the stove after each meal. They had run out of detergent and Linnéa had learned to make soap from tallow. By the time the water had cooled off a little, the dishes were basically clean and could be rinsed with cold water.

Laundry was tough to do and both Mrs. Nordin and Linnéa sorely missed a washing machine, but they had no electricity and Joseph had informed them that they may never have electric power. The wash was put in a large plastic tub and soap was added. They usually left the laundry to soak for a few hours, then agitated it with a stick before finally wringing it out and rinsing it. The soap was easy to rinse out, but the whole process was still slow and tedious as well as hanging all the pieces on the wash-line.

They had both a root cellar and an ice house. A corner of the garage had been separated from the rest of the garage and functioned as a root cellar. It was well insulated and had a small window they used to regulate the temperature so it kept about forty degrees over the winter. Occasionally this makeshift root cellar got too cold and they had to open the door to the rest of the garage to bring in warm air.

The ice house was small, but sufficient, and very well insulated with straw bales. It was built into the north side of a hill with shade trees all around. A huge amount of large ice blocks was brought in over the winter, stacked together, and by the time the summer arrived the ice kept the food rather cold all summer long. The slanted floor allowed the melting ice water to flow into a drain and out. A vent in the ceiling prevented condensation. They had to be careful to keep the door closed all the time to preserve the ice. Mrs. Nordin also kept several zeer pots in the kitchen for the smaller items.

One cow, Rosie, supplied all the milk they needed, but they also had several dairy goats that were used mostly for breeding. A neighbor milked these goats and used the milk for cheese making. Mrs. Nordin did not charge the neighbor for the milk, but instead received cheese as a payment for the milk. Linnéa always milked the cow and enjoyed doing it. It was a quiet time and she leaned her head against the warm side of Rosie while she gently milked her. She felt a strong affection for the cow and they enjoyed their time together. After milking, Linnéa would put her arms around Rosie's neck and Rosie would respond by licking her arm and clearly showing her love for Linnéa.

Joseph and Sarah's boys spent many weekends with the Nordin family and loved the animals and life on the farm. Karl and Wesley were only one year apart and were best friends. Both loved everything mechanical and would take apart any motor they could get their hands on and then put it back together again. Derek was more of a dreamer and loved books. He had an outstanding voice and enjoyed singing and would happily comply if asked to sing. Even as a child, the power of his voice was impressive. The Nordins had an old piano and Derek taught himself to play. It was obvious that he would choose a career in the arts.

Grandpa Nordin had been rather sick, but was now well recovered. He had experienced terrible abdominal pain that grew worse and when he finally agreed to see Dr. Schultz, his pain was so agonizing he could not walk upright. Dr. Schultz quickly determined he had appendicitis and had his neighbor notify Sarah Thorpe to meet him at the hospital at once. The operating room had been refurbished and was ready to use. Even though Dr. Schultz was a general practitioner and had not been trained in surgery, he had found several textbooks in the hospital's library and spent many hours reading and practicing surgical techniques on smaller dead animals. He had no problem performing the operation on Grandpa Nordin and had found anesthesia medication at the hospital's pharmacy. All went well and after spending a few days recovering Grandpa was ready to go home.

PART TWO

REBUILDING AMERICA

CHAPTER 6

Shortly after Linnéa gave birth to Joy, a small airplane had landed at the little airport in town. Two men were onboard and they pulled out two bicycles from the plane. Together, they biked toward the center of town to find anyone in charge so they could deliver their message. A man walking on the road directed them to Joseph's house and he invited them in. After several hours of intense discussion Joseph sent one of his assistants to inform the people in town to gather in the auditorium the following day at nine o'clock in the morning. They only needed to inform the people in the first house on each street and the person would then go from house to house to deliver the message. Bjorn was in town and heard of the meeting and decided he and Linnéa should also attend.

The following morning in a packed auditorium, Joseph and the two men were on the stage.

"These two men, Mr. Lund and Mr. Tipton, arrived yesterday by plane and they would like to tell you the latest news from around the country and also from the world," Joseph said. "I let Mr. Lund start."

"Hello everybody," Mr. Lund said. "As you all know, our country, the United States of America, ceased to exist about seven years ago and most of the population died from a combination of the superbug and the hardship of living without electricity when the grid failed in 2035. At that time the population was about three hundred and seventy million and we're guessing the current population to be between fifty and seventy million people nationwide, a tremendous loss of life. Some areas do have electricity and are doing rather well, but all areas without electricity suffered terribly. There's no functioning government and no armed forces.

In Europe, we have been told the death toll came mostly from the superbug and some countries didn't lose electricity. However, even with electricity those countries did poorly and still went downhill as too many people with the necessary skills to run an advanced technological society were dead. As a comparison to our country, Europe did better than us and had at least more food available for the people than we had over here. The death toll in China, Russia and Africa is about two thirds of the population and in the rest of the world more than half of the population died, perhaps many more, we don't know exactly as there is very little communication. All countries suffered as societies fell apart from lack of food, electricity and loss of skilled people. Manufacturing of goods plummeted due to lack of raw materials or, should I say, the extraction of raw materials. The ability to safely ship whatever was produced was a hazardous affair. Pirates and thieves were and still are everywhere. The production of crops continued, but at a cut rate and much below what was needed for people and livestock. So, the world population has gone from over eight billion to about two billion. Please note, this number can't be confirmed and is based on guesswork, but is probably close to the actual number."

The audience gasped and Linnéa and Bjorn looked at each other trying to maintain courage, but both had a sense of drowning. What future did they and their children have? Would they have to labor as hard as they did now forever? Bjorn took Linnéa's hand to calm her as Mr. Tipton continued -

"I'm Mr. Tipton and I can see on your faces that you now have lost hope. STOP, let me give you the good news. We have assembled a team of electrical engineers and various skilled professionals who have promised to not rest until the electric grid is restored in all areas of our country. The European Union has promised to supply any spare parts we need to restore the grid at half price and we'll pay with gold from our gold reserves when the government is restored. We'll accept any help from any country to rebuild the United States. Now is not the time to refuse help due to national pride. If another country needs any parts that we may have in excess, we'll also supply that country what they need at half price. In the long run, every country will benefit. Manufacturing must start again and fuel supplies for cars and farm vehicles will be available eventually. A new government will be established and also some sort of money system. Armed forces will not be instituted as there is no threat from any country at this time. We all have enough just keeping our own countries above water."

The audience looked relieved and Mr. Tipton continued -

"Your area is next on the list and our team of professionals will start working on your grid next week and depending on the severity of the repairs, you may have electricity after a month or so. However, if spare parts are needed, they will most likely have to be transported by ship from Europe and then it could take six months to get your grid back in working order. From the East Coast, the parts will be unloaded from the ship and sent by truck to your area here in the West. After you have electricity, we expect that each community will have a better chance to reestablish food production, manufacturing and all necessary services to create a functioning society."

Now followed an hour of questions and answers and the meeting was over. Linnéa and Bjorn bicycled back home to tell the other Nordins all the news. Their feeling of despair was gone and they looked forward with childlike anticipation to the return of electricity.

******

Three months of intense activity took place. One crucial part had to be ordered from Europe and when it finally arrived, the team of experts successfully restarted the grid and the whole Inland Pacific Northwest had electricity. Some of the electric lines along the roads had to be repaired, but most of the lines had survived these years of non-use.

There was no cost for the electricity in the beginning and until a new currency was established, people had no way of paying for it anyway.

When Linnéa turned on the lights in their house, Karl stared mesmerized at the lit lightbulbs and asked over and over where the light came from. Bjorn explained as simply as he could how the system worked and this was the first of many lessons he gave Karl about modern technology. Karl was insatiable and never had enough of these lessons. He was intelligent and very mechanically inclined.

All modern equipment could now be used again in the Nordin household and the workload for Linnéa and Mrs. Nordin was noticeably less. Even though they had no detergent, the washing machine performed relatively well with Linnéa's home-made soap and so did the dishwasher. All of them treasured being able to take a hot shower and they were lucky enough to have electric heat in the house, so firewood was no longer the burden it had been. The gift of electricity filled them with gratitude.

******

Slowly, over two years, modern life returned in small packages. Farming and food production came back little by little. Many families became backyard farmers and started growing small fields of wheat and keeping a few animals as breeding stock hoping to increase the number of livestock. Meat and grain were sold and some of the farmers were able to enlarge their wheat production. Available land parcels were used and since the owners of the land were dead, whoever wanted to grow a crop and had seed available could cultivate any unused piece of land. Eventually, families moved out of town and settled on nearby fields and started farming. Most of them made sufficient income from the farming and sold their products at little farm stands that popped up all over the place. Buyers would bicycle to these farm stands to buy foods and everyone benefited. Gasoline was scarce and rationed, but small amounts were available for sale. People still paid with silver and sometimes gold for larger quantities of goods.

All foods were real and processed foods did not exist. No one missed the junk food that so many had been hooked on before the collapse and as a consequence, people's health had improved considerably. Prescription drugs as well as recreational drugs were unavailable and after a few years people with addictions were weaned off these substances and forgot about them. Food was first and foremost on everyone's agenda and even though there was now enough food available, there was no excess. As food supplies slowly increased, fertility rates improved and more children were born. This was seen as a positive sign and everyone understood the need to increase the population.

A small government of seven people had been established in Washington, D.C. and the country were governed according to the Constitution. Some changes were made to the Constitution and everyone over twenty years of age was allowed to vote. The Electoral College was abolished and majority rule introduced. There was no official party and the president and his six assistants were self-appointed. No one objected as there were few candidates for the job as president. It was considered an overwhelming task. The president was nicknamed the new Benjamin Franklin as his name was Benjamin Farnham. He had selflessly restarted the government and he and his government worked seven days a week with a minimal salary as compensation. This very intelligent man shunned the former corrupt government system and only had the country's best as his goal. His devotion was undeniable and so was the commitment of his assistants. Several hams had been engaged to broadcast daily messages to the population about everything the government was planning to do. As there was no other communication working for the time being, the people could not approve or disapprove of the government's decisions, but the hams often asked around and found most people agreed with the president and his plan. The goal of the government was a system that worked only for the benefit of the people.

The gold standard was brought back and only gold and silver coins were used, no paper money. The government had minted a sufficient number of coins and put into circulation. There were just slightly more coins in circulation than was needed and this enabled the economy to grow somewhat. Gold coins could be exchanged for silver coins and Linnéa had exchanged her gold coins for silver. The money system, however, was a work in progress and the government knew a more efficient system was needed. For the time being, resolving the issue of a new currency was put on the back burner as other more important matters had to be dealt with first. No taxes were collected and many worked for very small salaries just to get the country back into working condition again.

Medical and dental care were not available and most people learned to use herbal medicines for most of their needs. There were few doctors around and only a few hospitals performed surgeries; medical supplies were missing at every hospital. Some dentists had opened their offices when the electricity came back and had waiting lists. A small amount of over-the-counter pain medications were sold in most towns, but no stronger prescription pain relievers existed.

Everyone felt education of the children was of paramount importance and schools were opened in every town. The teaching was done by the best educated in the area. In Linnéa's community, Mr. Kwan and Mr. Tsang came forward and offered their services and the quality of education these two men gave the children was truly impressive. They were well educated and covered all subjects between the two of them and their quiet, loving demeanor was appreciated by the children. They refused payment, but would take food donations. Karl was in first grade and absolutely loved school. Grandpa Nordin drove him to school every day as they now had just enough gas to fill the old farm truck. Linnéa made sure to donate home-made bread, milk and eggs several times a week to pay for Karl's education. When they slaughtered one of the farm animals, she also donated meat which the teachers gratefully accepted. Some parents home-schooled their children the first years and then transferred them to the school in town.

Postal service was private and if someone needed a message sent to another town, there were a few people working as delivery men using motorcycles for travel. A small amount of gasoline was available for sale and the motorcycles were very economical to run. The cost of this service was rather high and the distance was limited to maximum two hundred miles. Each delivery person had a bag full of mail to distribute for each trip he made. The government had not resolved how to restart the postal system, so the private system was the only way for people to send out mail and packages.

All infrastructure was mostly intact and usable in much of the country. The cities were all burned down and so destroyed by the gangs that they were considered beyond help and since no one lived there, they were left as they were. Most of the gang members were dead and those who had survived had joined nearby towns and started new lives, this time without crime.

The crime rate all over the country was almost zero and the ten years since the collapse had changed the surviving people's outlook on life drastically. Everyone had been through enormous hardships and to harm another human being was not even considered. The population was so small compared to what it had been that every life was valued. No one feared invasion from other countries. Each country struggled to rebuild and with loss of population everywhere the concept of war was nonexistent in every country. There were no terrorists anywhere. Former terrorists who had survived the superbug had lost all will to fight and were now living in peace with their former enemies. The surviving people everywhere understood the importance of rebuilding and the need to cooperate with foreign countries.

Local train service was available a few times a week, but the trains were seldom full. Most people preferred to just stay home. Gasoline was still rationed and people used their cars locally for short distances only. Air travel had not restarted, but some small private planes could occasionally be seen in the air.

*****

Life had improved in Sandpoint and a small number of jobs were now available. Little shops continued to open and offered employment. Small scale manufacturing had started in various areas such as production of clothing, simple everyday items, dried foods and so on. A bakery opened and was very popular. Two repair shops offered to repair people's appliances since there was no manufacturing of new appliances. The key to this new wave of entrepreneurs was the free electricity. Both local governments and the federal government realized that the small cost of supplying free energy would pay for itself in the long run. Of paramount importance was to restart manufacturing to get the economy back on track.

Welfare did not exist, but if anyone did not have enough food to survive, their neighbors would always help out. People cared about each other in a way they had never done before the collapse, when people often felt their neighbor was the enemy.

Employment was hard to find and many of the men would shovel snow for a small payment and take any odd job they could find. Logging and hunting supplied some jobs and very slowly work opportunities arose as goods and services were exchanged. Those willing to work eventually found some type of employment, but it was never easy. Even though manufacturing had slowly started to make a comeback, raw materials were hard to find and the problem of transportation and distribution had not been solved yet.

Trade between countries started on a very small scale. Coffee and bananas were the first items imported by America and paid for with surplus grain. Most countries, however, strived to restart manufacturing and wanted to become independent of foreign goods. The importance of self-sufficiency was clear to most people. It would take decades before normal trade between countries was initiated and all the problems of shipping resolved. Even shipping within America was still difficult.

Everyone wanted both local and national news and Joseph had started a weekly newspaper. With electricity now available, he had the use of several printers he had rebuilt. He wrote most of the articles himself and sold the newspapers at the cost of printing. In one of the warehouses, he had found copy paper and calculated the supply would last two years at the current rate of use. Both national and overseas news were covered and the quality of his writing was excellent. Nothing was printed that was not totally accurate and a lot of research went into his writing. He knew people relied on his accuracy so guesswork or fabricated news was not even a thought. Television had not yet started and the only news people had access to was his newspaper. He had several reliable hams who supplied him with information and two of the hams provided news from abroad. Most of the countries were no better off than America and they received their news from local hams as well.

When Linnéa was twenty-three years old, she gave birth to fraternal twin boys. Bjorn and Linnéa loved their children, but felt that four made a nice family and neither of them wanted another child.

Linnéa, Bjorn and his parents had agreed that if Karl would ever ask why his mother was only fourteen years older than him, they would tell him the truth as gently as possible. Karl did ask when he was fifteen years old and he accepted the truth with relative calm. Nothing changed and he still loved Bjorn as his father. Bjorn and Karl had a strong bond between them that nothing could sever. Karl never asked about his biological father after that and the matter was not discussed ever again. They all felt it was in the past and no longer of any concern. Linnéa never thought of Jake and had healed from all emotional scars. Bjorn was the love of her life and she was very happy.

******

Ten years had passed with remarkable improvements in lifestyle. All services, including the Internet, had been restored and people lived relatively comfortable lives. Even though millions of professionals, technicians and skilled workers had perished, services throughout the country had been restored. Remote areas had to wait the longest, but teams of experts did eventually travel to rural areas and rebuilt the infrastructural needs of the towns. Local people were trained to maintain the infrastructure. Electricity was still free and functioned as a trigger to entrepreneurship. There was one change running through the whole population and that was people's mindset. People over thirty years old had some memories of the old society, but the older population remembered more in detail the corruption, wars, crime, rampant diseases, money printing with inflation as a result, huge taxes and especially the small group of super rich people with an ungodly stranglehold over both the government and the population. No one wanted that system back. The twenty years that had passed since the collapse of society and the hardship and misery the surviving population had endured had changed the way people looked at life and their fellow man. Before the collapse people lived immersed in a toxic day to day lifestyle, but the present population demanded freedom, respect for each individual and a society free of crime and oppression. The government was in full agreement with the people and worked to establish a new system totally different from the old ways.

A new government, still very small, had been elected and the new president, Perry Sparks, upheld the same political convictions as the former president, Mr. Farnham, who had stayed on as an advisor to the new president. The new government was debt free and declared it would remain so and live within its means. Government leaders were accountable to the people and there was no power elite exploiting the people. There was no Congress and people voted on issues directly over the Internet.

Linnéa celebrated when the Internet came back. Before the collapse, she had used her mother's computer and marveled at all the information she could find. All the programming and memory stored on the old computers were not lost and the programmers were able to restart the system and reload all the information back into various servers. People felt it was magic when they were able to take out their laptops from closets and storage bins and turn them on. The fiberoptic cables were not damaged and functioned well. Most websites were down, but more and more websites came back daily. Older programmers were training younger people to write software and how to run the system, but there was a definite shortage of well trained 'old-timers'. Once the Internet was up and running, younger people born after the collapse could access history websites and learn for themselves how life before the collapse had functioned. They were impressed by the technological advancements of the society, but also learned about the drawbacks such as pollution, crime, wars and the hate between ethnic groups of people. The travel websites were favored as no young person had ever been abroad and most of them had only traveled a few hundred miles from their homes.

Linnéa's interest in spirituality was the first topic she wanted to investigate. To her surprise, several websites dealing with reincarnation and various spiritual topics were alive and she read everything she could find. She understood life was a learning experience to be enjoyed rather than feared and that spiritual beings did exist. The knowledge she gained made her feel liberated.

CHAPTER 7

Karl was nineteen years old and looked intently at the computer screen. He was attending the second year of college and all courses were given over the Internet. Only a few universities were open in the whole country, but most students preferred to live and study from home. His dream was to become an aeronautics engineer. He had been well educated by Mr. Kwan and Mr. Tsang and when he entered high school, an engineer had joined the staff in his school and provided first-rate math and science education. Since the school did not have many students, the curriculum was individualized and very thorough. Karl was well prepared for college when he graduated from high school. His three siblings were all attending the local school and received the same quality education as Karl had been offered. All the teachers were now salaried and even though the local tax rate was very small and easily affordable by the community, it was sufficient to pay for the salaries of the three teachers. The community was frugal with tax money and no money was wasted on frivolous items.

Karl studied hard and had good grades. The Internet college courses were inexpensive and text books were free to download. Twice a year he traveled on his motorcycle to Coeur d'Alene to participate in a series of testing. There were usually at least a dozen other students present and Karl enjoyed meeting them and to discuss his favorite topic, a car capable of traveling above ground. He knew it was possible and he wanted to be part of the team inventing these future vehicles. He was driven with ambition and enthusiasm.

Last time he went to Coeur d'Alene a girl had been present and he was fixated on her. She was a Vietnamese American, also nineteen years old, and her name was Linh Chuong. She was hoping to become a pediatrician and she studied via the Internet as well. Only Linh and her mother had survived the superbug. Her mother worked as a teacher and

Linh made a little money as a freelance journalist writing whenever she had time between studying.

Karl and Linh emailed each other and Karl had found out that her great grandparents had been part of the boat people fleeing Saigon, Vietnam on a fishing boat in 1978. Karl had been taught about the Vietnam war in school. An American ship had picked them up after they had drifted on the water for weeks with no engine power and no food. Only a little drinking water was left when they were taken aboard the American ship. The refugees were transported to the Philippines and Linh's great grandparents had applied for asylum to America. To their surprise and gratitude, it was granted and after spending a few months in a camp, they flew to the United States aboard an army cargo plane. Linh's great grandfather had been a chemist and he managed to get a job as a chemist as soon as he had learned to speak English. He did well in his new country. Both her grandparents and parents had Vietnamese spouses and Linh was not of mixed race. She and her mother had survived the superbug, but her father and her sister had died. She seemed to be open-minded to Karl's interest in her. Karl was tall with sand colored hair, handsome and resembled Jake and Linh was petite with classic oriental features. Karl found her beautiful. They were not dating, but kept in contact by email.

Linnéa and Bjorn were busy running the farm and raising their children. With all modern amenities back, they found their lives to be relatively easy compared to what they had gone through just ten years ago. Most services were back and quality of life was considerably better than before the collapse. The crippling fear that had permeated society before the collapse was gone and people faced the future with anticipation. Life was good.

Lars and April had three children, two daughters, Annette and Emilee, and a son named Colin. They had tripled the size of their cabin. Lars still worked on the farm and he and Bjorn produced tons of food that they sold locally. They were best friends and worked well together. Financially, Bjorn and Lars easily made enough money to supply a good life for their families. Grandpa Nordin was semi-retired and only worked part time on the farm. He still drove all his grandchildren back and forth to school every day, a task he enjoyed and never tired of.

Wesley Thorpe was studying to become a mechanical engineer and, like Karl, lived at home and attended his courses over the Internet.

Derek had moved to San Francisco to attend a musical academy and was being trained by a maestro to become an opera singer. His baritone voice was magnificent.

Wesley found he was drawn to Joy. She was only thirteen years old, but he had strong feelings for her and had decided to wait and try to win her heart when she was old enough. Every weekend that he had visited the Nordin farm when he was a child, he had tried to spend time with her. She was lively, spontaneous, full of life and, oh, so cute with her auburn hair.

******

Five years passed and Karl and Linh had graduated from college. Right after their graduation they got married and moved into a little house in Coeur d'Alene. All unclaimed houses were sold at very low cost by the local towns and Karl and Linh could easily afford their house. The location of Coeur d'Alene had power of place meaning it had easy access to highways, the railroad, airport and a good supply of educated people. As a result, the town was growing rapidly. Karl was now an aeronautical engineer, but continued to study part time to earn his Master's degree. The standard work week was thirty hours and he worked for a local engineering firm that had started up just a few years earlier and specialized in propulsion systems. Karl was hoping to gain enough experience to pursue his dream to design a car that could travel above ground. Linh studied full time to become a doctor and was doing well with her courses.

Both Karl's extended family and Linh's mother were overjoyed when Karl and Linh got married. The wedding took place at the farm and Linnéa had invited Joseph and Sarah, Dr. Schulz and some of the neighbors who used to take care of Karl when he was a baby. Linh was just beautiful in her white dress and Karl could barely take his eyes off her. He loved her so. Linh was equally in love with her handsome husband and they hoped for a long life together.

Wesley had also graduated and was a mechanical engineer. Most weekends he would drive to Sandpoint and stay with his parents and then visit Joy. He had proposed to Joy and she accepted immediately and as soon as she had finished her studies to become a nurse, they would get married.

Joy and Wesley married three years after Karl's wedding took place and moved to Coeur d'Alene a few blocks from Karl and Linh. Wesley had secured a job as a mechanical engineer with a firm specializing in robotics and Joy was employed as a nurse at the local hospital. They often visited on weekends with Karl and Linh and enjoyed each other's company. Linh had recently given birth to a daughter, Leanna.

******

Life in America continued with huge changes taking place and new ideas were implemented all the time. Over the years, society went through a metamorphosis and the younger citizens pushed the hardest. A new government system eventually emerged called *People Democracy.* Misinformation and deceit were no longer an issue and people trusted their government. The two-party system was gone, but the three branches of the government had been kept with the executive, legislative and judicial branches serving the country. These three branches only employed enough people to make the system function and the whole government was very small. The system worked well and was free of corruption.

The legislative system had been simplified and the laws on the books were few, fair and easy to understand. No one was above the law and equal rights were universal. The whole court system functioned well and most cases were resolved by mediation and only the most complicated cases ended up in the court room. Personal lawsuits were rare and the loser was responsible for all court costs.

The government had asked the voters whether they wanted to have a Congress and the majority of the people voted no on the issue. People felt that the time for elected representatives was over forever and the older generation clearly remembered how corrupt the government had been and the negative influence of corrupt lobbyists on members of the Congress. Free speech had been removed, privacy reduced to a minimum, elections were dishonest and the economy non-functioning. The legislative branch functioned satisfactorily without Congress and all new laws and decisions of importance had to be approved by the voters. The citizens were encouraged to vote over the Internet on every issue and since there was no Congress, most people were involved with how the government ran the country and willingly voted on new laws. People who were less aware of the system would ask others for advice. A small percentage of the people refrained from voting and did not want to get involved, but most citizens did vote and majority rule decided the vote. The government had issued detailed information how the economy and money system worked and found that most citizens did comprehend both subjects.

The judicial branch also functioned well. There was accountability in the government at all times and no member of the government had ever been caught enriching himself or herself illegally while in office. For the time being the government system worked, but it was understood that as times changed a new system may be introduced. Elected members of the government served a four-year term and no one could serve more than two terms.

The Constitution had been modernized and was still the law of the land. To the people who claimed the Constitution was outdated, the president replied *the goal of the Constitution is freedom and since when is freedom outdated?* Then he added *the most important rule of a democracy is respect for each individual and to let the people rule, not the government.*

On the government blog, there was a steady interaction between the voters and the government about future improvements and the direction of the country. Disinformation by the government was never an issue and many practical solutions materialized as a result of the citizens' input. The various agencies within the government implemented the changes that the citizens had approved and they became law.

Some people with brains were irritated that the 'mob' had voting rights and hinted they were too ignorant to vote. In response, the government posted all voting issues on their website explaining in simple language the pros and cons of every issue to be voted on. To the government's action the people responded with a positive reaction showing they did indeed grasp the proposed ideas and after a while the self-appointed masterminds fell silent.

The Federal Reserve was terminated. It was a private institution made up of private banks in America and was not a federal agency.

Most banks were state owned, but there were a few privately owned banks around. To prevent an elite system from reemerging, the private banks had to adhere to the same strict rules as the state and federal banks. Only state and federal banks could legally charge interest and the rate was three percent for all loans. The profit from these loans was returned to the people by paying for various infrastructure. Mortgages could not be sold. Deposited money was stored by the private banks for a fee and no interest was earned by the depositor since there was no inflation and money did not lose its value. Deposited money could not legally be invested by the banks. The idea was that the bank should not make money on money. The private banks made sufficient money by offering many other services, but no bank was awash with money as had been the norm before the collapse.

Money was taken out of politics and candidates running for office did not have to raise funds. This process eliminated fraud. Each candidate was allotted equal time for free on television to present his or her views and buying of ads was illegal. There were no lobbyists allowed and lobby groups were no longer legal.

Starting at age 21, each citizen had a tax-free base income from the government freeing many people with creative talents to develop new ideas and inventions that could not have materialized had they been forced to worry about making a living. New wealth was created with money benefitting both the people and the government. Most people earning a good income opted out of the free base income. A few people preferred not to work and lived on their base income, but the majority of the people were employed and enjoyed their work. Since all had access to a free income, salaried employment was stress free and looked upon as a hobby by some and stimulating by others. The work week was four days and hard labor was done by robots. The robots were continuously improving and becoming more efficient.

To start a business was easy with only one form to fill out. Business loans to start a company were funded by the government and interest free. Delinquencies were rare and loans were repaid on time. Most companies remained small by choice and were usually owned by the employees who shared the profits. Creative people preferred working for the small companies and most new inventions came from these smaller businesses. There were some larger corporations around, but they had been forced to copy the business model of the smaller companies or risk losing their employees.

Patents were issued for seven years, which was considered a sufficient time to recover expenses and to make enough profit on the new invention. Some inventors did not patent their inventions, if they found there was a need for the product right away at an affordable price.

They considered the new invention a gift to humanity. Other inventors removed the patent after two, three years when they had recovered the cost of inventing the product, forgoing profits. There were also some companies that let the patent run the standard seven years, but offered the product at a fair price. Generosity trumped greed and this mindset was typical of the attitude held by the general population. The money hoarding and greed so common before the collapse was disapproved of and helping society grow was considered more valuable than financial gain. No patent could be sold.

Manufacturing was reinstated in America and factories were run by a mix of robots and employees, but the population in America was still small and overall manufacturing was much less than it had been before the collapse. Some goods were imported, but the government had set a goal to manufacture as many goods as possible domestically in order to be self-sufficient and to supply jobs.

One reason manufacturing had been slow to start was the difficulty finding parts. Local fabrication of parts was encouraged to speed up production. Hence foundries and small businesses making various parts opened up close to the new factories and eventually a large number of products were produced. Over the years, human employees were replaced with robots in the factories, but as society moved forward and new inventions were designed and fabricated, new jobs were created in fields that had not existed before. Everyone wanting to work could find a job. As new inventions were created, new raw materials never before extracted from Earth were needed and traded between different states. As a result, new jobs were created.

Any large company that failed was not bailed out by the government and the idea that a company was 'too big to fail' made no sense to the voters and consequently would never gain voter approval. Companies cooperated and competition between companies was mutually respectful. Free enterprise was the norm.

Electricity was still free for all. Every house had a little black box that received electricity and this box ran the electrical system of the house. The power came from outer space and was unlimited. A one-time fee paid for the box and no electrical lines to people's houses were needed. No additional fees had to be paid for electricity. The amount of electricity people could use was limitless and the free electricity created a booming economy as well as new jobs.

Scientists had discovered that space is not a vacuum, but a crowded whirlpool of subatomic particles briefly coming to life, combining with other subatomic particles and in the process exchanging energy. This subatomic exchange between the particles creates enormous amounts of energy and it is this energy that feeds the black boxes in people's homes. The process is called *Zero Point Field* and is referred to as *Natural Energy.* The concept of free energy was accepted without resistance from the business world. The energy producing companies were more openminded than before the collapse and did not object. Before the collapse, the idea of free energy would have provoked intense efforts from many companies to stop it as these companies would go out of business if free electricity was implemented. The oil companies did survive as oil was still used in manufacturing of plastics and other materials, but many companies selling energy-based items such as batteries, heaters and so on ceased to exist. Many jobs related to the energy field such as power plant workers, electricians and others also lost their jobs forever, but the free energy, or Natural Energy as it was called, also created many new jobs and business opportunities. The net result that evolved over a few decades was a second Industrial Revolution and in the long run people and businesses profited rather than lost money. More new jobs were created than lost.

The discovery of free natural electricity was one of the most important findings ever on Earth and advanced society tremendously. Natural energy was used by beings on inhabited planets everywhere in the universe, but somehow Earth took a long time to discover it.

Most countries around the world had no armed forces. Fear drives wars and since the various countries on Earth did not fear each other any longer, they dismantled their armed forces. An enormous amount of money was saved and instead spent on infrastructure, education, research and other projects benefitting the people. Moreover, no money was spent on inventing new weapons. A few countries did maintain a small army that was used when natural disasters occurred such as earthquakes and tornadoes. People, who in the past had been supporters of war to solve disputes between countries, had realized that war was not the answer and joined the majority who rejected the idea of war. Nuclear weapons had been deactivated and the uranium removed. The result was that most people looked to the future with positive anticipation, not fear. America was no longer the cop of the world and did not interfere with other countries' affairs in the name of spreading freedom and democracy. The citizens simply would not allow it.

Many countries copied America's new system of government and sent teams of experts over to Washington, D.C. to study the details. When they looked around and saw how well the system functioned, many were sold on the new ideas and recommended them to their home countries.

People Democracy could never have worked if the old power elite had been alive. It only worked because the survivors of the collapse rebuilt society from scratch and the survivors wanted no part of the old corrupt system. The Greek philosopher Aristotle referred to democracy as an imperfect form of government as the poor would vote to benefit only the poor. Perhaps this was true in Athens at the time he lived, but with a basic income for all citizens there were no poor people in America and the voters were all survivors of tremendous hardships. Their mindset was totally different compared to the Athenians of Aristotle's time.

There had been talk about forming a world government, but the suggestion did not gain much support. Instead, a global *Advisory Board* was formed with a member from each country participating. The sole purpose of the Board was to coordinate projects and ideas for the world and the Board had no power to dictate or interfere in sovereign affairs of any country. Each participant was carefully chosen on merit and experience and served a five-year term. The Board's recommendations were practical and common sense and most countries embraced them. United Nations had not existed since the collapse.

Race wars in America as well as in other countries had slowly just faded away. It was considered an outdated way of life and no longer accepted. Most people felt that tolerance of ethnic differences among people was just basic humanity and the elitist idea so common before the collapse that some people are 'more equal' than others was frowned upon. Obviously, everyone accepted that some individuals had more abilities and skills than others.

Limited trade between countries had started again and all countries had a currency backed by the gold standard. Money printing to artificially create money had been declared illegal many years ago. Money held its value and was thought of as a means to exchange goods and services, not to hoard, and money not spent would lower the economy. The massive debt owed by many governments before the collapse had been forgiven as there simply was no way of repaying it anyway. Paper money had been reintroduced in America and was the legal tender. The government released more money into circulation as the economy grew and since the money was backed by the gold standard, it held its value and there was no inflation.

No poverty and no homelessness existed. There were some affluent people who had accumulated money from successful businesses, but they were not super rich and had worked very hard for their income. Most people had comfortable lives and enough money to pay for all material needs. Before the collapse, only a few percent of the people owned all the money and the rest of the people ended up with less and less money. This unfair system had been eliminated and the assets of the country were spread out more evenly among the citizens.

The federal tax rate was a flat rate of fifteen percent on earned income with no deductions and there was no sales tax. Each employer deducted the tax and there was no need to fill out any tax forms on an annual basis. The state income tax was five percent, no deductions, but some states with income from natural resources had no income tax. The corporate tax rate was ten percent and business owners did have to file a tax return, but the forms were short and simple. Estate taxes had been eliminated. Homeowners paid real estate taxes, but the tax rate was very modest and covered only local services. Overall, the taxes people paid were small, fair and affordable. The government posted the budget online and the people could see for themselves how their tax dollars were spent. The government approval rate was very high.

An enormous amount of money was saved by keeping the size of the government to a minimum; there was no welfare and no pension money to pay out since the base income was enough to live on; no armed forces to maintain and few prisons existed that needed funding. Violent crimes were rare and the police force dealt mostly with accidents and occasional disputes among people. Tax money spent on research was limited to science that would truly advance society and frivolous scientific research received no tax funds. The government was truly frugal with the tax money.

Recreational drugs including narcotics were legalized. They were not available to buy, but the few people who were addicted to them made them themselves. Most people were of the opinion that if someone wanted to destroy himself or herself with drugs, it was that person's free will to do so and government authorities should stay out of it. This law eliminated all crime related to drugs as well as the enormous cost associated with convicting and incarcerating drug users and sellers. Millions of dollars were saved when the law was enacted. Many people overdosed and died setting an example for others that there are consequences to one's actions. Even alcohol consumption was less than it had been in the past and smoking was mostly a habit of older people, who saw no reason to quit.

Medical care was free, but people were healthier than in the past and many preferred natural cures they carried out at home and saw no need to consult a doctor. The old system with prescription drugs had been mostly abandoned and many drug companies had converted to herbal medicines. Some prescription medications were produced as well as drugs used by hospitals.

The hospitals were well equipped and holistic medicine was the norm. A new method of healing was to increase a patient's vibration, but not all patients could master this technique. Some people were able to receive more light into their chakras and found that their health and wellbeing improved with the additional light. People were also mentally healthier and more positive than in the past. Many people lived past one hundred years and were physically and mentally active until they passed away.

Traditional religion with church attendance had become less popular and had been replaced with spiritualism. The Catholic Church had gone through a drastic modernization to hold on to their members, but many people had abandoned Christian churches and found them outdated and unresponsive to people's needs. Celibacy was dispensed with and Catholic priests were allowed to marry. There were still people attending church, but people's consciousness had increased as they learned to find answers from within rather than from a priest. Most people believed in reincarnation and as a result felt they had a mission to fulfill in life. Death was not feared and considered a natural transfer from one embodiment to another with some time spent in the afterlife. The question so often asked in the old days "why do we live" was no longer relevant as people knew that each lifetime was a learning experience. Sanity levels were high and the fear driven lifestyles that had crippled many people in the past had been replaced with optimism, joy at being alive and a feeling of freedom.

Globally, people had stopped trying to force their religion onto others and tolerance was the general attitude. Religion was no longer fear based and no one believed in a punishing God serving as a dictator.

Marriage was slowly becoming outdated and many couples preferred a marriage contract when they decided to have children. Children were loved but not spoiled. All western countries had legalized gay marriages as everyone's free will was respected.

Public transportation was free. Airmobiles and groundmobiles as well as boats were all electric and powered by a black box. Airmobiles had a device that eliminated gravity allowing the car to rise from the ground and travel at several different altitudes, the highest levels reserved for long distance travel. The airmobiles were driverless and run by computers. They were a big hit with the people, even though the accident rate had been quite high when they were initially introduced. The problems had been addressed and the cars were now very safe. The highways were used mostly by the trucking companies and the few people who refused to travel above ground. Almost all vehicles traveling on the ground were driverless.

All large cities had been burned down during the collapse and they were not rebuilt. Everyone favored small towns and many of these towns were spread out over a large area. Commuting to work was so easy with the airmobile that people who preferred a rural setting could live further out in the countryside.

Every person's free will was honored and the government could not legally force anyone to accept services or rules that were against the person's beliefs, such as vaccinations and more. All technology had been retrieved from computers and servers from before the collapse and the programmers who had survived reinstated first the old Internet and then a new, more efficient Internet. The binary computer system had been replaced by quantum computers and the efficiency of these new computers was impressive.

America emerged as a humbler country and the old mindset that America must always win and be the best and the mightiest was gone. It was accepted that some countries were ahead and that America could learn a lesson from these countries. Occasional failures were looked upon as an opportunity to grow and nothing to fear.

******

It was 2072 and ten years had passed. Karl and Linh and Joy and Wesley enjoyed happy but busy lives. Karl and Lin were now the parents of three children, Leanna 10 years, Olivia 7 years, and a son Forrest 5 years. Wesley and Joy had two sons, Brandon 6 years and Drew 3 years. Karl was fond of his sister Joy and the two families were very close. The five cousins spent most weekends together and occasionally they would drive up to the Nordin farm and visit Linnéa, Bjorn and Lars and his family. It was always a happy occasion when Karl and Joy came to visit Linnéa and Bjorn with their families. Bjorn and Lars still ran the farm, but Grandma and Grandpa Nordin were retired and had built a small house for themselves a distance away from the main farm house. They were still in good health and enjoyed retirement.

PART THREE

———————

THE GOLDEN ERA

CHAPTER 8

Karl was strolling down the street in San Francisco during his lunch hour, a distinguished looking man and still handsome at sixty-one years old. The streets were seldom crowded as the airmobiles, or the Birds, all traveled in the air above him and the local traffic of groundmobiles was usually light. The city was quite small and had been fully rebuilt after the catastrophic earthquake that occurred twenty years ago. Several thousand people had perished and the rebuilding of the city had involved over a thousand people, from planners, engineers, contractors and, of course, all the robots that did most of the labor work. The new city was beautiful and had been nicely landscaped with bushes and flower arrangements. Derek had just moved out of the city when the earthquake struck and was spared.

Karl reflected on the fact that in only two years a new century would arrive, the year 2100, and how much that had happened during his lifetime. He had his own engineering firm with nineteen people hired. He deliberately kept his company below twenty employees to free up as much time for his family and grandchildren as possible.

His three children were all grown with families of their own. Linh had had an interesting career as a pediatrician and was now fully retired. She had never worked more than part time to ensure she would have enough time to spend with her children. Karl was planning to turn his business over to his employees and retire shortly and he and Linh wanted to travel both around the Earth and to the Moon. He had moved his business from Coeur d'Alene, Idaho to San Francisco only twelve years ago and they lived just outside the city. Commuting to work was so easy with the new generation of airmobiles that traveled through the air at high speed and once he had entered his destination into the airmobile's computer, he could just relax and let himself be transported to work. The black box that supplied electricity to the engine was very reliable and had never failed. His firm had designed part of the propulsion system for the airborne vehicles and several other engineering firms had been members of the team. It had not been an easy endeavor and the first models had been involved in several crashes. All the problems were eventually solved and the new airmobiles were selling at affordable prices and had replaced the old cars. The vehicles were manufactured almost totally by robots and practicality and efficiency were favored over luxury.

Technology was advancing even though there was a shortage of experienced scientists and engineers. If the collapse had not occurred, society would have been much more advanced, but if quality of life would have been better is questionable and most people preferred the present system. Artificial intelligence was slowly getting better, but even the most advanced robots could not design other robots. Some people felt concern that if the robots would become too advanced, competition between humans and robots may end with the robots taking over society and render humans unproductive and with no purpose. Perhaps even taking over all employment. This topic was endlessly discussed with pros and cons addressed and most people were unsure whether to limit the advancement of robots with artificial intelligence or not. All the research and files had been retrieved from the various Institutes of Technology and from cloud storage. Several of the professors who had been involved with the latest inventions before the collapse came forward offering their assistance. Some of them were old, but still mentally alert, and were able to explain all the details to the younger people taking over the files and continuing the research. Without the help of these professors and surviving members of the former research teams, the development of robots and all the new technology the world enjoyed would have taken a much longer time to invent.

Everything on Earth had improved. Extreme poverty was gone in all countries and the standard of living was good in all modern countries. There were, of course, people earning much less than the most successful people, but low-income earners still had a decent income and could afford all necessary amenities. No wars had taken place anywhere since the collapse and with all the money saved by not feeding the war apparatus and bloated governments, the money was spent on the citizens instead. The former Third World countries had been helped by experts from the more affluent countries and they were now able to run their own countries in a more efficient way. Industry and extraction of raw materials worked well and supplied their governments with the income they needed. Even in the former Third World countries citizens would not tolerate a power elite and no government had the audacity to try forcing their will on the people anymore. Many people referred to the years before the collapse as the Dark Ages. More children were born as a result of the new prosperity and the global population had recently passed three billion.

The crime rate was low and convicted criminals could choose either prison or treatment. The treatment centered on psychology and teaching the convict how the mind works and they were taught techniques to find out why they had chosen a criminal lifestyle. The success rate of the program was high and those convicts who did not respond to the rehabilitation treatment were sent to prisons where treatment continued. Many of the prison inmates were eventually reformed and could be released. The basic income of all convicts was sent to their victims while the convicts were locked up.

Over a thousand satellites in orbit supplied instant Internet service. Traveling by air was fast and efficient with the supersonic planes. For long distance air travel, a new fleet of planes were being designed and would soon be put into use. They were designed to cruise at Mach five at an altitude of a hundred thousand feet cutting long distance trips down to an hour or two. A plane cruising at Mach ten was possible to design, but the team of engineers had settled for a slower plane that could be built using less expensive and more available materials in order to lower the cost of the plane. Most people felt a plane cruising at almost four thousand miles per hour was fast enough for travel anywhere on Earth.

Recycling of all materials was mandatory and Earth had gone through an impressive upgrade. Most plastic items were recycled and reused and non-recyclable plastics were eaten by worms capable of digesting and breaking down the toxins in the plastic. In grocery stores some products were sold in glass jars and recyclable mylar bags, but newer and more lightweight materials were released all the time. The pollution of the planet that had been so destructive before the collapse had ended and the old landfills were covered. Households produced only a fraction of trash since so many items were recycled. As a result, fewer landfills were needed and the willingness of the citizens to comply with recycling made the system work well. Anyone looking at old pictures on the Internet showing the plastic items floating around in the oceans and the heaps of trash so often found in the cities felt the recycling process each family had to go through was a small price to pay for a clean planet.

Karl returned home early and was glad to be home. His parents had arrived during the day for a visit and he enjoyed their company. Lena, Karl and Linh's maid, welcomed him home and informed him his parents were in the backyard by the pool. Lena was an android, attractive to look at with brown hair and very humanoid features. Her personality was pleasant and her skills were truly remarkable. She was the latest model and equipped with artificial intelligence enabling her to think and make independent decisions. Her programming included everything that needed to be done in a home as well as some of the most common house repairs. Lena had basic feelings and as she spent more time with Karl and Linh, she continuously learned and adapted to human behavior. The cost to acquire her had been high, but her reliability and the time she saved them had been worth the expense. Linh had taught Lena Vietnamese cooking, which she mastered with ease and she was a good cook. Many people used the 3D food printers for quick meals, but they were not overly popular and most people preferred the taste of standard cooking. No printer could match the expertise of Lena's cooking. She kept perfect inventory of everything they needed so they never ran out of anything. All the groceries were delivered by cargo drones designed to carry heavy loads. To Karl and Linh, she was a dear friend.

"Hi Dad, hi Mom," Karl said with his pleasant smile. He gave them each a hug and thought to himself how good they still looked.

"We're so happy to see you," Linnéa said with an affectionate grin. At seventy-five years old, she was still attractive with silver colored hair and a face that had been spared the ravages of age.

"Karl, what a pleasure," Bjorn said. Even though Bjorn had worked hard his whole life, he looked ten years younger than his age and still maintained a youthful posture.

"How was the trip?" Karl asked.

"Easy, our Bird was fast and it only took four hours," Bjorn responded. "The top lane had very little traffic and the landing here went well also. We watched a movie and Mom took a nap after that, so the trip went well."

Linh came out and the four of them sat down together. A lively conversation followed and all the latest news about the children and grandchildren was discussed. The Nordin farm was run by Annette and her husband, the oldest daughter of April and Lars. When Bjorn and Lars retired, Annette and her husband were happy to take over the farm. They had been living in Seattle, but felt cramped living in a city and accepted right away when Lars asked them if they wanted to move back to the farm. Bjorn and Linnéa lived in the retirement house where Grandma and Grandpa Nordin had lived when they were alive, but April and Lars had bought a house in Montana not too far from Linnéa's cabin. Lars was an avid fisherman and often went fishing on the Clark Fork River. The whole valley in Montana following the river was sparsely populated and was again a good area for hunting. After the collapse the wildlife population had been decimated from hunting, but deer and other animals slowly returned to the area and had increased in numbers. Linnéa's cabin was used occasionally for weekend trips by the Nordin family members and even though the little cabin was over eighty years old by now, it was still structurally sound. Karl had spent many weekends there alone when he was a teenager and he remembered how he had loved to jump on his motorcycle, rev up the engine to full speed and travel down the center of the highway with the wind blowing in his face. There were so few vehicles on the road that all he needed to be on the lookout for were deer crossing the road. He had an emotional attachment to the cabin and even though he knew the sad circumstances under which he was conceived, he had decided to wipe those thoughts out of his mind. His mother had assured him she was over it. He wandered around on the same trails that Linnéa had used and felt an inner peace in the forest. His thoughts would clear and he felt one with nature. There were often deer and turkeys on the trails, but Karl had no interest in hunting and just as Linnéa had done, he would stop and talk to them. He made sure the supply of firewood was never running low and would often cut down a tree and slice it up. Occasionally Wesley would accompany him to the cabin, but Karl preferred to go there alone and wander around in the woods.

Not everything was rosy, however. Lars' son Colin was struggling with his son Clarence, who at 21 years old was a convict and serving a prison sentence. He had chosen prison over rehabilitation. Since early childhood he had been fascinated with computers and was a full-fledged hacker at the early age of fifteen. Without thinking of the consequences, he had hacked into the government's financial records and retrieved hundreds of financial accounts from various citizens. He was caught when he started to withdraw money from some of the accounts and was sentenced to five years in prison. The modern prisons had no resemblance to the old-style prisons and all the convicts were enrolled in rehabilitation programs. Clarence was brilliant with computers and Colin and his wife felt sure he would be able to work as a programmer when he was released from prison in two years.

The second tragedy in the Nordin family was that Brandon, Joy and Wesley's son, had died the year before at the age of only thirty-one years. His self-driving groundmobile had malfunctioned and ran off the road killing Brandon instantly. The computer controlling the vehicle just died and the backup computer had not been activated. Computer failures were so rare that Brandon felt a backup was unnecessary and he paid with his life for this mistake. He left a wife and daughter behind.

The conversation turned to the government's recent decision to allow the *Akashic Records*, a vibrational recording device or database of everything happening on Earth and the universe, to be released for viewing on the Internet. The Akashic Records could be found in the Zero Point Field realm. Even though each citizen could only view his or her own file, many felt it was only a matter of time until the rules would change and every citizen would be able to read other people's files. Some people were angry over the loss of privacy, but there had been a vote on the issue and the majority of the people wanted the records released. The Akashic Records contained an accurate history of every person's embodiment on Earth and reincarnation was accepted by most people as truth. Some people felt liberated when viewing their own file and were able to find answers to problems and hang-ups they had been working on. Others avoided their own file out of fear they would not be able to handle unpleasantries that had occurred in a former lifetime. Karl vented his annoyance about the release of the records and the loss of privacy many would experience if all the records would be open for all to read, but he knew that both Linh and his parents had welcomed it. They felt they had nothing to hide and were not concerned about privacy. The government felt release of the records would eliminate crime and corruption as the records recorded everything that happened on a daily basis. There was no way to lie about anything. The privacy issue was a sensitive matter and people felt strongly about it and they had recently voted against installing surveillance cameras on the streets.

In the meantime, Lena had cooked dinner and announced everything was ready. When Karl and Linh were alone, they always invited Lena to sit at the table with them and engaged her in their conversation, but any time guests were present she kept a respectful distance and only appeared when they called her. As always, her cooking was great and after dinner they enjoyed a 3D holographic movie. As a surprise, Karl had ordered an ice cream cake from a store in the city and it was delivered on time by a drone that landed right next to their pool. Most smaller packages were drone delivered and the efficiency and speed of the drones were amazing. Accidents and delivering to the wrong address hardly ever happened. Karl paid for the cake with a swipe of his wrist where his electronic microchip was implanted.

It was turning dark and they went inside to enjoy their cake and Linh brought up the subject of women's rights. In the Western countries, women had gained full equality with men over a century ago, but in the Muslim countries male dominance prevailed until the women had had enough and rose up and demanded equal rights. The Muslim men had no choice but to comply and granted the women full rights as the rest of the world focused their interest on the issue and shamed the men into modernizing their views. A few countries in Africa and some tribes in India, where women were still subjugated, soon followed suit and subsequently all women everywhere had equal rights. It was finally recognized and accepted that each person has free will and no one can force his or her will on someone else and no person can own another person. This concept had, of course, been in effect for a very long time in the more modern countries, but the Muslim countries had refused to adhere to those beliefs and when the change arrived, the women celebrated and felt they had been awarded a new life. They looked forward to the same independent lifestyle as the women in the western countries enjoyed. As part of their equal rights package, women did not have to cover themselves and no special dress code was in effect. In the western countries it was common for women to hold leadership positions in both the government and business world and these positions were awarded strictly based on merit and nothing else.

Karl took the following day off from work and they spent a leisurely day at the pool. They listened to a 3D holographic opera performance sung by Derek and admired his powerful voice. Derek was an accomplished performer and well known. He was married to another opera singer. Their frequent travels and busy lifestyle were perhaps the reason they had no children.

"Before we leave San Francisco, we'll take a day trip orbiting the Earth," Linnéa said. "Your city is the closest city that offers the tour and since we're here already, I booked the trip before we left home. We chose the tour that orbits at low orbit and the ship will orbit twice. I'll stay strapped into my seat, but Dad wants to experience zero gravity and float around a little. I would have liked to travel on a ship with artificial gravity, but there's none yet. At least it's pressurized."

"You'll have a fantastic trip and the first time we went we felt overwhelmed by the awesome beauty of Earth," Karl said. "We plan to vacation on the Moon next month and stay for a week. Both the hotel and he tour buses are pressurized and we'll take daily trips to see as much of the moon as we can fit into a week. We've never been on the Moon, so we're looking forward to it."

"We're too old for a Moon trip," Bjorn sighed. "We enjoy watching all the 3D holographic movies about space and it's so real that we feel we are there."

The space program had been slow to start due to the enormous cost and the difficulty to find experienced engineers and computer scientists. No country had their own space program and there were a few places around the world where all the countries worked together and shared the cost of developing space technology. So many of the best engineers and creative people had died from the superbug and the few that had survived had done their best to train new engineers. Luckily, all the courses and text books from various engineering schools were available on servers and there was a big drive to entice young people to study science and engineering. The space program had been set back many years due to the collapse, but people's interest in space had been revived and every advancement was celebrated. The Moon program and the spaceships needed to travel there had been a difficult endeavor to achieve. Tours to the Moon had only been offered the last few years and engineers were working intensely to improve tourism into space. Several teams were working on more advanced spaceships to be used for trips to Mars, but that would take more time to accomplish. Colonization of Mars was of big interest, but to develop a workable infrastructure had proven to be more difficult than first thought and the team working on this project had not been able to overcome all the obstacles yet.

Karl's son Forrest and his five-year-old daughter Hilma accompanied Bjorn and Linnéa on their orbit cruise. Forrest had slightly oriental features and looked more like Linh than Karl. Little Hilma was quite sophisticated for her age and had had a computer microchip implanted at birth under the skin behind her ear boosting her cognitive abilities. This was now standard procedure and all newborn children left the hospital with an implant suitable for a young child. Children's implants were carefully chosen to fit the child's age and were replaced every two years with a slightly more advanced model. Most adults had opted for implants and there were several models to choose between. Some of the more advanced implants featured dictionary, history and a variety of information as part of the chip while the simpler implants just boosted intelligence and cognition. Not everyone could tolerate the most advanced implants and opted for a basic model. Implants were not so common among the elderly and both Bjorn and Linnéa had still not decided whether to go ahead or not, but all members of the Nordin family had implants and loved the results. The implants made a huge difference in learning and comprehension and so far, no malfunctions had been reported. One attempt by a madman to plant a virus over the Internet into people's implants was immediately stopped by checking the Akashic Records and the person was caught the same day. Some adults could not adjust to the implant and felt so overwhelmed by it they chose to have it removed.

After they were strapped in, the ship took off and very quickly gained altitude until they reached 250 miles above Earth's surface and entered orbit. They felt the force of the acceleration on their bodies, but once they were in orbit and were cruising at seventeen thousand miles per hour, there was no pressure and they could just enjoy the awesome view of planet Earth. All of them marveled at the beauty of their planet and after one revolution they were glad that the trip offered two revolutions around Earth. Bjorn and Forrest took the opportunity to experience zero gravity, but Linnéa and Hilma stayed strapped into their seats. Both of them were grateful they did not need to use the restroom as floating over there seemed rather troublesome. There were handles and straps to grab onto for the passengers when they were ready to return to their seats, so no one needed to bump into anyone. Bjorn and Forrest were enjoying themselves immensely up at the ceiling of the ship, but found that returning to their seats was not as easy as they had thought and they had to pull themselves down little by little until they finally were back and securely strapped in. The beauty of Earth and the excitement of the trip left a big impression on all of them.

Forrest, Hilma, Linnéa and Bjorn returned back to Karl's home by a driverless groundmobile cab. Forrest entered Karl's address into the computer and the cab safely drove them to Karl's home. Forrest paid with a swipe of his wrist. Airborne cabs were also available, but for shorter distances the groundmobiles were fast and reliable and rather inexpensive. At home, Linh ran a medical scanner over Hilma's body to ensure the space flight had not in any way affected her and everything tested normal. Bjorn and Linnéa returned home the next morning with their Bird.

Forrest lived within walking distance of Karl and Linh and holding Hilma's little hand they slowly strolled back home. The neighborhood was well kept with average sized homes, not too crowded and each house had an acre of land. His wife Sheena was a flaming redhead with a freckled nose. She was waiting at the front door holding their two-year-old baby girl Cecily, or Cellie for short, and eager to hear about the trip. With great enthusiasm, Hilma told her mom all the details of the trip and showed her the film she had taken of Earth. Sheena had never been in space, so she enjoyed hearing all about it and her dark amber colored eyes were totally focused on her daughter. Hilma was able to express herself quite well for a five-year-old and her implant enabled her to comprehend topics that would have been impossible to understand for such a small child without the implant.

"How I wish Cellie could have come along," Hilma said and eagerly took her little sister from her mom and hugged her.

Cellie could master simple speech thanks to her implant and when Hilma put her down, they walked into the backyard to play. One of the toys the girls loved to play with was a robotic goat resembling Snow-White, a gift from grandpa Karl. Karl had strong memories of Snow-White and her kind disposition and he could still taste her wonderful, rich milk. After he and his mother moved to the Nordin farm, he had visited Snow-White many times and he would never forget her. Snow-White died of old age at thirteen years old and was missed by many people who had enjoyed her as a unique being of high intelligence. She had lived a pampered life filled with affection and in return delivered nine babies and tons of milk. Snow-White was fully aware people drank her milk as she often smelled her own milk on Linnéa's and Karl's breath and she held herself in high esteem.

The girls activated Snow-White and 'milked' her while enjoying listening to her voice. She had real fur and looked very much alive and from a distance it was hard to tell whether she was a live animal or not. Each day Sheena would fill Show-White's tank with a pint of milk so the girls could milk her and drink the milk. Her udder felt and looked like the real thing. Hilma did not play that much anymore, but when she was with Cellie, she did have fun playing little games suitable for a toddler.

The following morning the school bus arrived. It was driverless, but had a robot attendant onboard to assist the children and to keep order on the bus. The robot was a cheaper version of an android and not as advanced as Lena, but still fully capable of seeing to the children's needs. Children attended schools in their neighborhoods, but college courses were usually given over the Internet and only a few universities remained open. The efficiency of the Internet higher education was excellent and the courses were free. The universities maintained libraries and gave lectures as well as offered specific courses that required lab experiments. They also did the testing of the college students who studied at home using the Internet.

Hilma went to her study group of twelve children and her human teacher started the first lesson for the day with reading from a large screen located in the front of the room. All the children had implants and were able to read already and they took turns reading out loud and then discussing the topic. The next lesson was writing and they all practiced their skills writing on paper. The parents felt, and the teachers agreed, old-fashioned paper was better to use at this early stage of learning than the standard computer tablets. The parents wanted their children to master penmanship and not rely totally on the tablets. Cursive script would soon start. There was no set curriculum and each study group worked according to the needs and ability of the children in each group. Some groups were more advanced, but no stigma was attached to being in a lower group. There were no tests to pass and consequently no stress. Testing was, however, used to qualify for higher education and entry into these classes was based on merit. The overall result of the children's education was excellent and emphasis was placed on each student's aptitude. Whenever a student had mastered the skills in one study group, he or she moved up to the next level, sometimes with a few other children who also had qualified for the higher level.

After lunch, Hilma had a lesson in psychology and the lesson was over the Internet. This subject was a favorite with the children and was presented in an easygoing and humorous way. They were taught how to understand and master their feelings, the art of interacting with other children, respect for others and self and how needless fear could be avoided. As the children grew older the lessons became more sophisticated and the students understood how important the subject of psychology was. Psychological wounds were addressed and dealt with before they became a problem and each student was trained to recognize and correct any problem he or she had. The children gained self-control and a feeling of wellbeing and as a result behavior problems were rare.

The older children were taught to dare being themselves and refrain from building a false facade believing this improved appearance would make them more acceptable. This was not an easy concept for the children to understand at first, but they eventually saw that a false improved image of themselves would only lead to lies and insecurity.

Another topic the children struggled with was the ability to make their own decisions. Many feared making decisions and did not trust themselves. The teacher emphasized that a bad decision was better than avoiding making a decision as a wrong decision can be replaced by a good decision. The next step in their learning process was to understand that some decisions have unintended consequences, which forced the children to think ahead. The children understood if they allowed someone else to make their decisions for them, they would cease to grow.

The older children also dealt with overcoming fear and how to apply their minds to conquer this crippling feeling. They were taught to decide that they could actually bring all fears under control by using mind over matter. The teacher reminded them that fear is an illusion of the mind and there is no need to surrender to fear. Obviously, the concept referred to fears not involving situations of life and death.

The whole psychology program worked well and resulted in self-sufficient adults with sane minds.

Several years ago, a team of elderly scholars had dumped all history books and rewritten new textbooks based solely on original documents and records in order to teach the students the truth about history. They knew the books used before the collapse were inaccurate and had been written to suit the political agenda of that time. The team also carefully examined the textbooks covering the other subjects of the curriculum and removed all falsehoods and fabrications. It was recognized among scholars there was no ultimate system for education and new thoughts would replace outdated ideas. The system will always change and modernize.

Linh was a volunteer teacher and taught biology to the older students. She also gave a course in premed studies that was popular with the college students.

CHAPTER 9

Karl and Linh were preparing for their week-long trip to the Moon. They would travel onboard a spaceship, which was the only way to reach the Moon for now. Dreams of teleportation remained dreams and no one had been able to make the system work.

Another way people dreamed of reaching the Moon was a lunar space elevator. At present, engineers were working on designing a space elevator but, so far, the difficulties and problems involved had not been overcome. The elevator needed to reach an altitude of sixty-two thousand miles and have a super strong cable with several attached elevators climbing from Earth all the way to the top. A gigantic counterweight in space, possibly an asteroid, for the other end of the cable would also be necessary and the engineers had not been able to find a workable and affordable solution. The elevator would take at least a week to travel the full distance of the cable and perhaps the system would be better for cargo rather than for passengers. Weather and space debris added difficulties to the design as well as the vibrational issue referred to as vortex shedding. Moreover, the effect of solar wind and the Earth's wobble were additional issues and how they would affect the support system was unknown. A space elevator would be able to lift at least one hundred tons, but probably much more, and would cut the cost of launching cargo into space tremendously. The people working on the space elevator had not given up and reasoned if the elevator could be built the cost of sending cargo and passengers into space would be very affordable. If it worked well a lunar elevator could also be built. Both well-meaning citizens and experts in the field of space advised against pursuing the elevator and felt it was a waste of time and money, but the design team ignored such advice and stubbornly continued their work to create a safe elevator that would work flawlessly. They had just enough funding from the mining companies to continue their work.

It was six o'clock in the morning and Karl and Linh were safely strapped into their seats onboard the Moon spaceship. They were both excited and a little anxious. There were twenty passengers on the ship, two on each side of a center aisle and at the present time children and the elderly were not permitted due to the stress of the trip. As an extra precaution all passengers had to pass a basic medical check-up. The company offering the Moon trips had issued a news release that very soon their new fleet of ships would be faster and more comfortable and the age restrictions would be eliminated. The ship also carried the drinking water needed by the hotel. The mostly stainless-steel ship glimmered in the sun and as the passengers boarded, the ship was in a horizontal position. Outside the ship the tanker trucks pumped cooled fuels into the ship's tanks. Finally, everything was ready for take-off and the doors were safely closed. Linh noticed that the pilots were human, but the crew were androids and they seemed as advanced as their Lena. The journey would take about eleven, twelve hours and the ship would reach a maximum speed of twenty thousand miles per hour. To make the trip less stressful, the seats were very comfortable and could be lowered fully if the passenger wanted to sleep. In front of each seat, a flat screen offered Internet access and streaming movies. The ship was fully pressurized. Sturdy rails in the aisle and overhead handles to grab onto made navigating down to the restrooms easy.

The ship was now in a vertical position and the engines of the launch rocket ignited. The ship was well insulated so the roar of the engines was loud but bearable. Liftoff! The upward thrust of the liftoff was substantial and as acceleration increased, Karl and Linh were pushed back into their seats. The straps around their bodies held them firmly and limited the feel of vibration. The speed increased and soon they were mostly free of Earth's atmosphere and the launch rocket separated. The spaceship's engines ignited and slowly the ship adjusted to a horizontal position and they were on their way to the Moon. The windows on the ship were large and they watched the launch rocket travel back to Earth. All rockets were fully reusable and as soon as a rocket had returned to the launching pad and landed in a vertical position it could be refueled and reused.

Karl and Linh were a little overwhelmed by the excitement of the launch and enjoyed looking out the windows at the spectacular view of Earth and the blue oceans. Several hours went by and they were offered by the ship's crew to experience zero gravity. Five passengers at the time could float around in the ship for an hour and then return to their seats. They accepted the offer and unstrapped their harnesses. A slow push was all it took to lift themselves up and using the bars, they pulled themselves straight up in order not to bump into any passenger and were soon at the ceiling of the ship. What a feeling to be weightless, how free they felt. After an hour of playing around they pulled themselves slowly back above their seats and then down using the side bars. Both of them decided to visit the restroom before strapping themselves back into their seats. They felt a little unsteady after their hour of weightlessness and held onto the guard rails firmly to get down to the back of the ship where the restrooms were located. This was their first time using a toilet facility in zero gravity. They did not need to be concerned as the instructions were clear and everything was very clean. Linh put the strap around her waist to avoid floating away, put a sanitary plastic liner on the suction tube attached to a hose and relieved herself. The liner went into a waste receptacle and was sucked down. Linh entered her hands into another receptacle and her hands were sanitized with warm antiseptic steam. The whole experience was easy and well thought out.

It was now dinner time and the space crew attached a tray covered with a lid in front of their seats. The crew had a strap around their waist and the strap was attached to the handrail in the aisle. Each tray contained several labeled mylar bags and a bottle of juice with a plastic straw that could be shut off with a valve. Their dinner consisted of steak, potatoes, pureed peas and for dessert strawberries. The steak and potatoes were cut up and easy to eat. A small corner of the bag could be opened so they could insert a fork and they ate the pureed peas with a spoon. The dinner was tasty and the steak very tender.

As they were nearing the Moon, the ship fired the retro-propulsive thrusters and Karl and Linh felt how the ship slowed down as they entered Moon orbit. Their scheduled landing place was close to the Moon's North Pole and this area had almost constant sunlight and was relatively warm at fifty to sixty degrees below zero Fahrenheit. The ship was now close to the landing area and was braking, falling gently towards the surface with the ship's nose slightly up. They could now see far below them the hotel and the landing pad for the ship. It was the first and only hotel on the Moon, but several hotels were planned for the future. The thrusters were firing and the ship moved into a vertical position and was gently falling down and with the help of sensors they made a soft touchdown. A large shuttle bus hooked up with the ship and the androids could now safely open the door and welcome the passengers to the Moon. The passengers reached the base of the spaceship with the help of a steep spiral staircase.

Both Karl and Linh felt wobbly on their legs after the long trip and were glad to enter the bus. It was nicely warm inside the large bus and it was pressurized. An android on the bus welcomed them and after they were all seated the self-driving bus quickly drove them to the hotel. The hotel was a domed building and not overly large. As they all entered the lobby through the airlock, they felt for the first time the difference between Earth's gravity and the Moon's much lighter gravity - only seventeen percent of Earth's gravity. It was difficult to walk normally and they had to hold onto the handrail as they tried to get their bearings. Without the handrail, they felt they may lose their balance and they realized they had to walk slowly and concentrate on finding their footing.

The hotel was run by a mix of robots and androids and they saw only two humans, a man and a woman in their forties who appeared to be the managers. One of them welcomed them and introduced himself -

"I'm Mike Dillon, the hotel's manager, and this is my wife Sophie, my assistant. We're the only two humans here and all the work is done by our robots and androids. The androids are fully updated and can master all aspects of human interaction as well as speak several languages. I know you'll find walking around very strange until you get the knack of it and we advise you to wear a weight suit. They're easy to wear and will simplify your walking stability. We supply them for free.

"We keep the hotel around seventy degrees, but you can increase or decrease the temperature in your rooms, if you prefer," Mr. Dillon continued. "Dinner will be served in one hour and we will both be there to answer any questions you may have. For now, let's take you to your rooms. The weight suits are lined up over there on the shelves and just grab one. It will make your walking a little easier. We use them ourselves."

All the guests took a weight suit and after they had put them on, they felt more stable as they followed the Dillons to their rooms one floor below the lobby. Their names were posted on the doors and Karl and Linh were pleasantly surprised at the spaciousness of their room and the bathroom was nice and equipped with a shower. Above the shower was a reminder to limit showers to five minutes to save water. The scientists knew the craters on the Moon contained frozen water at both the south and north poles in addition to some water ice close to the surface. Millions, perhaps billions, of metric tons of water ice were available in the craters, but the method of mining and extracting it had not started yet. The cost was one of the major factors. Every spaceship carried several tanks of water and the hotel recycled shower and wash water, but not waste water. Since there was only one hotel on the Moon at the present time, it was easier to just bring the drinking water from Earth to the Moon, but in the future when the Moon was colonized, water extraction would begin.

The oxygen for the hotel was extracted from lunar soil and the process worked well. Other methods were being researched on Earth, but were not yet available.

The dinner was enjoyable even though all the foods were freeze dried except their salad bowl, which was a tasty mix of micro greens grown under a mix of red and blue lights in the hotel's kitchen. There were plans for the future to grow vegetables in indoor greenhouses, but those plans were still a few years off. The hotel's android chef grew a variety of hardy crickets in special breeding boxes in the kitchen and any guest adventurous enough to try stir fried crickets was served a protein rich insect dinner that was quite delicious. Karl and Linh tried it and were surprised at how good it tasted.

"We offer two bus trips daily, mornings or afternoons, in our pressurized excursion bus that will take you on a three-hour trip," Mr. Dillon explained. "You need to sign up for it the day before. We also have Exploration Rovers that seat four people. Obviously, you must wear a space suit to ride in a Rover and we supply them free of charge. The Rovers are driverless and run on an electric motor with a capacity to run at least ten hours on one charge. No one stays out that long so you don't have to worry about "running out of gas". If you want to try a trip with a Rover, you'll have to inform us the day before so we can have one fully charged for you. The bus leaves from the front of the hotel. The Rovers are parked behind the hotel and you put on your suits in a special equipment room before exiting outside. I suggest you visit the restrooms before any trip to avoid the discomfort of Nature."

The people smiled and nodded as Mr. Dillon continued -

"By the way, call me Mike and my wife Sophie. In addition to exterior excursions, we offer indoor activities for those who prefer to rest and just enjoy being on the Moon. We have two Holodecks with virtual reality that are very popular with our guests and you can create any environment you want. You get a two-hour session and you need to enter your name on the list. When everyone has had their turn, the Holodecks are available on a first come, first serve basis. For those of you who are science minded, we provide lectures about the latest space inventions going on as well as detailed information about the whole space program visiting other planets. These lectures are constantly updated so the information is the absolute latest and we take pride in the accuracy of the information. You'll be surprised how fast your five days here on the Moon will pass and in addition to the activities I have mentioned, we have game rooms and other entertainment for you to try out. Some of you may enjoy just conversing for a while with one of our androids. Believe me, they are both fun and interesting to interact with."

Now Sophie took over. She was of Chinese descent and looked very kind.

"A few of you may feel your digestion is not as normal as it would be on Earth and that is due to the low gravity. We have herbal remedies to help you out if you need it. I'm a registered nurse and I can attend to most medical problems that may come up with the exception of surgeries and severe injuries. In case of a life-threatening injury, we would return that guest with our space ship to Earth immediately at no charge. I did notice that Linh Nordin is a medical doctor and we often have doctors as guests. Let's just hope no one needs medical attention. Does anyone have a question for Mike or me?"

Now followed an hour of back-and-forth interaction between the guests and Mike and Sophie and after a nightcap of cognac everyone retired to bed. Before leaving the dining room, Karl put his and Linh's names on the list for the bus tour the following day. Both Karl and Linh felt exhausted and longed to collapse in bed. It had been a long day with the most excitement they had ever experienced. Back again in their room, they were glad to find out that the toilet was power assisted and functioned well. They both slept like dead that first night.

The next morning after breakfast, they boarded the bus and took off. One female android functioned as guide and explained what they saw and answered questions. She was pleasant with a clear voice but humorless. Outside the bus was a freezing fifty-five degrees below zero Fahrenheit temperature, but it was nice and cozy inside the bus. Everywhere were stones and boulders and the clingy dust soon coated the bus even though the bus followed a scraped path. The tour was fascinating and both Karl and Linh decided that their next trip would be with the Rover.

The afternoon was spent attending a lecture about the Mars program and it was presented with a mix of 3D holographic images and standard film on a large screen. Karl and Linh found it most interesting.

The next day they donned their space suits and helmets and as soon as they were able to breathe, the doors opened and they were allowed to climb into their Rover together with two other guests. An android sat in a single seat at the back behind the passengers. The space suits were heavy, but not uncomfortable, and they could communicate via the built-in radio. They were required to wear diapers to protect the expensive suits and Linh and Karl smiled at each other when they put them on, both determined not to allow an accident to occur. The Rover traveled in the opposite direction of the bus tour and the landscape was almost the same, but with more craters and several steep bluffs. It was cold outside, but the suits kept them warm. The dust stirred up by the Rover was all over them and they had to wipe the faceplates of their helmets off to be able to see. They stopped the Rover to go for a short walk to get the feel of walking on the surface and found that the weight of the suit made it easier to move and hopping rather than walking was the way to move forward. It was time to return to the hotel and the android entered the code into the Rover's computer. Back at the hotel, the suits were cleaned and sanitized by a team of robots. It had been an overwhelming excursion and Karl and Linh decided to just enjoy the many amenities of the hotel for the rest of the day.

Before going to bed, they tried out the shower and found that the water fell slowly and gently from the shower head, just fast enough to qualify as a shower but, obviously, not with the same pressure as on Earth.

The Holodeck was an adventure and Karl and Linh had reserved both, one for each of them. Karl wanted to experience the deep part of the Pacific Ocean while Linh opted for Jupiter's moon Europa and Saturn's moon Enceladus. Both of these moons had water below the frozen surface and Linh was interested to find out more about them.

They were both impressed by the lifelike graphics and felt they had actually been there.

The five days passed very quickly and with daily outings and other activities, Karl and Linh were pleased with their vacation and ready to return to Earth. The Moon trip had been the biggest adventure of their lives and very expensive, but Karl was a man of means and could afford it. They both felt once was enough and they had no plans for a second trip to the Moon.

The return flight went well and the reentry into Earth's atmosphere was easy with the ceramic tiles providing an effective heat shield. They landed vertically, but there were other space ships around that landed by gliding down to Earth in a horizontal position. Karl and Linh were glad to be back on Earth and would savor the trip for the rest of their lives. As a precaution, Linh ran her medical scanner over them to ensure no abnormalities had emerged from the trip, but all the signs were normal. Lena welcomed them back and had spent the week cleaning the house and finishing all the chores on her to-do list. Linh showed her all the holographic images from the Moon and Lena enjoyed them a lot.

******

Hilma wanted to hear everything about her grandparents' trip to the Moon. Forrest had bought a powerful telescope for Hilma and together they studied the Moon's surface.

"Every time we look, we see the same side of the Moon," Hilma said confused. "Why don't we see the other side?"

"Because it takes the same time for the Moon to rotate one time around its own axis as it takes to travel once around Earth. The timing is the same. It takes the Moon about 27 days to orbit the Earth. You can only see the far side of the Moon from a spaceship," Forrest explained. "By the way, why do we have tides in the ocean?"

Hilma thought hard and finally said -

"Is it the force of the Moon on the ocean?"

"Right you are, Hilma." Forrest was pleasantly surprised that Hilma figured it out. "The gravitational pull of the Moon causes the tides on Earth."

"Tell me more about the Moon."

"You're about forty pounds, but on the Moon, you would only weigh six, seven pounds. Guess, how high you'd be able to jump! There's no atmosphere and no wind on the Moon so the sky is black."

"How big is the Moon?"

"About one quarter of Earth. That means four Moons can fit inside Earth."

"Where did the Moon come from?"

"It's believed that a long time ago a huge object crashed into Earth and a large piece of Earth came off and all the pieces from the crash eventually formed the Moon. This happened by gravitational force. Gravity pulls matter together and all the little pieces were pulled into one large piece, which became the Moon. Do you understand?"

"I think so, Dad," Hilma said.

"It hasn't been proven, but that's what the scientists believe happened."

Forrest was glad Hilma had been able to grasp the whole topic of the Moon and they returned home.

CHAPTER 10

Back at the Nordin farm, Linnéa and Bjorn had finally decided to go ahead and have a computer microchip implanted. The procedure was done at a doctor's office and was quick and painless. The chip could easily be removed if they had trouble adjusting to it. Slowly over a week their brains interacted with the chip and as their memory and cognition increased, they felt as if they went through an awakening. The experience was mind-boggling, but very exciting and every day they discovered they had new abilities. Their thinking capacity and problem solving felt effortless and they said to each other that they should have gone through with the procedure years ago when the chip was first introduced.

******

Two years passed and a new century arrived. Karl had turned his business over to his employees, who he cared about and respected, in exchange for a modest compensation package and he and Linh were now fully retired. They had many years of retirement to look forward to as the lifespan of most people had increased to around one hundred years and most people enjoyed good health and cognition.

Clarence Nordin had been released from prison and was now twenty-three years old. He had promised himself to never commit any crime again and even though modern prisons were a far cry from the dangerous places they had been in the past, he had still been locked up and lost his freedom. No one had abused him or attacked him in prison and he was grateful for that. His parents had invited him to live at home, but he had decided to move to San Francisco and try to find employment with one of the numerous tech companies. He had applied to the government for his basic income and would be able to live just fine on that money until he was able to find a challenging job. His goal was to work with artificial intelligence and he had great trust in his own abilities and knew he was capable of almost any job in the computer industry. Another dream he had was to work on human teleportation, but he realized development of such sophisticated software was far off in the future. In prison he had studied programming and computer science and advanced quite a lot. He knew he was welcome in Karl's home, his father's cousin, and also in Forrest's family. Clarence and Forrest were second cousins and even though Forrest was ten years older than Clarence, they had met many times at family gatherings and got along well.

Clarence arrived in San Francisco with his two suitcases. He had taken an airmobile taxi from the prison and Forrest had rented a small apartment for him in the outskirts of the city. The apartment was fully furnished with a well-equipped kitchen, bright and sunny, and he was very pleased with it. Now, all he needed was to find a job and that turned out to be trickier than Clarence had expected. Most companies hired former convicts, but Clarence had used the money from the accounts he had hacked into and that fact added an extra problem to his trustworthiness. Several companies turned him away. As he sat in front of the hiring manager of the company he desperately wanted to work for, he felt worried. After the interview, the manager kept looking at his application.

"Do you have any computer problem right now in your office? I'll fix it for you to show you what I can do. I'll work for free," Clarence blurted out.

The manager hesitated as he slowly lifted his eyes from the application on the computer screen built into his desk and said -

"Actually, we do. We're writing a new program in artificial intelligence and have run into a problem none of our programmers has been able to solve. If you can resolve the issue, you're hired."

As Clarence sat down at the desk and started to analyze the software, he had a rough idea what the obstacle was. After consulting with the other programmers and listening to their input, he worked for four days and rewrote parts of the program. To his relief, it worked and he was hired.

Clarence walked joyfully home to his apartment, but first he stopped by a food store and bought the ingredients for a pizza neatly packaged into five mylar bags. He paid with his wrist implant and back in his apartment he emptied the contents of each bag into the canisters of the 3D food printer and pressed start. His kitchen did not have an electric range and he had decided to buy one. For now, he would have to use the printer, but he planned to teach himself to cook the old-fashioned way and that required a range. His mother had enjoyed cooking and he grew up on foods cooked the traditional way. Electric ranges were still available and robotic maids were fully capable of using them. The 3D printers were indispensable in the manufacturing and medical industries where they were shining stars, but for cooking many people still swore by the old-fashioned range.

While he was waiting for the printer to cook his pizza, Clarence gave a voice command to his wrist communicator to call his parents and his father Colin answered. Clarence told him the good news that he had landed his dream job and the holographic image of his father grinning ear to ear as he listened to the news felt heartwarming to Clarence. He knew he had caused his parents enormous grief when he was convicted of his crime and it was a relief to finally deliver good news.

Clarence continued working on the artificial intelligence software program and earned respect from his team members for his ingenious solutions to any setback they encountered. The software was complicated and involved designing an artificial brain with much more capacity than Lena's model had, but Clarence was the right man for the job. He had a special 'feel' for computers and was first-rate.

Clarence finished his first four-day work week and had accepted an invitation to spend the weekend with Karl and his family. He knew them rather well from the family gatherings at the farm. Joy's son Drew, Clarence' second cousin, was also invited and he looked forward to seeing him. Clarence and Drew had played together as kids when both were visiting the farm. Drew was thirty-one years old, unmarried, and worked as a fisherman. He owned his own fishing boat and had it anchored in San Francisco harbor. The waters outside the city had been cleaned up years ago and was safe for fishing. Drew was a free spirit preferring life on the water rather than being cooped up in an office.

It was a happy reunion to meet Karl and his family and Drew was already there. Drew was a bearded, somewhat scruffy looking guy, but handsome in a masculine way. He had a laid-back nature and while smiling warmly at Clarence, he gave him a bear hug and immediately invited him for a trip on his boat. No one mentioned Clarence' prison time and what was ahead of them was more important than the past.

Clarence took the opportunity to chat with Lena to compare her skills with the model he was hoping to design and realized she was more advanced than he had expected. He found her charming and easy to communicate with and so lifelike he almost forgot she was a machine. Lena listened attentively when Clarence explained he was working on designing a more advanced model of herself and offered several suggestions that were of interest to Clarence. In the future, he often consulted with her for tips and she always had interesting ideas that he was able to incorporate into his design.

The second day, Karl took Clarence into his garage and showed him his 2019 Harley-Davidson motorcycle, a dark blue twin engine Low Rider. It was an antique and over eighty years old, but still ridable and a beauty.

"Remember this one?" Karl asked. Clarence nodded excitedly. Of course, he remembered. He had admired it when he was a kid and Karl had kept it stored in the Nordin barn until he moved to San Francisco and decided to take it along.

"You can use it anytime you want," Karl continued. "I'll teach you how to run it and the country roads are perfect for a motor bike. Very little traffic and beautiful scenery. It tops out at ninety miles per hour, but I would ask you not to ride that fast."

"Wow, Karl, how cool and thanks a lot. I'm dying to ride it," Clarence said with enthusiasm. He could hardly contain himself in his excitement.

Karl spent the next few hours going over the bike with Clarence and then took him for a spin. It was hard to believe the bike was over eighty years old and the old gasoline engines had been replaced by twin electric engines. Karl drove the bike to a secluded road and let Clarence take over. Clarence had no trouble balancing the bike, but he stumbled with the controls and realized that it would take a while until he would master it. To say he loved the bike was an understatement. There were few motorcycles around, but they were still made for the dedicated enthusiasts. The following day he drove the bike alone and kept the speed slow to get the feel of the bike and after a few hours he was able to relax a little. As Karl had told him, the country roads were indeed beautiful and he saw only one groundmobile on the road. He kept the speed below sixty miles per hour and with the wind blowing in his face he felt a touch of euphoria. This was the first of many such rides Clarence enjoyed with the Low Rider.

Clarence returned to his apartment after promising Drew to spend the next Saturday on his fishing boat.

Early next Saturday Clarence met Drew on the pier and jumped aboard his forty-foot fishing boat Liberty. It was a relatively new boat equipped with all the latest technology and was powered by twin electric engines. A large generator that was hooked up to a black box emitting electricity supplied the power to the engines. A galley and twin cabins made it a temporary home. On the deck was standard fishing equipment and built-in coolers for the fish. Drew's girlfriend Tina was onboard and Clarence liked her right away. A pretty ponytailed girl in her mid twenties with brown hair and a quick smile. As they talked, Tina told Clarence she had a small business manufacturing herbal medicines and supplements. Being her own boss, she could take days off and share Drew's fishing life. They were planning to apply for a marriage contract in the near future. Clarence noticed she wore an engagement ring.

Drew had cast his net the day before and was hoping for a big catch of herring. He drove a short distance from shore until reaching the little buoy identifying his net and pulled it up. His electric winch slowly pulled the net up and separated the fish from the net and then neatly rolled up the net onto a reel. A lucky day for Drew with abundant herring in the net. Drew and Clarence raked the fish into the refrigerated coolers while Tina made lunch for them. The galley was well equipped with both an electric range and large refrigerator and a table that seated six people.

After lunch, they spent an hour just sitting around and talking. Some fishermen had robots working as crew members, but Drew was a traditional man and preferred humans. When fishing in the bay, Drew and Tina did the work themselves, but for offshore fishing Drew had two men helping out.

As they returned to the harbor, about a mile from the shore Clarence noticed a dozen floating homes forming a circle and moored to a floating dock tying the homes together. They were rather attractive, dome shaped with lots of glass windows and seemed to extend below the surface of the water. Each home had a large deck and most of them had planters with vegetables growing. There was also a fishing line hanging in the water from each home supplying, hopefully, dinner for the owner.

"Those homes are mostly for retired people," Drew explained. "The people move from area to area and the homes can move at a slow speed. The bedrooms are below the water line and they can watch the fish from their beds. I've been in one and they're really fun for people who prefer an aquatic lifestyle. All waste is incinerated so there is no pollution discharged into the ocean. They're built to withstand rough weather, but in case of a severe storm they can easily be moved close to shore. The drones deliver groceries and fresh water for their tanks and also pick up their trash. It's all well thought out."

They returned to shore and Drew quickly sold his catch to a buyer waiting for him. The two men knew each other well and this man bought most of the fish Drew caught. Drew's boat was not big enough to handle canning or freezing of the fish onboard, but he still made a good living and was able to enjoy a free lifestyle.

A few months later, Clarence was invited to Drew and Tina's marriage contract ceremony and Clarence wondered within himself when it would be his turn. Even though he was only in his early twenties, he felt ready to settle down, but he did not even have a girlfriend. Drew and Tina had signed a fifteen-year marriage contract hoping to have children soon. Some couples renewed their marriage contract when it expired and some went their separate ways. About half of the people tying the knot chose a marriage contract over traditional marriage.

Drew and Tina spent their honeymoon at an orbiting space hotel, a rotating wheel with simulated gravity and fully pressurized. The rooms for the guests were located at the perimeter of the wheel where the gravity was the highest resembling the gravity of the Moon. The accommodations were luxurious and the view of Earth breathtaking and slowly changing as they traveled around the planet. Drew and Tina would cherish the memory of their space trip for years to come.

******

Three years had passed and Karl and Linh were onboard a supersonic plane cruising at a hundred thousand feet elevation at Mach five. Finally, Linh would visit the country where her ancestors came from and the trip from San Francisco to Vietnam took about two hours. They planned to stay for a few days in Saigon, formerly called Ho Chi Minh City, and then tour the countryside. The plane trip was very smooth at the altitude they were flying and went by quickly.

After Karl and Linh checked into their hotel, they went for a walk in the busy area surrounding the hotel. Vietnam had suffered a tremendous loss of people from the superbug and loss of electricity. The people had worked hard to rebuild. Even though Saigon seemed to be a bustling city, the countryside was very sparsely populated. The country had no army and was run by the same system as America, People Democracy. Vietnam had accepted help from the western countries and manufacturing and tourism had slowly improved their economy. The size of the population was increasing, but still far below what it had been before the superbug hit. The standard of living was good at the present time and all technological modernities had been reintroduced. Vietnam and all neighboring countries had fared about the same with severe losses and hardships and all of them had faced the same struggle to rebuild. The threat of war between the countries was nonexistent as they had entered into an agreement to honor peace at all costs. There was no threat from China or Japan either and southeast Asia had become a peace-loving area.

Karl and Linh enjoyed touring Saigon and ate at the street restaurants. The food was good and Linh planned to cook some of the dishes they sampled at home. They saw few robots and when they asked why, they were told most people could not afford them.

On the third day, they hired a car with chauffeur, who also acted as a guide. They saw no groundmobiles and the car they rode in was an old-style gasoline car. These types of cars had disappeared in the western countries, but were in full use in the less affluent countries. It was hot and steamy outside and the air-conditioning worked hard at full blast. Karl and Linh were fascinated and enjoyed the scenery tremendously. Fields planted with rice and other crops as well as tea were frequent sights and the farm workers they saw were all human, no robots. They stopped at a country restaurant for dinner and then found a small hotel, where they and the chauffeur stayed overnight. The accommodations were not fancy, by no means up to the standard they were used to, but they knew that fact when they booked their trip. Linh mentioned to Karl that she was grateful to live in America and not Vietnam, but she had wanted to see where her ancestors came from for years and was willing to travel in less comfort.

They returned home after a memorable trip and Karl had a wound on his leg. He had stumbled and fallen down while they were exploring a path in the country and neither of them thought it was serious. Linh had cleaned the wound and it seemed to heal well, but a week after their return Karl's leg was swollen and painful. After she had given him a local anesthetic, Linh cut an opening into his leg with a scalpel and pus was visible. Linh immediately contacted the hospital and within fifteen minutes a drone delivered a package containing live maggots. They were placed on Karl's leg and crawled inside the wound. The sight of the maggots was nauseating to watch, but Karl hardened himself and tried to ignore the itching they caused. Finally, after two hours the maggots had consumed all the pus and emerged from his leg tripled in size. Linh quickly collected them and dropped them into a chemical solution that killed them instantly together with any bacteria from the wound. She applied a surgical glue to close the incision and Karl was totally recovered after a few days.

******

Clarence was in love. The girl who stole his heart was a twenty-two-year-old blond named Lotte and she had spent the first part of her life in Holland. Her family moved to the Bay Area of San Francisco when she was ten years old. Her father was a pilot flying the supersonic planes. By moving to America, the family could spend more time together as most of his flights originated from the United States. Lotte had just finished school and was working as an airmobile diagnostic mechanic. She was quite feminine but preferred a masculine type job and trying to analyze airmobile engine problems was right up her alley. She was good at it and usually found what was wrong. The worker robots then carried out the repair according to her instructions. Lotte was well trained and knew exactly how both airmobile and groundmobile engines worked and when the computer could not diagnose the problem, Lotte could. She had worked part time in a garage while going to school and had several years of experience already.

Clarence was riding the Low Rider with Lotte on the passenger seat. The engines were purring as Lotte had recently fine-tuned them. They had been dating a year and in his pocket was a ring he hoped Lotte would accept. After their lunch break, he popped the question and Lotte accepted with an elated smile and gave him a hug. They both wanted a traditional marriage rather than a marriage contract and decided to go ahead with the ceremony the next month. There was no reason to wait as they knew each other rather well by now. A month was all they needed to find the right house and move their belongings into it.

A relatively new 3D printed house was available in a convenient location and Clarence and Lotte bought it. They only needed to buy some weight bearing furniture as most of the walls were LED and would display any decoration they wanted. The home was situated on a rented acre of land and could be transported by a cargo drone to a new site, if they would prefer a new location in the future. Smart technology ran the home, but the kitchen was equipped with a traditional electric range, which pleased Clarence, and it even included a step-in medical pod for scanning of diseases or injuries of any kind. Lotte enjoyed changing the LED display on the walls from tropical to snow landscapes, then space features and sometimes dinosaurs and Clarence could not help but laughing at her ingenuity.

Clarence and Lotte had a lovely wedding with most of the Nordin family attending as well as Lotte's sister and parents. Linnéa and Bjorn did not attend as they were now in their eighties and even though they were still in relatively good health, they felt the trip was too strenuous. For their honeymoon, they had chosen to spend a week at an underwater ocean hotel off the coast of Washington state. The hotel was sitting on the ocean floor at a depth of fifty feet, which was shallow enough to allow bright sunlight to come through. They boarded a submarine shuttle at the shore and reached the hotel after about an hour. The sight of the spherical structure with huge window panels and bathing in sun was so stunning that Clarence and Lotte were amazed. After the shuttle docked with the hotel they entered through the airlock into the sphere. The lobby was awesome with fish swimming outside and the large acrylic windows made the visitors feel as if they were inside an aquarium. A robot bellboy took them to their room and even though it was small, it was comfortable with a spectacular view of the marine life and a shark peeking into their window made them laugh.

An information brochure describing the hotel's mechanical systems was on the night table and they read that the ventilation system supplied fresh air through a duct to the surface. The hotel supplied the same atmospheric pressure as the surface which removed any health concern about decompression. Waste was incinerated ensuring no pollution from the hotel entered the water. Wash water was filtered before it was released into the ocean. Lastly, the drinking water was desalinated ocean water and after purification the water was remineralized. Lotte found the information intriguing and decided to check out the mechanical system just for the fun of it.

The week went by too fast and Clarence and Lotte would have liked to stay longer. They had made daily trips with a submarine and encountered a diving whale that was twice as large as their submarine; an unexpected but awesome sight that all the passengers enjoyed.

Back home again, Clarence and Lotte settled into their new home and started their lives as a married couple. During their honeymoon they had discovered that they were able to communicate without words. Neither of them knew if the transmission of thoughts was due to their computer implants, but they discovered that if one of them would think about a topic, the other one had the ability to detect it and translate the electrical signals into words. They found it entertaining and engaged in it often to increase their psychic abilities. As they started to investigate this phenomenon, they found there were other people who could master this art as well.

******

Trouble was brewing on America's southern border. A psychopath Mexican man in his late twenties had managed to corrupt a small army of men with a promise of monetary gain and power if they joined him in overthrowing the government. The Mexican government was a peace-loving administration that had adopted the same style of governing as America. Pepe Guerra had big plans once he had toppled the government. The American states of Texas, New Mexico, Arizona and southern California were next on his list and he did not anticipate any resistance as he had heard America had no army. In his perverted mind, these southern states should belong to Mexico. His army of seven thousand men and a few women was well armed with assault weapons and hand grenades that they had found in a forgotten armory.

Guerra led his army to the government buildings and boldly marched inside and shot the president and the members of his cabinet. Thirty-three people were lying dead on the floor and Guerra commanded the rest of the employees to remain calm and wait for instructions. Soldiers were posted in every room and the people were told that Guerra was now de facto president.

There had been no war on planet Earth since the collapse and very few countries had an army, but a few years back America had decided to assemble a small military reserve unit to be activated in emergency situations. The decision had been approved by the American voters and the government was hoping they would never have to deploy the troops. America had no intention to ever start a war.

Guerra successfully established leadership over his country and had increased his army to fifteen thousand troops. The Mexican citizens were frightened and strongly disapproved of the coup and Guerra's plan to also invade America. Many had notified America and asked for help to return their country to its former peaceful state.

The American troops flew into the Mexican capital and stormed the government buildings. Guerra and his team were totally unprepared and surrendered without a fight. The troops were disarmed, heavily fined and sentenced to two years of community service after they had served their prison term. The coup was over and peace restored and the world was reminded that aggression against a peaceful country was a thing of the past and would not be tolerated.

CHAPTER 11

Forrest was working in the asteroid mining industry and his company was one of about a dozen involved with different mining techniques. It was a thirty-man company and hundred percent employee owned. Asteroid mining was in the beginning of its development and was still considered experimental and dangerous. Several accidents had occurred involving other companies with total loss of the spaceships, but no loss of human lives as all the workers had been robots. The minerals the companies were looking for were rare and some were non-existent on Earth. Gold, platinum, palladium, iridium and other exotic metals needed for manufacturing of everything from robots, spaceships, LCDs, medical equipment and other important applications were mined. Forrest was working with a team planning new and better ways to retrieve smaller, easy to manage asteroids. His company also had two spaceships capable of mining on large asteroids using robotic workers and then delivering the ore to a large workstation his company owned orbiting the Earth. On the workstation, the rare minerals were extracted and then shipped to Earth by spaceships. Another workstation was in the planning stages for lunar orbit with the extracted minerals to be used on the Moon. Other lunar workstations, not owned by Forrest's company, were already orbiting the Moon and they extracted water from retrieved asteroids containing water. Rocket fuel was made by separating the water into hydrogen and oxygen and the plan was to offer this rocket fuel for sale to spaceships. At the present time the cost of a lunar workstation was beyond what Forrest's company could afford, but they were hoping the income from the mining of small asteroids would eventually be sufficient to build an orbiting lunar workstation. If the space elevators would be in service in the future, they would reduce the cost of asteroid mining tremendously.

Only near-Earth asteroids were targeted and the asteroid belt between Mars and Jupiter was too far from Earth to be considered.

Perhaps they would be mined in the future when faster spaceships had been invented and the cost of space mining had been lowered. Forrest's company was mostly involved with small asteroids, up to twenty feet in diameter. They could be fetched by towing them whole to the workstation orbiting Earth using smaller spaceships under rocket power. Very small asteroids were towed in bags while the larger ones were towed by an elaborate system of cables encircling the whole asteroid.

The present system worked well, but Forrest and his team were looking for ideas to cut the cost of mining. Another problem they were working on was safety. Losing an asteroid in tow and have it crash into Earth had never happened and Forrest and his team were designing methods to ensure it would never happen. Since they only worked with small asteroids, the damage such a small asteroid could inflict would be minor unless it landed in the middle of a city. Some asteroids caught for mining were very dense and may hit Earth without burning up in the atmosphere, so to increase safety was important.

Hilma had announced to Forrest that she would be an asteroid miner when she grew up and that put a smile on her dad's face.

******

Clarence and his team had made a breakthrough in the design of their next android model. This model had feelings, could think independently and would be capable of performing almost any task or profession. It would also be able to teach itself additional skills. Male androids were programmed to be masculine and female androids feminine. Clarence' company had not publicly announced their accomplishment as they were unsure how the news would affect the people. Most people accepted the worker robots, as they were needed for hard labor work, but there was resistance among many citizens towards the advanced androids. Many feared they could take over society and even be a physical threat to humans. Clarence was now a senior partner in the company and together with his partners the decision was finally made to release the news and, as expected, it was met with a mix of cheer and apprehension.

The design of the new, updated android was done mostly by Clarence. The other partners had finally realized how brilliant he was and he was now part owner of the company with a secure income. Both he and Lotte had cancelled their base income from the government as they earned more than enough money to enjoy a comfortable lifestyle. The new design had been patented and would last the standard seven years. Clarence had informed his partners that it was necessary for these new androids to go through a 'childhood' and allow them to evolve into mature adults. At first, his statement was met with skepticism, but as he explained how similar the android brain was to a human brain, they finally understood and agreed with Clarence. Since the patent was only seven years, they decided on a three-year initial education program for the androids until they would be available for sale. That would give them a de facto four years of exclusive selling rights before the patent expired. The manufacturing of the androids was made by a separate company that Clarence' company was part owner of and the two companies were located in the same area. They usually had at least a dozen finished android bodies in stock that only needed the programming inserted, so the first models would be ready within a few days. Everyone looked forward to checking out the new androids.

Clarence told Lena about the new design and asked her if she would like an update to her emotional package and an improved voice box. Her voice was not very melodious and one of the few things Clarence did not like about her design. Lena agreed and with Karl and Linh's approval, Clarence wrote a software program updating her emotions as well as her understanding of humor. She had expansion slots in her back for additional software so Clarence had no trouble inserting an additional software package. He also found her voice box and replaced it with a pleasant female voice capable of singing. The result was a success and Lena as well as Karl and Linh were delighted. From that day on, Lena caught most jokes and joined Karl and Linh when they laughed at something funny. Her feelings had doubled in intensity and came close to those of a human being. Perhaps the most valued asset she had acquired was her beautiful voice and she often sang by herself in the kitchen with a powerful musical voice. When Clarence asked her if she could feel love, she responded without hesitation that she loved him, Karl and Linh as well as the grandchildren who came to visit. Her answer warmed Clarence' heart and brought a tear to his eye.

A year had passed and Lotte was expecting and overjoyed with happiness. After years of hits and misses, the artificial womb had been perfected and about half of the mothers-to-be chose not to carry their babies and opted for the external womb. Lotte wanted no part of it and Clarence, being unusually old-fashioned in many ways, was delighted with her decision. They were hoping for three children and were now able to afford a late model android to help out with the housework and care of the children. Tina and Drew were the happy parents of two boys, Brandon, three years old, and baby James, one year old. They named their first son after Drew's brother who had succumbed in a car accident. Drew's parents, Joy and Wesley, had never fully recovered from the grief of losing their son and were loving grandparents to Brandon and James. Clarence and Lotte and Drew and Tina were close and often visited each other. Tina had also carried her two children to term and delivered them the natural way. The physical pain associated with childbirth was a thing of the past and full pain relief was administered to the mother. Tina had nursed both her babies, which was not that common anymore and she had recommended to Lotte to do the same. Lotte agreed. The last few years infant formula had been perfected and was almost identical to mother's milk. Mothers who chose not to breastfeed would still pump out their colostrum and feed it to the baby to ensure the baby received the antibodies. Lotte enjoyed all the different phases of her pregnancy and was excited when she felt the first kick of the fetus. She also sent loving thoughts to the baby telepathically.

Clarence bought an android and chose his own design. The android, Eva, had only lived through a 'childhood' of a year and a half, but since Clarence had designed her, he was not concerned with that fact and would finish her education himself. He brought her home and got her started with housework to make it easier for Lotte, who by now was only a few months away from delivery. Lotte had quit her job and would stay at home while the children were small. Eva was a hit from day one and bonded with both Lotte and Clarence right away. She was smart, pretty, humorous and carried herself with grace. Her voice was dark, but sweet sounding, and occasionally she would sing a tune while working. She had been programmed to handle all facets of infant care as well as illnesses and emergencies. Her physical strength matched a well-trained man's strength and she could easily pick up an item weighing a hundred pounds. Eva knew Clarence had created her and thought fondly of Clarence as 'father'.

Lotte went into labor and Clarence took her to the hospital with their airmobile. The pain was intense, but as soon as they arrived at the hospital, she was given pain medication and could relax somewhat. The birth went well and Clarence was present. Together they welcomed their first born, a daughter who they named Brianna, a healthy-looking baby with a commanding voice and energetic kicking of her little legs. Vaccinations were no longer administered and parents had refused them for years, but a tiny computer microchip was implanted behind the baby's ear.

Lotte and Eva shared in the care of the baby and while doing so they bonded and became very close. Eva was in the process of improving her cooking skills and often surprised them with delightful dinners. As she noticed how much they appreciated her efforts, she continued her self-education and eventually became a master, just like Lena was. Clarence hated 3D printed food and was pleased with her performance.

******

Seven years had passed since Karl and Linh had vacationed on the Moon and finally serious colonization of the Moon had started. The area selected for a colony was not far from the Moon hotel, since there was water in the craters that could be extracted, and the constant sunlight made the climate more tolerable. Until now, there had been limited interest in living on the Moon even though the technology to settle the Moon had been available for several years. Many citizens had vacationed on the Moon and found it rather nasty and without beauty, so there was no interest from the private sector to live on the Moon. The reason why the decision was made to build a colony was that asteroid mining had increased and the processing of the minerals could be done easier on the Moon than on Earth. Funding for the Moon colonization came from several participating countries working as a team, but private investors had also been invited to join as junior partners in the program.

Two manned workstations had been in lunar orbit for months already as the first step toward colonization of the Moon and later on for space travel. One of the stations would act as a refueling station and sell rocket fuel made from water mined from the craters of the Moon. Larger asteroids intended for mineral and water extraction were towed to the second workstation and secured outside the station until the asteroid could be safely dropped onto the Moon's far side, the side facing away from Earth. Small asteroids were pulled inside the workstation and the minerals were extracted by a team of robots and then sent down to the Moon by a space shuttle. A tremendous variety of precious metals were found on the smaller asteroids and the metals were very pure.

The first village was built rather quickly from lunar soil mixed with magnesium oxide using industrial sized 3D printers. The design of the printers had been complicated as they had to perform under the harsh conditions of the Moon, but eventually a group of inventors succeeded to manufacture a printer that could work in extreme cold and low gravity conditions. A team of robot laborers worked around the clock to erect the buildings. The 'glue' holding the buildings together was a type of salt that hardened the material. Large solar panels supplied the electricity, but the black boxes would be installed later on. Natural Energy was so much easier to work with.

Six dome shaped homes, three large factory type buildings and a few storage buildings completed the first village. A crew of twenty-four people, sixteen males and eight females, as well as fifty robot laborers were sent from Earth to take up residence on the Moon on an annual basis. After one year, each person could choose to renew his or her contract for another year or return to Earth. The pay was very good and many had volunteered for the jobs. Six married couples, two single women and ten single men made up the first employees. Karl's granddaughter Dawn, only twenty-two years old, was one of the two single females. Both Dawn's mother Leanna and her grandparents Karl and Linh had pleaded with Dawn not to go, but Dawn was not listening and determined to be part of the lunar mission. She was to head the greenhouse and with her degree in horticulture she was qualified for the job. Dawn was a good-looking girl with slightly oriental features and her mother Leanna looked like Linh. The family often referred to Dawn in a loving way as 'the mule' as she often would not budge once she had made up her mind on something.

The greenhouse was a hydroponic model resembling an octopus with a center body and six tubular arms for growing plants. Each arm was a hoop structure made from a strong alloy and covered with a double layer of fabric. The arms were buried under a thick layer of lunar soil to protect the plants from radiation and debris. At the end of each arm was an airlock for entrance from the outside. LED light supplied bright light for the plants. The design was not new, but it worked well and this model was chosen among several other available greenhouse designs.

Robots would do most of the daily work and Dawn was hired as the manager and troubleshooter should problems arise.

The trip to the Moon went well and Dawn had moved into her tiny little room, barely larger than a walk-in closet, but it was her own room and supplied the privacy she needed. At times, she preferred solitude and to be alone with her thoughts. A cot for sleeping, a tiny dresser, a shelf and chair to be used as a desk completed the furniture. Dawn did not mind the cramped conditions and knew she would adjust to it. All the buildings were connected and there was no need to put on a space suit when the employees had to move between buildings. Even the greenhouse was connected making it very convenient for Dawn to start her workday. Three robots worked with her inside the greenhouse watering and tending the plants. They did a good job and Dawn could concentrate on fine-tuning the system, hand pollination when the plants bloomed and experimenting with growing various new plants from seed. It was pleasant inside the greenhouse and about seventy degrees Fahrenheit and the very bright lights made her feel as if she was in the sun on Earth. She loved her job and was glad she had insisted on signing up.

Dawn adjusted quickly to the low gravity of the Moon and to ensure she did not lose muscle tissue, she worked out every day in the gym. The buildings were all pressurized and in addition to the well-equipped gym, a holodeck, large lobby with a small bar and a library with computers and even a small supply of old-fashioned printed books, a rarity, were among the amenities. Other entertainment rooms were also provided and Dawn found the whole setup easy to live with.

Dawn sat in the lobby talking to Alexa, the second single girl, and they enjoyed each other's company. They thought on the same wavelength and had become rather close. Alexa had a degree in metallurgy and worked mostly in the lab. She was a pleasant looking blond the same age as Dawn.

"Tomorrow Keith and his team will go and pick up the first asteroid that is scheduled to be dropped from the workstation," Alexa told Dawn. "I asked Keith if I could come along and just watch and he agreed."

Keith was the master mechanic and oversaw maintenance of all vehicles as well as participating in retrieval of dropped asteroids. He always joined the crew with his tool kit ready to jump in should any mechanical system fail.

"Do you think there is a chance I could come along to watch?" Dawn asked in a hopeful voice. "The robots do a good job in the greenhouse and I can easily be gone for a day."

"Let's go over to Keith and ask," Alexa suggested.

They walked over to one of the factory buildings where Keith and a few robots worked on repairing one of the Rovers. Keith was in his early thirties, dark hair and with a friendly nature. Dawn had met him several times already and liked him.

"What's up, ladies?" he asked.

When Alexa asked if Dawn could come along, he smiled and said "of course she can".

Early the next morning they all pulled on space suits and the obligatory diapers. The girls, Keith and his crew of one man and two robot laborers climbed aboard two over-sized Rovers, each vehicle towing a long flatbed trailer. The trip would take two hours and the top speed of the Rovers was twenty miles per hour. Keith and the second human crew member each drove one of the vehicles and it was easy to maneuver as it had a standard steering wheel. The asteroid had been dropped from the workstation to the Moon during the night and was expected to shatter upon impact with the Moon's surface. A lunar drone had been sent to the landing place after the asteroid had been dropped and Keith knew from its cameras exactly how many pieces they were supposed to pick up.

The ride was bumpy, but the Rovers had a wide wheelbase and were very stable even when they ran over large rocks. Dawn enjoyed the scenery even in the absence of anything green and soon they found the landing site and the shattered asteroid, a nineteen-foot-wide rock that had broken into several small pieces except for one piece that looked huge. Dawn wondered how the larger piece could possibly be lifted onto the trailer. Keith lined up the trailer with each rock and launched a robotic arm from the trailer gently scooping up the rock into its bucket. The robots assisted in guiding the rock into place. The first trailer was loaded and the second trailer was now ready for the large boulder. Keith used the robotic arm from the first trailer to shove the boulder into the bucket of the second arm and dropped the boulder onto the trailer. The whole process went well and thanks to the low gravity of the Moon, the robotic arms could handle the weight of the rocks.

The return drive was a little slower and the electric solar powered engines did not seem to labor too hard from the heavily loaded trailers. Dawn had enjoyed the learning experience, but was glad when they were safely back at the home station. Both Alexa and Dawn had to run to the restroom as soon as they had their spacesuits off as neither of them wanted to use their diaper.

The trailers had been parked inside the factory building and the processing of the rocks would start the following day. Dawn heard later from Alexa that the elements extracted from the asteroid were mostly platinum but also several other precious metals of great value and usability. Small asteroids that were bagged and processed inside the workstation in orbit often had very valuable metals and the last asteroid, only seven feet wide, had contained a large amount of pure gold. Some of these metals were used on the Moon and some were sent back to Earth. The mining had not been in operation more than a few years, but it was obvious that the value of the various minerals found was exceeding the cost of the operation. Anyone could start a mining business and there were no restrictions as no one owned anything in space.

Each afternoon Dawn picked enough vegetables for the evening's dinner, loaded them onto a cart and walked over to the kitchen. She took pride in the quality of the produce. The kitchen was run by a human chef assisted by two other human cooks and several robot laborers handling cleanup and dishes. A huge amount of dried and freeze-dried foods had been sent up from Earth to the Moon and with the produce from the greenhouse, people were happy with the selection offered. Fresh yeast bread was baked daily and since the buildings were pressurized, the bread dough did rise.

It was apparent that Alexa and Keith were more than friends, but dating was not encouraged among the crew. Everyone had accepted the company's rules when they were hired, so Alexa and Keith limited their mutual interest in each other to a strong friendship. Neither of them intended to renew their contract, so they had decided to postpone any romantic involvement until they were back on Earth. Dawn had no interest in dating and felt her work was enough to keep her busy until her year was up. She also had decided not to renew her contract. Living on the Moon was not easy and the trips away from the home station were exacerbated by the need to wear a space suite. She had six months left and any dreams she had had in the past to live on Mars were abandoned.

The monotony of space travel and being restricted to indoor living on both Mars and the Moon was too confining for Dawn.

The six months passed quickly and Dawn was back on Earth. After living a year with Moon's low gravity, she had trouble adjusting to the full gravity on Earth and she felt like a lead weight. Just moving around was cumbersome and she dragged her feet with no spring in her step. Her digestion was also affected by Earth's heavier gravity and it took her several weeks to feel well. Even though she had exercised daily on the Moon she did notice she had lost muscle strength. After a few months of exercise and working out with weights, she finally felt like her normal self again. She had truly relished her year on the Moon and the experience she had gained, but she had decided not to go back. Earth with its green flora, flowers and trees was stunning compared to the bare landscape on the Moon.

Keith and Alexa got married soon after they returned to Earth and Dawn attended the ceremony. Dawn herself did not feel ready to settle down and had a business project in mind. Her salary from her Moon job had been deposited into her account and she had almost enough funds to start an insect business. A small interest free loan from a government bank would supply the rest of the cash she needed.

Her preference would have been to start a vertical hydroponic farm growing vegetables the same way as she had done on the Moon, but when she did a market analysis, she found there were almost too many of them around the San Francisco area where she lived. The population of America was only one hundred and twenty million people, barely a third of what it had been before the collapse. Conventional vegetable farms growing crops in soil were still around producing vegetables that did not do well as hydroponic crops. There were many benefits to vertical farms; they were popular, no pesticides or herbicides were needed, the produce was highly nutritious and they were located close to the consumers. A medium sized building could grow several levels of vegetables and LED lights supplied all the light the plants needed.

Dawn bought an abandoned small building and had it remodeled to house thousands of growing insects of various kinds. She was looking for a business partner, but for the time being her cousin Hilma, by now thirteen years old, would be her helper. Dawn liked Hilma and her willingness to do a good job. Hilma had agreed to work at Dawn's factory two hours after school every day and on weekends.

The insect eggs were delivered and carefully nursed in the hatchery. After a few weeks, thousands of bugs were crawling around and grasshoppers, crickets, various worms and slugs were thriving on the nutritious feed they received. At maturity, they were put to sleep, sanitized, dried and then ground into powder for the 3D printers and steam ovens. Some of the powders became flour and was used for breads and pastas. Various natural flavors and spices were added and Dawn's customers were enthusiastic about the interesting flavors she offered. The insect powders were highly nutritious and supplied a well-balanced and quite tasty meal. People were no longer squeamish about eating insects and they were accepted as normal food. Hilma was very efficient and was in charge of blending the powders with flavors and spices and then packaging them into mylar bags. Some customers picked up their insect powders at the factory and some wanted it delivered to their homes, so Dawn had bought a delivery drone that was very reliable and had not missed one address so far. Dawn was pleased and enjoyed her business and was grateful it had worked out so well. Without her salary from the Moon job, she could not have afforded to start a business at her young age. She was hoping to pay back her business loan within five years and judging from the good response she had from her customers, it looked favorable. Hilma put her heart and soul into her job and Dawn made her a junior partner. She could easily juggle work and school and truly enjoyed working. Even though Dawn was ten years older than Hilma, they were great friends and got along well.

Standard beef, hog and chicken farms were still in operation, but the methods were totally changed. Since land was easily available due to the smaller population, all livestock lived outside and factory farms and feedlots were a thing of the past. Farm work was done mostly by robots. Many people had switched to a vegetarian diet, but some people consumed at least some meat. Vegetarians did accept insect powders as part of their diet.

The farm fields had recovered from being fallow for years and much of the damage caused by former farming methods was gone. Cereal crops were no longer genetically modified. People stopped buying these foods and regular heirloom seeds were back in use. Farms, even large ones, were often run by just one farmer and several robots. Tractors and combines were autonomous and the farmer could communicate with the machines as well as watch the process from his computer. Additional visual aid was supplied by drones if more detail was needed. With the automated system, no farm needed more than one or two human operators and a crew of worker robots.

CHAPTER 12

A year passed and Dawn was in love. The man who had captured her heart was a designer of holodeck programs a few years older than herself named Kai. An artistic man with a vivid imagination and bohemian temperament, intensely private by nature, but with a big-hearted soul. Although not handsome, his sharp features gave him a distinct manly look that appealed to Dawn. They had recently met and both knew they were meant for each other. Kai had already proposed and Dawn said yes with no doubt in her mind and they had decided to apply for a ten-year marriage contract. Dawn's family liked him. Kai was an orphan without any relatives and had been raised in foster care, so Kai had no one to introduce Dawn to. He had not suffered growing up, but perhaps living in foster care had attributed to his hermit tendencies and solitude enabled him to look for peace from within to escape often chaotic living conditions.

Dawn and Kai's wedding was lovely with Dawn's parents and grandparents attending and, of course, Hilma and her family. Kai and Dawn skipped a honeymoon and instead spent their money on a house not too far from Dawn's business. Kai worked from home and moved his studio into the basement.

*****

The unthinkable was happening. A fifteen-foot asteroid under tow to the workstation in lunar orbit was on its way to Earth. The cable towing the asteroid had snapped and Earth's gravity had pulled the asteroid to Earth. With a core of mostly iron, the mining company knew the asteroid would not break up in Earth's atmosphere, but land mostly intact somewhere on Earth's surface. To Forrest's relief, the asteroid did not belong to his company, but in emergencies all the mining companies cooperated. The asteroid travelled at almost twenty thousand miles per hour and there was no time to deflect it or apply standard defense methods. Thankfully, the asteroid fell into the Atlantic Ocean and no damage occurred. Had it hit a city, it would have caused many deaths. After this accident, all mining companies used dual cables to ensure that if one cable broke, the second cable would be able to secure the asteroid.

******

It was the year 2107 and the Mars colonization was finally underway. Before the collapse, the Mars program was planning to bring humans to Mars by 2040 or so, but when electricity came back there was very little interest in space travel. Just to rebuild Earth to its former condition with services and restored manufacturing had been an immense project that took decades to finish. It was only in the last twenty years that renewed interest in space travel had sparked some businesses to start designing and building spaceships for long distance travel suitable for humans. The plan was to move one million humans to Mars starting with one hundred people per trip and then adding more people depending on the success of the first inhabitants. No one knew exactly how the first Mars colony would fare. Conditions such as radiation, claustrophobia, the extreme cold climate and possible problems with water and food supplies were obstacles that the settlers would have to adjust to. The five-month journey in a cramped space ship may take a toll on the travelers' physical health. One problem had been solved and that was insulation of the ships from radiation.

Only ten thousand people had so far committed themselves to permanently move to Mars, a far cry from a hundred thousand people needed to start a new community on another planet. It was at least a start and the team of companies working as a partnership felt sure more people would eventually sign up. Funding had been shared by the participating companies and several governments. Various media outlets had bought the rights to broadcast life on Mars, but the fee they had paid was small compared to the total cost of the program. Eventually, mining on Mars would probably generate some money for the colonists and profits from future manufacturing would also be used to pay back the funding to the companies and governments that had originally paid for the whole project. It was understood that the Mars citizens would need at least a decade to pay back the money. If the settlement would ever be able to become financially self-sufficient was unknown.

Two spaceships with a crew of worker robots and supplies had already been sent to Mars and the housing and basic infrastructure was in place. The 3D printed houses were medium tall and rounded and the building material was made with Martian soil and sulfur. The outer shell was as strong as concrete and had been thoroughly tested for strength in an Earth laboratory before the decision was made to use it in the printing of the buildings. Inside the buildings an airtight liner was installed as a radiation shield. The buildings were pressurized and encircling the complex was a covered tunnel system tying the homes and supply buildings together to eliminate the need for a spacesuit while moving between buildings. These buildings were just a prototype and future homes would perhaps be constructed of other materials and with a changed design. Electricity was supplied by a combination of solar energy and by tapping in to the Zero Point Field energy, referred to as Natural Energy. A wall was built around the whole complex to shield as much as possible from sand storms.

Next to the colony, huge amounts of ice only three feet below the surface supplied potable drinking water and with the help of solar energy, the ice was melted and pumped to the homes. Waste was pumped to an incinerator and the remaining ash was nonpolluting. Two large greenhouses similar to the ones on the Moon would supply daily greens to the Martians. A huge amount of insect eggs and fertile fish eggs that would not hatch for seven months would accompany the first shipment of people and would supply protein. Large tanks were in place already on Mars to receive the fish eggs. In addition, mushroom spores to grow fresh mushrooms were onboard. It was expected that some kind of livestock could be kept in the future. Rabbits and chickens had been suggested and if they survived the journey to Mars, they could be cloned to increase the population until natural breeding could start. Any livestock would require artificial gravity during transit, such as a slowly rotating centrifugal wheel, and to fit even a small wheel inside a spaceship would be a challenge as well as the daily care of the animals. It was hoped that livestock of some kind would be shipped to Mars within a year or as soon as the difficulties with the shipping could be resolved.

The first hundred people boarded the spaceship and with no regrets they strapped themselves into their seats. They would never set foot on

Earth again. The ship was very large and would allow the passengers to move around once they were out of Earth's atmosphere. Most of the people were married couples in their twenties and nine half grown children were aboard. These children, five girls and four boys, had been thoroughly informed and had not hesitated to accompany their parents to a new life on another planet. More children were waiting to move to Mars in the next shipments.

The ship had been racing through space for three months and two more months were left before they would see Mars. Being weightless had weakened all of them and daily exercising with weights were required in groups of twenty per session. So far, no one had become sick or succumbed to depression or claustrophobia, but it was two more months to endure and to be busy was essential to cope with the conditions. Reading, movie watching, daily exercise, playing various board games, caring for one's hygiene took a good part of every day, but most of them needed a mild sedative to be able to sleep. The trip dragged on and everyone looked forward to touchdown on their new home planet.

The ship was in orbit around Mars and the colony was visible from space. The location was in the north close to water and the possibility of future mining was favorable in that area. The pilots fired the reverse thrusters to slow down the ship and they were gently falling towards the surface. The ship was now in a vertical position and with the help of the thrusters they made a gentle landing. All the passengers had survived the trip and the mood was ecstatic. A large bus was waiting for them. It hooked up with the spaceship and the robot onboard the bus directed the passengers to their seats. Everyone cooperated and the unloading was swift. Each home had three floors and housed six couples per floor. The furniture was sparse but practical and with 3D printers already on the ground, additional furniture could be printed as per need.

After a few weeks, everyone had settled in and started their assigned jobs. Work assignments and the basic routine had been worked out carefully on Earth, so everyone knew already what was expected of them. All the buildings and large vehicles were pressurized, but gravity was only a third of Earth's gravity and it took weeks for the people to get used to it. Sunlight was reduced because of the dust and also made the sky look orange, but inside bright light made the indoors appear sunny and Earth like.

Juliet and Darrel and their eight-year-old son Cliff were African Americans and were slowly learning to appreciate life on Mars. Juliet was working as a nurse and Darrel was a chef. Both of them were adventurers and eager to try life on another planet, but since they had a young son, they had spent hours educating him about Mars and also the risks involved. Cliff was well informed and had a bright mind. After weighing the pros and cons in his mind, he informed his parents he agreed to going. He understood it was not totally safe, but he was not afraid. Juliet enjoyed her work as a nurse and Darrel turned the insects into breads, stir-fries and other dishes that were welcomed by the people. Everyone ate in the communal dining room, but it was understood that later on when food was more available, people who wanted to do their own cooking would be allowed to do so and each housing unit had a kitchen. Cliff was attending school and with only nine students the teacher had lots of time for each student.

More houses were being built and the second group of people arrived. One person had died from the stress during the journey to Mars and the mood of the new people was less optimistic compared to the first arrivals.

Life on Mars was not easy, but so far, the new population was coping well with the difficulties. They were pioneers and dedicated to making their new lives a success. Inside the buildings life was not that different from Earth, but the lack of freedom to venture outside without a spacesuit did take a toll on some people. Several Rovers were available to rent at a small fee and many did make excursions lasting half a day to a day. The volcanos were popular with sightseers and deep canyons that stretched endlessly were interesting to explore. Six buildings had been built away from the colony, where people could stay overnight for free. It was recognized that some people had to get away from the colony occasionally to be able to cope with the monotony of life on Mars. A dozen people had arranged to return to Earth and they had not been able to acclimate to the confined lifestyle on Mars.

A horrendous sand storm lasting two weeks had almost buried the colony and when it finally ended, the homes were half covered in sand. The exterior wall around the colony had shielded them from the worst of the storm, but enough sand had still blown over the wall and a thorough cleanup was needed. A team of robots had to clear the sand away with robotic arms attached to the Rovers and haul the sand away from the homes. This was the first sand storm to hit and even though the Martians knew all about the storms, it was frightening when they had to witness the intensity of the first storm. The solar panels had not been damaged to everyone's relief.

Mining started on Mars and some rare minerals were found in addition to more common metals. The work was all done by robot laborers and supervised by two humans in spacesuits. Factory buildings to process the ores were built and slowly manufacturing of electronics and different tools was started. The goal of becoming a self-sufficient planet was no longer a dream, but perceived by most Martians as reality. Some simple household appliances were manufactured on Mars and it was hoped that eventually all needed machines would be built locally. Importing heavy appliances from Earth was expensive and waiting for shipments from Earth was impractical.

******

Five years had passed and the colony was doing well at five thousand citizens. Many spaceships had departed from Earth filled with people moving to the new planet. The community had grown to a city and the colonists named it Martia. Several commercial buildings and many homes had been added. They were all tied together with tunnels. A transportation system existed between buildings and electric vehicles were used to transport people anywhere within the city for a modest fee.

More people on Earth had signed up to move to Mars and the goal was to increase the population to at least half a million people, hopefully more. A small government had formed based on the same system as America with People Democracy. A hospital had been built, a school system was in place and all the basic infrastructure needed to support a modern community. The food supply was adequate with various vegetables from the greenhouses, farmed fish, insects and rabbits. Surprisingly, the rabbits had survived the journey to Mars and had adjusted to living with less gravity. The breeding of the rabbits was a success and the meat was popular. Every shipment of egg laying chickens from Earth had failed until a small rotating enclosure had been invented supplying at least some gravity through centrifugal force and the chicks survived the trip from Earth. More baby chicks were scheduled for shipment on the very next spaceship leaving for Mars. Everyone was hoping the chicks would survive and supply eggs for the colonists. Once established on Mars, breeding would begin to increase their numbers.

Back on Earth, Dawn and Kai had discussed moving to Mars and since they had no children yet, they had nothing tying them to Earth. Neither of them had felt ready to start a family and had decided to wait. Their five-year marriage had been happy and they enjoyed a laid-back lifestyle. Even though Dawn had felt that life on the Moon was barren and restricted, she was willing to give Mars a chance and colonists were now allowed to sign up for just a few years and then return to Earth. The newer spaceships were more comfortable and Dawn and Kai did not feel the trip would be a hardship. They decided to take the plunge and signed up for two years. Their decision was not popular with Dawn's parents and Karl and Linh were equally worried about their granddaughter. Strangely enough, both Bjorn and Linnéa took an opposite view and they promptly contacted Dawn with their communicator. Dawn was happy to see the holographic image of her great grandparents and listened to their words of encouragement. She was very fond of her great grandparents and had been to the farm in Sandpoint several times. Linnéa was now eighty-nine years old and Bjorn ninety-three, but both were still healthy and enjoyed life immensely. Modern marvels of technology and new inventions had always fascinated both of them and they had followed life on Mars with interest and were well acquainted with what was going on there. Dawn had a warm feeling inside when she ended her conversation with them.

Dawn gave her business to Hilma, who she loved like a sister. Hilma was now nineteen years old and had worked side by side with Dawn since the start of the business. By now, Dawn's insect business was thriving and generated a nice profit and Hilma was grateful to become the owner of the business. She still attended school and had a year to go until she would graduate with a degree in genetics.

Even though the trip to Mars was tedious and often boring, Dawn and Kai endured the hardships and arrived at Mars full of excitement. Their bones and muscles had deteriorated somewhat from being weightless, but they intended to start a vigorous exercise program to get back into shape once they were settled in. Landing went well and by now the spaceship pilots were very experienced and the whole trip back and forth between Earth and Mars had become routine.

Dawn and Kai liked their apartment and adjusted rather quickly to the low gravity. Dawn worked in the greenhouse and her degree in horticulture came in handy as she constantly aimed at improving production and quality of the produce. Kai worked designing new software and with his experience writing holodeck programs, he was well qualified for his job. Dawn and Kai were happy with their new life and faced each day with enthusiasm. They made friends, went on many excursions with a Rover and started to feel at home on Mars. Juliet and Darrel and their son Cliff had the apartment below them and they also became friends. They had made the final decision not to return to Earth and they let Cliff decide for himself whether to stay or leave. Cliff had told them he wanted to stay on Mars.

A few months passed and Dawn was pregnant. The news was not welcome and Dawn and Kai had planned to delay starting a family until they were back on Earth, but Nature wanted differently. Several children had been born on Mars, but these people had no intention to return to Earth and would not have to deal with the physical problems that Earth's gravity would impose on children born on a planet with only one third of Earth's gravity. Dawn and Kai were not religious, but they felt abortion was wrong. If they allowed the baby to be born, they had two choices - stay on Mars or return to Earth and hope the child could grow stronger bones and muscles and safely adapt to Earth's gravity. Only one child, a two-year-old boy, had tried to return to Earth with his parents and that child had died during the return trip aboard the spaceship. Dawn and Kai struggled over the decision and had several talks with the doctors on Mars, but finally they decided to allow the baby to be born. They simply could not get themselves to abort the baby. Once the decision had been made, they felt more at ease and actually were looking forward to the birth.

Dawn's pregnancy proceeded normally and she did not leave the colony to go outside. Even though the spacesuits were designed to fully shield against radiation, there was a possibility that a small amount would leak through the suit and damage the baby. The artificial womb was not available on Mars, but Dawn would not have chosen it anyway. Dawn continued working in the greenhouse until two weeks before delivery. The hospital was close to their apartment and the transportation within the colony was excellent and fast. Dawn just rested the last two weeks of her pregnancy and enjoyed feeling the baby kick. She felt a strong maternal love for her baby girl and according to her doctor, the baby was in excellent health and had gained proper weight. Not all pregnancies on Mars had had a happy outcome and several miscarriages had occurred. One baby had been born severely handicapped and died shortly after birth. When the magic day came and Dawn went into labor, the birth proceeded without incidents and with the help of medication the birth was totally pain free. Kai was present and together they welcomed little Adora to planet Mars. They were very grateful the baby was normal. Being traditional, Dawn had decided to nurse her baby and forgo the bottle.

Dawn had arranged to stay home with the baby. Living expenses were not high on Mars and Kai's income was more than sufficient to pay for their needs. Becoming parents was exciting for Dawn and Kai and seeing Adora grow and develop was captivating. Every day Dawn performed exercises on the baby to build muscles and strengthen her bones. She strapped weights onto the baby's legs, arms and around her waist and Adora kicked and giggled. She had been fitted with a standard microchip implant suitable for a baby and developed normally. At nine months, she was able to walk and she always wore her weight belts. Dawn had visited with the other parents in the colony who had become parents on Mars and their children were healthy and developing normally. If they had undergone any kind of mutation was unknown, but as more experienced scientists moved to Mars, it was hoped that future tests of the children would reveal whether Martian children were different from Earth children and if they were infertile.

Only three months was left of Dawn and Kai's contract and they were discussing the pros and cons of returning to Earth or stay on Mars. It was a difficult decision and they wavered back and forth. If they stayed, Adora would most likely live out her natural life while returning to Earth may kill her. They just did not know what her chances would be since only one child had returned and then sadly died in transit. Finally, Dawn made up her mind and informed Kai they should take their chances and return to Earth and hope Adora would survive. Kai had to think about her decision for several days and then agreed. Once they had made the decision, they did not look back or change their mind. Dawn had vigorously exercised her little girl with heavy weights and Adora was unusually muscular and strong compared to the other Martian children, so Dawn could see that her workout sessions with

Adora had had an impact. She did not take Adora outside as she did not want to risk exposing her to radiation.

The space ship was waiting for takeoff with full fuel tanks. Dawn, Kai and Adora were onboard and looking forward to returning to Earth. They had been lucky to find that their planned return trip coincided with the scheduled departure of a spaceship. A large factory had been built next to the colony manufacturing the propellant used by the spaceship's engines. The abundant supply of carbon dioxide and water ice produced liquid methane and liquid oxygen and large amounts were needed to fill the tanks of a spaceship. The electricity to produce the fuel came from Natural Energy. During the launch window, every twenty-four to twenty-six months when the distance between Mars and Earth was the shortest, many spaceships arrived and left and lots of fuel was needed. Some spaceships launched from Earth with minimal amount of fuel in their tanks and instead filled up at one of the many orbiting fuel stations before takeoff to Mars. This enabled the ship to reach orbit with less weight to carry through the atmosphere and cut the cost of the launch quite a bit. Some of the orbiting fuel stations were enormous in size and made their own fuel from harvested asteroids containing water ice. Smaller space ships would dock with the fuel station while large ships were fueled by a tanker spaceship a distance away from the fuel station. Since the gravity on Mars is low, the spaceships did not need as much power for liftoff and could depart with their tanks filled.

Dawn, Kai and Adora had traveled for three months onboard the spaceship and Adora was still alive and actually doing as well as her parents. She had adjusted to weightlessness and both Dawn and Kai spent several hours every day exercising her with heavy weights to the point that Adora almost buckled. She was strapped down so she would not float up while exercising. Since she had the boost of an implant, she functioned at the level of a three-year-old even though she was only a year and a half. Her command of speech was good and she was able to speak simple sentences and understood what her parents told her. When Dawn loaded her up with weights, she laughed out loud and understood she was supposed to 'become strong'. Without all the physical training Dawn had subjected her to on Mars, Adora's little body could never have carried the weights she now carried with relative ease. Onboard the spaceship was only three other people, but the ship carried a maximum load of processed minerals destined for Earth. The minerals were one of the many installments to pay off the loan Mars owed planet Earth. Only two androids and four human pilots were onboard as crew. The efficiency of the androids was impressive and they handled all the chores onboard effortlessly.

Dawn's grandmother Linh communicated often with Dawn during the return trip to Earth and as a former pediatrician, she strongly advised to keep Adora quarantined for at least a month to allow her to build up immunity to the unfamiliar germs on Earth. Dawn had already decided that and agreed.

The magic moment arrived and the spaceship landed gently on Earth's surface. Dawn had asked that no relative should be at the landing site to protect Adora from germs. Kai had rented a groundmobile while in transit and a bus took them to the parking lot. As they exited the bus and felt Earth's crushing gravity, they felt both dizzy and unsure if they would be able to stay upright. Kai was carrying Adora and struggled to keep his balance and Dawn was also in trouble feeling as if she weighed a ton. Their luggage would be sent straight to their house, which had been empty these two years, and they slowly, very slowly, and with great difficulty walked over to the rented groundmobile waiting for them. They were able to walk upright, but it took all their willpower and concentration to not fall down. Both of them were dizzy, but the distance they needed to walk was very short. They entered the groundmobile and when Kai gave their address to the computer, he noticed that even speech was strange to produce and his tongue and lips were almost numb. In addition, they noticed a reduction in their visual acuity. Adora was carried and did not seem to be badly affected at all.

Hilma had looked after their house and everything was in order with food in the refrigerator and the house looked tidy and welcoming. She had placed two canes by the front door in case they needed the extra help and both Kai and Dawn gratefully took a cane each. Finally, Kai put Adora on the floor and she promptly fell down. But she smiled and tried very hard to get back up again. As soon as she was upright, she fell down. She resorted to creeping on her knees and that she was able to creep was a good sign that all her exercising was now paying off. All of them drank several glasses of water to ensure they were hydrated and Dawn served a cold salad dinner that Hilma had put in the refrigerator. They noticed their stomachs felt strange and to digest food in the heavy gravity made them feel slightly nauseous, but they were able to finish their meal. Adora was fed a small portion of baby food and was able to keep it down. There was a crib in their bedroom and they gently put Adora to bed and then quickly got ready for bed themselves. As they lay down, the room was spinning at first, but to their relief it did not last long and they were able to fall asleep.

The first month on Earth, Dawn did not allow anyone to visit and the time was spent on rehabilitation. Each day she and Kai increased their exercising and with weight lifting and aggressive workouts, they started to feel stronger. It would take another month to be back to full strength and as they noticed their stamina increasing, they eagerly continued their efforts. Adora was exercised as well and was now able to walk around slowly. As small as she was, she understood that she would soon be strong again. The whole issue of moving from one planet to another was too much for her to understand, but she did comprehend that she was far away from the apartment on Mars. The dizziness, vision problem and digestive issues were gone and it was time for the first visitor.

Grandma Linh eagerly entered the house and after she had been briefed in person on their life on Mars, she did a thorough exam of Adora. Linh was pleasantly surprised when she checked her bone structure and muscle mass and informed Dawn and Kai that Adora was not far behind children born on Earth and with continued exercise she would be as strong as any child on Earth. Dawn and Kai breathed a sigh of relief hearing the good news. One more problem remained and that was to strengthen Adora's immune system and slowly expose her to common germs living on Earth but not on Mars. This had to be done slowly by introducing a new visitor every few weeks and possibly get her a live pet. Linh suggested a kitten and Kai found a healthy month-old kitten in the neighborhood with a gentle temperament. It worked. Adora was healthy and did not succumb to even a cold. After another month she actually ran in the house on her muscular little legs with her white kitten Icy in hot pursuit. Her adjustment to life on Earth had been successful only because her parents had spent so much time preparing her and not relied on luck.

By now, Dawn and Kai were almost back to normal and many of the relatives had visited. Kai had started a programming job, but was planning to start his own business later on. Dawn was home with the baby and had not made any plans for the future. Adora's welfare was all she cared about and any career plans could wait. Hilma had asked if she would come back to their insect business, but Dawn had told her no. Hilma now ran the business in partnership with her younger sister Cellie, who by now was a young lady nineteen years old. Hilma also had a part time job in a laboratory working in genetics while Cellie, enjoying more practical things, had quit school at eighteen years old and ran the insect business mostly alone and with gusto.

CHAPTER 13

The sad news arrived that Bjorn had died at the age of ninety-six and he was missed by all the Nordins. His brother Lars and his wife April were still alive. Linnéa grieved, but her strong spiritual faith and belief in reincarnation made the loss more tolerable. She was still able to run her own house with the help of her newly bought android and to walk around the farm on her daily outings.

Drew and Tina were doing well and had bought a larger fishing boat. Tina still had her herbal business, but took days off to work with Drew on their boat. Brandon, their oldest son, was already fourteen years old and James twelve and both boys looked forward to the weekends when the whole family was together on the boat. Drew was able to make a good living as a fisherman and the free lifestyle suited both him and Tina well.

Clarence and Lotte had three children and the oldest, Brianna, was ten years old. Lotte had not gone back to work as a mechanic and preferred to stay home and together with Eva, their trusted android, she enjoyed seeing her children grow up. Eva took great interest in the children and the bond between her and Lotte was strong and loving. Clarence was working with artificial intelligence and his designs were in high demand. Clarence and Lotte were close with Drew and Tina and often spent weekends on the fishing boat and their children got along well. Eva usually came along and loved the boat.

Brianna was horse crazy and had a little Arab mare named Misty stabled not far from their house. Every day after school she would jump on her electric scooter and race over to the stable for her daily outing with Misty. There were bridle paths around the stable and even though Misty had lots of temperament, she had common sense and did not scare easily. She loved her young owner and felt responsible for her and Brianna rode Misty with just a nose band, skipping the bit. These rides were treasured by both of them.

A year back, however, Brianna had taken a terrible spill and as Misty galloped through the field at top speed, her front foot had entered a hole in the ground and Misty fell with Brianna hitting the ground hard, face down, and both her upper front teeth were knocked out. All horse riders accept there is a certain risk riding a horse and most riders will encounter at least one accident during their horse life. Misty was not injured at all and was back on her feet immediately and anxiously sniffing on Brianna lying on the ground. Misty was very agile and surefooted and had never fallen before. Brianna dragged herself up and had the presence of mind to collect her two teeth and put them in her pocket for the dentist to inspect. She hugged Misty and reassured the worried mare that she was alive and still loved her. They walked back to the stable and Brianna had her hankie over the gap where her teeth had been to catch the blood. Back home, Lotte was shaken to find out what had happened, but she was at the same time a practical person and immediately contacted Brianna's dentist and notified her what had happened. The stem cells from Brianna's baby teeth were all cryogenically frozen and could easily regrow Brianna's teeth after implantation in the tooth socket. First, the dentist inserted a small support system for the new teeth and soon two brand new front teeth started to grow. A couple of months later Brianna proudly showed off her regrown teeth. Without fear, she was right back in the saddle, but did not allow Misty an all-out gallop anymore unless she had checked the field beforehand for holes.

To slowly strengthen Adora's immune system, Dawn took her daughter to Misty's stable and spent several hours playing with the horse. Adora had never seen a horse and was totally fascinated by the mare. She laughed and patted her and Misty enjoyed the affection from the baby and licked her hands. Dawn let it happen and knew she had to subject Adora to all the common germs on Earth and farm animals were one of the best ways to stimulate Adora's immune system. The baby did not have an adverse reaction and Dawn realized it was now safe to allow Adora to mingle freely with other children and even animals.

******

Clarence had once brought his android Eva over to Karl's android Lena. Lena was not as sophisticated as Eva, but Clarence had updated her twice and her thinking ability was almost as advanced as Eva's. Manual performance, physical agility and emotions were the same for both of them. Lena had often played ball with Karl and Linh's grandchildren and could run as fast as any of them. After the introduction the two androids communicated in their own robot language, which had been designed by the androids themselves. It was a fast non-human language only understood in written form by humans trained to translate it. It sounded like gibberish to the human ear, but was very specific and powerful when used between robots. Many people were intimidated by this interaction between androids and wanted to pull the plug on artificial intelligence and only use the simpler worker robots that had limited intelligence. But the new models of super performing androids were used in many fields such as delicate surgeries, where they outperformed the human surgeons, as well as being the designers of various complicated tools, software, engines and many other highly complex inventions. They accomplished successful designs faster than any human could and to pull the plug would affect many areas of modern life. Programmers of the androids were aware of the danger and wrote strict safety codes into all their programs. They did know, however, that there was a real danger in the future that the androids could try to take over and destroy humans, so they were always on the lookout for unusual behavior.

When Clarence returned home with Eva, he hooked up to her and retrieved her conversation with Lena. As he expected, Eva and Lena had compared notes about their daily lives as well as given each other their favorite recipes. Eva smiled at Clarence and said -

"Do you really think I would concoct a plan to hurt you, my Creator, in any way or my own family that I love so much?"

Clarence could not help but feeling embarrassed and gave Eva a bear hug and assured her that she was a loved and trusted family member. Eva enjoyed being hugged and Lotte would often show her affection for Eva by embracing her. Deep within himself Clarence knew that there was a true possibility of losing control over all the androids and as a designer of artificial intelligence he also knew it would be almost impossible to stop out-of-control androids once they decided to destroy humans. As a safety measurement, all androids were equipped with a separate program inaccessible by the android or any other android containing a 'kill-switch' that could be activated by a remote radio signal. Moreover, the prime-directive of the programming was to never injure a human being ever. No android had ever harmed a person since they were released and thousands were working all around the globe. With all the safety features already in place, Clarence still felt uneasy and made the decision to add even stronger safety codes to all his designs.

******

The world was at peace and minor terrorist attacks had been squelched without delay. Trade between countries did take place, but at a much smaller scale than in the past. Self-sufficiency was important to all countries and manufacturing supplied needed jobs. Some countries had merged into one country and there was still no world government. The Advisory Board was relied upon for unbiased advice and their consistently fair and logical solutions to some very complicated issues were valued by all countries.

Everyday life for the citizens of America was rewarding and people were optimistic. Competition and the drive to win at any cost in all areas of life was less important than it had been before the collapse. The new mindset was to accept yourself as you are, but apply your best efforts when needed. The political system of People Democracy had been in effect for over fifty years and the citizens did not want to introduce another system. Many countries had converted their government to People Democracy and no country had a monarchy in effect. The former Third World countries were self-sufficient and needed no help from the more affluent countries. Some people moved between countries, but the reason was mostly to experience a new area rather than escape poor living conditions.

Both the Moon and Mars colonies were prospering. Mining on the Moon was successful and the income earned easily covered the expenses to run the community. A small local government had been formed to handle day to day decisions and to implement new ideas, but the Moon was considered part of Earth and major decisions were usually handled by The Advisory Board. The population was only around two thousand people, but if the Moon population increased and the Moon citizens declared their independence, perhaps then a formal government would be formed. The Moon colony was still too small to be considered a separate planet with independent citizens. So far, the present system worked and there was no talk of declaring independency. Earth governments did not interfere with life on the Moon and allowed the residents total freedom to make their own decisions.

The Mars colony was equally flourishing and with a population of twenty thousand people and more waiting to become Martians, it looked promising that Mars would become an alternative place for humans to live. During the window of travel to Mars, many ships transported new people to the planet. The dream to terraform Mars, or making it more Earth-like with plants and forests growing, had not come true. It would involve raising the Mars temperature quite a bit and introduce greenhouse gases such as carbon dioxide into the atmosphere to thicken it and try to keep water in a liquid form. It was finally recognized that there was not enough carbon dioxide on Mars to convert it to resemble Earth and at the present time there was no technology available to terraform Mars. Mining was done on Mars' surface and in the canyons, but any thought of traveling to the asteroid belt to mine was unrealistic and not even considered. The distance was too far. The two Moons Phobos and Deimos were a remote possibility, but not yet seriously considered. No one had been there and actually taken soil samples to ascertain whether it would be worth the effort. For the time being, the colony was able to make enough income from mining to slowly pay back the huge debt they owed to their sponsors.

The last shipment of baby chicks had been successful and the chicks had survived the journey to Mars. They were now living in a greenhouse style building. The artificial gravity created on the spaceship, though small, seemed to have made the difference between life and death. They appeared to have adapted to the low gravity on Mars and within a few months they would start laying eggs. More baby chicks were scheduled to arrive from Earth.

The mushroom spawns had been planted and had also survived and the first crop of mushrooms were very appreciated by the colonists. The variety of foods was adequate, but many missed wheat bread. So far wheat had not survived several trial plantings in the greenhouses, but when trying a small planting of rye grain, the plants survived. They were grown in Martian soil, regolith, and fertilized with composted, cleaned waste consisting of digested human waste and plant materials from the greenhouses. The first planting of rye was now growing in a very large greenhouse and the growers had high hopes the crop would supply quality bread flour. Experiments trying to grow wheat had not stopped and trial plantings using older heritage varieties of wheat were ongoing. Emmer and spelt would be tried next. There were some heavy metals in the regolith, but the amount present in the produce grown in the Martian soil was not high enough to cause alarm. Further testing to inexpensively remove unwanted metals from the Martian soil were in progress and all sorts of new ideas were waiting to be tried. Several scientists specializing in botany were on the waiting list to move to Mars, so eventually any problems with the crop production would most likely be resolved.

******

Forrest was devastated with grief. His beloved wife Sheena was dead. She had drowned in a surfing accident. For years, Sheena had met with friends on the beach once a week and engaged in her favorite sport surfing. She was very good at it and not afraid of riding high waves. The day of the accident she was riding the last wave for that day and she was physically tired. Then it happened. The leash broke and the other surfers told Forrest she had slid off her board and was dragged under the wave and never surfaced again. By the time the other surfers dove down and recovered her body, she was dead. She had apparently hit her head on the sea floor and lost consciousness and then drowned. She was only forty-six years old and full of life.

Forrest and the girls were inconsolable and weeks after the funeral they still walked around in a daze. Hilma and Cellie shared a house and Forrest and Sheena were empty nesters still living in the same house they had bought as newlyweds. Forrest dreaded coming home to an empty house and often stayed in his office after the work day was over and only went home to sleep. This did not go unnoticed by his co-workers and they suggested he take some time off and live on their company's orbiting workstation for a year. Forrest agreed after only a few minutes of thinking. After he came home that evening and thought it over, he knew it was necessary to have a change of scenery to be able to function again. His daughters would look after the house while he was gone.

Forrest was strapped into his spaceship seat and as he lifted off from Earth, he felt excitement for the first time since his wife died. This was his second time flying into space. He and Sheena had spent a weekend on the orbiting space hotel five years ago and had found it very entertaining. This flight was not vacation and he planned to immerse himself in work. The spaceship was owned by his company and flew regularly between Earth and the orbiting workstation supplying foods and equipment to the crew and returning with extracted minerals to Earth.

It only took eight minutes to reach orbit and now the catch-up started to line the spaceship up with the workstation, which was in an orbit of higher elevation. The spaceship fired several short burns to get into an orbit closer to the workstation and was traveling at a slightly faster rate than the workstation. After completing a few additional orbits around Earth, the spaceship was at the magic spot and fired another burn, turned around and was now facing the workstation. Another burn was fired to slow down the spaceship and now they were ready for docking with the workstation. The docking port was located below the center of the huge wheel-type structure. The experienced pilots had the whole process down to a routine, but it was actually not easy to 'catch' an orbiting workstation traveling at close to twenty thousand miles per hour and it was not a job for a novice. To add to the difficulty, the workstation was slowly rotating to simulate gravity through centrifugal force and the lineup with the docking port had to be exact for the docking to work.

Forrest was greeted by the crew and shown to his room, a tiny room at the outer edge of the workstation. He did not mind that his room was small as long as he had a single. The workstation was pressurized and the gravity onboard was about the same as on the Moon. Forrest decided to wear a weight suit to avoid losing too much muscle. He was aware that no matter what he did both his bones and muscles would be affected by living in low gravity, but a year was not that long and he would exercise with weights when he returned to Earth.

The workstation was large and had a crew of twelve people and twelve worker robots plus a foreman, a late model android with years of experience and very loyal to the company. The cook, an android somewhat less advanced than Lena named Annie, had great cooking skills and everyone enjoyed her meals. Forrest performed similar work on the work station as he had done on Earth concentrating on streamlining all facets of the mining process, from towing the asteroids to the workstation to the most efficient way of extracting the precious metals from the asteroid. He enjoyed the work and was good at it. Every time the spaceship docked with the work station and the robots unloaded a small asteroid, he was filled with excitement to find out what precious metals it would contain. He worked hard and wanted it that way; it was the only way to suppress his grief. The human crew onboard was male except for two middle aged women working as metallurgists. All crew members signed up for a one-year tour of duty and then returned to Earth for one year. If they so desired, they could then apply for another year on the workstation. No one was allowed to work longer than one year at the time in space for health reasons.

Almost a year had passed, but before he was scheduled to return, Forrest was determined to accompany one of the two spaceships his company used for mining directly on the larger asteroids. Most of the time these mining missions only had robotic workers as crew and only occasionally a human to solve a specific problem the robots could not handle. Forrest knew it was very risky to be part of the robotic crew and land on the asteroid. Over the years several spaceships had been lost and some had crashed when landing on the asteroid. Landing was always dangerous as the asteroid had no gravity. The spaceship would maneuver itself above the asteroid and then lower a cable with a huge anchor as well as a set of grappling hooks that would, hopefully, grab on to the surface so the ship could dock alongside the asteroid. A three-mile-wide oblong asteroid with a large vein of almost pure gold was being mined. Many loads had already been sent to the workstation for processing and the refined gold shipped to Forrest's company on Earth and offered for sale. It was a lucrative business and easily paid for all the expenses of mining.

Forrest had his space suit on and a small jet engine strapped to the back of his suit. After docking with the asteroid, the robot pilot declared it was safe to exit and Forrest carefully floated out of the ship's docking port holding on to the handle outside the ship. The jet engine started right away and he released his grip from the handle and steered himself to the work area where the mining was taking place, about half a mile from the ship. He was not tethered to the ship. In the back of his mind, he thought he probably should be, but the jet engines had never failed over the years they had been in use and he decided to just take off. The engine was powerful and Forrest had full control over where he traveled. Large hooks had already been anchored into the surface of the asteroid by the robots, since the mining had been going on for months already.

Forrest attached his tether to one of the hooks and turned off his engine. He was now able to easily float above the surface and study the mining process and by now the robots were all in place and started working. They had a long day ahead of them and Forrest carefully observed every detail and recorded improvements in his mind how to speed up the mining process. He noticed several details that could be done more efficiently and would save time and money. Above the work site was a gigantic fabric roof held in place by sturdy posts and the mined ore was just pushed upwards and caught inside the fabric roof. At the end of the workday, the fabric would be detached from the posts and folded up with the ore inside. Since the ore was weightless it was relatively easy to tow it back to the ship and unload the ore and then reuse the fabric roof.

It was about two hours left of the workday and Forrest signaled to the foreman that he would return to the ship and write his report. The foreman nodded in agreement and saluted him showing he understood. Forrest started his engine, unhooked his tether and took off. He saw the ship and then it happened. *The engine died.* He was four feet above the surface of the asteroid and with no atmosphere to slow him down he could not stop his forward momentum. To his horror, he floated past the ship without being close enough to grab hold of any handle and just continued floating out into space. Panic set in and his thoughts tumbled around in his head. His air tank had only two hours of oxygen left and he knew by the time the foreman returned to the ship and discovered he was gone he would be dead already. He forced himself to shake off the panic and try to be calm and meet his death with dignity. He saw Sheena's smiling face in front of him, her red hair glistening in the sun and the warmth of her amber eyes. How he loved her and how he missed her. Suddenly, a serene feeling came over him and he felt Sheena's presence as she transferred divine strength to him. He knew that soon he would be with her in the afterlife. Calmly and without fear he drifted further and further out into space. He felt no physical pain and when he took his last breath, he simply lost consciousness and after a few seconds he was dead.

The foreman noticed immediately that Forrest was gone and realized his engine had failed. At record speed they loaded the ore and took off. They followed the direction they knew Forrest must have been traveling and after an hour they caught up with him and saw him. The foreman slowed down the ship, strapped a jet engine onto his back and attached a tether between himself and the ship. He opened the docking port and took off after Forrest and within minutes he had him in his hands. He saw Forrest was dead and shook his head to the crew onboard signaling the bad news. Holding Forrest in a bearhug grip he returned to the ship and entered the cargo bay. The robots working in space were more advanced than the common worker robots on Earth and had been programmed with basic emotions and the mood was sorrowful when they saw Forrest's dead body. They took off again and were soon back at the workstation. The crew was shocked when they were told what had happened. Forrest had been well liked by everybody and the crew members grieved his death.

Forrest's body was transported back to Earth and his daughters were overcome with sorrow as were his parents Karl and Linh. Hilma and Cellie had lost both parents over a period of one and a half years, but they were grateful their grandparents were still alive and in good health. Karl and Linh were eighty-one years old, but looked years younger. They gave the emotional support the girls needed to get through the funeral and in doing so they were better able to cope with their own grief. Even Lena mourned and was present at the funeral. She had helped to raise Forrest and had seen him grow up.

At Forrest's company a new set of ironclad safety rules were added to the existing rules to ensure a tragedy like this would never happen again. The other mining companies adopted the same rules.

******

Drew was almost back in harbor with his boat full of fish. He noticed a group of people on the dock leaning down and watching something. He quickly docked his boat and spotted Lewie, an old salt with limited tolerance for landlubbers. He had been a fisherman his whole life, but he was now in his eighties and retired.

"Hey, Lewie, what happened?" Drew asked.

Lewie turned his weather-beaten face to Drew and responded -

"A kid just had his arm ripped off by a shark. The arm is gone so the shark must have eaten it. The ambulance is on its way."

Drew shuddered with horror and peeked at the boy lying on the dock barely conscious with blood dripping from his shoulder. He knew an artificial arm with full functionality would replace the missing arm, but he still felt shaken by the sight. The sharks would sometimes come close to shore where people were swimming, but rarely would an attack such as this one happen. Research was going on to regrow missing limbs, but the scientists were still working on it and had not finished the project yet.

Lewie helped Drew unload his catch and the buyer arrived with a refrigerated truck. Drew had a reputation for selling high quality fish kept under clean and cooled conditions and his buyers usually sold the whole catch to the local restaurants. Since the waters around the Bay Area had been cleaned up, fish had become very popular and many preferred fish over meat. Drew locked up his boat, said goodbye to Lewie and walked the short distance home to his and Tina's house. It was a stick built house, not 3D printed, and resembled a New England farm house, all white with a large front porch. A one-acre backyard with fruit trees, berry bushes and a vegetable garden made it homey. Tina had her herbal business in the basement and the house was rather large. She grew many of her herbs in the garden and processed them herself.

Drew always felt a jolt of happiness when he entered the front door and saw his family. He and Tina had recently renewed their marriage contract for another fifteen years and both knew the marriage would last. Brandon, by now sixteen years and almost as tall as his dad, and James, fourteen years, greeted him and Tina came out from the kitchen with their android maid and gave him a hug. She looked much younger than her forty-two years and every time Drew came home from a long day on the water, the sight of his family was the best part of his life. Drew and Tina were easy going parents and had allowed their sons to grow up with lots of freedom and both boys were independent and mentally strong. James had inherited Drew's bohemian ways and had told his father he wanted nothing more than to take over the fishing business. Drew was pleased with the news and was training James in all facets of fishing. Brandon was space crazy and kept rambling on about the universe and planets and being an astronaut. Drew and Tina just smiled and had no intention of holding him back. His future was his choice.

CHAPTER 14

The monarchies of the Middle East countries had been replaced by democracies and the lives of the royal families had been spared when they agreed to give up power without engaging in war. Over the years, there had been conflicts and minor wars in the Middle East since the discovery of the Zero Point Field, when free electricity was introduced worldwide over fifty years ago. Demand for oil and gas was diminished and the citizens of the oil and gas producing countries had to tighten their belts and adjust to a more frugal lifestyle. There was still demand for oil in manufacturing of goods, enough so that their economies did not collapse, but they were no longer affluent countries. Women's rights had added another irritant to the men's lives and even though women had attained full equality with men twenty years ago, some of the male population still felt it was the wrong decision and had a hard time accepting it. When one of the Muslim countries elected a woman as president a few years back, the Middle East took a big leap forward. It was soon evident that the new president was a capable leader and had full understanding of economics and all other internal affairs. Under her leadership the country prospered and there were no conflicts. She introduced a strictly secular government declaring faith should not be part of government and a secular government was the norm for most countries when she took office.

The first time a Muslim girl appeared on the beach clad only in a bikini, the older generation gasped in disapproval while the younger generation followed suit and within a short time all girls who wanted to could wear a bikini without being condemned. Traditional clothing was abolished for good.

India lost seventy percent of its population from the superbug and loss of electricity and during the slow rebuilding of their country, animosity between Hindus and Muslims faded away. Both Pakistan and

India had deactivated their nuclear weapons years earlier and were at peace with each other.

Israel was a peaceful and prosperous country and had slowly rebuilt their society. The population was still small and half the citizens had died from the superbug and loss of electricity. The country was technologically advanced and involved in many aspects of space travel. It was also a popular tourist destination.

Russia and China were also peaceful and had slowly gained population. China was no longer the factory of the world as self-sufficiency was considered important and most countries favored domestic manufacturing over imports. The standard of living in China was increasing and jobs were plentiful.

The African countries were not as affluent as America and Europe, but people could afford the basics of life and did not need help from the more advanced nations. The whole African continent was at peace and it had not been a war anywhere in Africa since the collapse. The populace of Africa was estimated to be around three hundred million, a severe drop from the one and a half billion that lived in Africa before the collapse.

The South American countries were also doing well and even though the border to the United States was open and no wall was ever built, immigration from the south into America had stopped. People preferred to stay in their native countries.

The United States had not split up as some had predicted before the collapse and, so far, no state had formerly seceded from the Union.

It had taken many years, but the immigrants to Europe had finally integrated with the customs of their new countries and abandoned Jihad. The high crime rate that had dominated Europe before the collapse was now down to almost nothing and the deaths and suffering from the collapse had changed everyone. Many people realized cooperation was the only way to achieve quality of life and whether a person was a Christian, Jew or Muslim was irrelevant. The world had entered a period of peace and prosperity and people referred to it as The Golden Era. Worldwide people wore an implant boosting cognition as well as adding the ability to look at matters from an objective point of view.

******

The male voice was gentle and came in clear and the people who had for years been assigned to listen for signals from outer space almost fell off their chairs.

"We're Cosmic Beings from Venus and we greet you as friends. For many years we have been watching you and followed your advancements in technology and how you finally have achieved global peace and abandoned wars as a way of resolving problems. We're your elder brothers and sisters and have contacted you to offer our assistance in your continued prosperity and also to aid you in your spiritual development. "

The voice was deep and melodious. One of the people had the presence of mind to respond, stammering -

"How, how … how did you connect to us? You sound as if you are right here."

"We use the Zero Point Field and so are you right now. When we're connected to the field, we can communicate without time delay. We could have contacted you years ago, but we felt it would be better if you as a species would mature and advance on your own first. You have now reached the point when you're ready to interact with us. My name is Zarem and I hope you'll accept our help."

"You say you are from Venus, but no human can survive on Venus."

"We're not biological beings; we're beings of pure light and vibration," Zarem explained. "We usually communicate telepathically between ourselves, but we're also capable of speech. Many of the issues you're struggling with, we've been through ourselves and you may find our help and experience useful. We're ahead of you in development and feel we can help you if you accept our help."

"I'm sure your help will be appreciated by our leaders here on Earth. How do we contact you when we need help?"

"We will contact you as we follow you and know when you need us," Zarem said. The men in the room were transfixed by his engaging voice.

"My female assistant Tholiika or myself will respond when you need us. Some of you may be able to communicate directly with us telepathically. We're always here, ready to be of service."

This was the first of many interactions between the Venusians and people on Earth. The Advisory Board when faced with complex ethical issues would always consult with Zarem and Tholiika and their consistently wise and practical solutions were deeply appreciated by the Board. The solutions were posted on the Internet for all to read and the Board listed the guidance given by the Venusians. After the initial surprise that Venus had a population, people on Earth got used to them and were grateful for their assistance.

People on Earth had become more spiritual and the majority of the population accepted they were not the only living beings around and many planets had intelligent life. Clarence and Lotte had for years communicated telepathically with each other and both found they were able to contact beings on Venus. The interactions were most rewarding and educational. The advice they received was always practical and common sense. Clarence' Venusian friend was named Polaris, a young male being, and Lotte had a female elderly friend with the name of Chismara. Lotte and Clarence connected often with their new friends and both felt they were growing and developing spiritually with their assistance. Of the three children, only Brianna, now fourteen years old, had the ability to communicate telepathically and she would sometimes connect with Polaris on Venus.

"Why does Earth orbit the sun?" Brianna asked telepathically.

"The sun's gravity causes it. Earth does not orbit the sun, but the sun's center of gravity," Polaris explained. "The sun moves all the time to offset the gravitational forces of the planets in our solar system and depending on the location of the planets the sun must move to keep balance. You can call the center of gravity the barycenter. When all the planets line up on one side, the sun must move away from the barycenter to keep balance. Depending on the location of the planets in their orbit around the barycenter, the sun moves accordingly in its own orbit. Think of a seesaw. If one person is heavier, the balance point moves from the center of the seesaw towards the heavy person. Otherwise, the seesaw wouldn't be balanced."

"Does our solar system orbit anything?" Brianna continued asking.

"Yes, our solar system, meaning our sun and planets, orbits around the center of the Milky Way galaxy and it takes about two hundred and thirty million years plus/minus to travel once around the Milky Way at the speed of almost half a million miles per hour. In the center of the Milky Way, it is believed there is a massive black hole."

"Why does gravity occur?"

"We know *how* gravity works, but it's not fully clear *what causes* gravity. Many theories have been suggested, but none has been proven yet."

This was just one of the complexities of space that Polaris clarified for Brianna and she often returned to him with science and astronomy questions.

******

Adora was now five years old and just as strong as any Earth child her age. She was athletic and loved to run, play ball with her dad and had just learned to ride her little bicycle. She had only hazy memories of Mars, but would probably not remember anything from Mars and her trip to Earth in a year or two. Hilma and Cellie's insect business had grown and Dawn enjoyed working with them a few days a week. Dawn had recently become the mother of a second child, a boy named Darren. She had chosen to use the artificial womb for this pregnancy and Kai left the decision to Dawn. She and Kai would visit the lab every week to check on the fetus and were present when the baby was removed from the womb. It was a strong, healthy boy and as Dawn washed him and dressed him for the first time, her maternal bond with him was just as strong as if she had carried him the natural way for nine months. The artificial womb had all the sounds of a human mother with heartbeat and other natural sounds, so the baby developed in an environment almost identical to a human womb. Dawn had been injected with low doses of hormones the last few months to enable her to nurse the baby.

******

A female android had become 'insane' and at first no one noticed. This android had been redesigned illegally by another android and lacked a kill-switch and safety programming that was mandatory for all androids designed by humans. New programming ordering the android to kill human beings had been inserted by the second android. The killer android would stalk humans walking alone and then strangle the person. Six persons were killed and the police had no clue at first how to find the perpetrator.

When nothing could be found in the Akashic Records, the police realized it must be an android they were looking for and installed cameras in various areas of the city. They were lucky and found the killer android within a day and deactivated it. All the programming was pulled and destroyed. The next problem was to find and destroy the android that had redesigned the killer android and determine how this android had bypassed its own safety programming. The Akashic Records revealed that a teenage hacker was responsible and had hacked into the first android and deactivated its safety programming. The hacker then reprogrammed him to find another android and redesign this android to become a criminal. The crime was of such severity that the court showed no mercy and sentenced the hacker to twenty years in jail without parole. When the judge asked the hacker why he had perpetrated such a vicious crime, the hacker responded without remorse he had done it 'for fun'. Not hesitating, the judge added five more years to his sentence and slammed his gavel down hard to show his anger with the hacker.

Clarence was asked to look into how the hacker could have bypassed the strict safety programming of the android and found one unprotected entry into the code that the hacker had used. He closed the entry and added another set of safety codes and for many years there were no more attempts at hacking into an android and the system worked safely.

******

Hilma was newly married to a man twelve years her senior, a wheat farmer from the Palouse in Idaho. Hilma had an Internet job and was able to work as a geneticist from home. Both Hilma and her husband asked Cellie to live with them as long as she wanted, but Cellie felt lost, still grieving her parents and she continued running the insect business alone with the help of her worker robots. She immersed herself in work, but felt chaos inside. The two sisters had always been very close and Cellie had trouble accepting that Hilma was not at her side anymore. She was twenty-three years old and found herself questioning if life was worth living. Her deep depression was noticed by both Linh and Lena. A worried Linh brought Cellie back to a more positive outlook on life and using her sensitivity and listening skills, Linh eventually was able to reach Cellie's heart. It was not a fast recovery, but once Cellie was back to her normal self again she emerged a stronger person. She went to visit

Hilma and her husband and when she saw how happy Hilma was and her joy at the tranquility of rural life, Cellie felt peace in her heart and was ready to live her own life again. Hilma was expecting and Cellie promised to visit after the baby was born.

Cellie enjoyed watching the holographic news from Mars. She would make her dinner, usually 3D printed food, and sitting on her sofa with a tray in her lap she closely followed the events on Mars. At the end of the newscast available jobs were announced and as Cellie watched with interest, an employment as manager of the insect growing business was announced. Cellie jumped, almost losing the tray in her lap. She knew she was fully qualified for the job having worked in the insect business for years. The job was available immediately, but required signing a two-year contract. Cellie did not mind that and applied for the job. After a week, she was offered the job and accepted right away. The next spaceship would leave in four weeks and in that time, Cellie had to sell her insect business and also her house. She offered both her business and house at a fair price and was able to sell both within two weeks. Hilma was sad to hear the news, but realized Cellie needed a change of scenery and wished her luck. Karl and Linh were not happy to hear the news either as they talked about it among themselves and Lena was also concerned. Karl and Linh always included Lena in their decisions as she was so close to both of them and they valued her common sense and logical advice. The three of them decided not to let Cellie know about their concerns, but to stay in close contact with her through holographic visits. The trip to Mars was safe and life on Mars was comfortable. There was enough food for sale, housing was nice and most services were available such as medical care, education for the children and recreational opportunities.

Cellie endured the trip to Mars and exercised vigorously to stay in shape. The speed of the spaceships had increased and the journey took only four months and Cellie kept herself busy with Internet studies, keeping a diary, visiting with the other passengers and watching holographic movies. She did not think the trip was that bad.

The landing went well and she settled into her little apartment and after a while she adjusted to the light gravity on Mars. When she was alone in her apartment, she wore a weight suit. She had not decided whether she would stay for good on Mars and Dawn had advised her to carefully monitor her bones and muscles. Cellie found her job as manager of the insect business enjoyable and was totally engaged in her work. She was efficient and introduced several improvements that were recognized by her superior. Her work week was five days and five hours a day and if she needed to take a day off, all she had to do was ask. The worker robots handled all the basic care of the insects. For the first time since her parents died Cellie was happy and she felt an inner peace that was soothing. She was not religious, but had certain spiritual beliefs that aided her when she was under stress.

Cellie made several excursions around Mars and loved the trips. Even though the landscape was without trees, she still found it enjoyable and signed up for many of the trips that were announced. The food was quite good and adequate from a nutritional point of view and she ate in the dining room. There was a small kitchen in her apartment, but she only used it to make breakfast. All sorts of recreational activities were available and a brand-new swimming pool had just been built that Cellie used several times a week. Jumping in caused a big splash as the water weighed less than on Earth and she found she could float on top of the water with ease. The pool was rather large and had taken months to fill, but it was very appreciated by the people using it.

She communicated at least once a week with Linh and Hilma and sometimes with Dawn, who had many good tips for her when they talked. Hilma had just given birth to a girl and Cellie smiled to herself when she heard she was now an aunt. She had no boyfriend, but several of the young men had tried to date her. She politely declined their invitations. Cellie was pretty and looked like Sheena. She had a quick wit and her humor caused many to erupt in laughter. There was one man she found interesting and would date if he approached her. She had heard he was a mechanic and oversaw all the equipment used in the mining industry. He was a blond guy in his late twenties and Cellie knew his name was Gordon.

One evening when she sat in the lobby and had a glass of wine, Gordon sat down next to her and started talking. Cellie did not know if he deliberately sought her company or just sat down next to her to make small talk. She was intrigued by his presence and listened intently. He had been on Mars two years and had signed a contract for four years and if he decided to return to Earth, it would be the same year as Cellie returned.

"I love Mars and the challenges here," Gordon confided to Cellie. "Whether I stay for good or return to Earth, I don't know yet. I'll decide when my contract is up."

"The same for me," Cellie responded. "The odds are I will most likely return to Earth even though I also like Mars a lot. I do miss my sister and grandparents. My parents have passed away."

"Sorry to hear that. How did it happen?"

Cellie told him how Sheena had drowned while surfing and the sad story of her father floating out into space. Gordon listened with great interest and when he saw a tear in Cellie's eye, he put his arm around her to console her.

They started dating and saw each other as often as they could. Gordon enjoyed cooking and would often invite her to his apartment for dinner. He did not use the 3D printer but used an old-fashioned range and his cooking skills were impressive. Cellie could not cook at all and was delighted with his tasty meals.

Gordon proposed after a year and Cellie accepted knowing he was the right man for her. They opted for a traditional marriage license and the following week Cellie became Gordon's wife. It was a simple ceremony with only a few friends present. Cellie moved into Gordon's apartment and although a little small, they made do. Cellie found Gordon to be a caring and considerate husband and very kindhearted. He was by nature calm while Cellie was impulsive and spontaneous and their opposite personalities complemented their union. They were happy and their families back on Earth were also pleased when they heard the good news.

Mining on Mars was not without mishaps and Gordon was involved in many of the safety features of the mining. Right now, he oversaw the extracting of water ice, purifying and storing it, but he also was involved with the mining of precious metals, which was more dangerous. Now that he had a wife, he did not want to take unnecessary risks the way he had done in the past.

A spaceship had been sent to investigate the surface of Phobos, the larger of Mars' two tiny moons and only fourteen miles across, to ascertain whether it was worth mining there. Phobos is orbiting Mars at an elevation of slightly less than six thousand miles and travels across the Martian sky three times a day. The surface is coated with fine dust, at least three feet deep. A huge crater as well as two smaller craters cover the surface of Phobos. There were also plans to investigate the second moon Deimos, only eight miles across and orbiting Mars once a day at an elevation of fourteen thousand miles. Nothing conclusive was determined from the samples taken from Phobos and the metallurgists and geologists announced they needed more samples taken from a lower depth to finalize their research. There was only minor interest to start serious mining on the two moons. A final decision would be made after the samples from Deimos had been more thoroughly examined and it would be several more years before a ship would be sent to Deimos to explore its mining possibilities. The Martians had to watch their expenses and were still paying back the initial loan that had funded their settlement. The government on Mars was very frugal and all expenses were carefully considered to ensure no money was wasted. The new swimming pool had been expensive, but the government decided to fund it deeming it necessary for the citizens' enjoyment.

The Martians paid ten percent tax until the loan from Earth was paid off and then it was hoped a smaller tax rate would be sufficient to pay for all services. Education and health care were free and the government paid for all infrastructure and its maintenance as well as salaries for those working for the government. A steady income was generated from making fuel for the spaceships and the income from mining on Mars was continuously growing. The population had grown to twenty-five thousand citizens and housing was added all the time to accommodate new arrivals. Mars had become popular and even though life on Earth was pleasant, many people wanted to try out life on Mars, at least for a couple of years. Many of them stayed and never returned to Earth.

There were now a variety of little shops on Mars and those who preferred to cook their own meals could find reasonably priced fresh foods of high quality. Cellie and Gordon always went shopping for food together. The communal dining hall on Mars also served up excellent food and Darrel still worked there as a chef. He, Juliet and their son Cliff had now been Martians for fourteen years and had no plans to return to Earth. Cliff was now a young man of twenty-two years and had just started working as a teacher. They had been among the first people from Earth to settle on Mars.

Cellie was expecting and when she and Gordon found out the happy news they decided to stay on Mars. They knew what Dawn had gone through to adapt Adora to Earth's gravity and felt it was too complicated. Their Martian life was pleasant and improvements were made all the time and as they weighed the pros and cons of life on Earth versus Mars, they both agreed Earth was more beautiful, but Mars had its own attributes. Gordon found a bigger apartment and they decorated it with 3D printed furniture and made a corner of their bedroom into a nursery. The artificial womb was still not available on Mars so Cellie had to carry her baby to term the natural way.

There were already talks about exploring other planets suitable for future settlements. This idea intrigued both Cellie and Gordon. Teleportation was the hottest new research area and several methods were being explored. Clarence was involved in teleportation and felt confident that eventually humans would be able to teleport from one planet to the next.

Every week Cellie and Gordon communicated with their Earth relatives. Hilma's girl was already a year and a half and Hilma was expecting her second child at about the same time Cellie was due. Dawn and Kai were a happy family. Adora was now seven years old, a lively girl with a big appetite for life. Darren was doing well and Dawn had just 'given birth' to a third child using the artificial womb for the second time.

Cellie always communicated with her grandparents Karl and Linh and when they heard Cellie would not come back they were very sad. They enjoyed visits from Clarence, Drew and Dawn and their families, but they would still miss Cellie. Karl and Linh would sometimes spend a few days with Hilma and her family on their farm and enjoyed the peaceful countryside and watching all the animals on the farm. Lena always accompanied them and relished these visits as much as Karl and Linh. She loved the animals and would often watch in delight when the wind swept through the wheat fields gently moving the wheat like waves on the ocean. She also got along splendid with Hilma's android, a very advanced model, and the two of them usually cooked together. Lena was so close to being human that both Karl and Linh seldom thought of her as a machine but viewed her as a friend they loved. Lena was fully aware of Karl and Linh's affection for her and responded by always giving her best. She ran the household with the efficiency of a CEO. Hilma's husband was an affluent man and could afford to provide a comfortable lifestyle for his family. The farm was fully automated and Hilma's husband oversaw the whole operation from his office.

Hilma and Cellie gave birth within a week of each other and both had boys. On Mars, Gordon was a proud father and they named their son Arvin.

CHAPTER 15

Back on Earth, Clarence was heavily involved with teleportation and several methods were on his drawing board. The idea of slipping through a wormhole or a portal was his favorite method, but he was also working on the Quantum Teleportation method. The end goal was to enable humans to travel through space between planets almost instantly. Clarence was not a physicist, but still had a good understanding of wormholes and the problems with passage through them. At the same time, he was working with a teleportation device that would transport humans long distances. His team had several androids doing the calculations and two humans, a physicist and a highly skilled computer scientist. Clarence and his team were one of several companies working on interplanetary travel and several other companies were trying to solve the problem as well.

The sad news arrived that Linnéa had passed away at the age of one hundred years. Her android that had lovingly cared for her for twenty years found her slumped in her chair and saw she was dead. Linnéa never moved away from the farm in Colburn and had lived in her own house on the property ever since she and Bjorn retired. She had enjoyed good health most of her life and it was assumed she died of old age. Her seventy-five-year marriage to Bjorn had been very happy. All the relatives mourned the death of Old Grandma Linnéa.

An intense sandstorm hit Mars and lasted a full month. The sky darkened and no one could go outside. Mining had to stop while the storm raged on, but the Martians were prepared for these storms and large quantities of water were in the storage tanks and the food production was all indoors, so most people took the storms in stride and just waited them out. When the storm was over, the worker robots would clear off the sand rather quickly and life was back to normal within a few days.

Cellie went back to her old job as manager of the insect department and enrolled Arvin in daycare. She only worked twenty hours a week so she had plenty of time to spend with Arvin. On Dawn's advice she strapped weights onto Arvin's arms and legs even though Arvin would probably never travel to Earth, but Cellie felt it could not hurt to make him physically strong. Every day she bicycled an hour with Arvin strapped behind her. Next to the regular traffic in the tunnel system that tied the whole community together were bicycle lanes. The tunnels had windows and every few miles there were rest areas with flower arrangements and benches that were popular with the bikers. All the people from Earth had lost some of their bones and muscles because of the lighter gravity on Mars, but those who had decided to stay on Mars were not overly concerned about it. Only the people who had traveled to Mars for a limited time walked around with weight belts or weight suits and engaged in heavy exercise to maintain as much bone density as possible. Both Cellie and Gordon wore weight belts when they were in their apartment to maintain physical strength and Cellie enjoyed the strenuous biking.

The last year, two Holodecks had been built and were immensely popular. They could be rented for two hours per session by appointment only and the waiting time was usually a week. The programs available were very varied and the person could immerse in almost any fantasy imaginable. Cellie's favorites were other planets in the solar system as well as going back in time to medieval times while Gordon preferred being aboard old-fashioned sail ships fighting horrendous storms, climbing mountains and occasionally just wandering around in jungles on Earth.

Pets had been introduced and initially all the kittens and puppies had died in transit to Mars, but when they were transported with low gravity on the rotating wheel aboard the spaceship, many of them did survive. Some families wanted a pet for their children, but the overall interest in owning a cat or dog was not that great. No large animals could exist on Mars, but rabbits and chickens did well as did fish. The chickens were for egg production only as there were not enough fodder and space available to raise chickens for meat, but the option was open to raise chickens in the future. Fresh milk was not available, only powdered milk imported from Earth. The overall health of the Martians was good and malnutrition was not an issue. The Martian government gratefully accepted guidance from the Venusians.

******

Before the collapse, a team of inventors had worked on the idea of launching helium-filled airships from a spaceship above Venus' atmosphere. The idea was to create a spectacular vacation for tourists from Earth. To land on the surface of Venus was out of the question as the surface temperature was almost nine hundred degrees Fahrenheit and its atmospheric pressure ninety times higher than Earth - truly hellish conditions. But, thirty miles above the surface of Venus above the cloud cover the conditions are sunny and more friendly. The atmospheric pressure is about the same as on Earth and the temperature range is from 32 degrees to roughly 150 degrees Fahrenheit depending on the altitude.

The Advisory Board had been asked by the team to consult with the Venusians whether the airship idea was worth pursuing and also if it was ethical since the ships would hover above Venus' surface.

Zarem and Tholiika took turns answering.

"In principle, we have nothing against the idea," Tholiika said calmly. "As biological beings, you would not be able to land on Venus' surface, but above the cloud level you should be able to create airships that could sustain human life. The whole project is by no means easy and would require your brightest minds."

"It would be an enormous expense to create a workable business model out of this venture and you may not get a high return on your investment for many years and even then, the profit may not be as high as you had expected," Zarem added. "I don't mean to discourage you, but we suggest you look into the details carefully before you start."

When the Board conveyed the message from the Venusians, the team of inventors promptly decided to scrap the idea, at least for the time being.

******

Devotion and care for planet Earth had increased and big efforts had been put into action to thoroughly remove all trash, toxic substances, debris of all kinds from both the ground and oceans. Included in the project was the burned down cities that had been left in a state of ruin since the collapse. Most countries agreed to the proposal and financed their own implementation of the project and many ideas were shared between the different countries. Big sweepers cleared the oceans of plastics and the cost was shared by all countries when they swept international waters. The whole campaign was a huge affair and very costly, but it was agreed that each country would tackle the project according to its financial ability and spread the work out over several years. Leveling the cities and removing various building materials were complicated tasks and involved the creation of many jobs for both robots and humans. Some new landfills had to be created for dumping and they were later filled with soil and landscaped. Plastics were put into huge pits and plastic eating worms were added feeding on the edible plastic. It took years, but eventually all the plastic was gone and the worms were saved for future use. The plastics that were not edible by the worms were recycled and reused. Most people had recycled and cared about the planet for many years, but a full clean-up had never taken place globally and the beautification of Earth was visible for all to see. Most people felt it was worth the cost.

'Clean-up' of people's minds was also considered important. Simple psychology lessons started in the first grades of school and gradually became more sophisticated as the students understood how their psyche worked, why they harbored certain negative feelings and the origin of these feelings. The Akashic Records were available on an individual basis to explore former embodiments. Events from past embodiments may have followed the lifestream to this present embodiment and caused fears and negative feelings. Most students used the Akashic Records without fear, but a handful of students never got up the nerve to explore their former embodiments and were not forced to do so. The mood of the population was optimistic and various fears had faded away. As a result, creativity increased and society was moving forward. Before the collapse, suicides and insanity were increasing and many people suffered from a variety of fears and indecision.

Old archived news videos were available on the Internet and had been converted to 3D format. When people watched videos of Black Friday and the shopping mania, they were amazed at people's obsession with 'things' and the value attributed to these items. Most people concluded that these shoppers suffered from mental illness and had lost touch with reality. It was now the year 2123 and the videos were from the 2020s. People felt the population a hundred years ago had valued the wrong things in life. The present population looked upon material abundance differently and only strived to own what they needed without feeling the need to show off luxuries and hoarding. Personal growth and inner peace, achieving mental self-sufficiency and independence were goals people tried to achieve.

It was now known that humans receive light from the universe measured in Hertz, cycles per second, and that most humans were not able to receive sufficient amount of light to achieve full brain capacity due to mental blocks and filters. The maximum light a human can use is 25,000 Hertz, but most people only functioned with a mere 5,000 Hertz and often less. Before the collapse, many humans could only receive 1,000 to 2,000 Hertz with lowered quality of life as a result. The more light a person is able to receive, the more use the person has of his or her brain and hence creativity and cognition are enhanced. Large parts of the brain are simply dormant when low amounts of light is present. Many people were deeply involved with increasing their light reception by mentally removing their blocks and filters and using 'mind over matter' to overcome mental obstacles and raising their vibration. Higher vibration resulted in less disease. Even atheists not open-minded to anything spiritual understood and accepted the concept of light entering the human body and some of these people were as enthusiastic as spiritual people. The implants that most people carried increased brain capacity, but had nothing to do with receipt of light.

Scientists understood more and more how the complex human body functioned and some interesting diagnostic tools had been invented. One valuable tool was a very small one-time use camera for diagnostic purposes, small enough to swallow and too small to create an intestinal blockage. The patient was hooked up to a communicator and the transit images through the system were available through the communicator. If disease was present, the location and severity of the disease was visible on the 3D images retrieved from the communicator. Recently a similar tool, a mini size camera, had been invented to be injected into a person's blood stream to diagnose abnormal conditions. This camera had to be removed by a doctor, but it was a simple procedure and the same type syringe that injected the camera was used to retrieve it.

Replacement organs grown in laboratories using the patient's stem cells had become routine. People in general enjoyed better health than before the collapse, but when disease occurred the doctors were very capable and seldom lost a patient. The median age was one hundred years and some lived even longer and usually in relatively good health until the end. Cognitive decline was not common and most people lived out their lives with normal brain capacity. People who could afford it either bought or rented an android to help them towards the end of their lives. Nursing homes were a thing of the past and elderly people preferred to live out their lives in their own homes with the assistance of an android.

Genetic work was advancing and involved crops and plants of all sorts as well as pets and humans. Lately the subject of having a 'designer baby' was discussed among the population. Most people were against changing babies and stated people should refrain from 'playing God'. The Advisory Board had several consultations with the Venusians and finally posted their advice on the Internet. The Venusians declared that they strongly deterred the geneticists from pursuing genetic editing of embryos and to abandon all work on germ line gene editing and allow babies to be born without changing their genes. They announced they found germ line gene editing unethical and that it may upset the natural balance. In addition, unintended consequences that no one could foresee in advance may occur.

They further stated that removal of certain disease-causing genes in humans was recommended if the process could be done without altering the rest of the DNA. There had been a few incidents where removal of some genes had changed the DNA and caused unexpected outcome, in a few cases serious changes.

The Board also announced gene splicing on food crops to improve a species was recommended as long as the plant could reproduce and not become sterile and that the gene splicing only involved plants from the same genus.

Many farmers had already abandoned genetically modified food crops and successfully used predatory insects to fight destructive insects on various crops and fruit trees with good results.

******

Exploratory spaceships had been sent to Jupiter's and Saturn's moons. They were launched from Mars, but the government of Mars had refused to contribute any funding to the project citing they were still in debt to Earth and could not afford additional debts. America and several other countries had shared the cost to send two spaceships to orbit Jupiter's moon Europa and Saturn's moon Enceladus. It was a small project and the interest from the public was limited as the conditions on these moons were too severe to support human life. Before the collapse unmanned spacecraft had visited these moons and scientists had gained some knowledge about their surface conditions, but no details were known. This space mission was launched to obtain as many facts as possible. It would be several years before the mission was completed and all the pictures and facts analyzed. The end result was that the moons were judged uninhabitable and perhaps in the future mankind would rekindle interest in these moons, but at the present time no more exploratory missions were planned.

******

Ollie, short for Olivera, walked slowly through the brightly lit tunnel deep below the surface of Mars holding a bucket of ore that she had chipped off the wall of the tunnel. Her spacesuit was cumbersome to wear and slowed her down. She was part of a team of geologists exploring natural elements on Mars and she often ventured down into the tunnels alone to take her samples. There was always a risk involved to enter the tunnels, but Ollie was never afraid. Some tunnels had collapsed with loss of human life and the miners had run out of oxygen and were dead before the rescue team could reach them.

Ollie was in her early thirties, newly married and even though she was plain looking, she generated a strong personal aura that made her attractive. She had a gentle but commanding voice that mirrored her self-confidence. As she turned around to start her walk back to the elevator that would take her to the surface, she felt a slight tremor under her feet. It was about half a mile to the elevator and Ollie hastened her step. The trembling increased in intensity and she moved as fast as her spacesuit would allow. She was out of luck. A strong quake shook the tunnel and it collapsed all around her. Rocks and soil rained all over her and she fell to the floor of the tunnel with one of her legs trapped under a boulder. She could not move and it was all dark around her. The ground was still shaking, but with less intensity now and after fifteen minutes it finally stopped. Marsquakes were not a common event and when they occurred, they were mild and most people disregarded them. She remembered her head lamp and switched it on. The sight made her gasp. She was in a small hollow and the tunnel leading to the elevator seemed to be totally filled in with rocks. All lights were out and it was pitch-black everywhere. The boulder on her leg was too large to move and she knew her leg was broken. She was trapped. Her communicator was dead and she was praying the rescue team would reach her before her air supply ran out. She forced herself to remain calm and to trust she would be found alive.

It took about an hour until she heard the familiar sound of the earth drill and she knew the team of rescue workers was on the way. Her thoughts wandered to her husband Koto, an easygoing man of Japanese descent, and how happy they were together. She was carrying their first child and she was in the beginning of her pregnancy. Koto was a mathematician teaching both high school and college students and had signed a two-year contract to work on Mars. They liked life on Mars, but felt two years were enough and had decided to return to Earth. Dawn had written a detailed report on how she trained Adora with weights to prepare her for Earth's higher gravity and all parents with plans to return to Earth followed her instructions. Ollie and Koto had read Dawn's report and planned to follow it to the letter.

Three hours went by and Ollie estimated she had about an hour left of oxygen. The electronic display on her sleeve was broken and she could only guess how much oxygen she had left. Her leg throbbed with pain, but she was not aware of any other damage to her body and she felt sure the baby was unharmed. She lay quietly on the cold ground trying to breathe as slowly as possible to preserve oxygen and commanded herself to remain calm and trust she would be saved in time. To her dismay, her bladder emptied and she simply could not stop it from happening, but the obligatory diaper worn with a spacesuit came to her rescue. Ollie was strong-minded and was able to block out the worst of the pain from her leg, so much so that she actually dozed off.

The rescue team was working frantically and when they reached Ollie and saw her on the ground, not moving, they expected the worst. Ollie was popular and a group of friends had gathered together with Koto by the mine's entrance anxiously waiting for news. When the elevator emerged with the rescue team and Ollie on a stretcher, awake but exhausted, everybody jumped with relief. The medic explained to Koto that she had been unconscious when they found her and with only minutes left of oxygen. They had resupplied her air tank and were able to wake her up. Together the team had pried off the boulder and saw that her leg was broken. Ollie was rushed to the hospital and upon examination, the doctors found she had a complete fracture of the bone with the bone snapped into two parts. She was given local anesthesia and the bone was successfully lined up and glued back together. Another type of glue closed the incision on her leg. This technique had been around for years and worked well, but on Earth medical researchers were experimenting with even faster methods of fusing bones together, however, these new procedures were not available on Mars. Ollie was fitted with a leg brace and was able to leave the hospital sitting in a wheel chair. The following day she would start physical exercises to regain the use of her leg and full recovery usually took about two weeks.

Three weeks after the accident, Ollie was back at work. She felt well and her leg was mostly back to normal. Koto had taken time off from work and stayed home with Ollie while she was recovering and their emotional bond grew even stronger. Koto had psychic abilities and had sensed Ollie was in trouble when the tunnel collapsed and the thought of losing her had shaken him to the core. Life without her would not be worth living and Ollie felt the same about Koto.

Ollie gave birth to a small, but healthy little girl and they named her Takara. She looked just like her father but had her mother's blue eyes. Ollie and Koto had one year left to stay on Mars and started with Dawn's exercise program for the baby. Ollie worked only a few hours a day while Takara was in daycare so she would be able to spend time with her baby and ensure the weights strapped onto the baby did no harm.

The year went by quickly and the return trip to Earth was only a few days away. Koto and Ollie were glad to return. They had enjoyed Mars, but felt it was entirely too confined to live mostly indoors and both of them looked forward to spending time in Nature on Earth, walking barefoot in green grass and seeing flowers and trees again and to be rid of the spacesuit. They felt sure Takara would adjust to Earth's gravity and her bones and muscles would strengthen. The space flight back to Earth was uneventful, but long and tedious. Takara had adapted well to being weightless and showed no sign of illness to her parents' relief. Many children had already gone through Dawn's program and survived the trip from Mars to Earth and only one child had died in transit. One other child had become infected with Earth bacteria, but survived and the overall success rate of moving children back to Earth had been more favorable than expected.

Ollie and Koto soon acclimated to Earth's gravity and little Takara did well also. Her bones and muscles were not as strong as those of Earth children, but just like Adora, she caught up after a year and was able to keep up with her Earth friends. The family settled in Pennsylvania and Ollie and Koto loved the rolling hills and the pleasant landscape. Ollie was pregnant again and stayed home and Koto was hired as a math professor at a nearby university. Most of his teaching was over the Internet, but he also offered private lessons at the university for students seeking more advanced math lessons.

******

Karl and Linh had reached the respectable age of eighty-nine years but felt twenty years younger thanks to improvements in geriatric research. They looked good and functioned well and there was no slowdown in their cognitive abilities or physical mobility. Linh had had her heart replaced and the organ was grown in a laboratory from her own stem cells. She had also had one hip replaced and Karl had been fitted with two knee replacements. Medical science had discovered ways to delay aging and some of their achievements dealt with vision, hair loss, teeth, memory, skin and organ replacements to name a few. To prevent baldness had been more difficult than the medical researchers had expected and this problem was not totally resolved yet. Various methods had been tried with partial success, but it looked hopeful that eventually hair loss would be a thing of the past.

People often lived past a hundred years and some reached the age of one hundred and ten years. Medical scientists sometimes joked they would raise the average life span to two hundred years and as more and more medical problems were resolved, perhaps they had a point.

Lena was still living with Karl and Linh and her loyalty and dedication were highly valued by Karl and Linh. Lena assured them that she loved her work and even though she did all the housework and errands, she told them her work load was not too much. Lena always accompanied them on vacations and family visits and enjoyed the different sceneries. Her intelligent input during family discussions was well received by Karl, Linh and their relatives. Even though she was an android, she had her own very specific personality which differed from any other android and she evolved and matured just by living and facing new experiences.

The year before, Clarence had asked Lena if she wanted to have a 'baby' and go through motherhood and to his surprise she had nodded enthusiastically. Lena's software included maximum feelings and her abilities were almost as advanced as Eva's. Clarence designed a new android resembling Lena in both appearance and personality, but did not equip the new android with a full package of software. She was full size, but still a youngster in mind. Lena took enormous delight in raising her 'daughter', whom she named Miracle, and taught her many valuable lessons. Clarence incorporated all the lessons into a software package and inserted into her memory banks for permanent storage. He also fitted her with a full package of feelings. Miracle stayed with Lena five years and then she was given as a gift to a close friend of Linh's. Miracle would visit Lena on and off for years and the two were very close.

******

The world had been at peace for close to a hundred years with the exception of the failed coup in Mexico in 2103, twenty-three years ago. Unrest was building in the Middle East all over again and many men could not accept the new modern lifestyle and women's equality, which had been in effect for close to thirty years. Women in the Muslim countries were not about to go back to the 'dark ages' and totally ignored the pleas of the men to cover up. The men had no choice but to accept the women's decision, but waves of irritation swept the area and was probably one of the reasons why a war broke out between two of the Muslim countries. On Zarem's and Tholiika's advice, the rest of the world did not interfere and stayed out of it. The bloody war lasted three long years with thousands killed and when both the leaders and the soldiers finally realized there was no gain or merit to the war, it ended with a truce in effect that became a final peace agreement. The rest of the world breathed a sigh of relief as did the Muslim women. Life returned slowly to the new modern lifestyle and the men eventually accepted the idea that women were equal to men. Rebuilding of the two countries lasted several years and took a big bite out of their budgets. Witnessing the destruction of this war reinforced the belief in the rest of the world that war never solved any problem and whatever difficulties arose, there were better ways to resolve them.

Many countries now had a small army and air force and the soldiers were required to report for training once a year. No one wanted war and the soldiers of these armies had never been in combat, but would be called upon during natural disasters such as earthquakes and severe storms to aid the population. The cost to maintain these armies was minimal for each country as the soldiers were only paid when they were on duty.

There were no armed forces on the Moon and Mars as they were deemed unnecessary. The Moon colony was growing and many worked a year or two and then returned to Earth. The pay was more than they could earn back home on Earth and many signed up to work on the Moon both to earn extra income and enjoy a new adventure. No one stayed on permanently.

Two police officers ensured that law and order was maintained on Mars, but the crime rate among the citizens was extremely low. Both of them had a regular job and the police officers were only called upon as needed.

******

Brandon was now twenty-five years old and an astronaut in training. He was able to fly most spaceships, but lacked sufficient flight hours. His passion for space had never diminished and he loved his work. To his surprise Brianna, who was four years younger, had also enrolled to become an astronaut. The two of them had spent many hours talking about space travel and the universe when Brianna and her family were guests on Drew's fishing boat, but Brandon never thought Brianna would follow through and embrace such a dangerous and demanding career. Brianna looked feminine, but had inherited her mother Lotte's enthusiasm for a male oriented career and she was fiercely independent with a strong personality. A traditional lifestyle was not for her. She was still in school, but practiced often in various flight simulators learning how to fly both standard planes and spaceships. Clarence and Lotte supported her choice of lifestyle and kept their worries to themselves.

Brandon and Brianna were close friends and were hoping to work together in the future. Brandon was working as copilot on the Moon spaceships, but had been offered to switch over to the Martian spaceships. He accepted and his first flight was scheduled for the following month.

Two years passed and Brianna had graduated from school and entered flight school. She was now ready to be part of the crew on the Moon spaceships as a cadet and her first flight filled her with awe. The many hours she had spent studying had been worth it, she felt. Between her space flights she would continue taking different courses related to space and the mastering of the new updated spaceships. She had barely any free time, a fact that did not concern her at all. Dating and boyfriends could wait. After a year working as a cadet, she was offered to become a copilot and after two years she easily mastered flying the spaceship with no help from the senior pilot.

Between flights Brianna dated Brandon and their friendship had become a matter of the heart. They were distantly related as their fathers Drew and Clarence were second cousins. Both of them hoped to serve on the same Martian spaceship in the future as a husband-and-wife team and their wish was soon granted. Brandon was offered the position of senior pilot with Brianna as his copilot and both were overjoyed. They tied the knot without delay and their parents were truly pleased when they heard the news. Their first flight together was scheduled to leave in two days so there was no time for family and friends to attend their wedding. When Brandon put the ring on Brianna's finger, she felt the same euphoria as she had felt the first time she flew the Moon spaceship by herself. Their love for each other was as deep as their friendship.

Clarence was very interested in Brianna's career and he knew of her ambitions to pursue space travel to distant planets in the future. His work with teleportation had turned out to be much more complicated than anyone had foreseen and was still just in the beginning stages. He was in his mid-fifties and knew that he would not realize his dream of building a functioning teleportation device in this lifetime and perhaps it would take another hundred years to perfect the invention. In addition to his work with teleportation, Clarence had worked on suspended animation or hibernation for astronauts and had had some success in that field. Even this scientific field had proven to be more complicated than expected and only some achievements had been reached.

Brandon and Brianna had adjusted to living on the Martian spaceship and even though their cabin was small, it was cozy and homey. Since the launch window for space flight to Mars only occurred every twenty-six months when the two planets were at their closest distance to each other, Brandon and Brianna made one round trip to Mars every two years with a layover in Martia lasting a week. There was now a hotel in Martia where they stayed and on Earth, they owned an apartment. When they returned from Mars, they had two months off before working as astronauts on the Moon cargo ships until the next launch window opened for Mars travel again. Their work schedule was not easy, but both of them were resilient and able to adapt to the different gravities of Earth, the Moon and Mars with less physical problems than most.

During their two months off Brandon and Brianna often spent time on Drew's boat helping Drew and James with the fishing. Drew and James were partners with similar personalities and seldom disagreed on how to run the business. James was divorced and did not feel ready to commit himself to marriage again. His ex-wife disliked the whole business of fishing and had left him after a year of marriage. They had no children. James loved the ocean and the free lifestyle as much as Drew and he would only remarry if the girl shared his interest in his way of life. Tina would always come along on the boat when Brandon and Brianna were onboard and they all worked well together as a team. When Clarence' work schedule allowed, he and Lotte would join them for a day or two.

Brandon and Brianna had lived through a frightening experience during their last trip to the Moon when one of the three engines just quit. They were close to the Moon when it happened and Brandon saw on the instrument panel the symbol for the fuel pump flashing and realized it had stopped pumping fuel into the engine. The spaceship started to slowly veer off course. Brandon was able to adjust the engines and fins to maintain symmetrical thrust, but until he had managed to steer the spaceship back on course, he and Brianna lived through a nerve-wracking experience. Only Brandon's quick reactions and 'feel' for the spaceship saved them from a potential disaster. Landing the spaceship was tense with one engine out, but went well without additional problems. Afterwards, Brandon told Brianna exactly how he had adjusted the spaceship to return to its original course and they also repeated the lesson in the spaceship simulator. With Brandon's help, she was able to repeat the whole incident and felt she had learned one of her most important lessons of her career.

Brianna really wanted to experience motherhood, but being away from home most of the time, she saw no way to have a baby. To her surprise, her mother Lotte proposed a solution when she mentioned her longing to have children by offering to raise Brianna's children when she was away. Lotte suggested she would use the artificial womb and time the birth of the baby to coincide with her two months off after a Martian trip so she could nurse the baby. Brianna hugged her mother and accepted her generous offer and also gave Eva a hug. She knew Eva would be part of raising the baby and she was very good with children and enjoyed being around them.

Everything worked out according to plan and a year later Brandon and Brianna were the happy parents of a baby boy they named Rigel after a star in the constellation Orion. In addition to her scheduled two months off from work, Brianna's employer had allowed her an additional two months before she was scheduled to return to work. By the time Rigel was four months old, Brianna felt ready to start working and she resumed her work as astronaut with Brandon flying back and forth to the Moon until they were scheduled to travel to Mars again. Between Moon trips, they spent all their time with Rigel. Brandon's parents, Drew and Tina, often took care of Rigel on weekends and the two sets of grandparents relished caring for their grandson.

CHAPTER 16

Karol walked at a quick pace down the corridor in the White House where she worked. She was in her mid-twenties and although rather plain looking, she radiated an aura of elegance that was noticeable. With a slender figure and long, shapely legs she was an attractive person, but hidden within she harbored a frozen soul that tormented her and had prevented her from engaging in a relationship with a man. She had been orphaned at the age of five years old when her parents' airmobile had encountered severe engine trouble and fell from the sky killing both her parents. Karol was an only child and had grown up in foster care as her only relatives were elderly and unable to care for a child. Although she had not been physically abused, the three foster homes she had lived in were far from ideal and she had suffered daily verbal abuse and total neglect. As a child, she had never experienced love from any of her foster parents and she became cold and reserved. Her teenage years had been spent alone in her room with her Internet books and she finished college at the age of twenty at the top of her class.

The old White House had been burned down after the collapse and the new White House was much smaller, but since the government was still very small, the size of the new building was adequate. Karol had landed a job as assistant to the director of the space program and she had gained an impressive knowledge about most things related to space; the Moon and Mars colonies, asteroid mining and future exploratory trips to planets beyond Mars. It was a dream job and she worked hard to learn as much as possible. She had an apartment close to the White House and her private life was uneventful and lonely. She had no friends and no boyfriend. Sometimes she wished she had a husband, but she also knew that her career came first and she was determined to rise through the ranks.

Her boss, Ryan Clifford, was in his early forties with a calm disposition and easy to be around. He was a widower with two small boys and his wife had passed away a year ago. Karol and Ryan worked well together and he often took her out for lunch, but for the first time he had invited Karol for dinner to his home to meet his boys, four-year-old Elliot and six-year-old Kenny. Karol entered his house feeling slightly anxious as she had no experience with children and felt awkward when interacting with them. She did not have to worry as Ryan and his boys were cooking when she arrived and made her feel right at home. She truly enjoyed the peaceful atmosphere in Ryan's neat home and that was the first of many days she spent with Ryan and his family. To her surprise, she found she loved his children and when the boys gave her a hug her frozen soul mellowed. She had never had a boyfriend and never been in love, but when Ryan proposed she accepted and she knew that the deep friendship they had would mature into love. After they married the boys started calling her 'mom' and Karol's love for them was as strong as if they had been her biological children. Once she was married to Ryan, she adopted them and became their legal mother. It was a happy marriage and the age difference was not a concern for either of them. Karol had jokingly said to Ryan that one day she would run for president and with his usual calmness he responded "I'll support you, honey". He was proud of his new wife.

******

Adora was a strong-minded teenager at eighteen years old, athletic and very independent. Her parents Dawn and Kai watched her grow into a freethinking, self-confident young lady who prided herself in being self-sufficient. Her dream was to become a medical doctor like her great grandmother Linh and even though she had no memories of her life on Mars, she had watched her parents' holographic images of her as a baby on Mars. Returning back to Mars as a medical doctor had entered her mind, but for now she was fully immersed in her education. The everyday lessons were conducted over the Internet with the professors appearing holographically, but she also attended conferences and instructions held at the university in her area. She still lived at home with her family and she was especially close to her brother Darren, who was now thirteen years and with a personality matching Adora's. She was less close to her sister Hazel and perhaps the age difference of ten years was part of the problem. The two sisters were opposites in temperament and viewed life very differently. Hazel was an intellectual, disliked sports and preferred being alone in her room with her Internet books devouring history, classics and even spiritual material. She had no friends and preferred it that way. Her parents worried about her hermit tendencies, but never said anything to their daughter and on the advice of Linh, Dawn and Kai allowed her to discover her own ways in life.

Adora jumped into her groundmobile and gave the address to the university. Her boyfriend Drujin waited for her and helped her out. Adora was infatuated with him and he with her. Drujin had a Greek father and a Chinese mother and they had combined the Greek name Dru and the Chinese name Jin when naming their son. Drujin was strongly built and looked more Greek than Chinese. He was studying robotics and was a few years older than Adora.

"I see you for lunch at my place," Drujin reminded Adora. Neither of them knew much about cooking, but had decided to learn together and old-fashioned Chinese cooking was the latest on their menu. Sometimes they just used the 3D food printer to save time.

"I can't wait," Adora responded and gave him a quick hug.

Drujin's bachelor pad was small but cozy and since he lived on the government basic income until he graduated, he had to watch his expenses. His parents were not affluent and financially he was on his own. Drujin looked forward to working in robotics and had even considered going to Mars.

Together they concocted a stir-fry lunch cooked on an antique range that they had found at an estate sale. After lunch, Drujin took Adora's hand and said hesitatingly -

"I know you're only eighteen, but I love you and would be very happy if you agreed to marry me. I'll wait for you until you're ready."

Adora was taken aback by his unexpected proposal, but recovered quickly and without any doubt in her voice she responded firmly -

"Being your wife would make me the happiest girl in the world and my answer is yes".

When they broke the news to their parents, they were surprised but not against it and both Adora's and Drujin's parents felt it was not their right to interfere in any way. The wedding date was decided to be on Adora's twentieth birthday and by that time Drujin would have graduated and be able to support a wife. Adora would continue studying to become a doctor and until then they had plenty of time to plan for their future.

******

Three years had passed and Adora and Drujin were happily married. Brianna and Brandon had become parents of a second child, a boy named Orion, and the arrangement with Lotte as second mother had worked out surprisingly well. Tina often looked after the children on weekends.

Perhaps the most interesting news of the day was that Karol was running for president and at the age of twenty-nine, she would become the youngest president in American history if elected. She was well qualified with both leadership abilities and an impressive knowledge of history and politics from her endless studying and self-education during most of her life. Her dedication to honesty and serving the citizens was apparent to anyone who knew her. Ryan was fully supporting her and because money and raising of funds to run for office was a thing of the past, the campaigning was not as stressful as it had been before the collapse. Karol had overcome her shyness and gave a favorable impression when interviewed. Ryan's love for her and his sons' devotion to their new mother had totally healed her emotional scars. She was the clear favorite of the candidates.

To no one's surprise she won the election and was now President Karol Clifford. After the inauguration, the Clifford family moved into the White House and Karol appointed Ryan as her advisor. They still worked very well together and had never had a serious argument and their marriage was happy. In the office, Ryan often called Karol 'Madam President' with a smile on his face, but Karol was devoid of personal vanity and promptly told him to stop. Her goals as president were many and to increase space exploration, maintain global peace, increase domestic manufacturing and to ensure the country remained debt free were some of her aspirations. The basic infrastructure of the country worked well and health care, education, transportation and clean food production also functioned satisfactorily. The economy was stable and although America had no debts, there was no surplus of funds to aid the country should hard times come about in the future. Raising taxes was out of the question and Karol asked Ryan to scrutinize all expenses and notify her of any cuts that could be made. Karol agreed to keep two secret service men for her personal safety and dismissed the rest. Her predecessor had been a good president and honest, but he had allowed his government to grow larger than needed and Karol terminated all jobs she found unnecessary. Every employee that was discharged received a generous severance pay and they understood the new president desired a smaller government. There were no hard feelings and they were assured the White House would give each of them a favorable endorsement when they looked for another employment.

Ryan returned with a list of cuts and Karol approved all of them. The end result was that the government shrunk considerably and was now building up a surplus of funds, some of which would be invested by buying gold and the rest of the money would be spent on various improvements in the country. Gold was not so rare anymore as many of the mined asteroids had veins containing deposits of pure gold, which was offered for sale. The government maintained enough gold to back the currency and when they released more money into circulation, they made sure there was a sufficient amount of gold to cover the added money. The changes and money saved were posted on the government website for all citizens to see and Karol's approval rate was high. She was totally unpretentious and only cared about making America strong and self-sufficient. All the systems that performed well and were not corrupt she left alone. The usury law was made stricter to protect borrowers and the banking system was in general well run and honest.

Global trade was not popular anymore and domestic manufacturing and self-sufficiency were favored. Some imports were still necessary, but the overall trade between countries was minimal compared to before the collapse, when almost all goods the world used was made in China and other Asian countries.

Karol had weekly meetings with her economic advisor, Mr. Parker, a corpulent man forgoing looks for safety by wearing belt and suspenders. Equipped with a brilliant mind, he shared Karol's views that the government should be small and frugal. He had a special knack for finding wasteful spending of tax dollars and Karol was grateful for his input. Thanks to Mr. Parker the budget was kept lean and Karol was hoping to cut taxes before she was out of office.

One of Karol's concerns was to limit the power of artificial intelligence, but reducing the abilities of the androids may result in unintended consequences. The most difficult surgeries and other delicate tasks were often performed by specialized androids and to lower their capabilities may backfire. Karol was planning to consult with the leading designers of androids to ascertain whether the safety programming of the androids could be increased. She was aware that many of the citizens were intimidated by the androids.

Clarence and his colleagues were summoned to the White House and Ryan and Karol's closest advisors were present. America had a small army, but the troops had never been in combat. One of Karol's first questions was if the robotic soldiers that were part of the American army were capable of turning against the human soldiers and if their remote kill-switch was adequate as a safety measure. Clarence explained that the robotic soldiers did not have the intelligence of androids and they did most of the grunt work. They simply did not have the ability to think independently and their safety programming was very strict. Moreover, they could be shut down remotely by their supervisor through the kill-switch. Karol had many questions about the most advanced androids and their safety programming and Clarence and his team did admit that in principle the androids could turn on humans and become a threat. The only recorded incident had occurred sixteen years ago when a human hacker had entered the programming of an android and reprogrammed it. The hacker was still in jail and as a result of that crime the safety programming of both androids and robots had been scrutinized and improved. Clarence and his team members assured Karol they would take another look at the safety of the androids and report back to the White House.

******

Adora and Drujin had signed a contract to work on Mars for two years. Neither of them wanted to remain on Mars for good, but Drujin had been offered an interesting job in robotics and Adora would be able to continue her medical studies on Mars. She was a few years away from receiving her medical degree.

They endured the journey to Mars and were relieved when it finally ended. Both Adora and Drujin enjoyed being physically active and the boredom onboard the ship was hard to get used to. They settled in a small apartment and it took them several weeks to get acclimated to the low gravity and to have to wear a space suit when outside the compound. Both of them were used to the Martian lifestyle from watching newscasts from Mars, but to actually be there and live there was still a very different experience. They knew the low gravity would take a toll on their bones and muscles so they wore weight suits in their apartment.

Drujin found his job fascinating and he was part of a team assembling androids. He had nothing to do with the programming and he and his team handled all the mechanics of the robots, which was quite a challenge. The model they were working on was a very advanced android that looked and functioned almost like a live human being. Drujin found the Martians assembled their androids somewhat differently than he had done on Earth and looked forward to go to work. Adora adjusted to attending a Martian university and realized the quality of education on Mars was just as good as on Earth, even the higher education. Mars now had a population of forty thousand people and Martia had spread out over a very large area. Everything was available and whatever the Martians could not manufacture or grow themselves they imported from Earth. The cargo spaceships were huge and during the window when Mars and Earth were at their closest distance, many ships arrived from Earth filled with goods and then departed with Martian made goods and precious metals to Earth. This trade benefitted both planets.

After being in debt to Earth for almost thirty years, the Martian government proudly announced to the citizens that the loan was now fully paid off and the Martians were debt free. As a result, taxes would be cut from ten percent to only five percent. Cost of living was low on Mars and quality of life was rated high by the citizens. The government placed great emphasis on personal freedom and more and more Earth people signed up to move to Mars, many of them permanently. Even seniors showed interest. The Martian people were pleased with People Democracy and the government was small, frugal and honest and valued the citizens' happiness. Martia was a sovereign city/country and Mars a free and independent planet. There were no armed forces, but the government would not hesitate to form an army should there be any threats against the community from another planet.

The crime rate was low, but three murders had occurred during the last ten years and four suicides. Other than that, no crime had been committed. Women did not have to worry about being violated and could safely walk around the community even at night.

The food supply had increased and many items that had not been available in the beginning were now imported from Earth. Several restaurants offered interesting menus and even steak was available. Mars imported frozen meat and even though half of the population ate mostly a vegetarian diet with processed insects for protein, few could resist a grilled steak as a treat.

A sewage system had been established converting waste to clean fertilizers. Recycling was mandatory and the government found that trash collection was needed as well. A dumping area several hours away from Martia was designated for trash and a road was built between the community and the refuse area. Eventually the dumping area would be filled in and covered.

Two years had passed and Drujin was totally absorbed in his work and Adora had received her medical degree. Neither of them felt ready to return to Earth and they signed a two-year extension to their contract. They liked life on Mars more than they had anticipated. Drujin's colleagues were happy to hear that he would stay for two more years. Adora started working at the hospital as a general practitioner as soon as she graduated and found the work very interesting and rewarding. In spite of having no experience, she was encouraged to attend surgeries, receive patients with minor injuries as well as attend conferences and as a result, she was able to advance faster than she would have on Earth. She had to force herself to increase her emotional stamina during surgeries and watching an amputation the first time made her almost faint. Eventually, she learned to disconnect her feelings and just concentrate on getting the job done.

Back on Earth, their parents were not happy to hear they would stay on for another two years, but kept their feelings to themselves. Dawn was wondering to herself if they would ever return to Earth.

Adora became very close to her mother's cousin Cellie and the age difference of eighteen years was not important to either of them. Adora also enjoyed visiting with Cellie's son Arvin who at twelve years was a bright and energetic boy. Cellie and Gordon only had one child. Cellie still worked as manager of the insect breeding department and Gordon had kept his job as chief mechanic. Cellie was both substitute mother and girlfriend to Adora and Gordon and Drujin got along well. When Brandon and Brianna stayed on Mars for a week every two years, they would all get together and enjoyed spending time with each other. They were distantly related. Most people agreed Mars could not compare in scenic beauty to Earth, but Martia offered unique learning opportunities as a new and developing country that acted as a magnet for adventurers. The population continued to grow at a slow but steady pace and many decided to stay on Mars. Life was comfortable, cost of living low, barely any crime and the robots were quick to remove sand after the storms had passed. The drawback was no flora and fauna outside the community, but indoors were many areas with flower beds and mini trees planted in Martian soil. The spacesuits had gone through several updates and were not as cumbersome to wear as the old suits had been. Weekly day trips were always available to sightseers free of charge and for most people that was enough as a diversion from their indoor lives.

There were more men than women on Mars and men looking for female company could visit with an android. These 'comfort stations' were sanitary and a savior for lonely men. Discreetly located, visitors could enter with their privacy intact.

To be fair, life on Earth everywhere was enormously improved compared to the misery before the collapse. Food was adequate for all, there were no wars and quality of life was good. Personal freedom was granted to all citizens and no country was governed by a dictator. Services such as healthcare and education were free and the mood of the people optimistic.

Small cities had replaced large cities in America and even Washington D.C. was much smaller than before the collapse. Hundreds of old buildings had been torn down and not rebuilt and the land converted to parks instead. Most people preferred smaller communities. The countryside was rather sparsely populated and open land for recreation was plentiful.

CHAPTER 17

Tina was inconsolable and the grief she felt was beyond words. Drew and James had been fishing miles from shore when dark storm clouds started to form and quickly developed into a full storm. They had planned to stay on the water overnight and do some morning fishing before returning to shore the following day. The change in weather had not been in the forecast and surprised both of them. Drew immediately turned the boat around heading for shore, but the waves grew taller and taller and their boat was sitting low in the water with the coolers heavily loaded with fish. The boat was bobbing up and down and the waves were crushing over the deck. Drew tried to remain calm and assured James they would make it back safely. They were alone onboard. At full speed it would take at least four hours to reach the shore, but fighting the waves and a headwind slowed them down and they barely moved forward. Drew instructed James to put on a survival suit in case the worst scenario would occur and then asked James to take the wheel while he put his suit on. At that moment, with one leg only into his suit, the boat rolled over and started to sink and Drew lost his balance and fell down. Within a minute the boat was under water and as they were sinking, James grabbed Drew hoping he would be able to hold his father up in the water and that the flotation of his suit would be sufficient for two people. It did not turn out that way. Just the fight to get the door open under water caused James to lose his grip on Drew and as James floated up and reached the surface, he had already inhaled water and was gasping for air. The boat and Drew were gone.

The suit kept James floating, but the waves were merciless and he had big trouble breathing. He was coughing wildly to get the water out of his lungs. It was dark and almost midnight and he knew that his mother did not expect them back until the following day. No boats were visible. All night James was fighting for his life in the water and when daylight finally arrived, he saw a search helicopter in the distance. The waves had calmed down a little overnight and his bright orange suit was visible to the pilot. Within minutes the helicopter was above him and a basket was lowered. With the last of his strength James managed to grab the basket and crawl inside. What he did not know was that Tina had become very worried when she saw the storm clouds and when she did not get a response from Drew as she tried to contact him on the boat, she knew something was wrong and she notified the Coast Guard. Drew was unaware of her tries to reach him and with the storm roaring he paid no attention to his communicator.

James was transported to the hospital and stayed overnight for observation, but was released the following day. He was told that one other fishing boat had capsized and all three men onboard had drowned. The storm had taken the fishermen by surprise and no experienced fisherman would by choice go way off shore when a storm was in the forecast.

Some of the houseboats along the shore had been damaged due to the storm, but no one had died and no boat had sunk.

The Coast Guard made two attempts to find Drew's body and the boat to no avail. The depth was several hundred feet and the water murky from the storm and they had to give up.

Tina and James grieved together. James and Drew had been each other's best friend in addition to being father and son. Brandon was on his way to Mars and was not expected back for six months. They contacted him onboard his spaceship and conveyed the sad news. Brandon was totally shaken and so was Brianna. Lotte came over to stay with Tina and support her and let Eva take care of Brianna's children in the meantime.

When Karl and Linh heard the bad news, Karl suffered a heart attack and only Linh's quick reaction saved his life. She restarted his heart using her defibrillator and he survived, weak, but grateful for Linh's medical skills. They were now one hundred years old and no longer as robust as they had been just a few years earlier. Karl had always liked his nephew Drew and he mourned his death deeply. Linh and Lena nursed Karl back to health, but he was frail and the spark in his eye was gone. He told Linh he had dreams about Drew and the storm and when they happened, he was too upset to be able to sleep.

James took several months off from working and when he finally regained some of his emotional strength, he bought a new boat using the insurance money and with the help of two robotic workers he went back to fishing. He stayed closer to shore and abandoned the deep-sea fishing that he had done with Drew. He would never forget Drew and would always love him as a father and friend.

James did after some time meet a widow, Beth, who shared his love for the ocean and the independent lifestyle of a fisherman. Her half-grown son, Sidney, was a pleasant kid without hang-ups, always willing to help and seemed to genuinely like James. It was mutual - James took a liking to Sidney and enjoyed his company more and more. Beth and James got married and James adopted Sidney. Beth became James' fishing partner and joined him as often as she could on their boat. Life with James was the only happiness Beth and Sidney had experienced after Beth had endured a nightmare marriage to a heroin user who had beaten her and Sidney several times. He refused treatment and when he finally died in the gutter from an overdose, all Beth and Sidney felt was relief and neither of them shed a tear when they buried him.

Tina had a hard time adjusting to life without Drew. Her android was a great friend and Tina was grateful for her company. She was sixty-two years old and had still many years left of her life, but she could not focus on anything and had lost interest in living. Drew had been the center point in her life. Lotte did not bring her grandchildren over as Tina was emotionally unable to care for them. After months of grieving, Linh finally got involved and was able to connect with Tina and her broken soul. At first Linh was unsure whether she should impose herself on Tina, but when she noticed she seemed to sink deeper into depression Linh decided she had to do something. Drew had been dear to her and Karl and they were also very fond of Tina. Linh was one hundred and one years old, but young in mind and still able to move around with relative ease. Karl was frail after his heart attack and never left home. Linh and Lena met with Tina a few times a week and eventually Linh was able to convince Tina to start over and accept Drew's death.

It took time, but Tina slowly returned to normal and expanded her herbal business to keep busy. Her android helped her and the business was doing well. Brandon was back on Earth and invited her to stay on the Moon for a week. He and Brianna were now flying cargo spaceships back and forth to the Moon so it was no problem to let Tina be a passenger. Tina had never been on the Moon and when she arrived, she felt alive for the first time since she became a widow. She enjoyed her week on the Moon immensely and when she returned to Earth, she knew she was on the mend.

******

Should humans be cloned? The citizens were asked to approve or disapprove by voting on the issue. This was the final vote on the cloning issue that had started with farm animals, then proceeded to pets and now was ending with whether or not humans should be cloned. The whole topic of cloning had been discussed for years and always induced strong feelings among people, perhaps becoming the most emotional question needing an urgent response from the citizens. Farm animals had successfully been cloned for years, but many farmers and ranchers were not excited about using the practice and favored the natural way. Voters had approved the method, so it was legal and some farmers used it. Then the voters were asked to vote on cloning of pets and with a narrow margin the voters approved pet cloning. The human cloning issue was a different matter, however, and the people voted overwhelmingly against it.

Though illegal, some humans had had themselves cloned, but most of them had been discovered and the clones were euthanized and the doctors involved were incarcerated without parole. Most people felt cloning of humans was ethically unacceptable and that humans would not take a leap forward in evolution by allowing it.

******

Karol had completed her four years in office and was running for a second term, but without campaigning. She did, however, accept to be interviewed and never turned down these requests. When asked why she did not campaign, she responded with the honesty she was known for -

"If the voters approve of my performance in office these past four years, they will vote for me with or without campaigning. If my accomplishments have been a disappointment to the voters, I deserve to be replaced." She thought a minute and then added -

"Some people may prefer to vote with their heart and that's a good thing."

"Please explain what you mean with that."

"The people know what I mean," Karol said quietly with a smile on her face that mirrored her soul.

Karol was easily reelected and her approval rating was high. In spite of her young age, only thirty-three years old, her maturity and emotional intelligence enabled her to lead the country with a fairness that could not be denied by anyone. America was doing well and though no longer a super power, it was by no means a wimp. The country was moving forward at a steady pace, debt free, not engaged in any war and with a population that was optimistic.

******

Takara played the piano as her younger sister Mio was banging on her drum. Neither of them was a natural musician, but enjoyed making a racket, as mother Ollie called it. The two sisters were very close and shared similar interests. Takara wanted to become a farmer, perhaps inspired by all the farms surrounding their rural home in Pennsylvania, while Mio opted for veterinarian. Mio had declared she would spend a few years being a vet on Mars as she knew they were needed on Mars. At only eleven years old, she had plenty of time to decide and perhaps change her mind a few times. Ollie taught geology at the university and she and Koto were financially comfortable but not affluent. They did not have the financial means to buy a farm for Takara and she understood that. The family had two horses and the girls rode them around the neighborhood. Horseback riding was not popular anymore and people preferred motorized vehicles. The girls were average riders and their sense of balance needed improvement, but so far, they had never taken a serious spill.

Takara was in the lead on a winding trail in the forest and hollered to Mio, who was a distance back on her horse -

"Full speed ahead!"

"*Yahoo!*" Mio shouted back.

Off they went at a full gallop ducking low tree branches. What a thrill! With loose reins signaling to the horses they could run as fast as they wanted, Takara leaned forward jockey style in her English saddle with a firm grip on the horse's neck strap and cleared all branches. Mio did the same, but had trouble with her balance and as she struggled to stay on her horse, she did not see a large branch and galloped straight into it and was hit on the forehead at full force. She was almost decapitated and fell hard to the ground with a broken neck. Within minutes she was dead.

At first, Takara was unaware of Mio's fall and only realized it after a few minutes when she looked back and failed to see her. She pulled her horse to a stop and returned to find Mio. When she spotted her lifeless body on the trail her heart almost stopped and she jumped off and ran to her sister. The grim sight of Mio's dead body made Takara scream in horror and she fell down next to Mio crying violently.

Ollie and Koto were home and saw the horses come running toward the stable without the girls. They both froze. In panic mode they jumped into their groundmobile and followed the trail until they found the girls. Takara was devastated and kept screaming "I killed her" between her sobbing attacks.

For Takara's sake, Ollie and Koto managed to regain their composure after the initial shock and loaded Mio's body into their groundmobile with trembling hands. They had to lift Takara into the vehicle. She did not respond to anything they said and was ready to collapse emotionally.

After Mio's funeral, Takara and her parents went through a period of intense mourning. They gave away the horses and closed up the stable. A year went by and Ollie and Koto went through a slow reawakening, still grieving and feeling severe emotional pain in their souls, but they were able to work and get through the day. Not so with Takara. She had become a zombie and was unable to study and live normally. She barely ate anything and was just skin and bones and did not respond to her parents' efforts to bring her back to normal. They told Takara over and over it was not her fault, it was an accident, but to no avail. Takara had decided it was her fault. Mio had been her best friend and she had killed her.

Ollie hired a psychiatrist, Dr. Freed, who agreed to treat Takara at their home as Takara refused to go out. This elderly, female doctor had years of experience and finally managed to turn Takara around and bring her back to life, but it took six months before Takara responded to treatment. She understood that she was only partially to blame and a full gallop on a winding trail was too dangerous. Mio's death was the unintended consequence of her decision. Dr. Freed did not exclude Takara from all blame as that would only result in Takara living a lie for the rest of her life. After facing the consequences of her decision Takara had to learn to forgive herself. That was the hardest part.

"Takara, if Mio had survived, do you think she would have forgiven you?" Dr. Freed asked.

"With her big heart, she would have," Takara responded after thinking about it for a while.

"So why can't you forgive yourself?"

"I will try," Takara said in a low voice.

"Most people find it easier to forgive others than themselves," Dr. Freed explained. "When you forgive yourself, you gain emotional freedom. Without emotional freedom, you'll never grow in character and your creativity will also be impaired."

On their last appointment, Dr. Freed arrived at their house with a younger woman and introduced her as Nina.

"This is my good friend Nina. She is a psychic and we'll attempt to communicate with Mio and hear her version of the accident."

They sat down at the kitchen table and Ollie and Koto were also present. Within minutes Nina made contact with Mio and Mio started talking through Nina -

"Takara, my dear sister, *what are you doing to yourself!* I forgave you immediately after my death. It was an accident and with my lousy riding skills, I didn't belong on a horse. I never had the balance a good rider should have. You were a much better rider than me. I have watched you grieving and ask you to forgive yourself and go on with your life. You are only fourteen years old - do you really want to throw away your life by grieving over an accident that happened and can't be undone? I ask you, beloved sister, to forgive yourself and stop grieving. I'm fine here where I am. I don't grieve. My death was painless and without fear. I do have a request though and that is that you become a psychiatrist and help other victims of grief return to a normal life. *Do that for me.*"

The transmission ended and they all sat quietly at the table. None of them could speak and they all felt overwhelmed by emotion. Finally, Dr. Freed said -

"Takara, will you now forgive yourself as your sister clearly wants you to do?"

"Yes, and I will become a psychiatrist," Takara whispered trying not to cry.

The turning point had arrived and Takara slowly bounced back to life. She gained back the weight she had lost and dedicated herself to her education with an interest she had not had before the accident. Emotionally, she had become an adult from going through the tragedy of Mio's death and she promised herself to become an effective doctor in honor of Mio's memory. The emotional pain she had experienced had matured her and from this inner pain grew wisdom that guided her.

******

Linh was mourning Karl's death. He had died peacefully in his sleep at the age of one hundred and three years. Lena comforted Linh and she silently grieved the death of Karl as much as Linh, but tried to be strong for Linh's sake. The two of them were as close as sisters and Linh never left the house without Lena. Hilma and her husband attended the funeral and invited Linh and Lena to stay with them for a month. Linh accepted and the four of them returned to the farm. It was spring and everything was blooming and the animals had given birth. Linh and Lena sat by the pond watching the ducks and Hilma's son Thomas and daughter Annie joined them. Thomas was working the farm with his father and would take over the farm when his father retired. Annie had a year left of college and studied biology. She had been promised a job in the pet cloning business and being a farm girl, she had no objections to animal cloning. Linh liked her great grandchildren and had seen them grow up.

"When I have worked a few years and gained experience, I'll go to Mars for two years," Annie told Linh. "Cloning is big on Mars and it would be interesting to see what Martian life is all about. Aunt Cellie seems to love it there. I wouldn't want to stay there forever, but two years would be fun."

"Look around you, this is heaven. There's nothing like this on Mars, but I guess two years isn't a long time and you would gain practical knowledge from a different environment. Just don't remain there," Linh said. "I felt very sad when Cellie announced she would make Mars her home."

"Oh no, only two years," Annie responded. "I also love the greenery on Earth and to be able to be outside without a spacesuit. Martia has become huge and more and more people move there. It will be interesting to see how it develops."

"I would never want to go there," Thomas interjected. "My God, you freeze your butt off and no air to breathe and sand everywhere. I fail to see the attraction of that place."

Linh chuckled and said "I'm with you, Thomas. I'm Earthbound forever."

When Linh and Lena returned home, they felt whole again. Hilma's nurturing and loving care had been just what they needed and both of them were grateful.

CHAPTER 18

Karol was working at her desk when the message on her communicator came in. As she read it, a chill ran down her spine. The Yellowstone Caldera had erupted and it looked severe! The thoughts tumbled around in her head and she remembered reading a long time ago about Mount Tambora, an Indonesian stratovolcano that erupted in 1815 in the largest eruption in recorded history. Cubic miles of ash, rock and debris as well as sulfur reached all the way to the stratosphere and caused misery around the globe. The temperature dropped and the sun was blocked out causing severe crop failures the following growing season. 1816 was called 'the year without a summer' and frost occurred on and off the whole summer. With this dark scenario in her head, she called for Ryan and her advisors to come to her office. Together, they closely monitored the developments and found that it was a serious eruption, but still far from a full-blown emission. The Yellowstone Caldera had had several small eruptions and steam explosions during the last hundred years and people living in the area were used to it and were not overly afraid any more. Now, however, a severe eruption was taking place and people had to be evacuated for miles around the area. The initial explosion was gigantic spewing ash and debris high up into the atmosphere and lava was flowing from the Caldera.

The lava continued to flow for weeks following the initial eruption and the sky was darkened. The sun could not penetrate the ash in the atmosphere. It was early spring and farmers were ready to plant their crops, but now they were wondering if anything would grow with such limited sunlight. The ash in the atmosphere and stratosphere was all around the planet and affected spring planting on a global scale. The eruption, though not full scale, had been severe enough to block out the sun all around the planet causing farmers everywhere to ask themselves if it was any use to plant a crop.

Karol's advisors were tasked with reporting back to her the exact stock pile of foods held in the country including amounts of grain stored in silos and fodder for livestock. She asked them to be very exact so preparatory work could start should the available food supply be dangerously low. The report came back showing food supplies were adequate for about one year, including feed for livestock, and if no crops were planted that year there would still be sufficient supplies so no one would starve. Karol sighed with relief. Some countries elsewhere were not so lucky and had very little surplus of grain and other food supplies, so some sharing of available foods between countries would probably be necessary.

Hilma's farmer husband decided he would plant all his fields and just gamble on getting a crop and that was the decision made by many American farmers. Home gardens were not as common anymore as it had been in the past, but there were still some hardcore backyarders who enjoyed planting a garden every spring. By necessity, interesting inventions were made. People lucky enough to have a stone wall facing south, planted their vegetables along the wall using it as a 'growing wall'. The stones heated up in the daytime and gave off heat overnight preventing the plants from freezing. Some people erected a wall of reflective material, such as mylar, on the north side of the garden so any available light would reflect back from the wall and increase the light to the plants. Many of these home gardens did produce an average amount of produce, making the effort of removing the ash from the soil worth their time.

There was no real summer to speak of and ash was slowly raining from the sky. The sun did peek through the ash, but the available light was much below normal. Everyone was hoping that by next summer all the ash would have fallen and conditions returned to normal. Some crops failed and others were much smaller than normal. Hay for livestock did grow, but the plants were short. Greenhouses with full lighting produced close to normal amounts of vegetables, but the orchards were not doing so well. Hardy fruit trees produced smaller fruits, but in some areas the spring temperatures had been severe and the blossoms froze before pollination.

Hilma's husband produced a small wheat crop and enough hay for his livestock to feed them for the winter. He was lucky enough to have a surplus of grain and hay leftover from the previous year and being a generous man, he was prepared to donate some of it to his farmer neighbors if they needed assistance.

In the fall, when the harvest season was over, America donated half of its crops to other countries that were in trouble. Karol's frugal government had enough funds saved so they could compensate the farmers for their crops. Other countries with surplus food supplies followed America's example and shared both food and fodder and all supplies were given away for free.

The following year the sun appeared again and normal conditions returned. Farmers and citizens alike felt enormous relief. Yellowstone was quiet and no more lava was flowing. There had not been many natural disasters for years and people were hoping they would be spared any more events in the future.

******

Some smaller countries around the world had decided to consolidate into one larger country pooling resources. The idea caught on and through diplomatic channels Karol's government received discreet inquiries from Canada and Mexico whether America would be open to the idea of merging and thereby create a country called North America. Karol liked the idea and posted it on the government website for the citizens to mull over. Canada and Mexico did the same. The citizens of all three countries were excited over the idea and since Mexico and Canada had adopted the same type of government as America, People Democracy, the political changes would be minor. Mexico and Canada were both governed by frugal, small governments and doing well economically, so there would be no drain on America by merging with them.

All three countries asked their citizens to vote on the issue and the majority vote was affirmative. *North America was born*! Both Mexico and Canada as well as America would retain their local laws.

Work began to decide all the details and it was decided the new government should remain in Washington D.C. with a governor replacing the terminated governments in Mexico and Canada. Both countries had suffered huge losses of people from the superbug and loss of electricity and Mexico's population was thirty million and Canada had only nine million citizens. Together with America's one hundred and twenty-one million people, North America had a combined citizenry of one hundred and sixty million. The future showed that the new country functioned well and the benefits more than trumped the drawbacks.

Europe had also merged into one country with a population of one hundred and ten million citizens and they had kept the name The European Union. Iceland was part of this new country.

Other countries also merged and it was an ongoing process with borders changing all the time. There was no World Government, but the Advisory Board was frequently consulted for advice and their fair and unbiased recommendations were highly respected. They never forced their guidance on any country, merely offered an informed opinion.

******

Science worldwide was moving forward and discoveries about how planet Earth functioned were released through the media and Internet. The latest topic of discussion was control of the weather and many people felt emotional about it. A common slogan among the citizens was *Leave Nature Alone*, but some scientists had developed new ways to dim sunlight, create clouds and disperse clouds and other weather-related phenomena and were itching to manifest these ideas, often without considering unintended consequences. Everyone understood there were benefits to creating rain in a drought-stricken area as well as stopping excessive rain and prevent flooding, but the methods to be used were experimental and involved releasing chemical elements and substances into the atmosphere without knowing the long-term effect of these elements. After months of discussion, the topic was finally put to a vote and the reply from the people was NO by an overwhelming majority. The idea was mothballed.

Science dealing with people's psyche was popular and so was brain research. Overcoming negative feelings such as fear, narcissism and excessive personal pride was taught on the Internet and ability to feel emotional freedom was also among help topics people wanted to learn more about. Not all people were interested in these self-improving courses, but those willing to improve themselves and their psyche found all the information they needed on the Internet presented holographically. One area of interest was fear and how to cope with it. Defeating fear was achieved by finding the root of the fear; fear of death, fear of change and so on. It was found that certain changes in life were beneficial and if there were no changes, a person's life would come to a standstill and a false feeling of being secure. Adjusting to change leads to personal growth.

Another popular area of study for people with low self-esteem was to accept yourself as you are and resist building a false facade to appear perfect while concealing inner despair. Spiritual studies and soul research were sought after by some. Because most people had a computer microchip implanted behind the ear enhancing cognition, comprehension of the psyche and its intricacies was understandable. Many people were able to see 'the whole picture' of why they felt a certain way and what motivated them. Once they understood and removed the cause, the effect was also eliminated.

Philosophy was another subject people appreciated. As an example, what is truth? One scholar defined it as twofold; both a human and a spiritual concept. The human definition is that truth is the opposite of false and refers to an evaluation of ethics while the spiritual definition of truth is harder to explain, but can be described as 'all life is one' meaning we are all interconnected and there is no opposite.

New brain research found cures for several mental illnesses saving patients from disappearing into non-reality. Some of the cures were simple and involved just mega doses of certain supplements while others required surgery. Treatment of mental illness had advanced tremendously and there was no stigma attached to a diagnosis of mental illness.

All surgeries had become safer and often laparoscopic procedures were sufficient. The most delicate surgeries were performed by androids such as eye and brain operations. These androids were highly trained and their skills surpassed human doctors. Patients had no objections to android surgeons and they were recognized as more skillful than human doctors.

Advancements in agriculture had also occurred and stronger hybrids of various plants had been developed without resorting to genetically modifying the plants. The orchards had benefitted from the discoveries and new hybrids of fruits and berries more resistant to destructive insects were now available. No plants were fully immune to insect attacks, but there had been many improvements and farmers often had no need to spray their crops. Bees had made a comeback and were no longer a threatened species. The cleanup of the environment and elimination of genetically modified plants had helped to bring them back.

*****

Karol had finished her second term as president and she, Ryan and the boys moved into a country house several miles outside Washington D.C. Elliot and Kenny were almost adults at fifteen and seventeen years respectively. Karol and Ryan refused secret service protection as the other former presidents had also done. Karol was dreaming of having a baby and just be home. Ryan had accepted an interesting job related to space as he had years of experience in that field.

The fertility rate was down among women, but Karol did conceive and chose the artificial womb. A girl was developing and she and Ryan looked forward to her birth. It was en exciting moment when they brought her home and felt the joy of being parents. They named her Alison. Karol had decided to nurse her baby rather than bottle feeding and had received the hormonal injections necessary for lactation. Elliot and Kenny thought it was cool to have a baby sister and enjoyed carrying the baby around the backyard.

Baby Alison was six months old and dragged herself along the floor while happily babbling da-da-da to herself. Karol was watching with a smile and felt truly happy to just be a housewife. She had worked so hard these eight years and had no desire to start working again for several years. Ryan agreed with Karol that it was now time for her to enjoy motherhood and live without pressure. Her communicator vibrated and Karol checked the incoming message. She jumped when she saw the message came from Mars. She did not know anyone living on Mars and felt sure it must be a mistake, but she activated her communicator and the holographic image displayed the president of Martia, Mr. Shepherd.

"Mrs. Clifford, please accept my apologies for intruding like this, but I need to discuss an urgent matter with you. My second term as president of Martia is over in six months and Martia needs a new president with experience and ability to lead the people. The members of my government believe you would be a perfect leader. In two months, the window of travel to Mars is open and if you accept, you would have two months to prepare for your departure to Mars. We would add your name to the list of candidates and ask the citizens to vote in two weeks. There are only two candidates running for the presidency and both of them are inexperienced, so we believe you would easily be elected. You have a first-rate reputation and the Martians know your excellent performance in office and how well you handled the Yellowstone crisis. Is there any chance that you would you be interested?"

"I have a six-month-old baby," Karol said hesitatingly.

"We know that," Mr. Shepherd responded. "We did a search and found that four babies have successfully made the trip from Earth to Mars the last few years and all of them survived in perfect health. The new spaceships are more comfortable and the trip takes only four months now. You would get a private suite on the ship and whatever you need for the baby would be supplied. Mr. Clifford would be offered a cabinet position as we know you two have always worked together. We also intend to ask Mr. Parker if he would be interested in serving on Mars. We know he performed with excellence as your economic advisor. As president, you would of course pick your Cabinet yourself, but since this is a different planet, we feel we must make a preliminary inquiry whether any of you would consider moving to Mars for up to eight years, which is two presidential terms. The required working hours are only four hours a day since Martia is still just a city/country and you would have enough time to raise your baby girl."

Karol felt speechless. She had never been to Mars and neither had Ryan. Both of them were familiar with living conditions on Mars, but to live there for four or eight years had never occurred to her and her first thought was to say no, but something within her prompted her to refrain from refusing the offer.

"Mr. President, I need to discuss this with my husband and I'll contact you in one week with my answer," Karol finally said. "It's a big decision and we also have two sons that may not be willing to move to Mars."

"I fully understand," Mr. Shepherd said and they ended the conversation.

The following days several family meetings took place and Karol and her family spent hours discussing pros and cons of living on Mars as well as investigating quality of life on Mars. It was an opportunity with some risks involved, but also an adventure. Elliot wanted to go, but Kenny flatly refused. Ryan was open minded and said he would be happy to go if Karol wanted the presidency.

Karol mulled over the decision for almost a week and then decided. She was only thirty-eight years old and after two presidential terms she would be forty-six years with many years left of her lifetime. Ryan would be sixty-two, still not considered old as most people lived past a hundred years.

She contacted Mr. Shepherd and asked him to put her name on the list of candidates running for president. Mr. Shepherd was excited to hear her decision and responded he would organize all details for their trip in the event she won the election. He also informed Karol that Mr. Parker had accepted the offer and would also go to Mars. He was not married. The Martians voted the following week and Karol won by a landslide as expected. Now followed a dizzying period of selling their house and personal items and arranging for Kenny. At seventeen, he was almost an adult and very capable of taking care of himself. Ryan rented an apartment for him and in a few months, he would start college studying from home using the Internet services. Ryan's sister and her family lived only a short distance away and promised Ryan Kenny could stay with them on weekends and holidays and they would check on him often. Kenny reassured Ryan and Karol that he would be fine and would communicate with them every week.

Karol and her family as well as Mr. Parker boarded the spaceship and adjusted soon to the conditions. None of them had been on a spaceship before. All of them followed the recommended exercise programs. Their suite was small but comfortable with two bedrooms, bathroom and a little kitchenette. Alison adapted remarkably well to weightlessness and maintained her health throughout the journey. The first three months passed quickly as everything was novel and interesting, but all of them found the last month tedious and dragging on forever.

The landing went well and they moved into the president's living quarters. Mr. Shepherd and his wife were ready to return to Earth on the same spaceship that Karol had traveled on and would depart in one week. He briefed Karol, Ryan and Mr. Parker on a daily basis how the government worked and by the end of the week Karol felt she was ready to take over. Mr. Shepherd had been very thorough informing them how the Martian government functioned and all the details were electronically stored.

Karol went to work as President of Martia with Ryan and Mr. Parker as her advisors. She picked the rest of her cabinet using Mr. Shepherd's recommendations. The whole government system was a copy of Earth's government and Karol had no problem adjusting to her new position. The four-hour work day was easy and Alison was in daycare while Karol worked. Elliot attended high school and found Mars very exciting. He had no regrets moving to Mars.

The whole family enjoyed life on Mars and the first year went by quickly. Karol, Ryan, Elliot and Mr. Parker spent every weekend sightseeing. A neighbor, Mrs. Webster, looked after Alison. She was an elderly, childless woman who adored the baby. Karol found their weekly excursions fascinating and the new lightweight spacesuits were easy to wear. Her presidential duties were uncomplicated and easy to perform thanks to her experience. She occasionally contacted Mr. Shepherd and he told her that he and his wife had a hard time adjusting to Earth's gravity and eight years on Mars had weakened their bones. They were working out in the gym to regain physical strength and he advised Karol to exercise with weights. Other than that, they were happy to be back on Earth and visit with their family and friends.

******

Ryan had looked into Martia's space program and found that they were no further along than Earth. What was missing was a different propulsion system that would shorten the time to travel to distant planets, but there had been no new inventions in space travel for years. The spaceships to Mars had increased their speed and reduced travel time from five to four months, but that was due to more efficiency, not a new propulsion system. Ryan had asked the Venusians once if they knew of a faster way to travel in space and they had responded there were better ways than our spaceships, but humans were not ready for this new technology yet. Ryan found the answer a little odd and asked himself 'why not, why aren't we ready'. Ryan put the dream of finding new planets aside for the future when more details may be available and concentrated on the new venture the Martians had started.

Following Earth's example, the Martians had started mining on several nearby smaller asteroids and with no orbiting work stations in place, the spaceships either towed the larger asteroids back to Mars and dropped them onto Mars' surface in safe areas away from Martia or dragged the very small asteroids inside the cargo bay of their ships and traveled back to Mars to extract the valuable minerals. Both silicate and metallic asteroids were harvested and gold, platinum and some rare minerals had been found making the cost of the mining well worth it. One tiny asteroid, only twelve feet long, had consisted of mostly gold. These asteroids were not part of the Asteroid Belt and travel time from Mars was only two months. The distance to the Asteroid Belt was entirely too far to reach with the propulsion system of the existing spaceships, so the Martians only went after the nearby asteroids and there were plenty of them.

The spaceships were government owned and the profits benefitted all Martians. No government member enriched himself or herself illegally. Some of the minerals were traded with companies on Earth and some were used in manufacturing on Mars. The good news was that Mars was slowly becoming rich and the prosperity was used to improve everything on the planet from availability of goods, low prices on everything, only five percent income tax and free education, healthcare and transportation. Elaborate flower and tree plantings were everywhere as it now had become affordable to beautify Martia. The population had grown to sixty thousand people and many who had signed up for two years became permanent citizens. There were some people who found Mars too confined and returned to Earth, but most adjusted to living within 'the bubble'. All excursion trips to various places on Mars were free and people found they did not miss Nature that much.

The arts were doing well and Martia now had an orchestra that gave performances. An art gallery had also opened and a space museum featuring replicas of the oldest space probes from Earth as well as elaborate holographic images of the planets and moons in the solar system.   People had lots of leisure time to take up hobbies of all kinds.

Hard core Earthlings, as a comparison, would never give up Earth for Mars and they felt recreation such as skiing, camping, going to the beach and other nature activities could never be replaced by anything available on Mars.

******

Karol and Ryan were in the lobby outside the government offices when they noticed the little speck in the sky that was fast approaching Mars. It was not an Earth spaceship; they were all cylindrical and this object was a gigantic disk. Karol said in a trembling voice to Ryan -

"Star Trek is coming." Karol had once seen a documentary of the spaceships featured in the twentieth century space movies and whatever this object was, it looked like one of those ships.

"I think they will land," Ryan responded. He tried to stay calm, but felt the anxiety building. Were they enemies? Would they destroy Martia? Would they all be killed?

A group of people had joined Karol and Ryan and they were all transfixed by the object coming closer to the ground. It was a white saucer with a glass dome on top, a short wing on each side of the ship and a short tail. It had a tubular hull resembling a rudder and the diameter of the saucer was about five hundred feet. The huge ship was hovering above ground and four landing feet were lowered and touched the ground. Ryan quickly put on his spacesuit and went outside come what may. He had to find out who they were. As he approached the ship he was awestruck by its enormous size. There appeared to be a door at the base of the saucer and it opened slowly. A staircase was lowered from the door opening and four humanoid beings dressed in spacesuits climbed down to the ground. Ryan saw clearly through the face plate of their helmets that they were humans of some sort and stretched out his hand as a greeting. All four shook his hand and Ryan gestured towards the government building that they should go inside. They nodded and followed Ryan. Inside, they all took their helmets off and Ryan and the people in the lobby watched in fascination. They were around six feet tall, all of them had blond, short hair and one of them had a beard. They were pleasant looking and Ryan thought to himself that they reminded him of the old Vikings from long ago. The leader spoke first in an unusual language with guttural sounds. He held an electronic device that translated his speech to English. It had a mechanical voice, but was easy to understand.

"This is a translation device as we don't speak your language. It translates our language to yours as I speak. I am Emrak and these men are my crew members. We come from a planet called Frejja orbiting the star Velarus, which is seven light years from Mars. We come in peace." Emrak now handed another translation device to Ryan so they could communicate.

"How can you travel seven light years, I mean, it would take many lifetimes to travel that distance?" Ryan asked perplexed.

"There are shortcuts in space. We call them tunnels and we go through several of them to reach your solar system. Referring to your time, it takes us only two months to travel from Frejja to Mars."

Ryan suggested they should take their spacesuits off and continue their discussion in private in Karol's office. The four men had dark blue uniforms under their spacesuits and when all of them were seated Emrak explained -

"I'm the Captain of the ship. We know who you are through the Venusians. There are several reasons why we're here and one of them is to trade or buy minerals from you. There's limited mining in our area and we could, of course, travel longer distances to mine asteroids, but if you're willing to trade with us, it would be a better way."

"Our planet has about forty million citizens and there are substantially more women than men. It's not clear why more females are born than males, but we're trying to import men to our planet in order to balance the number of males to females. We know there is a surplus of men on Mars and we extend an invitation to any man who is willing to move to our planet. Quality of life is good and there are plenty of jobs. We're ahead of you technologically, but we're humans like you and it wouldn't be difficult for a man from Mars to get acclimated to our planet."

"There are only sixty thousand of us here," Karol said slowly wondering within herself how many men they would lose. "Earth may be a better place for you to find more men."

"We'll go to Earth also, but we were hoping to return to our planet with a hundred men from Martia," Emrak said. "We're also extending our hand in friendship and we're willing to provide you with our technology."

"Our planet Frejja is a little smaller than Mars, no Moon, and it's similar to planet Earth with liquid water and oxygen to breathe. The atmosphere has slightly less oxygen than Earth, about what you would find at eight thousand feet elevation on Earth. There are two more planets in our solar system orbiting our star Velarus, but they're not habitable. Our climate is temperate and very pleasant. The gravity is about the same as here on Mars. A year on our planet is ten months and a day lasts twenty hours. We have no winter, only summer and a rainy season that lasts three months."

The following week the four aliens engaged in conversation with the Martians and also presented a discourse in the auditorium explaining life on their planet. By the end of the week, one hundred men had signed up and among them was Mr. Parker.

"I'm single and I have nothing to lose," he explained to Karol and Ryan. Mr. Parker had lost weight since he came to Mars and his appearance was much improved. "I would love to get married and have a family. This is my last chance. I'm already forty-three years old."

"We'll miss you, for sure," Karol sighed.

Then came the next bombshell. Cellie's son Arvin signed up. At twenty-two years of age he was now an adult and Cellie and Gordon were heartbroken when he announced the news. They did not try to stop him as they respected his free will, but they did let him know how much they would miss him. Cellie had chosen to only have one child, but now she regretted that decision and thought to herself that they may never see him again and they had no family left. She was forty-nine years old and she was still able to have another child. She decided to test the waters and tossed out the question to Gordon -

"How would you feel about having a second child?"

To her surprise, he was enthusiastic and responded -

"Why not."

The spaceship left with a hundred Martians onboard. Emrak had signed a trade agreement with the Martian government to exchange minerals, mostly gold and silver, for technology and goods from Frejja. The legal tender on Frejja was gold and silver coins, no paper money. Cellie and Gordon had said goodbye to Arvin and watched the ship take off. Both felt numb with sadness.

CHAPTER 19

Arvin was strapped into his seat onboard the spaceship and as the ship gained elevation, he felt much less gravitational pull on his body than he had expected. Within minutes they were above Mars' atmosphere and gained speed rapidly. The main engines ignited sending a vibration through the ship and it took off at an unbelievable speed. The tremendous speed of the ship almost took Arvin's breath away. He had only been inside a spaceship on the holodeck on Mars and all he knew was life in 'the bubble'. He had not been to Earth either. A few months ago, he had graduated from college with a degree in engineering and being a recent graduate, he had no work experience. He looked forward to living on a planet where he could breathe the air outside and be without a spacesuit. His parents had told him about life on Earth and he may have moved to Earth if the Frejjans had not visited Mars first. He felt confined and almost trapped on Mars and was one of the first to accept Emrak's invitation to move to the new planet. The trip was free.

There were six crew members onboard and ten very advanced androids. He had his own tiny cabin with a bed, desk and a chair, private bathroom, also very small, and a window. The ship was pressurized and he did not need a suit, but there was no gravity on the ship and the weightlessness was uncomfortable. He was able to communicate with the androids as they had been programmed with language skills and spoke English with a slight Frejjan accent. They supplied him with heavy weights that he could strap on while he exercised.

There was a shower in Arvin's bathroom and it was totally enclosed. It was a marvel of ingenuity. As he turned on the water standing on a grid, a powerful suction started from below the grid forcing the water to fall straight down. The toilet was a standard spaceship version also functioning by suction. There were two straps on his bed that prevented him from floating off the bed.

The food onboard was all freeze-dried and not bad at all. Arvin had no idea what he ate, but it tasted rather good and had no adverse effect on his digestion. The passengers were not allowed on the Bridge, but the ship was so enormous that they still had plenty of room to move around. All the bedrooms were located at the outer edges of the ship and dining area, sitting rooms, a holodeck, galley, a large auditorium and sick bay were all at the center of the ship. The passengers attended daily school to learn the new language and the lessons were taught by an android that spoke almost fluent English. The classes lasted four hours per day and they were assigned homework as well. The Frejjan language was difficult to learn with an alphabet that had no resemblance to the English alphabet and Arvin struggled with it. Mr. Parker, on the contrary, picked up the nuances of the strange language and with his adept mind, he was the first of the Martians to almost be able to speak the foreign language when they arrived on Frejja, not fluently, but well enough to be understood. Arvin gave it his best and was advancing and spent several hours practicing the pronunciation when he was alone in his cabin. To produce the guttural sounds was the hardest.

The ship traveled smoothly without shaking, but when they approached the first of the four tunnels they had to go through, all passengers were ordered to strap themselves into their seats. The androids cautioned that they would experience severe vibration while in the tunnels, but there was no danger and all should remain calm. Arvin tried to look out the glass dome in the ceiling, but could not see anything and just told himself he must not be afraid. The ship entered the tunnel and it shook with such a force that Arvin held on to his seat with all his might. He estimated the trip through the tunnel lasted about fifteen minutes and as they exited the tunnel, he felt the ship had accelerated tremendously in speed. He had studied black holes in his astronomy courses, but he was not sure if a black hole and a tunnel was the same thing. They went through three additional tunnels and the ship was now moving through space at a fantastic speed, each tunnel increasing the ship's speed.

Frejja was now within sight of the ship and the two months' journey was over. Reverse thrusters were fired to slow down the ship and it started to descend towards the planet's surface. Arvin looked out the window and loved the sight. The landing field was straight ahead and, in the distance, he saw trees, green grass and houses with large lawns around them. He had spent many hours on the holodeck on Mars experiencing Earth's forests, beaches and nature, but now, here it was right in front of him and it was real. It seemed to be in the middle of the day and the sun was straight up in the blue sky. Not a cloud could be seen.

After the gentle landing, the passengers whistled and applauded to the delight of the crew. Everyone had packed already so it was only to grab one's personal belongings and follow the crew down the staircase and step onto Frejja's surface. Arvin took his first breath on his new home planet and the air was sweet smelling and fresh. It felt like around eighty degrees and Arvin thought to himself he had landed in heaven.

A large self-driving vehicle looking like a bus but without a roof came rolling over to the ship and a female Frejjan on the bus invited the passengers to board. She was tall, pretty and seemed genuinely kind. Her blond hair was neatly braided into one braid reaching almost to her waist.

The bus trip lasted about an hour and the men who had lived on Earth commented that it felt like being back on Earth. They arrived at a building that Arvin guessed was a hotel. Very modern design with large glass windows, stone siding and automatic entry doors. In the lobby a Frejjan man was waiting for them and he did speak English. He asked them to sit down and with a strong accent he introduced himself as Kovan.

"I know you feel overwhelmed from your trip to Frejja and now having to adjust to a new life on our planet. You'll be our guests at this hotel for one month so you can get used to your new life. There is, of course, no charge for staying here. Each one of you will have several consultations with our team so we can get to know you, your skills and what aspirations you have. There are job opportunities in many fields including our government and anyone who wants to work will get a job. We'll give daily lectures to inform you how society functions on Frejja and we ask that you continue to learn our language. Very few speak foreign languages on Frejja and the people who do, like myself, work with our immigrants. At present, we have only immigrants who are genetically identical to us such as people from Mars and a few other planets with human inhabitants, but we intend to invite beings from some planets who are slightly different but still compatible as husbands. This will introduce diversity. We're also planning to send a ship to Earth and hope some men will agree to come here to live."

"Our communication system is excellent and you'll be able to contact your relatives on Mars and Earth through the Zero Point Field. Our technology is ahead of yours and those of you who are technically inclined will find it interesting to discover our inventions. When your stay here at the hotel is over, we hope you will take the job we'll offer you and with it comes living arrangements, usually a starter house. Once a week we'll invite the local people to come over here and visit with you and that way you can practice your language skills."

"Our way of life isn't that different from the way people live on Earth. We have families, go to work, enjoy nature and so on. Our diet is similar to what you eat already and there's no shortage of food. Our government needs updating, but we know Mr. Parker over there is an expert in finances and other government business and we hope he'll help us address these issues. The work week is usually thirty hours and jobs are offered based on merit alone. There is full equality between men and women. For the time being, our society is homogenous, but, as I said, we plan to introduce more diversity by inviting beings from other planets. We don't expect racial complications by doing so, but we have found that some diversity is necessary to prevent stagnation in society."

"Our economy is doing well. We use no paper money, only silver and gold coins and for larger purchases, if you buy a house for example, we use smaller gold bars. By using silver and gold as the legal tender we have no inflation. Education, healthcare and transportation are free services. We wear implants similar to yours to aid in cognition and memory. Electricity comes from the Zero Point Field and is obviously free. Our tax rate is fifteen percent and no other taxes are charged. The government makes a good income from the natural resources on this planet and there's no need to increase the taxes. There is virtually no crime here. Drugs, alcohol, smoking are all legal as we feel every person's free will must be respected, but these problems are minor. Life here on Frejja is not that different than life on Earth, but we have admittedly some complications that we need to resolve."

Kovan ended the meeting and five robot bellboys arrived and showed the men to their rooms. The rooms were small, but each man had his own room and private bath. They were told dinner would be served in two hours.

Arvin just put his luggage on the floor and quietly went out to go for a walk. He needed to be alone and digest all the new impressions.

As he walked around the hotel grounds and admired the flowers planted along the path, he felt a joy from within he had never felt before. To be outside without a spacesuit and be able to breathe naturally gave him a feeling of freedom that felt liberating. Gravity was the same as on Mars and the slightly thinner atmosphere was not noticeable to Arvin. He was not religious, but had always felt a strong connection within himself to a higher power and he said in a low voice "to whoever is listening up there, thank you, thank you for bringing me here".

When he returned to the hotel it was time for dinner and they were served fish, something looking like potatoes and a plate of various cut-up vegetables. It was quite good. After dinner, most of the men retired to their rooms and went to bed. Everyone was exhausted.

The first week went by fast with lectures, language classes, interviews by androids to find out their skills and what they themselves were hoping to accomplish. Visitor night arrived and mostly young girls and a few slightly older women arrived at the hotel in airmobiles. Arvin had only been in an airmobile on the holodeck as they did not exist on Mars. The first impression Arvin had when he watched the girls was how kind they looked and almost all of them were pretty with clean features, long hair either braided or tied into a ponytail. Most of them were blond. All of them wore dresses, flat sturdy shoes and no one had makeup. The girls were not shy and mingled with the men in a natural way, smiling good-heartedly at the men's attempt at speaking Frejjan. None of them spoke English. Arvin spotted a petite girl that made his heart jump and walked up to her and said in his broken Frejjan -

"I'm Arvin. What's your name?"

"Maija, welcome to Frejja. Do you think you'll like it here?"

Arvin guessed her to be eighteen, nineteen years old. She was not as tall as the other women. Her blond hair was tied into a ponytail that reached to her waist.

"I know I will," responded Arvin. "I need to learn your language and start working. That way I'll become used to how life is here. Would you want to be my tutor?"

"Of course," Maija said. "Give me your communicator and I'll enter my code so you can contact me." Kovan had handed out communicators to all the men and they were worn as a bracelet. "I'm still in school, but if you contact me in the evening, you'll always reach me."

"What are you studying?"

"History, I would like to become a teacher. I know some of Earth's history and how the community started on Mars. I have only a year left of school."

"Can I teach you English?" Arvin asked. "That way we'll both be bilingual."

Maija laughed and responded -

"Sure, you can."

After that evening, they met every day at the hotel and as Arvin gained mastery of the Frejjan language, Maija's tutoring was a great help. Maija was intelligent and was slowly learning English and her pronunciation was good with less of an accent than Kovan's. Only a few days remained of the free month's stay at the hotel and Arvin was offered a job as beginner engineer at a smaller firm not far from the hotel. A small house was part of his salary and it was rent free. Arvin accepted the job and moved in. The house was furnished and neat and clean. He liked it.

With no work experience and still some language difficulties, Arvin had to work very hard to fulfill his duties. His fifteen coworkers, both male and female, noticed his efforts and tried to help him. Arvin also struggled to master the written language, which was very different from written English and seemed so much harder both to read and write. Maija was an invaluable helper and through her efforts Arvin advanced faster than he ever could have on his own. He had met her parents and two sisters and felt comfortable in her home. Arvin knew what he wanted and one evening he took her hand and asked her to marry him. They had been seeing each other for only four months, but Maija said yes right away. On Mars Arvin had dated a few girls, but never been in love. He adored Maija and could not wait to be married to her. Maija had never had a boyfriend as there were too few males around.

Marriage contracts did not exist and they were married by a government official two weeks later. Neither of them wanted to wait. Maija moved in with Arvin in his house and continued her education. She would graduate in less than a year.

They were happy and each other's best friend. Arvin had learned how to communicate with his parents using the Zero Point Field and Cellie and Gordon were relieved and thankful that Arvin had survived the trip and was now happily married. Cellie disclosed the good news to Arvin that she was expecting and that she had chosen the artificial womb, which was now available on Mars. Arvin was surprised, but realized that with him gone his parents had no family. He congratulated his mother and then, just for fun, he said -

"Mom, why don't you, Dad and the new baby move to Frejja also?"

To his surprise Cellie responded -

"We may do just that."

******

Mr. Parker had been offered a government job as advisor to the president of Frejja. They had contacted Karol and she had given them a rundown of Mr. Parker's brilliance, efficiency and leadership abilities. His command of the language was sufficient to handle the job and he accepted it. There was only one country on Frejja, the State of Frejja, and the capital where the government was located was called Raano. Mr. Parker was totally absorbed in his work and stayed late every night in order to learn as fast as possible how the Frejjan government functioned. After a couple of months, he had a full picture of the situation in his mind and saw several areas where money was wasted and efficiency was way down. He knew how to solve the problems and asked his assistant to write a full report to the President outlining his plan. It was well received and the president agreed to adopt it.

The Frejjan government was honest, but the biggest problem was the size of it. Without losing efficiency, it could be reduced to half the size. Mr. Parker found no corruption within the government. In addition to the solutions he had presented to the immediate problems, he had also outlined in his report in full detail how the government on Earth and Mars functioned, such as People Democracy, elections, banking system, basic income and so on. The President had not yet discussed those details with Mr. Parker and he did not know if the Frejjan government would want to change their way of running the country.

Mr. Parker was dating a Frejjan woman named Tolli in her early thirties and was really fond of her. He had lost his belly and was now in better physical shape and he had promised himself never to get fat again. Mr. Parker was pleasant looking and his girlfriend seemed very interested. She was taller than him, but this did not bother either of them. Tolli also worked for the government and, unfortunately, if the government 'slimmed down' her job would be lost. Mr. Parker had told her that, but

Tolli was not concerned and just said she would find another job. Tolli spoke no English and sometimes they struggled when discussing certain topics. She did not have a language ear and Mr. Parker's efforts to teach her English left him frustrated. He realized that he had to become fluent in Frejjan in order to eliminate the language barrier.

******

Brandon and Brianna had just landed their spaceship on Mars and for the first time they saw the Frejjan spaceship. Emrak and his crew visited Mars twice a year to trade and bring back Martian immigrants to Frejja. This was the fourth time Emrak's ship landed on Mars and so far, they had returned to Frejja with one hundred men as passengers every time. Karol was somewhat concerned about losing citizens, but she knew there was no way of stopping people from leaving. The saving grace was that every spaceship from Earth was full of new immigrants and in spite of losing people to Frejja, the population on Mars was still increasing.

Brandon and Brianna met Emrak in the lobby and asked for a tour of his ship. He was more than happy to oblige. The Bridge was impressive and left Brandon and Brianna awestruck and when Emrak noticed their reaction he tossed out an offer -

"We desperately need pilots and if you two move to Frejja with your children and any family members you have on Earth that you want to bring along, I'll train the two of you to run this ship."

"Yes!" Brandon blurted out. "Brianna, what do you say?"

Brianna only needed to reflect on the idea a few seconds and said -

"I'm in, my answer is yes."

Space travel into deep space had always been the ultimate goal for both Brandon and Brianna and the trips back and forth to the Moon and Mars had become too easy for them. They were ready for more. They were in the prime of life; Brandon was forty-five years old and Brianna forty-one. They were young, but still experienced.

"All costs related to your move to Frejja are free for you and your family members and that includes any charge for the trip from Earth to Mars," Emrak explained. "All immigrants travel for free. We leave in one week and if you want to, you can come with us and we'll start your training right away. Since you already are experienced astronauts, I don't expect your training to take more than six months to a year. The hardest part is traveling through the tunnels and that requires a steady hand at the helm. The next ship from Earth could bring replacement pilots for your ship. You also have to arrange for your family to leave Earth in this window of travel to Mars and they will have to wait on Mars until our next ship arrives here in six months, which is a waiting time of only two months until our ship lands. By the way, how old are your children?"

"We have two boys, Rigel fourteen years and Orion eleven years," Brianna said.

Emrak smiled and said -

"I can see where your heart is, both boys have star names."

The following week was a frenzy of activity and to the astonishment of Brianna, her parents Clarence and Lotte announced they would also move to Frejja. They could not emotionally part with their grandsons, who they had raised mostly without Brianna and Brandon, but Clarence was also dying to find out about the advanced technology on Frejja and he was ready for a new adventure. He was by now sixty-nine years, but still young in mind and perfectly capable of learning a new language and work for a few years. Lotte would stay home with the children and just enjoy a new environment. They would also bring Eva, their beloved android. Their two other children were now adults and on their own and assured Lotte and Clarence they did not mind.

"Just go and have fun," they said. They would take care of selling the house and personal belongings.

Tina was also asked if she wanted to come along, but she politely declined. She was seventy-one years old and felt the whole move to a distant planet was too much for her.

Within a week Clarence, Lotte, the boys and Eva were on their way to Mars. This was their second time onboard a spaceship. They had visited the Moon as tourists, but this spaceship was much bigger than the Moon ship and they found it exciting. They would stay at a hotel on Mars until the Frejja ship returned to pick them up.

Back on Mars, Brandon had notified their employer that they wanted to resign. He was relieved to hear that there were no hard feelings and his employer agreed to send a replacement crew to fly the ship back to Earth.

Departure day arrived and Brandon and Brianna were strapped into their seats on the Frejjan ship. They wore Frejjan uniforms with the rank insignia of 'pilots in training'. Both of them felt almost giddy with excitement. The Bridge was a marvel of technology with equipment they had never seen before. As the ship gained elevation and was free of Mars' atmosphere, the main engines ignited and off they went. Brandon memorized every move the pilot made and knew he was finally home. He belonged here, piloting this ship and did not for a second regret his decision to move to Frejja. He knew Brianna felt the same.

Going through the first tunnel navigating the narrow passage was mind-blowing. A very steady hand on the helm kept the ship straight on course and Emrak piloted the ship through the tunnels. There were three other pilots who ran the ship while cruising through space. Brandon felt he would quickly learn how to run the ship at cruising speed, but to master the tunnels would not be easy and one mistake could blow up the ship. As they exited the first tunnel and picked up speed, Emrak turned over the controls to the other pilots and sat down next to Brandon and Brianna. He handed them a translation device.

"What force in the tunnel makes the ship gain speed?" Brandon asked excitedly.

"To be honest, we're not sure why it happens," Emrak said with a smile. "These tunnels or black holes, as some call them, are mysteries to science and the first time a spaceship traveled through a tunnel, the pilot was not sure what would happen or even if they would survive. They carried no passengers and just took a chance and went through. When they exited the tunnel, they realized the ship had almost doubled its speed and found that the tunnel had been a shortcut and moved the ship several light years forward in space. They finally figured out where they were. These tunnels are all over the universe and are used by all the ships to shorten the distance of travel. There have been accidents when ships have blown up in the tunnel and that's why your training may take a full year until you master the technique. My copilots are still not ready to control the ship in the tunnels, but I feel a few more months of training is all they need."

Throughout the trip, Emrak spent hours every day instructing Brandon and Brianna and at the end of the journey both felt rather familiar with the equipment on the Bridge. They were fascinated and eager to go through the formal training that would take place on Frejja at a flight school. They also mingled with the passengers and the two months went by rather quickly.

After they had landed on Frejja, they were picked up by a Frejjan woman and taken directly by airmobile to the campus where they would go through their training for the next six months. Since they were already licensed astronauts, they did not have to go through basic training. They had their own room with bath and kitchenette, small, but comfortable. As soon as they had signed a contract their classes began as well as language classes and their days were long and demanding. The best part was the time they spent in the flight simulator and that is when they really gained the feel for the ship. They spent hours practicing piloting the ship through the tunnels and after a while they were able to keep the ship straight on course in spite of the shaking. The Frejjan language was a challenge to learn as well as reading and writing. They always brought the translation device, but found they started to understand the spoken language better and better and could carry on a conversation using 'simple' language. To master the guttural sounds had been difficult, but they learned and the other students had no trouble understanding them. The six months were an intense period of learning and acclimating to new ways, but rewarding and challenging.

Brandon and Brianna graduated and were now employees of the State of Frejja, the official owners of the star fleet. Their dark blue pilot uniforms had one gold insignia on the sleeves. They stayed on campus another week so they could welcome their family members, who were expected to arrive from Mars in the next few days. They would stay at the same hotel where Arvin had stayed for the first month and then transfer to a private house in the area of their choosing. Brandon and Brianna would stay with Lotte and Clarence in their house between flights.

Brandon and Brianna waited for them at the hotel and to see the children and Brianna's parents were a joy that brought tears to their eyes. They had only one day before they had to board the spaceship to Mars and they spent the day with the family and Eva. After a tearful goodbye Brandon and Brianna had to leave and board the ship. They spent the night on the ship as the departure was at dawn. Emrak had told them they would travel to several other planets in addition to Mars in the future.

******

Clarence, Lotte, Eva and the boys settled in a house outside the capital Raano. Eva had been programmed with the Frejjan language and was practicing the pronunciation. She mastered the language within a few weeks and then started tutoring her family. Every day they got together in the living room and took lessons from Eva including reading and writing skills. They worked hard and practiced talking Frejjan with each other. Clarence was the most ambitious as he was planning to look for a job in electronics and had to be proficient in the new language. Brandon and Brianna would return in four months and be home on leave for three weeks and they all hoped to be able to speak at least some Frejjan by then. If there was a need, Brandon and Brianna were allowed a longer leave than three weeks, but the standard off-time was only three weeks between flights.

Clarence easily landed a job with an electronics company and the pay was good. Cost of living on Frejja was moderate with many services free. As he discovered the new technology he was amazed and thought to himself the inventions he could have brought forward had he only known about these discoveries. He was told that some of the Frejjan technology was sold to both Mars and Earth in exchange for precious metals. Clarence estimated the Frejjans were about a hundred years ahead of Earth. He considered his job a hobby and never for a minute regretted moving to Frejja.

Lotte and Eva enjoyed being home and go for discovery trips with their groundmobile, an advanced version of the model used on Earth. The Frejjan vehicle was both an airmobile and groundmobile combined, self-driving, whisper quiet and very comfortable. It was equipped with full electronics and Internet capability. Reclining seats invited the passengers to take a snooze. When traveling above ground, the vehicle easily reached two hundred miles an hour and that was not top speed. The countryside was beautiful with lakes everywhere and trees and flowers that were similar to the flora on Earth. There were no wild animals on Frejja, no snakes and reptiles and only some insects, but there were wild birds of many varieties. The whole planet was sparsely populated and there were only forty million citizens on Frejja. The planet could support a billion people with ease and still not be overpopulated.

Outside the city of Raano were many large farms growing grain crops as well as smaller farms growing mostly vegetables. They saw no dairy cows and it seemed animals similar to goats supplied milk for the population. There were no oceans on the planet and all fish came from the many lakes where fishermen used nets to catch the fish. They were surprised to see fishermen doing manual work on such an advanced planet, but were told there were people who truly enjoyed working with their hands and living what was called an 'old-fashioned lifestyle'. Beef did not exist, but smaller animals the size of sheep were grazing in many places and they were used for meat. Flocks of birds looking like a mix of chickens and ducks were raised on many farms for meat and eggs. They saw no pigs.

Lotte and Eva loved their outings and continued until the rainy season started. A Frejjan year was ten months, slightly shorter than a year on Earth, and the summer season lasted seven months with moderate rain. Then came the rainy season with heavy downpour and when the three months of rain finally ended, people looked forward to dry weather and sunshine. Fresh water for drinking was plentiful and fires were rare as the ground stayed hydrated.

Rigel and Orion started school and had to work hard at first to overcome the language barrier, but they learned fast and within a year they were fluent in the new language. They liked their school and stopped talking about Earth. There was one ball game similar to football that was popular and both boys joined the team, but competition was not important. The kids played for fun and it did not matter much if they won or not. The curriculum was similar to what they had had on Earth, but the tempo was faster and the teachers demanded more of the students. Discipline was strict and rules enforced. By the time the students reached middle school they had learned the hard way that disobedience did not pay and bad habits were corrected in the early years of school by withdrawing privileges.

CHAPTER 20

Arvin and Maija sat outside their home and enjoyed the evening sun. Maija was playfully removing one petal at the time from a flower she had picked from their yard.

"One, two, three," she counted.

"It'll be a Fibonacci number," Arvin said with a grin. "Nature is mathematical."

"Please explain."

"Fibonacci was an Italian mathematician living in the thirteenth century on Earth and his mathematical formula is a sequence of numbers, where the sum of the last two numbers becomes the new number. For example, one plus one equals two; one plus two equals three; two plus three equals five and so on."

"i have twenty-one petals," Maija announced.

"That's a Fibonacci number. Do the math," Arvin said.

After they had played with several flowers their thoughts drifted to other things.

"Are there no pets on Frejja? Cats, dogs?" Arvin asked in English. They alternated between English and Frejjan so both of them could practice their language skills.

"No," responded Maija. "In addition, there are no horses here either. I had never heard about horses until you told me about them. The animals we eat are just part of our food supply and the farmers are not emotionally attached to them. They're treated well and don't suffer, but they are not pets."

Lately, she had watched several holographic programs about life on Earth. Arvin had no practical experience of Earth either, but Cellie had spent many hours describing her home planet to Arvin so he had a good idea how life functioned on Earth. Maija was a history buff and with a Martian husband and in-laws from Earth, she wanted to know everything about the two planets including being fluent in their language.

"What's the life span of Frejjans?" Arvin wondered.

"Most people live to one hundred and twenty years or so, which is a little longer than the lifespan on Earth," Maija explained. "They're usually healthy in body and mind their whole lives and there is no such thing as vaccinations here. Frejjans have strong immune systems."

Arvin had another question he had pondered over.

"I have never seen a church anywhere. Are people atheists on Frejja?"

"Organized religion similar to what Earth has doesn't exist here," Maija said. "Instead, people have strong beliefs in spirituality, reincarnation, reaching higher vibration and self-improvement. To us, reincarnation is a reality and we feel each lifetime is a learning opportunity and has a mission we should try to fulfill. We're taught to listen to our intuitive sense, not to silence it. We all must learn to make decisions without fear and acknowledge the consequences of our choices. Wrong decisions can be replaced with better decisions and fear of making decisions should never enter the picture. Many strive to achieve the ability to communicate telepathically with beings who have passed on, but only some people can master this skill. It's complicated. Spirituality is considered a private, personal matter and that's why you will not find any clergy here. There's no need for an outside teacher such as a priest. You'll find your guidance from within."

"Do you believe in a higher power?"

"Of course, don't you?"

"I am not sure what I believe. Somewhere within me I feel a connection to a higher power, but my parents are not religious and the whole idea of God seems so alien to me. I'm open to the idea of a higher power and several times in my life I've become aware of advice that seems to originate from within myself. The advice is always right so I tend to follow it. You can tutor me, if you want. I'm openminded."

Maija smiled and agreed.

"Do you have proof God exists?" Arvin asked.

"It can't be proven. Belief in God must be experienced and it's individual. It is a feeling, a knowing that comes from within. No outside person needs to be involved."

"You're more spiritual than you think you are, you just haven't awakened to faith yet," Maija continued. "There are ascended masters who guide us while we are in embodiment. We can't see them, because they vibrate at a higher frequency than we do, but they're here, right now, all around us. Think of it as a parallel universe. Some people can communicate with them, some can't. I haven't been in direct contact with them, but I can pick up messages and thoughts from them. I perceive the messages as an inner knowing and I always follow them. Faith removes fear and liberates you. You're free. But, and listen carefully, Arvin, there are dark forces that will try to manipulate you and take over your mind. As long as you have no fear and remain neutral, they can't hurt you. Fear is self-deception and will paralyze you. Fear opens an entry into your mind the dark forces can use. If you ever find yourself overcome with fear, immediately remind yourself fear is only a fantasy of your mind. If you need to protect yourself against danger, your escape will be more successful without fear. The ascended masters will remove the dark forces eventually. All they need is permission from us humans to do so. They respect our free will."

Arvin listened intently, reflecting on Maija's beliefs and finally said -

"Something is missing in my life. It's as if I'm not whole. We live to old age and learn all the lessons of life, then we die and all our wisdom is lost. What was that all about? With your beliefs, we reincarnate and the wisdom from past lives are still within us and guide us in the next life. There is no loss. I have to admit it makes more sense and I'm open to learning more about it. Life with peace of mind and no fear is a life of joy. I think you need to teach me more about this, Maija."

Maija nodded in agreement. She felt contented. A new life was growing in her and very soon it was time to transfer the embryo to the artificial womb. This was standard procedure on Frejja and all women used the artificial womb. It was considered safer as no miscarriages could occur.

"Are you ready to become a dad?" she said with a smile to Arvin.

"Are you sure?" Arvin asked with excitement. "Of course, I'm ready."

"I'm sure," Maija said and hugged Arvin.

The embryo was transferred to the artificial womb and it was a boy.

******

Clarence and Lotte were visiting Arvin and Maija and they had a good time exchanging their impressions of Frejja. Arvin had never met Clarence and Lotte, but he knew Clarence was related to his mother Cellie. Maija loved meeting them and to have Earth relatives nearby. They spoke English and Maija had no problem following the conversation. Arvin hinted that his parents may move to Frejja and Clarence and Lotte were excited to hear the news.

Maija graduated from school with a degree in history. She delayed looking for employment as the baby was soon due and she wanted to be home for a while to care for the baby herself. The nursery was ready and Maija and Arvin were both excited and humbled when they brought their son Fenul home. Maija's parents were visiting to greet their first grandchild.

Maija stayed home for six months and then started working part time as a history teacher. Arvin had bought an android, Vega, to take care of the baby and help with household chores. Vega was even more advanced than Eva and spoke fluent English with no accent. Her skill set was endless and she could master almost anything around the house. To boot, she had a lovely personality and soon she was a trusted family member and very appreciated. She had been programmed with a full package of feelings and was so 'human' they forgot most of the time she was a machine. She took excellent care of Fenul and Maija was touched when she saw Vega hugging the baby.

******

Brandon and Brianna took turns under Emrak's watchful eyes to pilot the spaceship with manual controls. He would transfer auto control to manual several times a day and allow Brandon and Brianna to run the ship so they would get the feel for how the ship traveled and responded to their manual adjustments. They learned quickly and became fully skilled at piloting the ship. The tunnels were another story and Emrak would not allow them control of the ship through the tunnels. He carefully explained every maneuver he performed as he skillfully took the ship through the tunnels with perfect aim and Brandon and Brianna knew it would take several more training sessions with the flight simulator to achieve mastery of the tunnels.

Life onboard the ship was pleasant and they had a big cabin with their own bathroom and a little kitchenette in case they wanted to make a cup of tea and a sandwich. They could take anything they wanted from the ship's galley and a 3D food printer made cooking easy. The cabin was equipped with full electronics and a library of holograms for entertainment and learning.

Emrak, Brandon and Brianna were sitting in the ship's dining room while the ship was on autopilot. Two pilots were on the Bridge to keep a watchful eye on the controls.

"Are there any hostile, warlike planets capable of attacking Frejja?" Brianna asked.

"There is one planet, unfortunately, named Morekia orbiting the star Zester and the inhabitants are a threat to Frejja. Morekia is located eleven light years from us, but with the tunnels they can reach our planet in four months. They're humanoids, but there are quite a few differences between them and us and their genetic code is too different from ours to produce offspring with a Frejjan female. That's what the doctors say, but it's actually unknown. They have never attacked Frejja, but they have raided and almost destroyed several smaller planets close to their planet. To use an Earth expression, they're terrorists and when they attack, they show no mercy whatsoever. Frejja only has a fleet of fighter spaceships, no ground troops as we've never been attacked. Our fleet is rather small and may not be able to defend our planet against the Morekians, we simply don't know. We have nothing to do with them and hope they never set foot on our planet."

"How do you know all this?" Brandon asked with interest.

"Oh, we have spies out there in the universe and bad news travel far," Emrak said with a smile. "For example, there are orbiting workstations where spaceships can dock for refueling and repair and that's a good place to pick up news. We also travel to a few other planets in addition to Mars and Earth and if anything has happened, we get briefed on the details. The majority of the planets have peaceful citizens, but Morekia with its cruel people is the exception to the rule. They take what they want by stealing rather than supplying their needs through work."

Brandon and Brianna felt distressed hearing Emrak's report and decided to find out more about Frejja's defense system when they returned home.

Brandon landed the ship with ease on Mars and they stayed a week in Martia. They visited Cellie and Gordon as they always did when on Mars and they talked about Arvin's new life on Frejja. Cellie and Gordon's son Jonas was a month old and doing well.

"In six months when your ship returns, we will move to Frejja. By that time Jonas is strong enough to survive the trip," Cellie declared. "The Frejjans have placed an android here in Martia who gives lectures and language lessons and both of us participate."

"Wow!" Brianna exclaimed with surprise and clapped her hands. "This is big news! Does Arvin know?"

"We just told him," Gordon said. "We really look forward to moving and the android told me that I will easily get a job and Cellie could start an insect business on Frejja importing the insect eggs from Earth. The android said there was no such business on Frejja and would most likely be a success. We're working hard to learn their language and practice talking with each other here at home. My God, it's a difficult language, but we're learning and are also working on reading and writing Frejjan."

They switched their conversation to the Frejjan language and had fun laughing at each other's mistakes and pronunciations.

When the ship departed for Frejja, Brianna was at the controls and mastered takeoff with ease. As usual, they had a hundred men onboard as passengers and this time there were a few African Americans and Chinese men among the passengers. Racism had faded away and not been an issue for many years both on Earth and Mars and the Frejjan recruiter had welcomed these men warmly.

The Frejjan ships had also visited Earth and the first time the ship landed outside Washington DC the people were as amazed as the Martians had been. The trip from Frejja to Earth had taken three months and a Frejjan android remained on Earth as a recruiter. He also gave lectures and language lessons. Quality of life on Earth was very good, but there were a large number of men who could not resist the adventure of space travel and living on another planet and after only a few days one hundred men had signed up. Within a short time, there was a waiting list of five thousand men. There were only six starships in the Frejjan fleet, but Frejja was in the process of manufacturing several more ships. A few families had also signed up and were warmly received.

******

Back on Earth, the sad news reached Linh's relatives that she had died peacefully in her sleep at the age of one hundred and ten years. Lena had found her dead in her bed and was mourning her death. The two of them had been as close as sisters for many years and Lena grieved with the intensity of a human. She had loved Linh more than any person she had been associated with and felt totally empty without Linh. Linh had been mentally alert her whole life and as her body became weaker with age, her mind never declined. Linh and Lena had enjoyed each other's company and Linh's keen intellect never ceased to amaze Lena.

Lena's daughter Miracle found a new home for Lena only a few houses away from her own home. Lena felt her lifespan should end in a few decades. She had had a long life and her model would soon be outdated. She would give her best to this new family, but she had no desire to continue her existence after her employment ended with this new family.

******

Mr. Parker had married Tolli and was very happy with her. At work, he was studying all branches of the Frejjan government. He had worked out a plan to shrink the government waste and if People Democracy would be implemented, he could literally cut the cost of government in half. The president was very interested in his ideas, but hesitated if the citizens would agree to all the changes that would have to be implemented. Mr. Parker suggested to put a summary of the plan on the Internet with explanations to the citizens how the money saved would be used. The idea caught on and the feedback was positive. The government put the whole package to a vote and the result was an overwhelming yes from the citizens.

Mr. Parker told the president he would change one department at the time, terminate those departments that were no longer needed and the whole switchover would take about a year. Tolli lost her job but found another, just as she had said. The new government was similar to Earth's government, but there were differences that had to do with the way of life on Frejja and old traditions that Mr. Parker felt had to be respected.

Lots of money was saved and the taxes were cut almost in half. Services that had not been free of charge were now free and when all was said and done and the new system was in place the people were grateful. The new government was small, frugal and very efficient. Money could now be saved for emergencies while before only a small amount of money was in the government's bank account. Mr. Parker felt relieved that everything functioned the way it should without problems. He loved his work and to him it was more a hobby than work.

Tolli had also told him she was pregnant and the thought of becoming a father had put tears in his eyes. He was looking forward so much to the baby's birth.

The rainy season had arrived and for three months it poured heavily. The lakes were slowly refilling, farm fields were thoroughly watered and nature was rinsed clean. The force of the rain was intense and buckets came down. All the wells had their fresh water replenished.

******

Emrak had carefully watched Brandon's and Brianna's practice runs with the flight simulator on Frejja and how they navigated the tunnels. He was impressed with their skills and when they made the return trip from Mars to Frejja he offered both of them to pilot the ship through one of the tunnels. The ship had dual manual controls, so he could take over instantly should anything go wrong. Brandon was first and forcing himself to stay calm, he flew the ship without mishap through the tunnel. Brianna had no trouble either and felt self-confident. Their skills were equal and they had advanced considerably compared to just a year before. Emrak told them that they were now ready to visit other planets and their very next trip would be to a planet called Arrynia orbiting the star Pyrester. Emrak would be the captain of the ship and Brandon and Brianna copilots. Emrak felt they should now learn the different travel routes in the universe and how to navigate to the planets that Frejja was trading with.

Upon return to Frejja, Brandon and Brianna enjoyed immensely to visit with Lotte, Clarence and their boys and the three weeks between flights went by too quickly, but they were also looking forward to learning the travel route to Arrynia and meeting the inhabitants of the planet.

Emrak was already onboard and this time the ship was a cargo ship. It looked identical to the passenger ships, but had only cargo space and no seats for passengers. After takeoff with Brianna at the controls, he explained that spaceships followed established routes in space to make use of the tunnels. The distance from Frejja to Arrynia was five light years and they would go through three tunnels. The whole trip would take about five weeks as the tunnels would almost double their speed. Emrak displayed their route as a holographic huge image. They would have to familiarize themselves with a large area of the universe and where all the tunnels were located. Brianna and Brandon studied the map for a long time and memorized the route.

"Do you ever see another spaceship when you travel through the universe?" Brandon asked in the Frejjan language.

"Very seldom. The universe is so enormous and the number of ships so small that I myself have only seen one single spaceship during my thirty years of space travel. We passed each other many miles apart and flashed our lights as a greeting to each other."

"This may sound silly," Brianna said "but what would you do if you enter a tunnel and another ship has entered the same tunnel from the opposite direction?"

Emrak laughed and said -

"You would be in deep trouble, my dear Brianna. As the ship enters the tunnel, it gains speed continuously and there's no way of stopping the ship at that speed. The tunnel isn't wide enough for two ships to pass each other inside the tunnel. There is, however, a safety measure that we all use and that is that we never enter a tunnel without sending a beam, similar to a laser beam, through the tunnel to search for objects inside the tunnel. If there would be a ship in the tunnel, there is enough time to bypass the tunnel and travel outside it. We would then make a turn and come back when the tunnel is clear. I have never in all my travels been in that situation and I sure hope it will never happen."

As they were nearing Arrynia, Emrak filled Brandon and Brianna in on life on the planet.

"The Arrynians are humanoids and their genetic code is close enough to ours so it is possible for a Frejjan and an Arrynian to produce offspring. They are short people, only about five feet tall, very kind and peaceful and they have no hair, small ears and rather large blue eyes. Other than those dissimilarities, they look just like us. However, there is one major difference between Arrynia and Frejja and that is that the Arrynian women are fully in charge of everything and run the country without ever consulting with the men. As I said, the people are dedicated to peace and it may be due to the female leadership that there has not been a war on Arrynia for a long, long time. The men don't seem to want to involve themselves with running the country and the females have been in charge for several hundred years. Full equality between men and women doesn't exist and the men accept that."

"Their planet is a little larger than Earth," Emrak continued "with heavy gravity, but they have an atmosphere of oxygen so we won't need spacesuits. The air quality is good. The Frejjans and Arrynians have traded for many years and technologically we are at the same level. We buy animal fodder, certain food products, platinum and a few other things from them and they buy mostly two of our minerals that we have in abundance but they don't have at all on their planet. They need our minerals for their manufacturing, mostly electronics. Their spaceships have a female crew, but there are some men onboard as navigators, overlooking the engines and so on."

Brandon and Brianna listened astonished to Emrak's description of Arrynia. Emrak continued -

"Don't ask too many questions about their society. Diplomacy reigns supreme among different planets and no one discusses rules and customs of another planet. Arrynia isn't that far from Morekia and the Arrynians have both an army and a fleet of spaceships for defense just in case the Morekians would invade. I don't know how skillful their female pilots are. I've heard they go through intense training, but they have never been tested in combat. The subject is touchy and all I know is what we pick up from our spies."

Brandon and Brianna were quietly reflecting on everything Emrak had explained and were excited to meet the Arrynians.

The ship landed and the planet was not as green as Frejja, but they saw planted farm fields and green grass, houses and little towns. In the distance they saw what looked like desert and Emrak acknowledged that it was.

"Not enough rain," he said.

Stepping down on Arrynia's surface was almost a shock with its crushing gravity. Emrak advised them to walk slowly and sort of drag their feet. It was pleasant temperature and the air was easy to breathe. Inside the building they were met by a woman looking just like Emrak had described - short, no hair and very large, blue eyes. She wore a uniform with pants. Brianna tried not to stare, but she could not help thinking to herself how unusual the woman looked. She held a translation device as neither she nor Emrak spoke each other's language.

"Welcome to Arrynia," she said in a language that sounded melodic, but had many clicking sounds. The device translated her speech into Frejjan. Emrak had told them that the language was very hard to learn and the written language used a system of pictorial characters.

"Please use our motorized chairs for moving around - I know how grueling our gravity is on your legs." Her voice was kind and so was her smile.

They sat down in the chairs and with a switch of a button they followed the woman to a conference room to discuss business.

"Emrak and I know each other, but let me introduce myself to you two," she started. "My name is Funina and I work with importing and exporting goods."

After Emrak had introduced Brandon and Brianna, she continued -

"It's always good to see you Frejjans." She turned to Brianna and Brandon and said -

"We look a little different from you, but we're still humans with heart and soul just like you. We have families and enjoy a lifestyle very similar to yours. Arrynia is a matriarchy and has been so for hundreds of years. Our men are valued citizens, but are excluded from working in government and the reason for this is that long time ago the men ran our country and bloody wars were commonplace. Only when the women took over leadership did the people finally experience peace and since then the men were removed from all positions of power."

Funina and Emrak chatted for a while and laughed together. Brianna was captivated by her charm, pearly white teeth and her laugh that sounded like little bells. *With hair on her head, she would look like an angel,* she thought to herself.

A vehicle took them a distance away to their hotel and they passed several towns with nice looking houses that were well maintained and neat looking. Children played outside and as Funina had said, their lifestyle was not that different from life on Frejja or Earth.

The dinner was good even though they had no idea what they ate and their hotel room was pleasant with full electronics equipment. At the hotel, they saw several men and at first, they had difficulty distinguishing between males and females, but after a few days they had learned to recognize the feminine features of the women and the more masculine appearance of the men.

Their stay lasted a week and, in the meantime, the Arrynians unloaded the Frejjan cargo and reloaded the ship with Arrynian goods. Emrak accompanied Brandon and Brianna on their excursions around the area and they found Arrynia to be a dry planet and farm fields had to be irrigated. They saw flocks of birds resembling geese and animals similar to sheep and Emrak pointed out that those animals were part of the meat supply. Arrynia was larger than Earth, but had only five hundred million citizens. The women preferred small families and Emrak told them he had heard rumors that the Arrynian government was contemplating starting an immigration program.

"Are there any overpopulated planets you know of?" Brandon wondered.

"Yes, I know of at least one, but there may be many more I haven't heard about yet. Fourteen light years from Frejja is a planet called Kodetsia orbiting the star Giisa. The people have a human body with a reptilian head like a lizard. Their planet is the size of Frejja, but the population is huge and they can hardly feed themselves. The Kodetsians are not hostile, technically as advanced as the Frejjans, but they don't believe in birth control and the population has soared as a result. Arrynia may welcome families from Kodetsia in the future, who knows. An Arrynian and a Kodetsian cannot produce children, but if whole families relocate to Arrynia, there would be no problem."

"Will you ever travel to Kodetsia?" Brianna asked.

"Probably not, as we don't trade with them. But if Arrynia would allow them to immigrate, you would meet them there," Emrak said. "Remember, our spaceships are only capable of travel within twenty light years more or less from Frejja and the size of the Milky Way is enormous. We only know a tiny little corner of our galaxy. There are millions of inhabited planets out there in the Milky Way. Just imagine if we were able to reach our neighboring galaxy, the Andromeda galaxy, with all the planets orbiting various stars over there. Sometime in the future, the ships will be fast enough to explore more of the Milky Way."

"Have you personally met a Kodetsian?"

"Yes, once at an orbiting workstation. We had to pull in there for emergency repairs and there was a ship from Kodetsia there. If they didn't have a reptilian head, they would look exactly like us. Their heads are intimidating to look at, but they are friendly and not at all mean. Their diet is mostly meat, usually consumed raw. They're intelligent and ambitious. Their language is easier to comprehend than the Arrynian language, but their vocal cords are different from ours and their voices are hard to understand. They speak with a wheezing sound. They are about six feet tall and strongly built. The women look the same as the men and you can only tell them apart by their clothes. The women wear skirts while the men always wear pants."

Their visit to Arrynia was over and the return trip went fast. Emrak had hinted that soon Brandon and Brianna would advance to full captains and pilot their own ship.

CHAPTER 21

Cellie, Gordon and baby Jonas were onboard the Frejjan passenger ship. The ship was not piloted by Brandon and Brianna as they were now working on the cargo ships. The whole trip went well and the baby was confined to a cushioned bassinet while they traveled through the tunnels and even though Jonas was shaking around in his little bed he did not cry. Cellie had imported thousands of insect eggs from Earth and they were onboard in the cargo bay.

The trip to Frejja was uneventful and they landed safely on their new planet. Stepping down on the Frejjan soil was very special to Cellie and Gordon and breathing in the fresh air felt exhilarating. They had lived on Mars over twenty-five years confined to indoor living. Cellie, Gordon and the baby stayed at the hotel for immigrants the standard month and then transferred to a house not too far from Arvin's house. It was a tearful and happy reunion when they all met again and Cellie and Gordon instantly liked Maija. Jonas and Fenul were almost the same age and Jonas was Fenul's uncle.

Gordon was proficient enough in the Frejjan language and was ready to start working right away. He was offered a job as chief mechanic doing repair work on the spaceships. It was a demanding job, but he loved it. It was a dream job.

Cellie rented a building nearby and started her insect business. She had years of experience and knew all the mechanics of the business. By the time she had built all the insect habitats the eggs were hatching and soon they were grown. She saved half of the insects for continuous egg production and started processing the rest. She did not advertise; the word was out and people would drop in to buy a bag of powdered insects and try it. The powder was pure protein, tasted good and could be used in the 3D printers as a flour for bread and pancakes and many other applications. She sold out in a few weeks and had to put in an order to Earth for another huge amount of insect eggs to be shipped on the next Frejjan spaceship returning from Earth. No Frejjan had ever eaten insects, but the idea had caught on and people were eager to try it. While she was waiting for the shipment, she expanded her business and hired a Frejjan girl, Saga, eager to make a little money. Cellie was able to speak Frejjan sufficiently well to instruct the girl and she was improving her command of the language all the time. Arvin's android Vega looked after both Fenul and Jonas. Cellie did not regret moving to Frejja and enjoyed being outside without a spacesuit.

Brianna and Brandon had bought their own translation device, but Cellie and Gordon felt they had to become fluent in the new language and decided they could do without it. The translation device was a complex machine and could be programmed with a huge number of languages, but it was expensive.

******

Karol was now on her second term as Martia's president and had easily won reelection. She and Ryan watched silently as five thousand Martian men left for Frejja and most of them were in their prime. Some of the men on Earth who had been planning to move to Mars changed their mind and instead emigrated to Frejja. The number of people on the waiting list to move to Mars was reduced from ten thousand to only four thousand. Martia had a stellar reputation for quality of life, inexpensive living and lots of free time for the citizens, but what was missing was the outdoors and that is why Frejja had such a big draw. The Frejjan women were also attractive and many men from Earth who had failed to find a wife were hoping to have better luck on the new planet.

Emrak had described the locations of all the tunnels he knew of between Frejja and Mars, Frejja and Earth as well as between Earth and Mars. Only one tunnel existed between Earth and Mars and with the help of that tunnel, the travel time from Earth to Mars was reduced from four months to three weeks. Because of the severe shaking in the tunnels, Emrak had cautioned that the design of the Martian spaceships, as well as the ships from Earth, would have to be changed to withstand the vibration. Frejja made an offer to both Earth and Mars to train their pilots to navigate through the tunnels for a modest fee and the offer was accepted with gratitude.

Karol decided Martia could now afford to build several more spaceships so the waiting time for people to move from Earth to Mars could be reduced. Ryan reviewed the Martian budget and found funding was more than adequate. Three additional spaceships with the latest electronics and expanded seating were soon under construction and would be ready to fly in about a year. All the ships were redesigned and capable of travel through the tunnels. Karol knew it was a necessity to have more ships available so people willing to move to Mars did not have to wait too long. Mars could not prosper in the long run if they did not have a sufficient number of citizens.

After the first Frejjan ship had landed on Mars, Karol and Ryan had often discussed privately how the Martians could ever defend their planet against an alien invading force. With all the tunnels in the universe acting as shortcuts the risk of invasion by hostile aliens was significant. Karol mulled over Martia's need for an air fleet of fighter spaceships. She asked Ryan to investigate the cost of the ships and how many ships they needed.

Next, Karol contacted the government on Earth and with great diplomacy she inquired whether Earth would consider entering into a defense alliance with Mars in case of invasion by hostile aliens. At first the Earth government said no, but then decided to ask the citizens how they felt about the matter and to their surprise the vote came back affirmative. All the Martians had been citizens of Earth and most of them had friends and family there and the bond between the two planets was very strong. Ryan worked out a detailed agreement with Earth and offered that Mars would supply all the funding if the fleet of spaceships from Earth would aid the Martians in a war situation. Most of the fighter spaceships were owned by North America, but several of the other countries on Earth agreed to send their ships to Mars in case of war. There had not been war on Earth for a very long time and the fighter spaceships had never engaged in defense of any kind. Ever since the first Frejjan ship landed on Earth and people learned about the tunnels in the universe, everyone now understood that there was a real possibility that even Earth could be invaded by an alien force and most countries had at least some armed forces.

When Ryan inquired whether Frejja would help defend Mars the answer was an immediate yes. The Frejjan people felt affection for the immigrants from Earth and Mars and they were of the opinion they should help to defend the home planets of the new citizens. Frejjan women had strong maternal instincts and without the immigrant men, many of them would never have found a husband as there were not enough Frejjan men around and they would not have experienced motherhood. Ryan was delighted to hear the news from Frejja and started right away to draw up a defense plan. He also asked the Frejjan government if they would sell six of their fighter spaceships to Martia and they agreed. The purchase of the ships and the cost of building three additional passenger ships would take a huge bite out of the Martian budget, but Karol considered it a necessity.

******

When Brandon and Brianna were back on Frejja, they stopped by their old school and asked one of the instructors about the fighter spaceships. They were told the fleet was twenty-two ships and there were thirty trained pilots capable of flying the ships.

"Any chance we could be trained to fly the fighter spaceships?" Brandon asked.

"Yes, we'll train you, but I advise you to first fly our standard ships one year to become fully skilled in piloting the ships through the tunnels and to get a feel for the ships that you can only gain through practice. Then, in one year, come back and we'll train both of you to fly the fighters. I estimate it will take six months to become proficient. You'll need at least a hundred hours of flying time to master a fighter. They're quite different from the large ships you now fly and the controls are also different. After you've been trained, you can return to fly the cargo ships and let's hope you'll never have to fly the fighters. If you do, it means we're under attack. If everything is peaceful, you're required to report for training two weeks every year to maintain your flying skills."

Brandon and Brianna thanked the instructor and told him they would be back in one year. They took an airmobile taxi to their house and spent the next three weeks with their family.

When they boarded the ship again, Emrak told them that this was their last trip as junior captains and after this trip they would be assigned to their own ship and become full captains. They could choose to continue working together and both would then be captain of the ship or split apart and work on separate ships.

"We will always work together," Brandon said firmly. "My wife is my best friend."

Both Emrak and Brianna smiled.

"This trip will be a standard cargo run to Arrynia, but on the way we'll have to stop at an orbiting workstation to pick up four passengers and drop them off on Arrynia. Guess what race they are?" Emrak chuckled to himself and looked at them.

"Kodetsians?" Brianna burst out with excitement in her voice.

"Right on target, Brianna," Emrak said with a smile. "This was unexpected and I only got the orders a few days ago to pick them up. They're part of the crew of a Kodetsian ship that needed repairs at the workstation and these three men and one woman asked if they could spend some time on Arrynia instead of hanging around on the workstation. We said yes, of course, and they offered to pay full passenger fee."

About half way to Arrynia Emrak changed course and after a day of travel they neared a planet with an enormous workstation in orbit. The station was rotating to create artificial gravity. Emrak explained the planet was uninhabited, but mining was done on the planet's surface. All the workers were robots as the atmosphere was toxic. The owners of the workstation, aliens of some sort, were in charge of the mining and processed the minerals on the workstation. The combined income from the mining and the repair work the crew performed on spaceships paid for the upkeep of the workstation and left the owners with a nice profit. Two spaceships were docked at the workstation, but there was plenty of room for Emrak to maneuver the ship to a docking port and connect. As Emrak skillfully docked with the rotating workstation, Brandon and Brianna memorized every move he made to line up the huge ship with the station and they knew they would have to go through some training in the flight simulator to practice docking, especially docking with a rotating object. The door opened and Emrak, Brandon and Brianna went out and into the workstation to look for the passengers. They left the engines idling and the navigator and a copilot stayed onboard to watch over the ship.

Brandon and Brianna were very excited to set foot on the workstation. It was pressurized and had light gravity, enough so they could walk naturally. It was a metal structure of gigantic size and they followed the signs pointing to the lobby. Several beings of different races walked around, all of them had two legs, but very different heads and features and even though Brandon and Brianna tried not to stare they probably did anyway, because Emrak was laughing quietly to himself when he watched them.

"I know, I know," he said in a low voice as he laughed. "I did the same myself the first time I saw aliens."

In the lobby they spotted the four Kodetsians and Brandon and Brianna felt a chill run down their spine. Three men and one woman, all around six feet tall and muscular, waved at them and talking into their translation device one of them said -

"Here we are, hi there".

Emrak hurried over and shook hands with all of them. He introduced Brandon and Brianna and they also shook hands. They had human bodies and they shook hands with a firm grip. There was a slight odor around them, not bad, but different. They had tan heads without hair, large yellowish eyes, leathery skin and their ears were a round hole. They resembled a lizard, just as Emrak had said, and they were not attractive. The woman was as tall as the men. She wore a knee length skirt and her legs were covered with fabric leggings.

"My name is Leol," the leader said "and this is Uven, Soher and Esta." His voice was a mix of wheezing and hissing, loud enough to be audible, but so strange Brianna thought to herself it was amazing the translation device could translate it to the Frejjan language.

"We appreciate you'll take us as passengers. Our ship will take another month to finish and then continue on to Arrynia to pick us up."

"Let's go aboard," Emrak told them and turning to Brandon and Brianna he continued "I give you an hour to walk around the workstation and look around and then please return to the ship so we can take off."

Brandon entered a code on his communicator to alert them when one hour had passed and they walked in to the restaurant of the workstation to have something to drink. Brandon pointed to what looked like tea and the alien nodded and served them two mugs of piping hot tea that smelled really good. Brandon paid with a silver coin which he knew was universally accepted as payment. The tea was as good as it smelled and while they drank it slowly, they observed the other beings in the restaurant. They saw no humans, only a variety of aliens. Most of them were variations of humanoids and some of them were rather similar to humans with only slightly different appearance. Only a few of them were not humanoids and even though they walked on two legs, they resembled animals more than humans. They finished their tea and walked around the workstation.

They found an auditorium, rooms for rent, two restaurants, a holodeck, several areas with seating so guests could mingle with each other and, big surprise, a small swimming pool. Two alien children were playing in the pool.

"They must have extracted the water from an asteroid they had towed into this workstation," Brandon said. "What a luxury, a pool out here in deep space."

"Just imagine to be stuck on this workstation for a month," Brianna reflected. "You do need some diversions to break up the monotony. The holodeck also helps."

The communicator beeped and they walked back to the ship and boarded. Emrak closed the door and took the controls. He revved up the engines and swiftly pulled the ship away from the workstation to avoid hitting the other two docked ships. His command of the ship was truly impressive. As the engines reached full speed, they soon entered a tunnel and picked up additional speed. He turned over the controls of the ship to one of the copilots and sat down with Brandon, Brianna and the Kodetsians.

"We've never been to Arrynia," Esta said. "You probably know how overpopulated our planet is and many of our citizens want to leave and move to a better planet. Our hope is that Arrynia will allow some of us to move to their planet. The young people all believe in birth control, but our elders forbid it. You can't convince them how wrong they are, so it's easier for the younger generation to just move away and start a new life somewhere else."

"How many of you would like to relocate to Arrynia?" Brandon asked.

"Several million, but I doubt Arrynia would want that many of us. We hope to discuss emigration from Kodetsia with them. It would be all families, no single people, as we know our species is too different from the Arrynians to produce children."

"We would work hard to show the Arrynians our gratitude for accepting us on their planet," Soher said nodding his head to emphasize his sincerity. "Our citizens are well educated and have many various skills. We would not become a burden on their society."

They continued their conversation until dinner time and Leol had informed the androids in the galley what foods they were accustomed to. They were served uncooked, ground meat that they ate with a spoon without chewing. They also ate a small piece of bread.

Brianna and Esta had several girl-to-girl talks and as Brianna got to know Esta she became fond of her. She sensed Esta's kind heart and soul and forgot her reptilian head. In spite of looking like a male, she was actually rather feminine. Esta explained that the was twenty-four years old and training to become a pilot for domestic travel. She had a boyfriend at home who she was planning to marry and both of them were hoping to move to Arrynia and start a new life.

"If so many of you want to change to a more modern lifestyle, why don't you just do it?" Brianna asked.

"The elders have total power over everything," Esta sighed. "If you disobey, they put you in jail. It is easier to just leave, but the problem is where to."

"I hope for your sake that Arrynia will allow you to immigrate." Brianna patted Esta's hand to show sympathy.

The ship touched down on Arrynia and the crew had five days off. Emrak joined the Kodetsians to negotiate with the Arrynian government officials whether they would consider immigration.

Brandon and Brianna were on their own and enjoyed exploring the countryside using a rented airmobile that was also a groundmobile. The planet was dry, but the irrigated areas were beautiful with little towns here and there. Walking around was hard because of the heavy gravity, but Brandon and Brianna were both strong and their leg muscles adjusted after a few days without giving them muscle pain.

When they returned to the ship, they found only Emrak onboard. The Kodetsians were at their hotel and sent regards through Emrak saying they hoped to meet Brandon and Brianna again in the future.

"They were lucky for sure," Emrak started explaining. "They were granted immigration of ten million Kodetsian citizens. The government officials prepared a contract and it said only families could immigrate; birth control had to be enforced to limit families to two children; full integration was expected and all immigrants must learn to speak, read and write the Arrynian language. To move ten million people will take a long time. Leol and the other three will stay on Arrynia and not go back. They will send for their families and Esta for her boyfriend."

"I'm happy for them," Brianna said. "That's really good news."

Back on Frejja, Brandon and Brianna practiced docking a spaceship with a rotating workstation over and over until they felt they had mastered the process. Their next trip was to Mars to pick up passengers and this time they would be captains of the ship. They knew they were ready. Emrak would continue to pilot the cargo ships for a few more years and then find work on Frejja.

A year had passed and Brandon and Brianna had piloted their own ship without problems and were now training at their former school to learn how to fly the fighters. It was a big adjustment to switch over to a tiny little fighter spaceship, learn how to use the controls and shoot down an enemy spaceship while flying at top speed. They worked hard and flew the ship every other day to gain experience. After six months of training, they graduated and returned to their full-size ship. They were required to report for training annually and practice their skills for two weeks.

CHAPTER 22

Life on Morekia was low quality and the citizens feared their government. A touch of cruelty ran through the society and many citizens were apathetic. It was a dictatorship masquerading as a democracy with rigged elections, corrupted government officials and hidden fees and taxes transferring wealth from the working people to the elite in charge. When government funds were running low, the solution was always to invade and take what they needed from nearby defenseless planets. Compassion for the victims was unheard of and generous salaries enticed the fighter pilots to bury their feelings and just obey orders regardless of the barbarity of the raids.

One of the pilots was a male called Thole. His conscience had started to bother him more and more and he confided in his wife Metissa.

"I can't do this anymore," he told Metissa. "I can't sleep at night. All I see are those dead bodies I have shot down with my weapons, some of them in two, three pieces in a pool of blood. Why do we attack other planets? Can't we supply for ourselves on this planet?"

"What's this all about? We've always been a war planet and you have never questioned the system before." Metissa seemed annoyed. Thole's income enabled them to live in comfort and their son Soren wanted to be a pilot like his father.

"I think I have woken up and I now see the situation from the victims' point of view. They are innocent minding their own business and here we come all of a sudden and kill them off and steal everything they own. How would you feel if it happened to us?"

"It can't happen to us," Metissa said in an angry voice. "We are warriors and would be able to defend ourselves."

Thole realized his wife was not sharing his feelings and ended the conversation. He had noticed Metissa had a cruel streak in her and totally lacked empathy. His gut told him he could not do another mission and kill more defenseless beings, but to quit his job meant a possible prison term and ending up in a labor camp for years.

Thole was thirty years old looking like a typical Morekian with a humanoid body, but his head was shaped slightly different from that of a human. He had no hair and his skull had two deep ridges running from his forehead to the back of his skull. He had large, green eyes, small nose and mouth and large prominent ears. His skin was mostly white with a hint of green and he was average height but with a strong frame. By Morekian standards, Thole was a handsome man.

A plan was forming in his head, a dangerous plan that may cost him his life. In a few weeks Morekia would celebrate an important holiday and everything would be closed for two days. The fighter spaceships would be parked in the aircraft hangars for the holiday. If he could just take the largest fighter, fill it with fuel and take off to Frejja, he could ask for asylum. He would not tell his wife anything and he knew he may never see her and their son again, but that was the price he must pay for peace of mind. He could not continue like this and something had to be done.

Thole was extremely careful in his research and to his surprise most of the ships were refueled before the holiday started. All he had to do was to open the hangar door and leave. The field where the ships were kept was a long distance away from any town, so most likely no one would notice him take off. He was an experienced pilot and would gain altitude as quickly as he could to avoid being seen from the ground. The larger ships had enough fuel to reach Frejja, which was eleven light years away, but with the help of the tunnels the ship would accelerate in speed. The whole trip would take four months and if he removed all trackers, no one would know which direction he had taken.

Everything went according to his plan and he told his wife he had to do some errands and left home. No one knew of his plan and he left with his airmobile. Hidden in the airmobile was a bag with clothes. The hangar door was unlocked and he entered. When he climbed aboard the largest ship, he removed all trackers and let them fall on the floor and then started the engines. He had checked the galley and knew it was enough food and water for a crew of five for several months and it was more than enough for one person. The ship slowly rolled out of the hangar and he steered it to the takeoff field. He revved up the engines and took off. There was no person anywhere and within a few minutes he was out of sight from the ground. His heart was banging from nerves and excitement, but once he had entered the course to Frejja into the computer system, he engaged the autopilot and was able to sit back and calm down. In one week, he would go through the first tunnel and accelerate in speed.

Thole was glad the trip would take four months. He needed time to think. The fact that he would most likely never see Metissa again did not upset him at all. After they married, he discovered her true personality and he had lost all feelings for her. She only loved herself and he even questioned if she had any love for their son. He had surprised her several times hitting Soren for minor disobedience and he had had to grab her and threaten her to make her stop. The true price he paid for his escape was the loss of his son. Soren had announced that he also wanted to be a pilot without having a clue about the savagery involved in the killing sprees. This fact was hidden from the Morekian people who were led to believe the people of the invaded planets willingly shared what they had with the Morekians. Many citizens sensed the truth, but were too afraid to talk about it.

Religion did not exist on Morekia, but Thole had always felt a strong connection to his soul and that's why he had to end his career as an invader and killer. Information was restricted on Morekia and the government only allowed the people to know what conformed with their agenda. Lifestyles on other planets were unknown to the Morekians. Thole felt he had to know and during each invasion he had tried to find information through the computer system. Sometimes he could not find anything of value, but several times he had found exactly what he needed and copied it. Alone at home, he would watch the holographic programs with amazement and understood finally what true democracy was and that Morekia was a full dictatorship. The more he learned, the angrier he became. He felt trapped and suffocated by the government, but he kept his feelings to himself. To speak out against the government elite meant severe punishment and probably loss of his life. He had destroyed all the holographic programs before he left; the less the government knew about him the better off he was.

The stifling mood running throughout the Morekian society had ended all creativity and nothing new was invented. Fear permeated people's minds. The population was intelligent, but endless propaganda and mind control had taken its toll and the citizens were apathetic.

They remained silent, obedient and just hoped to live out their lives in reasonable safety.

Thole spent his days meditating, exercising to stay in shape and just resting. He was flying with his lights off and only switched them on as he entered the tunnels. Slowly he reached a mental state of inner peace and he did not regret his decision to escape. If he would be killed as he landed on Frejja, so be it.

******

Metissa waited anxiously for Thole to return. Soren had asked several times where his dad was. It was holiday and they were supposed to visit with family, but without Thole home there was no point in going to their relatives. Finally, Metissa contacted Thole's supervisor at work and asked if Thole was working. She told him Thole had disappeared and she had no idea where he was. The supervisor had high regard for Thole and as one of his best pilots he felt he had to look for him. He also liked Thole a lot and he told Metissa he would check the aircraft area and report back to her. Metissa decided to stay home until she heard back from the supervisor.

When the supervisor saw the door to the hangar open, he knew something was very wrong. He saw right away that one ship was missing and then he spotted the trackers on the floor and realized Thole had run away.

"Why, Thole, you were part of the elite, you had a top salary and a privileged lifestyle. Why did you do this?" he half cried to himself.

He contacted the commanding officer of Thole's department hoping to find him home and sighed with relief when he answered his communicator. After he had explained the situation to the officer there was dead silence several minutes. Something like this had never happened before.

"Was he alone?" the officer barked.

"I don't know, but I believe he was. No one else seems to be missing," the supervisor responded nervously.

"With no trackers on the ship, there is no way we can find him even if our whole fleet would search for him. He could be anywhere by now. Can you guess what planet he went to?"

"No one seems to know anything about his plan and his wife had no clue either. She contacted me so it's obvious he didn't tell her either. I can't even guess why he did this. He seemed perfectly happy with his life so I'm as surprised as you are."

"I'll contact the government and we take it from there. This is outrageous. If we ever find the bastard he'll be hanged," he scoffed and ended the conversation.

Intense investigation followed and no information was found. Thole had been very careful and had left no evidence behind. The government interrogated Metissa and threatened her, but had to give up when they realized she spoke the truth and really had no idea where Thole was. There was nothing they could do and they understood they had to wait and see. No information was released to the public and Metissa was ordered to shut up or else. She fabricated a story that Thole was away on a mission and that solved the problem for the time being. The government suspected there was a chance they would be invaded and all the pilots were instructed to be ready for a possible war situation. Their orders were classified and the people knew nothing as usual.

******

Thole was landing on Frejja next to their fleet of spaceships. He was totally calm and trusted that the guidance he had received from within would protect him. He stopped the ship close to what looked like the official government building, opened the hatch and with a large white flag in his hand he slowly climbed down to the ground. His arrival had been spotted on the screen inside the building and an armed guard had assembled. Thole calmly stood next to his ship with his flag up and just waited. It was obvious to anyone looking that this was not a threatening situation and two of the officers walked out to him with the armed guard behind them but without weapons drawn.

"I am Thole from the planet Morekia orbiting the star Zester," he said using his translation device. "I come alone in peace and ask for asylum. I am unarmed and my ship has no trackers. I humbly ask you to allow me to stay and I turn my ship over to you to keep."

The officers needed a moment to recover from the surprise. A Morekian, known for the utmost cruelty and considered savages throughout the civilized universe, asking for asylum? Finally, one of them said with a welcoming voice -

"Thole, we welcome you and will grant you asylum." He stretched out his hand and shook hands with Thole. Both men felt the importance of the moment. This was perhaps the beginning of a new chapter in history for both the Morekians and the universe.

The officers waved the armed guard away and they walked into the conference room. The next several hours Thole explained everything and the president of Frejja had joined them together with the commanding officers of the space fleet. This was the first of many meetings Thole had with the Frejjan officials and he revealed how the government operated on his home planet, how they raided defenseless planets and terrorized the people, often killing them by the thousands. The suffering of the Morekian citizens who did not want to live in a dictatorship but had no way out. Everything he knew he revealed to them. He did not spare himself either and disclosed his own actions and how he finally had come to the realization that he could not continue with the raids and must escape to ask for help from other planets to put a stop to the Morekian insanity. Thole made sure to give the Frejjans the names of all the members of the elite he knew of.

Thole moved into a house in the neighborhood and was told to just rest and try to learn the Frejjan language. He had been offered to stay permanently on Frejja and work as a pilot and he had accepted, but he was told he must learn the Frejjan language before he could start working. His living expenses would be paid for by the government until he started working. Using his translation device, he struggled with pronunciation and learning the Frejjan vocabulary. The family living next to his house befriended him and when they heard his story, they went out of their way to help him. He spent many evenings in their house and enjoyed the warm atmosphere of the family and he realized that in his married life with Metissa, they had never had a truly loving home. With the help of this family, he started to become more and more proficient in the language and was able to make himself understood without the translation device. He found the Frejjan people very attractive with their warm personalities and good looks, especially the girls with their clean features. He had decided to divorce Metissa and had sent a message to her using the Internet, but if she had received it or not, he did not know. She had not responded. There was an Interstellar Internet, but it was not always reliable. He was fully aware he would probably never find a wife and he had resigned himself to that fact. What he did not know was that one of the daughters of the neighbor family, Terrin, thought he was quite handsome and was attracted to him.

Frejja contacted Arrynia and two other planets not too far from Morekia and briefed them on Thole and the surprising facts he had revealed about life on Morekia. An alliance was formed. Together they would take out the Morekian elite and liberate the citizens. Using the Zero Point Field, the alliance contacted the Morekian government and requested their presence on Frejja for negotiations. No response. A second try also failed. It was obvious that a peaceful solution using mediation would not work and the only way to deal with the elite on Morekia was by force. The alliance had a combined fleet of ninety fighter spaceships versus thirty Morekian ships. A final message was sent to the Morekian government that a full invasion consisting of ships from four planets would take place and this was their last chance to capitulate. *You don't stand a chance*, they were told. There was no response for two days and then, to everyone's surprise and relief, a message came in saying *we surrender*. The Morekian government understood Thole had informed the Frejjans how the Morekian government worked and the details of their defense system.

One passenger spaceship with government officials started the trip to Morekia from Frejja followed by the full fleet of fighter ships. Brandon and Brianna manned one of the ships. Ships from the other planets were also on the way. The pilots knew there would be no bloodshed, but all the ships were needed as a show of force. The passenger ship landed on Morekia and the fighters were hovering above the field. They were an impressive sight and filled the whole sky. Morekia had an oxygen atmosphere similar to Frejja and spacesuits were not needed. A team of Morekian generals accompanied by a battalion of troops met them and the senior general spoke through his translation device -

"The Morekian army and our fleet of ships are at your disposal. We take no orders from our government and from now on we will serve under your command. You may not believe it, but we're relieved you are here and will do everything to help you remove all of our corrupt government officials and form a fully democratic government. Our people have suffered enough and deserve to be set free."

A command was sent to the fleet of fighters to land and one by one they landed on the field. The Morekian troops escorted the pilots to the barracks at the outskirts of the field and food and drinks were offered.

The generals invited the government officials to a huge conference room right next to the hangars and negotiations started. The Frejjans showed the generals the list of names Thole had supplied and asked that they should immediately be removed from office. The senior general nodded and agreed and said that in addition to the names on the list at least another two hundred names could be added. After hours of talking, it was agreed that the whole government should be removed and a new government elected. The worst offenders of the government officials would be incarcerated and the rest would be permanently barred from ever serving in government again.

The citizens were informed that a new government would be formed and people could announce their candidacy for office. Certain educational standards had to be met, but otherwise anyone wanting to serve was welcome.

A busy period followed and hundreds of government people were imprisoned and the rest were let go with the understanding they would never again serve in government. There was no shortage of candidates willing to work for the government and an election took place. Many talented people who had never dared apply for a government job were now serving and full democracy with free speech, equal rights and freedom for all had finally been instated. The citizens were jubilant. Scholars came out of the closet to guide the process and all propaganda was banned. It was truly a new society starting from scratch. Morekia as a terrorist planet had been transformed to a free peace-loving planet. The first mission carried out by the new democratic government was to send formal apologies to every planet that had been a target of the preceding government's invasions assuring them that a new era had begun and Morekia was now a nonviolent and lawful planet.

Metissa had sent a message back to Thole that she agreed to divorce, but Soren stayed with her. She hated Thole and with the new government in place, she had no more entitlements than anyone else and her former privileged lifestyle was over.

Brandon and Brianna found Morekia very interesting and it was a beautiful planet with many similarities to Earth. Since they were on duty, they could not leave the immediate area, but they watched holographic images of the planet and found that Morekia was a lush planet with large trees, lawns and farm fields. Gravity was slightly heavier than on Frejja. On the horizon they saw tall mountains. They were told there were four seasons on Morekia, the same as on Earth.

Half the fighter ships were directed to return to their home planets and when the alliance officials felt confident everything was peaceful and the new government was capable of transforming society to a full democracy, the rest of the ships were ordered to return home. The alliance officials stayed another month to ensure there were no problems and then left Morekia. It had been a successful termination of a rogue government without bloodshed and the Morekians showed their gratitude by hanging Frejjan flags from their windows.

******

Thole followed the news from his home planet with peace in his heart. There were newscasts from Morekia on the Interstellar Internet. He had also received a response from Metissa she agreed to divorce and that Soren would stay with her.

Thole and Terrin spent time together and she showed him the area. They enjoyed each other's company and Thole's wit and humor made Terrin laugh. She found him so pleasant to be with that she always looked forward to their dates. Thole admired Terrin's beauty and loved her personality. They were sitting by a lake talking when Thole took her hand and kissed it. Terrin laughed softly and took his hand in hers.

"Is there a chance you would want me?" Thole said in a low voice in Frejjan. He had no idea what her reply would be.

"Are you blind, silly? I love you to death."

Terrin's straightforward answer startled Thole and he put his arms around Terrin and said -

"I love you, too. Will you marry me?"

"Yes, I look forward to being your wife," she responded.

"Would your parents agree? I am an alien."

"They have known for weeks I'm in love with you and have no objections. Yes, it will be an interracial marriage and I know we cannot have children together, but there are other solutions."

Terrin's parents welcomed Thole into their family and a month later they were married. When Thole tried to explain he had been married on Morekia and was not legally divorced, the government official that officiated at the wedding assured Thole that only Frejjan law was valid and his marital status on Morekia was of no legal consequence. Terrin moved into Thole's house next door and as they got to know each other better, they found there were more similarities between their two races than differences. Biologically, Thole had a human body with the same internal organs as a human and the only difference actually was the appearance of his head. They had been told they could not have children together, but Terrin was not so sure the scientists were right. She secretly hoped they would be rewarded with at least one child. They were so happy with each other and Thole was accepted by Terrin's friends. There was no discrimination.

Thole worked as a domestic pilot so he would not have to be away from Terrin and his trips were seldom longer than two days. Most of his journeys were cargo shipments. He missed space travel, but the thought of being away from home for months was unacceptable. Terrin was the owner of a clothing store and after she married, she only worked part time. Her employees were trustworthy and ran the business well. There was no need for Terrin to work full time.

Thole had been granted citizenship of Frejja. He never wanted to return to Morekia and he suspected that if he would go back even for a visit he would be assassinated by a former member of the elite. The loss of his son was the price he had to pay for peace of mind.

******

Arrynia signed a contract with Frejja and two other planets leasing their ships to facilitate the immigration of Kodetsian people to their planet. To move ten million people using only Arrynian ships would take entirely too long and without using extra ships the whole project would drag on for a lifetime or more. The Kodetsians would have to pay for the trip to their new planet and it was expensive. The size of the ships owned by the other two planets was much larger than the Frejjan and Arrynian ships and had seating for 500 people. The travel time was three months. Travel time in space always depended on the number of tunnels available.

Brandon and Brianna were assigned to make at least one trip between Kodetsia and Arrynia per year and since they had children additional trips were voluntary. Frejjans respected family life and the right of parents to be with their children.

Brandon landed their ship on Kodetsia and found a planet with an oxygen atmosphere and about the same gravity as on Frejja. He thought to himself that the Kodetsians would have to develop strong leg muscles to acclimate to Arrynia's heavy gravity. Everywhere were housing and people. Herds of animals resembling cattle were all over the place, but they also saw some farm fields with grain crops. It was obvious the Kodetsians favored meat. The landscape was mostly flat and there were no mountains visible. It was not a bad looking planet, but Brandon and Brianna found it uninspiring. Compared the beauty of both Earth and Frejja, Kodetsia was dull looking.

The ship was loaded and one hundred and fifty Kodetsians were onboard. They were mostly young people and full of anticipation. The ship took off and the three months went by rather fast. Brandon and Brianna often mingled with the passengers while their two copilots stayed on the Bridge. They found the Kodetsians very kind, highly intelligent and full of gratitude for the chance to start a new life with better conditions than back home. They ate mostly meat, but tried other foods that were offered and seemed to adjust to eating a more varied diet.

After unloading the passengers, Brandon and Brianna picked up cargo from Arrynia and returned to Frejja. It was only five weeks of travel time to Frejja and it would be a whole year until they were scheduled to return to Kodetsia. It had been an interesting trip.

******

With her usual frankness, Terrin turned to Thole and said -
"You're going to be a dad."
Thole looked at her not believing his ears.
"Is this a joke?" he finally said.
"No joke, just facts," Terrin said smiling. "The scientists were wrong, we are compatible. We have only been married four months and I am already expecting. "
Thole was overcome with excitement. The embryo was transferred to the artificial womb and it was a boy, healthy and growing well. Every week Thole and Terrin visited the lab and watched their son grow. The

doctors kept a watchful eye on him, but all was well and the baby was sturdy. When they brought him home, they could not stop admiring him. They named him Ranus and he looked human with just a hint of Morekian. He had blond hair as his mother, a human face and the only features from his father were his green eyes. It was obvious that Terrin's genes were dominant. Terrin's parents were thrilled to meet their grandson.

CHAPTER 23

A steady stream of ships landed on Kodetsia and departed after a few hours filled with people. At first the government, often referred to as The Elders, did not seem to care and felt it was not a bad thing to lower the population, but when a million people had left, they started to feel some concern. What was happening? Would it ever stop? Why did people leave?

Kodetsia was a mild dictatorship, by no means as bad as the former Morekia, but nevertheless ruled by an elitist government of mostly males with hardcore, rigid religious beliefs. The government was not elected by the people; senior members of the government appointed people when an empty seat had to be filled. Corruption and bribery were evident everywhere in the government and people feared the authorities.

One of the Elders, a man of advanced years named Pretos, finally approached a young man on his staff, Jonni, who he knew was very bright and well informed about what was happening in the society.

"Please come to my office and let's talk," he said to Jonni and when they were seated, he continued -

"What's going on and why are people leaving? Don't be afraid to speak your mind. All I ask for is the truth. You will not lose your job so don't hesitate to be straightforward."

Jonni felt he could trust Pretos and poured out his heart to the Elder. He told him how people struggled to feed themselves, how they wanted birth control to lessen the number of children they had, how they wished there would be universal suffrage, equal rights for all and not only for the elite, the citizens' fear of the government and that so many of them preferred a secular rather than a religious government. When he was finally finished Pretos sat silently for many minutes and then said -

"I'm old and have seen different variants of government. I really believed our government in its present form served the citizens, but listening to you I now understand that people suffer. Especially if they don't have enough to eat. I will request a meeting with the rest of the government members and see if we can come to an agreement to change the way this government operates."

Jonni left and returned to his desk. He knew Pretos would not fire him, but his supervisor might and, sure enough, he did fire him by a pretense that he had been negligent in his duties. As he was emptying his desk Pretos stopped by. He had heard that Jonni had been fired and was furious with Jonni's supervisor and fired him on the spot.

"Jonni, you're a valued employee. I fired your supervisor and ask you to stay on. I gave you my word you wouldn't be fired and I intend to keep it. By the way, would you consider becoming my personal assistant? I could use a young, bright guy like you to work for me."

"It would be an honor, sir," Jonni exclaimed enthusiastically.

"Now that you have packed, let's just take your belongings over to my office and you can have the office right next to mine. It's empty and from now on you are my personal assistant starting immediately. I double your salary."

This was the beginning of a productive working relationship between Pretos and Jonni; a merger between old wisdom and young ingenuity. Jonni was a genius at sniffing out the mood of the country and with his friendly, outgoing personality people often confided in him. Jonni never revealed his sources by name and was very discreet. Pretos valued his input and was pleased with his work. Jonni was full of ideas and most of them were implemented.

Some of the government members were inflexible and Pretos persuaded them to retire. The rest were won over on a one-by-one basis. The Elders finally understood the people were living in hardship and some changes had to be made. Three important decisions were agreed upon and became law. The government issued a news release declaring -

1.   *Birth control is legal.*

2.   *Universal suffrage with democratic elections and term limits for government officials will take effect immediately.*

3.   *Elections will be held within six months.*

4.   *Government must be secular.*

The news release astonished the society and many of the people on the waiting list to emigrate to Arrynia withdrew their names from the list. The government kept their promise and elections were held after a few months. Pretos and most of the Elders were reelected, but many new people won government seats and the end result was a secular, democratic government the people could live with. Best of all, the fear of the government was gone and the mood of the country was now optimistic and hopeful. Pretos and Jonni continued to fine-tune the workings of government and society and made sure the food supply was increased so no one had to go hungry. The number of citizens emigrating to Arrynia shrunk to five million instead of ten million and with birth control now legal the population continued to shrink in the coming decades.

******

The alliance between Frejja, Arrynia and the other two planets became permanent and a defense treaty was signed into effect. Mars and Earth were invited to join and both agreed to become members. To everyone's surprise Morekia humbly asked if they were allowed to join and the member planets all concurred. Interstellar news released the defense treaty and on Jonni's recommendation, Pretos applied on behalf of Kodetsia and they also were granted membership in the alliance. The combined fleet of fighter spaceships was formidable and any rogue planet trying to take over one of the member planets would face a combined force of eight planets. The defense treaty was named The Orion-Cygnus Alliance referring to the approximate location of the planets in the Milky Way.

******

Karol was reading her copy of the Alliance in her office when a guard stormed into her office.

"Mr. Clifford has had an accident. Come quickly to the hospital!" he shouted.

Karol tried to calm herself and followed the guard. They traveled in a small electric vehicle inside the tunnel system and reached the hospital within five minutes. She ran with the guard to Ryan's room and found him unconscious in his bed. The doctors worked frantically to restart his heart to no avail. He was dead. The doctors quietly left the room. There was nothing more they could do.

Karol was totally numb. Her beloved husband who she adored was gone. She collapsed in the chair next to his bed and cried uncontrollably. Finally, she was able to sit up and took his hand. Ryan had been the only man in her life and the love of her life. A doctor entered the room and sat down next to her and started to explain -

"Mr. Clifford was driving a Rover several miles from Martia. We believe he was on his way to inspect one of the mines. The Rover hit a large rock that was probably covered with sand and not visible and his vehicle overturned. His oxygen pack was crushed, but he was able to contact us with his communicator and we had a manned cargo drone there within five minutes. The medic found him dead when he arrived from lack of air and even though he had a tank of oxygen with him he couldn't revive him. We tried to restart his heart but he didn't respond. My deepest sympathy, Mrs. Clifford."

Karol nodded, too shaken to speak. After the funeral, Karol felt like a machine. She had six months left in office and was too numb to figure out what to do with the rest of her life. Alison was eight years old, but Elliot was now twenty-three and an adult. He had told her he would decide where he would live when Karol herself had figured out what planet she would live on. Elliot was very attached to his mother and preferred to live in close proximity to her. He was working as a male nurse.

A few months later Emrak landed his cargo ship on Mars and heard the sad news about Ryan. Emrak and Karol knew each other rather well and would always visit when he landed his ship on Mars. They respected each other and Emrak admired Karol's leadership abilities and her humble personality. Her status had never gone to her head and she remained unspoiled and gracious to all. She also had retained her femininity.

Emrak had one week to spend on Mars before he had to return to Frejja and they met every day. Karol found him comforting and was grateful for his company. Emrak was so calm and polite, never imposing.

He was nice looking with his blond hair starting to turn silver grey. At the end of his stay, he took Karol's hand and asked her if she would want to marry him. Karol was so surprised that she had to sit down.

Emrak had learned to speak English well enough to be understood.

"Karol, I am fifty-five years old and have never been married because of my work. If you would agree to marry me, I would be honored to take care of you and Alison and if Elliot would want to live with us, he would be more than welcome to do so. I would ask for a transfer from space travel and request to become a flight instructor so I would be home every night. You are very dear to me."

"Emrak, I don't know what to say," Karol responded in a surprised voice. "I have four months left of my presidential term. Can I give you an answer when you return to Mars?"

"I'm scheduled to be back here in four months. Can you at least give me a hint if you will say yes or no?"

"There's no man in my life except you and you have a special place in my heart, so it will probably be a 'yes'. But I need to talk to Elliot and sort out my feelings. If I decide before you are back, I will contact you wherever you are."

"You can always reach me over the Internet. Use this address." Emrak gave her an Interstellar address and hugged her.

After Emrak left, Karol talked to Elliot and his response was immediate -

"Dad is dead and you're only forty-five years old. You can't spend the rest of your life alone. Emrak is a great guy, I like him a lot and if you're asking for my consent, Mom, you have it. He would make a good husband and Dad wouldn't mind, I know that. He would want you to be happy. By the way, I would accept Emrak's offer to stay with you on Frejja for a few months and then look for a place of my own. This way the family stays together. I wouldn't mind at all to live on Frejja."

His frank answer enabled Karol to think through what she wanted and she found that her feelings for Emrak were very strong and a life with him would be better than spending the rest of her life alone. Alison needed a father and Karol was not too old to have another child. Frejjan men lived to one hundred and twenty years on average, slightly longer than men on Earth. She made up her mind and sent Emrak a message:

My answer is yes and I look forward to becoming your wife. Alison and Elliot both agree with my decision and all of us look forward to your return. We send our love. Karol.

A few days later Emrak responded:

I'm the happiest man on Frejja. Your Emrak.

By the time Emrak returned Karol had everything packed and organized. A new president, Mr. Taylor, had already taken over and Karol felt inner peace. She had said goodbye to Ryan in her heart and soul and asked for his approval. In two days, she and Emrak would be married on Mars and a Martian official would officiate. Emrak had bought a house on Frejja and some of the furniture and they would finish the house together.

When Emrak put the ring on her finger, Karol felt waves of love for him. She had no hesitation and looking into his loving eyes she saw he felt the same. Karol looked very attractive with her hair out and a light blue dress. Elliot and Alison were all smiles. It was the beginning of a marriage that would span more than half a century.

The return trip to Frejja went well and with Emrak as the captain they were allowed visits on the Bridge. Elliot was fascinated with the instrumentation even though he was not mechanically inclined and Karol enjoyed just sitting on the Bridge watching her new husband handle the ship. This was Emrak's last trip commanding a spaceship and he told Karol he would not miss it. He had had a long career and seen everything he wanted to see.

It was exciting to land on Frejja, their new home, and breathe fresh air without a spacesuit. When all the baggage was loaded into the airmobile, they took off. It took about two hours to reach their new home and Karol liked what she saw when she looked out the window. Frejja was a lovely looking planet, green and lush and not crowded. The airmobile gently descended and landed in front of a large house with a big lawn and flower arrangements.

"It's lovely! It's a house fit for a queen," Karol blurted out while admiring the house and the yard.

"But *you are* my queen, my dear wife," Emrak responded and kissed her on the cheek.

Alison jumped up and down and clapped hands and Elliot whistled to show his approval.

The inside of the house was just as lovely as the outside. It was almost new and Emrak showed Alison and Elliot their rooms. The master bedroom was huge and Karol was in love with the house already. Emrak had spent a small fortune for the property, but he could afford it. He had worked his whole life and as a single man he had had few expenses. Now he was glad he had saved his money so he could afford to supply for his new family.

Emrak had hired a tutor and every day Karol, Elliot and Alison had lessons in the Frejjan language as well as reading and writing. Emrak stayed home three weeks and he and Karol finished furnishing the house. After Emrak started working Karol found she looked forward to his homecoming and they enjoyed each other's company. He told Karol he really liked his new job training young pilots everything there was to know about space travel.

Karol, Alison and Elliot became Frejjan citizens automatically when Karol married Emrak and that would make it easier for Elliot to find employment.

Elliot worked very hard learning the new language and was advancing. He was eager to start working and finding a small starter house. He was taking nursing courses over the Internet to catch up with the medical technology on Frejja and he told Karol Mars and Earth were almost a hundred years behind Frejja. His days were long and after six months he felt ready to apply for a job. To his relief he got the job and moved out. The hospital was only half an hour from their house and through the hospital he found a house he could share with a Frejjan man who worked at the hospital lab. Most weekends he spent with his family, but Emrak and Karol knew that if he would meet a girl, they would not see him too often. Emrak and Elliot got along well and were great friends.

Emrak had asked Karol if he could adopt Alison and Karol told him she would be most grateful if he did. When the process was over, Alison started calling Emrak 'Dad'. It was her own idea and Emrak was touched when she snuggled up in his lap and they watched a hologram together. Alison would never forget Ryan, but he was dead and she now had a father who she could sense loved her and she loved him back.

Emrak considered her his daughter. He and Ryan had liked each other and he knew Ryan would have approved of him as Alison's new father.

Alison started school and was put in a special class where she received language lessons. She eventually caught up with the other children and enjoyed school. Karol continued taking lessons from the tutor and did not stop until she mastered speaking, reading and writing reasonably well. She was not fluent in the language, but was able to converse with Emrak in Frejjan without the translation device. Emrak continued with his English lessons and they sometimes talked in English so he could practice. Their married life was happy and they had a deep love for each other. Karol never regretted her decision to marry Emrak and make Frejja her new home. She liked the planet and the people, the easy climate and laid-back lifestyle.

To Karol's surprise she became pregnant after a few months of marriage. She had not expected she would conceive that easily considering her age. Emrak was thrilled when he heard the news and when the embryo was transferred to the artificial womb, they were told it was a healthy boy. Karol used the time while they were waiting for the baby to grow to full term to furnish the nursery. The magic day came when they picked their son up and Alison was waiting at home for her little brother. They named him Leo.

Emrak bought an android, Tyra, to help with the household chores and Karol appreciated her help. She needed a helper in the house and Tyra was the latest model with ability to speak English as well as Frejjan. She could handle cooking, cleaning, baby care, just about anything around the house. She was also very kind.

Karol had sent a message to Mr. Parker about Ryan's death and her remarriage to Emrak and that she now was a citizen of Frejja. He was truly surprised to hear the news and they decided to get together for a visit later on. It was quite a distance from Karol's area to the capital Raano, where Mr. Parker lived, so the visit would have to be postponed for a while. He told Karol he had two children, a daughter four years old and a son one year old. Karol congratulated him and felt so happy for him. She knew he had dreamt of having a family. Mr. Parker also mentioned that if she ever wanted a government job, there were several openings just below the presidential level that would fit her. Karol declined and told him that as a new mother all she wanted was to be home with her children.

CHAPTER 24

A strange looking spaceship, resembling a 'crocodile' without the tail, docked with the workstation where Emrak had picked up the four Kodetsian passengers. The ship needed some minor repairs and the crew of the ship did not resemble any beings the workstation crew had ever seen before. They were a variant of humanoid with human bodies, no hair on the sides of their heads, but with thick spiked, black hair running from the top of the forehead to the back of their skull and ending in a ponytail that was a foot long. The spiked hair was about three inches tall. Their eyes, nose, mouth and ears were human looking, but they had heavy, ridged eyebrows forming a 'v' starting between the eyes and ending above the ears. Each cheek had what looked like an animal ear growing out of the cheek. Their skin was slightly tanned in color. The men had beautiful, deep voices and the language sounded choppy and harsh. They were impressive looking, tall and muscular. Their brown uniforms were made of leather and they were apparently able to breathe oxygen, because they had no helmets on. They did not look overly friendly.

Using the translation device, the crew of the workstation asked what planet they came from and were told they were from the Pleiades group of stars in the constellation Taurus. The workstation crew was stunned. The Pleiades group was four hundred light years away! How was it possible? The mechanics of the workstation decided it was safest not to ask any more questions and quickly finished the repair work and the ship took off right away. The aliens paid with gold, which was one of several acceptable ways of payment among planets.

One of the mechanics on the workstation knew about The Orion-Cygnus Alliance and reported the incident to the Alliance. The workstation had only a minor defense system and the mechanic felt unsafe. The look of the aliens gave the impression that they were warriors and not merchants.

The message reached Frejja and the government contacted Emrak for advice. He had the most experience of all the pilots and knew every corner of space within twenty light years from Frejja. Together with several other pilots and the space fleet officials they looked at their maps of the universe and saw the huge distance the aliens had traveled.

"There must be a gigantic shortcut tunnel they use that we don't know about," Emrak concluded. "It would take more than a lifetime to travel that distance with just the standard number of tunnels that we know exist. The important thing is why are they in our area and are they a threat?"

A short time later the ship landed on Mars. The only defense the Martians had were the six fighter spaceships they had bought from Frejja and the Frejjans had trained twelve pilots how to fly the ships.

Mr. Taylor, the new president of Martia and Karol's successor, waited in the lobby of the government building as the aliens dressed in spacesuits walked towards the lobby. There were only two of them and the rest of the crew stayed on the ship. They entered the lobby and removed their helmets and the look of their faces gave Mr. Taylor the shivers. They had a translation device.

"We are from a planet in the Pleiades group of stars called Peturun orbiting the star Sentallius. I'm Tothellim. We're merchants looking to buy large amounts of the mineral terrynium, which we know is plentiful here on Mars. There is no terrynium left in our corner of the Milky Way and we need the mineral to produce a metal alloy that is used in manufacturing, especially our spaceships, but also in many other applications."

Mr. Taylor had managed to calm himself and responded through the translation device -

"Tothellim, I'm the president of Martia, Mr. Taylor. It's true that we have plenty of terrynium and we have no idea what to do with it so it hasn't been mined. It's easy to extract since the mine is open and within one week, we could probably fill your ship to capacity. We require payment in gold."

Tothellim looked pleased, even relieved, and agreed to pay with gold.

The following day a purchase agreement was arranged and mining started at full speed. All the available robots were ordered to work in the terrynium mine and load after load was wheeled out on the rail system and then transported to the ship. The cargo space of the ship was huge and terrynium was not a heavy metal by weight so the ship was filled to capacity.

The Peturuns stayed on their ship the whole time. Tothellim invited Mr. Taylor onboard and the ship was fully pressurized with good air quality. The Bridge was a marvelous showpiece with electronics that Mr. Taylor had never seen before and he realized that the aliens were perhaps a hundred, maybe two hundred years ahead of the Martians in technology development.

As Mr. Taylor and Tothellim sat and talked on the Bridge, Mr. Taylor asked -

"You told me it took you only six months to reach Mars. How can you travel four hundred light years in such a short time?"

"There's one tunnel just outside the Pleiades and it's an enormous shortcut. You go through it and end up not far from the workstation where we had repairs. We actually did experience a minor injury to the ship going through the tunnel and that's why we had to have repairs at the workstation. The tunnel takes one day to travel through and all ships going through the tunnel must be made with the terrynium metal alloy to withstand the vibration and heat in the tunnel. You fly through the tunnel with manual control as the tunnel is not straight and seems to almost float in space.   It takes an experienced pilot to control the ship through the tunnel. Let me show you the location of the tunnel."

Tothellim showed a holographic map of the Milky Way and the exact location of the tunnel and recorded the map for Mr. Taylor to keep. In spite of the fearsome appearance of the aliens, Mr. Taylor found Tothellim rather pleasant and by no means threatening. The aliens were humanoids breathing air like humans and looked like humans except for the look of their heads.

"Could you teach us how to make the terrynium alloy?" Mr. Taylor asked in a hopeful voice.

"We'll give you the formula," Tothellim replied "but you'll need special facilities to manufacture the alloy and I can see you are not as advanced as our people. For example, your spaceships would break apart in the tunnel and probably burn up. I need to discuss the matter with my people before I give you the formula and we can talk about it the next time we come here."

Tothellim had asked Mr. Taylor if they could return in six months for another shipment and Mr. Taylor had agreed. They were well paid in gold and the income would boost the Martian economy. Tothellim had contacted his planet and another spaceship had already departed from Peturun to pick up a second load of terrynium from Mars.

After the Peturuns left, Mr. Taylor assembled a team of geologists and asked them to map the locations of known deposits of terrynium and also try to find new areas where terrynium may be available. Their report came back two months later with positive results confirming that Mars had huge amounts of terrynium and all of it close to the surface and easy to extract. If Mars sold all of it, the Martians would become rich.

Mr. Taylor notified the member planets of the Alliance that the alien ship was not a threat but merchants buying terrynium and that he had received the location of the shortcut tunnel, which he included with his message.

Emrak read the message with interest and realized that he had seen the exit of the tunnel where the Peturuns came out of the tunnel. He had passed it several times without realizing it was a tunnel, but he had noticed strange vibrations in the area and had always made a wide passage around it to stay safe. None of the member planets in the Alliance had any knowledge of the terrynium alloy and all they could do was to wait and hope they would receive the formula from the Peturuns and start manufacturing the alloy. Emrak realized that even he, with thirty years of space travel under his belt, would need instructions how to navigate the tunnel. He also wondered to himself whether the Peturuns would be willing to share their knowledge with pilots of the Alliance. Were there rogue planets in the Pleiades area with knowledge of the tunnel? Would they invade planets in this corner of the Milky Way? Emrak felt concern and knew anything was possible.

Back home again, he forgot all worries with Alison and Leo in his lap. Being a father was the best experience he had ever been exposed to.

Karol had heard from her adopted son Kenny that he was now married and intended to stay on Earth. She knew she would probably never see him again, but she must respect his free will.

******

Adora and Drujin were still living on Mars and seventeen years had passed since they arrived. They had only one child, a ten-year-old daughter Ingrid. At thirty-eight years of age, Adora was an experienced doctor and enjoyed her work, but ever since Cellie, Gordon and Jonas moved to Frejja four years ago she felt sad. She had lost a close friend and her distant relatives Brandon and Brianna and Brianna's parents all lived on Frejja as did Arvin. Adora and Drujin had only made one trip to Earth to visit their families and lately Adora had made hints to Drujin she wanted to move to Frejja. Adora's parents, Dawn and Kai, had no interest in moving to Frejja and Dawn was now almost seventy years old and felt she and Kai were too old to relocate to another planet. Drujin was not against the idea and knew Frejja had advanced technology and he could probably get another job working with robots and androids. He announced to Adora -

"Let's do it. I'm ready for a new adventure."

Adora, Drujin and Ingrid all started taking Frejjan language lessons and booked seats on a Frejjan ship to leave in six months. Adora notified Cellie they were moving to Frejja and would settle in their area. It was not too far from Raano, the capital. Clarence and Lotte lived closer to Raano, but with an airmobile the distance was not far. Brandon's and Brianna's sons were almost adults and Rigel was twenty years old and Orion seventeen.

The three of them landed on Frejja and felt the magic of breathing fresh air and being without a spacesuit. Cellie and Gordon waited for them at the immigrants' hotel where they would stay the standard month to learn more of the language and Frejjan customs. When Adora saw Cellie she knew she had made the right decision and she gave Cellie a big hug. The first month passed very quickly and they found a house just ten minutes away from Cellie's.

Drujin bought a translation device to aid in his pronunciation and after they had furnished their house, he immediately looked for a job. His command of Frejjan was below par, but he was ambitious and his energetic personality came through when he discussed employment with his potential employer. He got the job. It was similar to his Martian job, but more demanding and the technology was more advanced than he was used to, so he knew he would have to work hard to just catch up with his coworkers. It was a challenge he welcomed.

Adora stayed home the first two months to get more proficient in the language and had hired a tutor to help her. She could manage a simple conversation and started looking for a job. There was a hospital not too far away and she inquired about work, but when they became aware of her poor language skills, she was told she had to be more fluent in Frejjan before she could be hired. Adora stayed home another two months working tirelessly to get better at speaking Frejjan and then reapplied for a job. This time she was hired. Adora was an excellent doctor, but the advanced medical equipment was new to her and she had to enroll in classes after work to learn how to handle the machines. It would take her a full year to master all the equipment. She worked four days a week so there was plenty of time to experience Frejja and make day trips.

Ingrid started school and liked it a lot. Cellie had promised Ingrid that whenever she wanted to she was welcome to work part time with Cellie in the insect business. Cellie's business was booming and she had four people hired and three worker robots. Ingrid had visited the building and was fascinated. As soon as she had mastered the Frejjan language she would start, she told Cellie.

All the relatives got together several times a year and relished seeing each other, comparing Frejja with Mars and Earth and enjoying speaking English. Maija was popular and liked Arvin's relatives and her English was good enough so she had no trouble understanding everything that was said. Fenul was already five years old and had also a newborn sister Rhea. Fenul and Jonas were growing up together as brothers even though they were uncle and nephew. They were both bilingual and spoke Frejjan and English fluently. They had just started school.

******

Elections were held on Frejja and Mr. Parker was running for president. As expected, Mr. Parker won by a landslide and people had great confidence in him. Everyone admired the new system Mr. Parker had organized and the free services the citizens benefitted from.

Once Mr. Parker was president, he asked Karol if she wanted to be his consultant and she agreed. There was no need to go to Raano and any advice she would offer Mr. Parker could be done using a communicator and a private channel over the Internet. Many aspects of the presidency were unfamiliar to Mr. Parker, but Karol knew them inside out. Their working relationship would last the two terms Mr. Parker was president.

******

The second spaceship arrived from Peturun and this time the terrynium had all been mined and was ready to be loaded. The captain of the ship brought with him the formula how to manufacture the terrynium alloy and detailed instructions how to build the manufacturing facility. All of it was complicated and required sophisticated machinery that Mars did not have. Mr. Taylor took a chance and tossed out a suggestion to the captain -

"You'll get this whole shipment of terrynium for free if you give us the machinery we need to set up a manufacturing plant to make the alloy. We'll pay for the buildings and all the materials ourselves. The minerals to make the alloy are also available here on Mars. The only thing you'll need to supply are the machines needed that we don't have. We'll also require a team of your experts to oversee the building of the plant and that they stay here on Mars until the plant is functioning properly. Let me summarize, you get a whole shipment of terrynium for free in exchange for the machines needed for the plant and a team of your experts. Your team will of course receive a salary."

The captain looked quite amused and thought about it for a while, then laughed heartily and said -

"It's a deal," and they shook hands.

Mr. Taylor was beyond delighted. They were swimming in terrynium and a free shipment was of no consequence in exchange for technology that was unavailable on Mars and probably on all the planets of the Alliance as well. The alloy was state of the art and would enable the Martians to build spaceships with ability to travel through the new shortcut tunnel and reach a part of the Milky Way that no one from this corner of the galaxy had ever seen.

The captain spent the next few days with several Martian engineers explaining the size of the buildings that would be needed and instructed them to start the project right away and in six months a Peturun spaceship would arrive with all the equipment they needed and the workmen from his planet. The ship would buy another load of terrynium so it would not return without a cargo and leave the workmen on Mars to oversee construction of the plant.

When Mr. Taylor inquired about what diet the workmen required, the captain replied that anything the Martians ate would be fine for the workmen. They were humanoids and had the same dietary needs as the Martians.

During the next six months the buildings were completed and by the time the Peturun ship arrived, the team of engineers and workmen on Mars were all ready to start. Eight Peturun specialists oversaw all details of the installation of the machines and layout of the interior. It was an exciting time for Martia. The terrynium had to be mixed with two other minerals that were also available in abundance on Mars and it was a magic day when production started. The Peturuns instructed the Martians about all the details of making the alloy, things to watch for, quality control and how to cut the finished alloy. They were truly thorough and Mr. Taylor was so pleased he decided to offer a second shipment of terrynium for free which the Peturuns gratefully accepted. Every six months a Peturun ship arrived and filled up with terrynium.

The plant was in full operation and the first spaceship was under construction built entirely with the new alloy. Emrak was aware of the new plant and the alloy and had questioned Mr. Taylor about the new terrynium spaceship and if they had any pilots capable of controlling the ship in the shortcut tunnel. Mr. Taylor had to admit that he had not yet addressed that problem, but was hoping to find a solution. Emrak suggested that Brandon and Brianna would be the best choice and were regarded as the most experienced pilots Frejja had. They were also fully trained fighter ship pilots. Mr. Taylor knew of Brandon and Brianna and asked Emrak to find out if they would be willing to start training to negotiate the tunnel.

Emrak found Brandon and Brianna home for the standard three weeks between flights and contacted them over the Internet. When they heard of the new spaceship and the shortcut tunnel their curiosity was instantly piqued.

"It's not risk free," Emrak cautioned. "It will be the maiden trip of a spaceship made with all new materials and there is no track record. You'll have to alternate controlling the ship through the tunnel and the tunnel is not straight. The smallest mistake and you'll damage the ship and possibly crash. It takes a whole day to travel through the tunnel and when you're out of it, you will be in a section of the Milky Way that's totally unfamiliar to you."

Brandon and Brianna looked at Emrak's holographic image in front of them and both knew they could not refuse to accept the challenge. Their sons were almost adults and not dependent on them anymore and this would be the adventure of a lifetime. They looked at each other and nodded.

"Tell Mr. Taylor we accept and will start training immediately," Brandon responded.

Emrak chuckled and said -

"I knew you couldn't resist."

Brandon and Brianna notified their supervisor they had to take some time off to train for the Martian project. The flight instructors at their former school reprogrammed the flight simulator to show a tunnel that resembled the shortcut tunnel as closely as possible and the training began. To travel through a standard tunnel in space seldom took longer than half an hour, but a tunnel long enough to require a full day of travel would be a challenge indeed and Brandon and Brianna had no illusions about the hardship they would endure controlling the ship manually a whole day.

They worked hard and after several months they were able to hold the ship steady in the center of the tunnel and gently follow the tunnel's curvature. Fast reactions were needed as the tunnel 'floated' slightly back and forth and the pilot could not ease off for a minute.

Brandon and Brianna flew as passengers to Mars and reported to Mr. Taylor. They had never met before and Mr. Taylor's first thought when he saw them was *what a handsome couple*. Indeed, they were in their dark blue uniforms with gold insignia. Brandon was fifty-two years and Brianna forty-eight and both were rather tall. They exuded self-confidence that only years of experience bring.

The maiden trip was planned for the following day and was a short day-trip to familiarize themselves with the ship. Brandon and Brianna would decide themselves when they felt ready to start the trip to the Pleiades and Mr. Taylor told them they could fly as many practice trips as they wanted. There was no rush.

It took six flights until Brandon and Brianna felt comfortable with the controls and how the ship handled. The ship had dual manual controls in addition to autopilot and it handled slightly different than the ships they were used to. It was a combined cargo and passenger ship and was twice as large as the cargo ships they had flown to the Moon, but smaller than the Frejjan passenger ships.

Finally, Brandon and Brianna embarked for the Pleiades and the ship was loaded with food, two copilots and twelve passengers. The voluntary passengers traveled for free and were fully aware of all the risks involved and had signed agreements they accepted the risk. They were all adventurers and considered the trip to Peturun the biggest event in their lives. The ship would land on Peturun to refuel and then return back to Mars. There was no cargo onboard as this was the maiden trip through the tunnel and Brandon and Brianna felt a light weight ship was preferable when they traveled through the tunnel.

After going through two standard tunnels, they reached the entry of the long tunnel. Outside the tunnel they felt strong vibrations and a strange gravitational pull towards the tunnel. Brandon was at the controls manually flying the spaceship and Brianna was at the second controls. They would have to take turns flying the ship through the demanding tunnel. Brandon nodded to Brianna and they entered the tunnel. The vibration was more powerful than they had ever experienced and required a firm grip on the control. Just as they had been told, the tunnel appeared to 'float' and waved back and forth requiring constant adjustment. To hold the ship steady in the center of the tunnel while the ship was shaking violently was difficult. It took twelve hours to cross the tunnel and towards the end both Brandon and Brianna were fatigued. They came out of the tunnel like a bomb at an accelerated speed and now they could safely engage the autopilot and turn the ship over to the copilots. Brandon and Brianna sat down and smiled at each other, relieved and humbled at the same time. It had truly been a challenging experience and the many hours in the flight simulator had paid off. Now it was only two months of easy travel to Peturun.

Brandon entered the coordinates of Peturun and the landing area into the computers and the rest of the trip was easy. Peturun was the size of Earth with an oxygen atmosphere and about the same gravity. As they neared the planet, they saw water bodies and realized it had at least one ocean and the planet appeared to be green and have a lot of vegetation. They made a soft landing and opened the hatch. Tothellim greeted them and he had been in touch with Brandon and Brianna several times during the trip to guide them and answer their questions. They were glad to meet him and were not intimidated by the looks of the Peturun people. Several Peturuns were still working on Mars in the alloy plant and Brandon and Brianna had seen them.

"You made it. Congratulations to you," Tothellim said with a big smile. "Welcome to our planet."

They shook hands and made small talk about the new ship, the alloy and the tunnel. Compared to Mars and Frejja, the gravity felt heavy and Brandon and Brianna had to flex their muscles to walk normally, but they were accustomed to switching between light and heavy gravity and adjusted after a few days. They were taken to a guest house and served dinner at the house as Tothellim knew they just wanted to relax after their long trip. The rest of the crew and passengers were taken to a hotel.

They spent a fascinating week on Peturun and were shown one of the many alloy manufacturing plants and several different models of their spaceships. The society was very modern with high-rise buildings in the cities and the countryside had towns and many farms. Everything seemed clean and orderly and the planet was beautiful. Tothellim told them the total population was three billion. Brandon and Brianna did not feel they should ask too many questions, but Tothellim was talkative and told them many facts about his planet.

"We're at peace now and have been for a hundred years with a democratic government, but in the past this planet was a war zone with endless wars between different groups of people. Everyone hated everyone and it came close to that the whole planet was destroyed and all its people killed. Then, out of nowhere, this man appears with ability to unite us all and to put a stop to the wars. His name was Megonim and we consider him our savior. Now we all live in peace with very little crime and we're lucky to have an honest government that respects the freedom of all citizens. "

"What caused the wars?" Brianna asked.

"Insane desire for power by a small group of elitist people who wouldn't accept defeat," Tothellim replied. "The war industry also made lots of money for the elite and they owned all the manufacturing plants that made the weaponry. They felt no remorse when people died. Then Megonim showed up and made us realize we're all one, one people, and no group of people should have the power to rule over other people. A country can't prosper if the citizens live in fear and have no freedom of speech. Megonim understood the mentality of the elite and with the help of the media and uncorrupted government officials, they were all put in jail. Most of the media had been paid off to support the wars, but there were some who did have the courage to tell the truth. We're all relieved those times are behind us."

Overall, Brandon and Brianna found Peturun attractive and a pleasant planet to live on and the people they met were friendly in spite of their fearsome appearance. There were no aliens on the planet, only the Peturun people. When Brandon asked if immigration was allowed, Tothellim responded that the present population of three billion was considered too small and they would welcome immigrants. Brandon and Brianna kept his comment in mind as they knew of some overcrowded planets with citizens looking for a new planet to move to.

The return trip went by without incidents and the trip through the tunnel seemed less intimidating this second time. They landed on Mars and were greeted by a beaming Mr. Taylor.

"Congratulations! We're so proud of you. Your trip is a milestone in space travel. Let's go to my office and please brief me on all the details."

They spent several hours updating Mr. Taylor and his advisors about Peturun and its people as well as the modern manufacturing plants they had seen. Several holographic images showed the planet and the different factories. Mr. Taylor was all ears and listened eagerly and finally asked -

"Would you consider working for the Martian government as pilots?"

"Our family and children live on Frejja so it wouldn't work. So sorry, but we have to decline your offer," Brianna said. "We would be willing to advise your pilots if they need help. If they go through the same training in the flight simulator as we did, your pilots will be able to learn how to fly through the tunnel safely. We recorded the tunnel and will give you a copy."

When Brandon and Brianna returned to Frejja they met with Emrak and gave him a full report. As flight instructor, he needed as much information as possible and Brandon had recorded the tunnel onto his communicator so Emrak had visual input how the tunnel looked and behaved. It was a holographic image that could be transferred to Emrak's flight simulators and facilitate the learning process for the new pilots. Emrak really appreciated this help and knew several of his student pilots were advanced enough to start learning.

Frejja decided to buy the terrynium alloy from Mars in ready to use sheets so they could start building new spaceships. The government decided it was easier to buy the terrynium sheets from Mars rather than importing the terrynium and building the manufacturing plant themselves. It was the beginning of a new export item for Martia and several of the member planets in the Alliance ordered the cut and ready to use sheets of terrynium alloy. The Martian economy was booming and after a decade of exporting Mars was a rich planet. Taxes were eliminated and the standard of living was the highest among the planets of the Alliance.

None of the planets in the Alliance had terrynium, but it was discovered that the Moon had plenty of it and mining started without delay. The terrynium was exported from the Moon directly to buyers and the profits were fairly divided between Earth and the Moon. Since the Moon belonged to Earth, all countries on Earth received some of the income from the terrynium according to a formula worked out by the economists in North America. It was a fair distribution and all countries agreed to it. The planets that bought the terrynium from the Moon also bought the technology and machines to manufacture the alloy from Peturun. This caused a big boom in the Peturun economy and the increased prosperity raised the standard of living for the citizens. All the member planets of the Alliance started building new spaceships using the terrynium alloy. These planets now had technology that may have taken them a hundred years to attain without the help from Peturun. Emrak instructed the member planets how to configure their flight simulators to negotiate the shortcut tunnel.

There was a lot of talk of what is next? The governments of the member planets now had a nice fleet of tunnel-ready spaceships ready to travel to a corner of the Milky Way that was four hundred light years away, but what to do there? Trade, exploration, tourism? With a travel time of only six months there were many possibilities. Morekia was the first planet to send a new spaceship through the tunnel and land on Peturun. They met with the government and agreed to a trade arrangement to exchange goods. Arrynia also sent a ship through the tunnel piloted by female pilots, but they chose to turn around and return without landing on Peturun. Their practice run was also successful. The new spaceships replaced the old fleet on all the alliance planets. They were superior and could handle vibration with more stability than the old ships. The other member planets also made practice runs through the tunnel and then decided to let it go for the time being until they knew more about the Pleiades area of the Milky Way.

******

The gold reserves on Mars were impressive and well-hidden below ground. Only the top government officials knew where it was and they all had to take an oath never to reveal the location. Somehow the richness of Mars was slowly entering the Internet, especially the Interstellar Internet, and Mr. Taylor was well aware of the danger. He sent encrypted messages to all the planets in the Alliance that there was a real danger that one day they would be attacked by rogue forces trying to obtain their gold by force. In his message he made it clear that any necessary response from the Alliance would be fully funded by Mars. To his relief, all the members responded they were ready and would send their fighter ships if there was a need. Mr. Taylor realized the Martian fleet of six fighter spaceships would only be able to hold back an invading force for a short time and he ordered ten more fighter ships from Frejja for immediate shipment. They were available and a Martian spaceship with three government officials, twenty pilots to fly the ships to Mars and gold bars in the cargo bay departed for Frejja.

Frejja was an exporter of ships and usually had a large inventory of various ships in stock. The transaction was sealed with a handshake and the ships were flown to Mars. The Martian payment in pure gold was appreciated by the Frejjan government. Gold was always needed to produce gold coins used as the legal tender on Frejja. In general, gold was not in short supply in the universe as it could be mined from asteroids, but all mining was dangerous and to find an asteroid with a rich supply of gold was not always easy. The asteroid mining companies often processed many asteroids without finding gold, but when they were lucky enough to come across an asteroid with plenty of gold, the profits were substantial from hundreds of pounds of pure gold.

A year passed and Mr. Taylor jumped when his advisor stormed into his office.

"We have detected a fleet of perhaps twenty fighter ships and it sure looks like they will land on Mars," he shouted. "We must deploy our fighters."

Mr. Taylor had prepared himself for this moment and had the levelheadedness to remain calm and he summoned the pilots. The ships were always ready for takeoff with full fuel tanks and within fifteen minutes all sixteen fighter spaceships took off and flew towards the incoming fleet of ships. In the meantime, Mr. Taylor sent emergency messages using a private Internet channel to all the member planets in the Alliance and within a short time he received replies that their fighters were on the way. They would arrive at various times depending on travel time, but the Martian pilots would be able to communicate to the invaders that backup forces were on the way.

The Martian fleet was by no means a wimp and was a force to be reckoned with. They were highly trained and the pilots ready to fight to the end to defend their home planet. When the invading ships were within sight, they hovered in space ready to release their weapons in case the invaders would not back off. The Martian captain in charge sent a message in English to the invaders that several hundred fighter spaceships from eight planets were on the way and they had no chance of taking over Mars. The English language was always used when the origin of the aliens was unknown. The invaders responded by firing on the closest ship. It was a hard hit, but the terrynium alloy held and the ship was not seriously damaged to the amazement of the invaders. Only the six original ships Mars had bought from Frejja were made with standard materials available at the time Ryan ordered the ships, but the new ships Mr. Taylor had bought were all made with terrynium. The older ships were kept in the back. The new Martian ships were equipped with powerful weapons designed by the Peturuns. In response to the firing by the invaders the Martian captain instantly fired on one of the invading ships. It blew up in a fireball. The message was clear and the whole fleet of invaders took off. When they were out of sight the Martian ships returned home and Mr. Taylor breathed a sigh of relief when he saw them land. He immediately sent a message to the spaceships on their way to Mars to return to their home planets as the invasion had been staved off. No Martian had been killed and only one of the enemy ships had perished.

True to his word, Mr. Taylor promptly reimbursed all the planets for their quick response to the emergency with greetings from the Martian people expressing their gratitude to the members of the Alliance. The interplanetary payments were sent electronically to each member planet.

News of the attempted invasion popped up on the Interstellar Internet with details of the powerful response from the Alliance. No one knew who the invaders were, but the strength of the Alliance became known and respected and for many years no one dared attack any planet that was a member of the Alliance.

CHAPTER 25

Tothellim was back on Mars for another shipment of terrynium and as he and Mr. Taylor were talking about the failed invasion of Mars, he told Mr. Taylor that there were many guerrilla bands of terrorists and gangsters out there in space and this must have been one of them. Tothellim also informed Mr. Taylor about a planet in the Pleiades group of stars called Bantizza. The citizens were slaves to the dictatorial government with nothing to look forward to but misery and the only way to survive was total obedience by the people. They had no freedom of speech, no way of fighting back and the well-paid armed forces sided with the government. The government owned everything and the people barely survived. His own government did not want to get involved and perhaps start a war so nothing was done. The dictatorship had existed for several hundred years.

Mr. Taylor sat quietly for a while contemplating the suffering of the Bantizza people.

"How big is the planet?" he finally asked.

"Same size as Earth," replied Tothellim.

"Your own planet has a similar background as Bantizza. Before your savior Megonim changed the conditions, life on Peturun wasn't much better. Do you think the Alliance could take out the Bantizza government?"

"Yes, most likely, and if the Alliance would decide to invade, I'm sure my own government would send some of our fighter ships to assist in the attack."

"It would be a costly affair considering the distance, but I'll brief the member planets. They may agree to liberate the people. It would be easier if some of the planets in your own area could form an alliance and take down the Bantizza government."

"It would, for sure, but Peturun and the planets close to us refuse to get involved," Tothellim said with a sigh.

After Tothellim left, Mr. Taylor sent encrypted messages to the member planets inquiring whether they would want to participate in the ousting of the Bantizza government. There was no funding available so the entire cost of the invasion had to be absorbed by the member planets. The replies were slow to return and only Kodetsia and Morekia agreed while the other planets stated the distance of travel was too far and it would be preferable if the planets closer to Bantizza would liberate the people.

Mr. Taylor scrapped the plan and even though he was disappointed, he understood why the members had rejected the idea. He wondered to himself if the Alliance should be the cop of the Universe or if each planet must fend for itself. If no one offered a helping hand the people were doomed to live in hell forever. He was a strong believer in each person's free will and the citizens of Bantizza had no free will. The elite government had the people in a vise-grip with no regard for their humanity. Mr. Taylor was a compassionate man and felt troubled by the situation. There was nothing he could do for now, but he would not forget the Bantizza people and he was hoping they would be rescued in the future.

******

Mr. Taylor usually scanned the Interstellar Internet to keep abreast of news in the universe and an ad caught his eye. *Mercenaries for hire. Contact Rasufilus.* Mr. Taylor's interest was fired up and as he communicated with Rasufilus over the Internet, they made an agreement to meet on Mars. A month later a fighter ship arrived and Rasufilus and his co-pilot exited the ship and walked towards the government building. As he took his helmet off, Mr. Taylor noticed he was a Morekian and so was his copilot. They shook hands and Mr. Taylor welcomed them into his office.

"'I'm Rasufilus and this is my copilot. I'm the commanding officer of our space fleet," Rasufilus said in broken English.

Mr. Taylor noticed Rasufilus carried himself with dignity and commanded respect. They sat down and Rasufilus started talking -

"We're mercenaries with a fleet of ninety ships and close to three hundred pilots, all of them fully trained to fly our ships. The pilots are from several different planets and all of them are loyal and trustworthy.

We don't engage in any illegal activities, but are often hired to help a planet in distress as an extra backup force. That's the majority of our work. We don't have a specific home planet, unfortunately, as many planets are uncomfortable with a mercenary force on their land so we rent space on a few different planets that allow it."

Mr. Taylor explained the situation on Bantizza and that he wanted to terminate the dictatorship on the planet.

"We're fully familiar with the planet," Rasufilus said. "I agree with you that the conditions are horrible."

"We would prefer if you could manage this military operation with minimal bloodshed. Incarcerate the government and oversee that a new democratic government is elected by the people, for the people."

"I didn't live on Morekia when the Alliance threw out our old government, but I know all the details of it and I would consult with the new Morekian government officials when forming a new government with free elections on Bantizza. I have several contacts in the Morekian government I will use. When I'm done it will be a free planet just like Morekia is now. I feel confident we can get the job done without harm to innocent people. Our fee will be less than normal, because this is a humanitarian operation."

The following days Mr. Taylor and Rasufilus worked out a detailed plan that covered all the facets of the military action. Mr. Taylor asked Rasufilus to stay for a while on Mars so he could ask the Martians to vote on the issue. The result of the vote was ninety percent affirmative. The funding of the project was easily affordable by the Martians as the export of terrynium was a continuous source of income.

Rasufilus left and would use the element of surprise to make his strike. His entire force of ships and pilots assembled and departed for Bantizza reaching the planet in the morning hours. They had flown through the twelve-hour tunnel several times before and were familiar with it. The ships hovered at low altitude above the government buildings almost filling the sky. Rasufilus activated his translation device and connected with the president. He ordered all government employees to exit their offices and stay together outside the buildings. The president was among them.

"Mr. President, use your communicator now and order your army to lay down their weapons and capitulate. Your presidency is now terminated permanently."

Rasufilus waited and nothing happened. Then he heard the president shout in an angry voice -

"I refuse to follow your orders, you lowlife."

Instantly, Rasufilus fired a shot and the president was lying dead on the ground. The vice president used his communicator and yelled in a fearful voice -

"I'm the vice president, I will do it. I will connect with the army generals right now."

Rasufilus followed the communication on his electronic device inside the ship and, as ordered, the vice president instructed the army generals to obey orders from the invading ships and not resist. After giving detailed orders to the generals, the vice president ended his instructions with -

"Our government no longer exists."

The seasoned generals did not respond immediately. They were used to being in charge of the people and to have their full obedience, but they were not stupid. They knew it was over. The invading force was too powerful to defeat and the generals also suspected their weapons could take out the whole army if they chose to do so. He was right. Rasufilus' ships were equipped with state-of-the-art weapons and the Bantizza weapons were no match for Rasufilus' ships. The commanding officer finally responded -

"We capitulate. We will not strike back."

He issued orders to his troops to follow commands given by the invading force and he and his top commanders entered an airmobile and within a few minutes landed next to the vice president.

Rasufilus landed his ship and instructed his pilots to land as well, but stay inside their ships. He walked over to the vice president and the generals accompanied by his two fully armed copilots. The Bantizza people looked identical to human beings except their eyes were illuminated giving a flashlight effect. In the meantime, a team of government officials from Morekia were on the way to Bantizza to work as consultants and help form a new, democratically elected government.

Rasufilus ordered the men to go back into the building and they entered the conference room. He demanded the names of the top government officials and as they assembled in front of him, he ordered the army generals to escort them to whatever prison facility they had and incarcerate every one of them for ten years. The rest of the government was dismissed and let go.

When the generals sized up Rasufilus they realized he was a man of considerable power and abandoned any surprise attack they had been toying with in their minds. Finally, they accepted their rule was over and the people of Bantizza were free. Only one life had been lost as a result of the military action.

The Morekians arrived within a few days and skillfully organized elections and full disclosure was made to the citizens about the termination of the dictatorship. The people were so unaccustomed to freedom that they could not really comprehend that they now had voting rights and free speech. The Morekians had been through the same thing and knew how to open the people's minds and to reeducate them. Daily Internet announcements were made and slowly the citizens started to understand that a new era had started and a life with possibilities was ahead of them. They had freedom of choice, unheard of for a couple of hundred years.

It took a whole year until a new fully democratic government was established and the Morekian team stayed the full year to ensure everything was running smoothly. The army was under the new president's command and adjusted to the new ways. Rasufilus stayed on and was awarded a large enough piece of land to permanently keep his fleet and he and his pilots were granted citizenship of Bantizza which they accepted. They declined to join the Bantizza army and preferred their independence as a mercenary fleet working for other planets needing reinforcement ships. The citizens discovered life with freedom, but it took years for the older generation to adjust to independence while the younger people were quick to adhere to a lifestyle where they were in charge and they themselves made all the choices using their free will.

Mr. Taylor followed the successful transformation of a dictatorship to a full democracy and reported the good news to the Martians as well as the members of the Alliance. Everyone cheered. When the whole thing was over Mr. Taylor felt peace of mind. He had paid Rasufilus in gold and when they shook hands the last time both men were touched and felt it was a divine moment.

The new government of Bantizza sent formal greetings of gratitude to the Martian people for liberating them. Mr. Taylor posted their message on the Internet for all citizens to see.

******

The members of the Alliance now had the knowledge of the shortcut tunnel, but what to do with the information? The government of Frejja asked Brandon and Brianna if they wanted to explore that part of the Milky Way just to see what was there. Perhaps they would find a new planet. The voyage would take a year and a half, possibly two years. As adventurous as they were, both of them hesitated knowing very well it was a dangerous, unpredictable trip. They mulled over the decision and weighed the pros and cons of the trip. It would be the culmination of their careers, an opportunity of a lifetime, but would they survive? Both felt the lure of exploring the unknown. Brianna made up her mind first.

"I vote we go," she declared to Brandon. "If we perish, so be it. Exploring space is what we have always wanted."

"If you want to go then I go, too. Decided."

They notified Emrak and the government officials they accepted the offer and were ready to go. A newly made passenger ship manufactured with terrynium was prepared. The ship was equipped with a sophisticated defense system designed by the Peturuns. There would be fifty passengers onboard, all volunteers. To run the ship, two copilots were needed in addition to the two captains. Four androids were also part of the crew. The fifty people were all married couples looking for adventure and most of them were assigned various tasks on the ship. The design of the ship was the same as Brandon and Brianna had piloted for years, resembling a saucer, but the equipment and technology were the latest available. Huge amounts of food and water were onboard, probably enough for a trip lasting four years, but this was a safety factor that Brandon insisted on. Water onboard was recycled, but the extra amount of fresh water gave a feeling of security. If the water filtration would fail, the stored water was available.

Brandon and Brianna hugged all the family members and reassured them they would be back safely. Emrak was onboard until they took off and wished them luck. He was emotional and if he had been a single man, he would have joined them, but as a married man and father it was out of the question.

The ship departed and they had six months of travel ahead of them until they reached the area of the Milky Way outside the Pleiades group of stars and at that point, they would start their search of the area for uninhabited as well as inhabited planets and map the area. On the ship, the equipment was impressive with a holodeck, all sorts of entertainment devices and a large library of holographic movies, history information, planetary information and just about anything they would ever need additional information about. The ship was fully pressurized with good air quality, but in the year 2155 when they left Frejja, no space ships had gravity, so the crew spent at least an hour a day exercising with heavy equipment. Only workstations orbiting a planet had slight gravity onboard from rotation of the station. The communication system was powerful and they had contact with their families and Emrak every day.

Brandon and Brianna skillfully piloted the ship through the twelve-hour shortcut tunnel. This ship was larger and wider than the ship they had used on their first trip through the tunnel and they had to concentrate to keep the ship centered in the tunnel. When they flew out of it they felt freed from a burden. They entered the coordinates opposite the Pleiades area into the computer system as they knew the Peturuns had mapped the area all around the Pleiades. As far as they knew, no one had traveled to the corner of the Milky Way that they would soon reach. There was one star in that area, far away but visible, and three planets orbiting the star. The second planet was at the right distance from its sun to possibly be habitable. It took three more months of travel time and the ship descended into orbit of the second planet.

The crew watched the landscape in amazement. The planet was almost a copy of Earth and about the same size. It was green with vegetation and forests and several large lakes were visible from space. It appeared to be empty of any living beings and looking through their powerful telescopes, they still could not find anything alive on the surface. At night, there were no lights coming from the planet. They named it Earth2. Brandon and Brianna had an important decision to make - should they land or continue their search for more planets? The third planet should also be investigated, but the planet closest to its sun was most likely too hot and they abandoned the idea of orbiting it. They still had plenty of fuel left, enough for the return trip.

The decision was made to use the space shuttle onboard and descend to the planet's surface. It seated six people and four people were chosen by lottery to accompany Brandon and Brianna to the surface. They could see the planet had an oxygen atmosphere, but they wore spacesuits to be sure. The shuttle descended quickly to the surface and landed on a field of tall grass moving slightly from a light wind. They saw from their instruments that the air temperature was seventy-four degrees Fahrenheit and Brandon opened the shuttle door and stepped out. Once outside, he removed his helmet and took a deep breath.

"Fresh air, hooray," he yelled out loud.

They all went outside and admired the landscape and the sweet air. The gravity was heavier than Mars, but less than Earth. It was truly lovely. They quickly removed their spacesuits and walked towards a lake in the distance, about a mile away. They saw flowers with buzzing insects as they walked to the lake, but no animals or reptiles of any kind. When they reached the lake, Brianna put her hand in the water and it was slightly cool. She smelled on it to make sure it was water and it was. Then she jumped and shouted -

"See the fish!"

A foot long fish swam right in front of them and it looked similar to a catfish. Brandon put a little water in his hand and tasted it. It was sweet water and probably potable. To be safe, he did not swallow it.

They walked around all day on the planet's surface and the tranquility of the place was addictive. Flocks of small size birds, totally unafraid, landed on their outstretched arms. Some were very colorful and gently pecked on them to figure out what they were. They knew the planet had insects, fish and birds, but they did not know if anything lived in the forest and decided to use the shuttle to investigate. Towards the evening, they returned to the shuttle and flying right above the treetops they carefully looked for anything alive. It was a healthy-looking deciduous forest with some evergreen trees here and there. They saw no animals of any kind.

Before dark they were back on the ship and relayed everything they had seen to the rest of the people onboard. The following day, they made another trip with the shuttle and this time they covered a large area of the planet without landing. The purpose was to find anything alive on the surface and they found nothing. No animals and no beings of any kind. The planet was empty except for birds, fish and insects.

They returned to the ship and sat down to discuss together. To the surprise of Brandon and Brianna one of the passengers, Manny, spoke out -

"All fifty of us and your two copilots would like to stay on this planet. We are all in agreement. We humbly ask for some of the supplies loaded onboard to help us establish a colony here."

After Brandon had recovered from the surprise, he thought for a while and finally said -

"Brianna and I can pilot this ship with the help of the androids. The androids are fully capable of most repair work on the engines and almost anything onboard except piloting the ship. We take that chance, because it's unlikely that both Brianna and I would become incapacitated during the return trip. Part of the cargo onboard was actually intended to help out an existing colony on a planet or to start a new one. We even have six black boxes with everything needed to generate electricity as well as an abundance of electronics and communication devices that you can have. We also have tools, weapons for self-defense, medical supplies, seeds for crops and household items. Best of all, you'll get two airmobiles so you can explore the planet. My answer is yes and what do you say, Brianna?"

"I agree," Brianna responded without hesitating.

"You're only fifty-two people," Brandon continued "and you would have to commit yourselves to living in peace with each other respecting everyone's free will. There can't be a self-appointed king or queen forcing his or her will on the others. Free will must be respected at all times. Decisions should be made by voting on various issues and not rammed down the other people's throat by a few considering themselves smarter than the rest. In other words, don't create an elite. You're all equals and you're all one. If you accept those terms, I'll unload everything we can spare and you'll have a new beginning on this pristine planet."

A round of applause and whistling followed.

"Words can't describe how grateful and excited we are," Manny exclaimed.

"If you prosper and generate income sometime in the future, you'll have to reimburse Frejja for the cost of all this equipment," Brandon added. He had made an inventory of the supplies he would unload for the people.

"Of course," Manny said in agreement. "We may find a mineral here that could be used instead of currency as payment. When we have the communication system running, we'll stay in touch with Frejja."

Some of the people were highly skilled in different areas and one of them was a medical doctor, a few were engineers and with their combined skill set their chances of surviving and prospering were very good.

The following week the shuttle was traveling back and forth between the ship and planet and it took a whole week to unload all the equipment, food and people. The first men landing on the planet started immediately to build wooden houses since they did not know if there was a winter season. It turned out there was a winter season, but so mild it was never a hardship.

Brandon and Brianna bid an emotional farewell to the fifty-two pioneers and told them they would probably be back some time in the future.

On the trip back to Frejja, they entered orbit of the third planet and found it was a gaseous planet unsuitable for human life. There was sufficient fuel in the tanks to last the full return trip and with no extra copilots onboard, Brandon and Brianna had to work hard and sleep in shifts to manage the ship. Returning through the shortcut tunnel was arduous and they were both very fatigued as they exited the tunnel and took turns catching a nap. With luck on their side, they returned to Frejja and landed where they had left. Emrak's smiling face greeted them and what a welcome sight he was. If anyone would understand what they had been through, he would. Brianna gave him a big hug and Emrak and Brandon shook hands with big smiles on their faces.

They walked inside the hangar to the sitting room where Karol and some Frejjan government officials waited. Brandon and Brianna had met Karol on Mars and were glad to see her and they knew she was now Emrak's wife. They spoke English as Emrak was now almost fluent in English and the Frejjan officials also spoke good English.

For three hours Brandon and Brianna took turns conveying all the news of the trip and the Frejjan officials did not object that Brandon had supplied the pioneers with all the equipment from the ship. They felt certain they would be reimbursed later on.

After dinner, Brandon and Brianna caught an airmobile taxi and went home to see their family. They had been gone a year and a half and the reunion was tearful and heartwarming. Lotte and Clarence knew they were on their way back, but did not know exactly when to expect them. Rigel and Orion were now young adults and Rigel was studying to become a pilot like his parents. Orion preferred life on land and had decided to work with programming and computers like his grandfather Clarence.

Brandon and Brianna took three months off and enjoyed their free time tremendously. They had a spacious room in Clarence and Lotte's house and Eva took care of most of the household chores. Rigel returned to his school, but Orion still lived at home and was happy to interact with his parents. He barely knew them and during the three months they were home, he spent a lot of time with them and discovered how truly fond of them he was. Clarence and Lotte had raised him and he loved them dearly, but to finally spend time with his biological parents was an emotional discovery that touched his heart. He was immensely proud of them and now, as a young adult, he understood how much they had accomplished.

******

News from Earth2 started to trickle in to Frejja's government and over the next few months daily messages arrived and they were all posted on the Internet. Earth2's communication system was installed; every couple had a simple house; electricity through the black boxes was functioning well; all the equipment was organized in a separate building and the food had been divided between the couples. No one had become sick from bacteria or a virus and if they existed the pioneers were immune. Fish, birds and insects appeared to be the only living things. The water from a spring next to their community had been diverted to the houses and was clean and good tasting. They did not have running water yet, but the engineers were working on it. It was spring on Earth2 and the first crops had been planted by hand as they did not have any farm equipment. Fish was abundant in the lakes and they were able to catch several dozen a day by hanging a hook in the water baited with cut-up fish heads. It was not an easy life, but very rewarding and none of the pioneers regretted their decision to stay on the planet. All the couples were relatively young and one of the women was expecting. That would be the first child in the community. The pioneers did miss eggs, milk and meat and made it known that farm animals would be highly appreciated if there was a way for them to survive the trip in the spaceship.

There had been no disputes within the community and they all got along well. Earth2 had four seasons. The winter had been easy with a light snow cover and it lasted only three months. There was one geologist among the pioneers, Ijakull, and he had excavated holes in the ground by hand to find out what minerals the planet had. He found a modest amount of terrynium, lots of silver and in one area close to the community a cave with a vein of pure gold. It was a promising start. They needed worker robots to aid in the mining and Ijakull added six robots to the list of items the community was planning to submit to Frejja. If the gold deposit was plentiful, they could pay Frejja in gold for all the new supplies as well as for the supplies they had received from the ship. The colony also needed at least two 3D printers for house construction. Mr. Parker, who had easily won reelection and had just started his second term as president, was fascinated by the colony and openminded to aid them as much as possible.

Mr. Parker asked Emrak for the list he had received from the colony and read through it. It was a reasonable list and he approved all the items and instructed Emrak to ask Brandon and Brianna if they were willing to return to Earth2. They agreed and the preparation of the spaceship began. A rotating cage was built to induce low gravity in the cage and chicks would be packed onboard. No one knew if they would survive, but it was worth a try. A much larger rotating cage was also built to house baby goats for milk supply. Three Frejjan goats, one male and two females, would be part of the shipment. They were not expected to survive, but if they did, it would improve the lives of the colonists a lot. When the ship was fully packed, there was room for thirty people and fifteen couples were chosen by lottery from a waiting list. These people were new settlers. There were two copilots in addition to Brandon and Brianna and six android crew members, a total of ten people working on the ship.

The ship departed and Emrak and Karol were at the ship to see them off. Mr. Parker was also present and felt very emotional when he wished Brandon and Brianna a good trip and safe return. They had nine months of travel ahead of them until they reached Earth2.

The nine months felt long to everyone onboard as time drew on, but finally they arrived safely at Earth2 and entered orbit. The chickens had died, but to everyone's amazement the goats were alive. Perhaps one of the reasons was that the goats had been loved endlessly by the passengers and were seldom left alone. Their little souls were nourished and their minds kept busy. Brandon and Brianna manned the shuttle on the first descent to the surface and then turned the shuttle over to the copilots. Brandon and Brianna enjoyed immensely visiting with the colonists and hearing their stories. Their houses were simple but functional and none of the colonists wanted to leave. There were no regrets. One baby boy had been born and another baby was on the way. Their crop of grain had been a success and several huge vegetable gardens were planted. Ten tiny apple trees were growing and had been planted from seed. The women missed appliances such as washing machines and dishwashers, but Brandon told them they would eventually be delivered once they had their water supply working with running hot water. Manny proudly showed Brandon several large buckets filled with almost pure gold nuggets and told him it was their first payment to Frejja. The gold needed to be processed, which could not be done on Earth2 as they lacked the equipment. Frejja always accepted both silver and gold as payment for goods since their currency was silver and gold coins.

After a few days, the ship was unloaded and the men were stacking everything neatly in the storage building they had built. The goats were kept in cages in the shuttle and remained mostly calm during the flight to the surface. The food had been divided and the people had enough food to last them close to two years. The only meat they had was the freeze-dried meat from Frejja and they were hoping they soon would get a shipment of Frejja's meat animals. There was plenty of pasture for herds of animals and egg laying chickens would also be welcome. The colonists were very excited to receive two 3D printers for house building and the six worker robots for mining. These were costly items, but with the minerals available on the planet, the people on Earth2 were confident they would be able to pay back the loan to Frejja in installments.

A few of the men voiced concern about self-defense and Brandon was well aware they were vulnerable. The weapons they had were powerful, but if a terrorist group of ships would invade them, they had no chance. Brandon and Brianna had been part of the defense team sent to defend

Mars from the invaders so they knew Earth2 was defenseless. The saving grace was that no one knew Earth2 was now settled. Brandon told the men that they could not afford to buy a fleet of spaceship fighters and would just have to hope an invasion would not take place. In the future, when the population had increased, a purchase of fighters was highly recommended if they had the means to pay for it.

The return trip to Frejja went well and the gold from Earth2 was refined. It turned out it was almost pure gold and amounted to a substantial payment. Mr. Parker sent a message to the colonists telling them how delighted he was that they were able to generate an income and if these payments continued, they would be debt free within a decade.

******

Nasha and Ares were in their mid-twenties and they were one of the couples from Frejja who had moved to Earth2. Their simple homestead was their castle and the pristine conditions on the new planet were of emotional value to them. They had had a pleasant life on Frejja and loved their home planet, but to be part of starting a colony on a distant planet was too intriguing to turn down and both of them had been eager to try a new lifestyle. After dinner they went for walks in the evening just to enjoy the sunset and the peace the nature offered. They had no children yet, but Nasha was expecting. Life was not easy and all household chores had to be done by hand. They both knew the hardships were temporary and modern appliances would eventually be in all the homes, but for now those conveniences were a few years away. Every house had electricity from the Zero Point Field and hot water was available in all the homes. Five washing machines had been delivered in the last shipment from Frejja and hooked up in one of the buildings, but they were used almost non stop and Nasha continued doing all the laundry by hand rather than waiting for a machine to become available. She had two electric burners for cooking, but no oven and had to use a solar oven for baking. It worked well even though it took a long time to bake anything. They had been promised 3D food printers to be delivered with the next shipment from Frejja. Electric heating was supplied through the black boxes.

The three goats were on pasture and thriving. They were adults now and both females were pregnant. A few more male goats were needed to avoid inbreeding and the colonists had also asked for meat animals to be included with the next shipment. When the baby goats had nursed their mothers for two months they would be weaned and the colonists could start milking the does. The milk would have to be shared and the herd needed to be increased. Cloning had been rejected by the colonists and they preferred the natural way.

Among the colonists was a pleasant man of very high intelligence, Ássurt, but with an annoying habit of trying to force his will on the others. He felt he knew better. His wife reminded him not to play king and each of them had free will, even if their free will would lead to mishaps. They had to learn on their own and from their own mistakes. Ássurt would shut his mouth for a while and then, to his wife's dismay, he started to impose his ideas again on the others. Each week all the colonists met to discuss strategy and plan for the future and at the next meeting Ássurt's wife addressed the colonists -

"I suggest we elect six people by voting to act as our advisory team and the team should be changed every six months, so that all of us have a chance to serve. Let's put all our names in a basket and then select six names. We can also vote on the ideas coming from this team and majority vote wins. It will be the beginning of a simple government."

Everyone agreed and six people were elected to become the first team. They were instructed to try to foresee future problems and to find possible solutions as well as improving quality of life for everyone. The new system worked well and each team took their responsibilities seriously. Ássurt finally stopped voicing his opinion and understood they all had equal rights. When his turn arrived to serve, he offered several brilliant ideas and all were implemented. Now his opinion was wanted and not forced upon the others, a distinction that had eluded him until he served on the team.

The men were working on the mechanical systems of the colony and had ordered an incinerator toilet for each home to replace their outhouses, which everyone was uncomfortable with. Running hot water was now available in all homes. A simple waste water system had been built and the used water filtered through a thick layer of sand. The pollution from the colony was minimal. Little by little the settlement was transformed into a village of modernity.

No organized religion existed. Divine beliefs were considered a private matter belonging in people's hearts. The colonists showed respect for each other and cooperated, which was necessary for the survival of them all.

Three baby goats had been born and the harvest season started. One field of tall grass had been cut as hay for the goats and the grain was now ready to cut. They still had no farm equipment and the work had to be done manually, but with so many people willing to chip in the processing of the harvest went fast. They were hoping to receive a modern tractor with implements soon, but other items such as household appliances were considered more important and the tractor would eventually be delivered and relieve them of heavy farm work. Many of the men actually liked working in the fields and build muscle. There was no real rush and they could even take a nap in the sun, if they wanted to. There was enough rain on the planet, but it tended to come down extremely heavy for several days in a row and then be absent for weeks with azure blue skies day after day.

Nasha gave birth to a girl, the second baby born on Earth2. The doctor had built a little clinic with five beds and he had all medical supplies to handle accidents and perform simple surgeries. He delivered Nasha's baby and she gave birth without pain thanks to the effective pain relief the doctor had. On Frejja women used the artificial womb, but everything on Earth2 had to be done the old way. Nasha had actually enjoyed her pregnancy and if given a choice in the future, she would reject the artificial womb and go through another natural pregnancy. To feel the baby kick had been magic for both her and Ares.

The six worker robots were hard at work extracting gold from the cave. They were not the latest model, but had ability to express themselves in simple speech in Frejjan and they worked hard all day long. Most of them had years of mining experience. Some of the men worked alongside the robots and an impressive amount of gold was harvested. The colonists were hoping the deposit of gold would be sufficient to pay off the whole debt they owed to Frejja.

The 3D industrial size printers worked all day to fabricate houses and used sandy soil from Earth2 mixed with an aggregate that came from Frejja. The minerals in the aggregate were not available on Earth2 and had to be bought from Frejja. Due to the heavy weight of the aggregate the shipments were small and goods shipped to Earth2 had to be prioritized. After only a month all the aggregate was used up and the printers were idle. Two of the engineers worked on inventing an alternative to the aggregate and with all the natural minerals available on the planet, they felt there must be some material that could be used to replace the costly aggregate. They tried dozens of mixes and all failed. The test houses crumbled and fell apart over the winter. Eventually they found a mix of minerals that worked and the houses survived the winter with no structural damage. This was a relief for the colony as the aggregate was too expensive to buy and always in short supply. Now the printers could be put to work and expand the community. The colonists knew many people wanted to join them and become citizens of Earth2. There had also been inquiries from other planets if immigration was allowed and the Earth2 people responded 'yes'. As soon as they had built more housing they would welcome as many people as the planet could handle without overcrowding it. No one wanted to jeopardize the serene landscape and there would be a definite limit to the number of immigrants. It was not clear how these other planets knew Earth2 was being settled.

There were no stores on Earth2 as everything was shared evenly, but the people knew stores would open and a money system would be needed as the population increased. It was decided gold and silver coins was the most practical currency to use and hence a mint was established. The front of the coins showed the name 'Earth2' with a bird and a fish intertwined to display the original 'inhabitants' of the planet. On the other side was an image of a man and a woman holding hands indicating a human population now resided on the planet. A pair of dies was made and the images meticulously created by an artist among the people. The images were truly beautiful. Blanks were first made from molten gold or silver and then the design was pressed under high pressure into each side of the coin, referred to as striking. It was a learning process that took time to master as none of the team had any prior knowledge how to make coins. They had to import the refined gold and silver from Frejja as they still could not refine the ore themselves, but they were determined to eventually have the equipment imported and process the minerals themselves. The coins the team made were by no means masterpieces, but as they gained more experience the look and feel of the coins improved. All coins were stored in a separate building under lock and key, a measure of safety that was probably not necessary as theft and crime did not exist on the planet.

Every eighteen months the supply ship arrived from Frejja and new pilots now manned the ships. Brandon and Brianna had made two trips to Earth2 and decided the time it took to make one roundtrip was too long and they did not want to be away from home for a year and a half, but they stayed in touch with the colony via the Internet and enjoyed hearing about their progress. They were now flying cargo ships between Frejja and Arrynia, a ten-week roundtrip and they had three weeks off between trips. It was an easy schedule both Brandon and Brianna could live with. They enjoyed visiting with Funina and they also met with Esta, the Kodetsian woman. Five million Kodetsians lived on Arrynia and had fully integrated into the Arrynian society and spoke the language well. There had been no problems so far. Esta told Brandon and Brianna that Kodetsia was now a totally changed planet with happy citizens thanks to all the improvements made by Pretos and Jonni. She also said that she had no intention to return to Kodetsia and was pleased with her life on Arrynia. She was married with a child.

******

Frejja was still importing single men from Earth and Mars, but the number of men from Mars had dwindled to a dozen or so per trip. Earth, however, had a large supply of men willing to make the move and every ship was full to capacity with men. They integrated well on Frejja and so far, there had been no problems. All of them found a wife and not a single one of the immigrants had returned to Earth. The trip from Earth to Frejja took three months and the Frejjan ships landed every two months on Earth. Frejja had only forty million citizens and could easily accept several million immigrants, single men as well as families. Earth was a nice place to live and not many families wanted to leave, but occasionally an adventurous family would sign up.

The population on Earth was now four billion and considered too low. The planet could support up to ten billion people, but fertility was down and women preferred to have just one or two children. Birth control was approved everywhere and the modernized Catholic Church had no objections to it. The population remained stable and did not increase.

In North America, the government system was still the same and People Democracy had been in effect for close to a hundred years. The government's promise to the people to remain small and frugal and to be fully accountable had been kept and that may be why the system had not changed for so long. The citizens liked the system and wanted to keep it. The Advisory Board was also active and working closely with the Venusians.

The base income had worked out well also and many working people chose to cancel it while they were working. They applied for it when they retired and the government had no problem paying it. The taxes collected plus the income from asteroid mining, which the government was part of, brought in sufficient funds so the government could meet its obligations and still remain debt free. Keeping the government as small as possible meant less bureaucracy, less salaries to be paid and the legalizing of drugs had saved many millions of dollars that were formerly spent on enforcing drug laws and incarcerating criminals involved in drugs.

Drug use was legal everywhere and making it legal had had the opposite effect than predicted. Instead of becoming addicts, young people shunned drugs. In the beginning when drugs were legalized there were thousands of people who overdosed and died, but this initial phase was ebbing away when young people saw their friends dying in the gutter. Anyone with self-preservation realized a high from drugs was not worth becoming a slave to addiction.

Crime had not been eradicated completely, but was not the big problem it once was. Hoarding money was no longer important and the simpler things in life were more attractive to people such as being in Nature, family life and soul searching. Everyone had enough money to pay for all their basic needs. Taking 'money baths' had lost its appeal.

The economy was doing well and some companies became very large. Two of these large companies dominated the market and tried to eliminate the smaller companies in the field thus removing competition. The government served the people, not the corporations, and had no intention to allow old history to repeat. They reminded the citizens that those who cannot remember the past are condemned to repeat it and promptly broke up the two large companies so smaller businesses had a chance to grow.

Mining of asteroids was going well and generated a good income for many of the companies engaged in the business. People envisioning space travel from Earth to various planets were proven wrong and ships from Earth had never been beyond Mars. No Earth ship had traveled to Frejja. The new ships were all made with terrynium alloy and the pilots had learned to travel safely through the tunnel to Mars, but there was no real interest in long distance space travel. Earth was pleasant and many felt space travel was not worth the cost and effort. People knew many planets were inhabited, but the interest to interact with the aliens was limited.

The space elevator project had finally been scrapped as an impossible dream and millions of dollars had been wasted trying to make the idea work. The team involved with the program was sad to see it end.

People from Earth continued to move to Mars and ships from both Earth and Mars were used for transporting. Now that the shortcut tunnel was in use, the trip took only three weeks and was easy. In spite of losing over five thousand men to Frejja, the population on Mars had increased to eighty thousand and Martia was very large and spread out. It was also affluent and the largest exporter of terrynium. The Moon had large deposits of terrynium, but not to be compared to what Mars had. Martia had everything to offer the citizens except the outdoors and many immigrants to Mars did not care about being outside. There were no taxes and most services were free. No one had to work hard. Life on Mars was easy.

The former third world countries had caught up with the western world and enjoyed a middle-class lifestyle. The shantytowns that existed before the collapse were all gone and had been replaced by good housing and there were work opportunities for everyone. Their governments were no longer self-serving and the income from natural resources was spent on infrastructure. Money was spread more evenly among the people rather than ending up in the pockets of a few. The power elite was gone.

The weapons industry on Earth had stagnated and many governments felt the cost to invent and manufacture lethal weapons was a waste of money. Earth was at peace and the idea that aliens may invade Earth was considered remote. Only North America had weapons for self-defense against aliens. The weapons were stored at a location known only to the top generals and the president and North America made it known to the Advisory Board that no country on Earth needed to fear an aggressive attack from them. The weapons would only be activated if an invasion of hostile aliens were to threaten Earth. Earth had been free of wars since the Middle East War thirty years earlier.

Since the superbug devastated Earth a hundred and twenty years ago, no virus or bacteria of that magnitude had popped up. People in general were also healthier than in the past and the quality of the food supply was superior to what had passed as 'food' in the old days.

Weather extremes had not stopped, but seemed less frequent than it had been. Earthquakes, volcanic eruptions and violent storms did occur and flooding from excessive rain was never easy to deal with, but overall, the climate was stable. The sun had an adequate number of sunspots and the cooling cycle was over. Starting around 2020 and lasting until the year 2050 the number of sunspots had been very low, some years none at all, and the cooling of the climate was evident. The winters had been very snowy and cold and the summers cool. Everyone was relieved that phase was now over.

With the present, smaller population on Earth more habitats were available for wildlife and extinction of animals and birds had become less common. Even fish had made a comeback since the oceans had been cleaned up and plastics removed. Elephant herds in Africa had recovered and the demand for ivory was nil. The worldwide campaign to save the majestic elephants had succeeded and the brutal slaughter was finally over.

Manufacturing plants could not legally discharge toxic waste and had to spend the money needed to ensure filters and scrubbers were in place.

People felt safe and with peace of mind creativity flourished. Many new inventions were created and some were released without patents as gifts to humanity. Being rich was less important than bringing an invention to fruition. Did stable living conditions lead to stagnation? Quite the opposite. Life in most countries continued to change with the times and people were transcending all the time.

Intermarriage had become more common between people of different ethnic origins as well as different faiths.

Maturity grew and spirituality increased people's mental freedom and removed fears. There were also many people who were atheists, materialists, who only believed in what could be scientifically proven. The good thing was that each person's beliefs were respected.

CHAPTER 26

Earth2 had been plundered and the colonists were frightened. The same group of gangsters who had tried to invade Mars got wind of the easy pickings on Earth2 with gold stored somewhere on the planet. No one ever found out how the information had leaked out, but it was a tragedy that the Earth2 people would never forget. It started in the morning with the landing of twenty spaceships and armed aliens not resembling any of the known peoples the colonists had seen on the Internet climbed out. They were humanoids, five feet tall, human noses, mouths and ears and deep facial furrows from the nose to the chin. Their heads were normal size and they had no hair, but their eyes were huge, yellow colored. They were dressed in black leather jackets and pants and their piercing eyes were cruel. The leader had a translation device and barked into it with a high-pitched, squeaky voice -

"Gold, where is it?"

The colonists knew they had to give up their gold or die and Manny quietly led them to the mined gold nuggets they had saved to be picked up by the next Frejjan ship. He had no intention to show them the gold coins and was hoping they would not find them. About five hundred gold coins had been minted and were under lock and key. They were worth a small fortune.

The gold nuggets were stored in steel buckets and each bucket could hold about a hundred pounds. There were two hundred buckets filled with gold. It was unprocessed, raw gold, but of high quality and had taken a year to extract from the cave. The terrorists eyed the gold with interest and the leader gave orders to the rest of them. They unloaded a large cargo drone from one of the ships and within a short time all the steel buckets had been loaded onto their ships.

"Show us your electronics," demanded the leader.

Manny showed them what they had and they took the Internet communication equipment ensuring the colonists could not summon help.

Without a word they took off and Manny sighed with relief they had not found the coins. The colonists were standing in a group too shaken to speak but grateful no one had been killed. The Frejjan ship was expected to land in six months and in the meantime, they had no way of reporting the crime.

"We did save the old communication system," one of the engineers finally said. "Let me work on it and see if I can transmit a message to Frejja."

The people returned to their homes and they felt despair. A whole year's worth of mining had been stolen. All they could do was to try to return to their daily routine and hope the Frejjan government would somehow help them recover the gold.

It took the engineer a whole month to rig the outdated communication system and a weak signal reached Frejja. The technicians recognized the signal came from Earth2 and even though they could not pick up the words, they pieced together that it was a distress call. The Frejjan ship had left and would land on Earth2 in five months.

Mr. Parker was notified and with his advisors they came to a conclusion. They realized Earth2 had probably been robbed and they suspected it may be the same gang that had invaded Mars. Earth2 was not part of the Alliance, but all the people were Frejjan. There was no way of knowing where the terrorists were right now and when Mr. Parker notified Mr. Taylor on Mars, he said he would talk to Tothellim of Peturun. Tothellim was very experienced and may know what planet the terrorists lived on.

"Tothellim is here on Mars right now and I'll talk to him," Mr. Taylor said. "I'll contact you when I have discussed the matter with him."

Tothellim stroked his chin and said after a while -

"I think they're from planet Humbrus, a medium size planet not too far from Peturun. I've heard rumors they have expelled loads of people who were troublemakers and refused to obey the laws of the planet. The people of Humbrus are good people. I've seen a few of them and if I had a sketch of the terrorists' faces, I would be able to tell you for sure if they are from Humbrus. The gangsters who left Humbrus are scattered on several planets and are bribing those planets to allow them to live there."

"The Frejjan supply ship will reach Earth2 in five months," Mr. Taylor explained. "I'll ask the captain of the ship to send us a sketch of the terrorists when the ship lands on Earth2. Then I'll send it to you."

Tothellim nodded and they sat around talking about how vulnerable Earth2 was and how badly they needed a defense system of some kind.

The Frejjan ship landed on Earth2 and was notified of the robbery. The captain asked the colonists if any of them could make a sketch of the invaders and one of the people had already done so from memory. It was a good sketch and the captain forwarded it to Tothellim. Within an hour he received an answer confirming the terrorists were from Humbrus and he would make some inquiries among his contacts as to which planet they were now living on.

The Frejjan ship had a spare communication system onboard and handed it over to the colonists. It was a powerful system, ultramodern, and they were told to hide it when not in use. Being without any means of reaching Frejja had left the colonists feeling totally defenseless and they knew they had to hide this expensive communication system. The old system could be left out to give the image it was all they had.

The captain promised the colonists he would discuss their defense with Mr. Parker and let them know when they had worked out a plan. The captain also said that if the terrorists could be found there was even a chance the gold could be returned. In the meantime, all they could do was to hide whatever gold nuggets they were mining and hope no more invasion would take place.

From that day on the gold stayed in the cave in a side tunnel well hidden from sight. The communication system was kept below the floor planks in the little building functioning as an office and the gold coins were stored below ground a distance from the houses. So far, the terrorists had not returned, but no one knew if they would come back in the future.

Mr. Parker knew from Mr. Taylor how efficient Rasufilus was and he contacted him via the Internet. Rasufilus agreed to take the job. An agreement was made that he would hunt down the terrorists and try to return the gold to Earth2. Rasufilus was not given a time line and Mr. Parker said the main thing was to catch them regardless of how long it took.

Rasufilus contacted Tothellim and was told of possible hiding places and one by one Rasufilus and his fleet checked them all out. They had no luck. Then, when they stopped at the orbiting work station, Rasufilus got a tip from one of the workmen who quietly told him the planet most of them, but not all, were hiding. Using heavy bribes, they had settled on this planet and intended to stay there. The workman was well paid in gold for his tip.

The planet was orbiting one of the stars in the Pleiades group of stars and Rasufilus knew the location of it. Rasufilus' and his fleet were now permanently living on Bantizza and he departed for the planet with all of his ninety ships. It took only a month of travel time and they easily found the government buildings. Only Rasufilus landed while the other ships hovered in the sky at low altitude. Rasufilus and his copilot were unarmed and walked into the building calmly telling the guards they needed to see the president. They had expected trouble from the guards, but they did not ask any questions, just checking them for weapons, and then walked them to the president's office.

"I'm Rasufilus," he explained "and I'm here to take out the terrorists you allow to live on your planet. We know you're thoroughly bribed to let them live here. If you cooperate with us we won't disclose this truth to your citizens, but if you warn the terrorists so they can leave before we get to them, we will for sure inform your people of the bribes and you'll be thrown out of office."

The president was in a mild state of shock. He had heard of Rasufilus and knew he was incorruptible and a man of integrity. He also knew of his fleet of fighter ships, always the latest model and equipped with incredible weapons. He had looked out his window and saw the sky filled with his ships just waiting for orders.

"I will cooperate," he said in a low, intimidated voice. He knew there was no other choice. Anyone keeping up with interstellar news had heard of Rasufilus' termination of Bantizza's dictatorship and many other military operations he had successfully participated in.

"Good," Rasufilus said calmly. "Here is the plan - we will destroy all their ships, find stolen property and return it to the owners and round up the terrorists. We expect you to deal with them according to the laws of this planet and charge them with interstellar terrorism. They tried to invade planet Mars but didn't succeed and they did invade another planet and stole natural resources from that planet." Rasufilus intentionally avoided mentioning the name of Earth2. The fewer who knew the planet was now inhabited the better.

"The sentence for terrorism on our planet is death by a firing squad," the president replied. A coward, he was relieved they would be put to death so none of the terrorists could come after him and take revenge.

"Have your police force ready to pick them up in two hours," Rasufilus instructed him.

The fleet took off and the snitch had given Rasufilus the location where the terrorists stayed on the planet. It was only an hour away and the ships were parked outside in full view, twenty-six ships total. Rasufilus and fifteen of his ships descended to a lower altitude while the rest of the ships stayed in the sky waiting for orders.

"Fire!" Rasufilus shouted. Bang! Every ship was engulfed in flames and soon reduced to ashes. The terrorists fired at the ships from inside their houses, but the terrynium fuselage was impenetrable and their weapons barely made a dent on the ships.

Rasufilus and his pilots landed and Rasufilus addressed the terrorists from the cockpit of his ship using the loudspeakers. They all stayed in their ships in case more firing was needed. Rasufilus activated the translation device.

"Come out unarmed and wait for the police force of your planet to pick you up," he commanded.

Slowly, hesitatingly they came out. Looking at the ships on the ground and the rest of the ships up in the sky convinced them they could not fight back. Within minutes the police were at the scene with several vans and handcuffed the terrorists. When they were removed, all the ships landed and the search for the stolen gold began. It was easy to find and all of it was stored in one of the buildings together with the stolen communication system from Earth2. They used the same drone to load the gold onto the ships that the terrorists had used and distributed the weight evenly between the ships. When all was done Rasufilus contacted the president and informed him they were leaving, but they had found a stash of weapons that could be used by his police force. The president understood and said he would send his force over there and collect anything they could use. The terrorists would face the firing squad the following day, he added. All of them had confessed to invasions on several planets.

The mission was over. It had been swift and successful, mostly thanks to Rasufilus' military experience and an inner knowing how to deal with other beings. He ordered his fleet to return to home base and after a month they were back on Bantizza. The Earth2 gold was stored in a safe building within the compound.

Rasufilus contacted Mr. Parker and informed him the mission had been successful with full recovery of all the gold and the communication system. Mr. Parker was elated to hear the news and said they would send a ship over to Bantizza within a few days to pick up the gold and pay Rasufilus for his services. It would take six months for the ship to reach Bantizza. He thanked Rasufilus profusely and ended the transmission. Mr. Parker then sent a message to Earth2 relaying the good news to the colonists. He also added that the cost of hiring Rasufilus would be paid by Frejja.

The colonists celebrated and their feelings of doom and gloom were instantly swept away. High hopes returned and they faced the future with optimism.

******

Brandon and Brianna were on their way from Frejja to Arrynia and they had precious cargo onboard - their son Rigel, now a licensed pilot and twenty-six years old. He had signed on as their copilot and with only two years of experience, he had a lot to learn, especially how to fly through the tunnels. Brandon was at the controls when they hit the first of the three tunnels and Rigel carefully followed every correction Brandon made with the controls. He knew he was not ready to fly the ship through the tunnel and needed to spend hours in the flight simulator to get the feel of the ship as it vibrated inside the tunnel. It was still informative to watch how easily his parents were able to keep the ship centered inside the tunnel and he was impressed.

This was Rigel's first trip to Arrynia and he looked forward to meeting Funina. He knew his mother was fond of her and that the planet was a matriarchy. When they were through the tunnel Rigel took the controls and flew the ship manually for a long distance to gain experience and he landed the ship on Arrynia. His parents could see that eventually he would become a fine pilot.

Rigel was not prepared for the heavy gravity on Arrynia and dragged his feet. Brandon and Brianna laughed and assured him he would have to get used to heavy and light gravity as no two planets were the same. Inside Funina and her young daughter Sillia waited to greet them. Sillia was very pretty and Rigel thought she looked like a little angel without hair. He had seen several aliens and was used to that most of them had no hair. Rigel was tall as his parents and Sillia only reached to his shoulder. His admiration for Sillia did not go unnoticed and both Funina and his parents smiled at each other. Rigel was a handsome guy and dated a girl on Frejja, but it was not serious and he had no intention of marrying her.

They stayed a week on Arrynia and Rigel and Sillia spent time together every day. Sillia was twenty years old and studied to be a teacher. She played the harp and Rigel enjoyed listening to her playing and how much feeling she put into her music. It appeared that Sillia was as attracted to Rigel as he was to her. They had to use a translation device to communicate.

"May I stay in touch with you over the Internet?" Rigel asked and took her hand.

"Of course," Sillia responded with a smile. "When will you be back here on Arrynia?"

"I'll be here once every thirteen weeks," Rigel responded. "Sillia, I think you have stolen my heart."

Sillia laughed and her laugh sounded like little bells, just like his mother used to say about Funina.

"Rigel, I reciprocate," Sillia said looking into his eyes.

Privately, Brianna asked Funina how she felt about Rigel's interest in her daughter and Funina smiled and said she approved, but it was up to Sillia to pick her future husband. Both Brandon and Brianna had no objections to a mixed marriage and Arrynians and humans were able to produce children.

This was the first of several trips the three made to Arrynia and after a year Rigel mastered the technique of flying the ship through the tunnel. His parents taught him many valuable lessons from a lifetime of flying and interacting with different aliens. They got along well together and Rigel now started to know his parents as friends. He had grown up barely seeing them and he felt he had a lot of catching up to do.

They were one day away from landing on Arrynia, when Rigel said -

"I'm gonna ask Sillia to marry me this time. I love her."

"We expected that," Brianna responded. "We like her and wish you well."

They landed and climbed out of the ship. Funina and Sillia waited in the lobby. Rigel lifted up Sillia and hugged her and suggested they go outside and talk for a while. Behind the building were benches and tables and they sat down. Rigel had tried to learn the Arrynian language to no avail. He did not have an ear for languages and had given up, but Sillia had taken lessons in Frejjan for a year and had worked diligently and was able to speak broken Frejjan. Rigel had only been fourteen years old when he moved to Frejja and was still young enough to learn the Frejjan language rather quickly. He also spoke fluent English, which was his native language.

"Sillia, please marry me, I love you," Rigel said in Frejjan.

"Yes, yes, I can't wait and I love you, too," Sillia replied.

"Are you willing to live on Frejja? You would be the only Arrynian I know of living on Frejja. I would only apply for shorter space trips and not be gone for years at the time. Between trips I have three weeks off. Do you think we can make it work?"

"I would like to live on Frejja and it wouldn't bother me to be the only Arrynian on your planet. I did some research about Frejja and immigration is open to several planets. Eventually there may be different peoples living on your planet and no one will think I'm that different. I look at the Kodetsians on our planet and, sure, they look very different from us, but they are nice people and I like them. I hope your people will accept me."

"I have never seen prejudice on Frejja. Earth, where I grew up, used to have race problems in the old days, but when I was a kid that problem didn't exist any longer. Would you be willing to marry me the next time I land here? When I have my three weeks off, I could find us a place to live."

"I would be happy to marry you when you come back next time and return with you on the ship to Frejja."

Rigel hugged her and they went inside to tell their parents the news. No one was surprised and Funina had a tear in her eye.

"I'll miss you so much," she said to her daughter.

"Mom, we'll see each other again. It's only five weeks of travel time."

Back on Frejja, Rigel found a starter house not too far from the air field and bought it. It was not too big, but cozy and he would pay for it in installments. He was well paid as a pilot and could easily afford it.

The three weeks on Frejja flew and Rigel and his parents spent the time tidying up the new house. They furnished it with a mix of printed and old-fashioned furniture, equipped the kitchen and even had time to prepare a little vegetable garden behind the house. When they were finished, all three thought the house was truly welcoming. The house was rather far from Clarence and Lotte's house, where Brandon and Brianna stayed when they had their time off, but it was only a two-hour trip with an airmobile.

The big day arrived and the wedding was a small affair with only family members attending. Sillia looked like an angel with her blue dress matching her big blue eyes and was truly attractive looking. Rigel said his vows without hesitation. The ceremony was simple but endearing and Rigel and Sillia spent the rest of the week in a country cabin that Funina had rented for them.

It was hard for Sillia to say farewell to her parents. She was their only child and had always been very close to her parents. Brianna assured Funina that she could travel for free on the supply ship any time she wanted to visit Frejja and that made the parting a little easier.

Sillia found the travel time on the spaceship fascinating. This was the first time she had been in a spaceship and even going through the tunnel did not scare her. Being weightless was also a new experience for her, but the ship had rails and handles everywhere so it was easy to prevent floating away. Artificial gravity onboard spaceships had still not been invented. The gravity on Frejja was much less than on Arrynia and that was also something Sillia would have to get used to. She was very flexible and took most things in stride. Not much bothered her and her easygoing personality was part of her attractiveness.

They landed and Rigel and Sillia said goodbye to Brandon and Brianna. Rigel would return to the ship in three weeks and make another trip to Arrynia. He had already planned to ask for a new route closer to Frejja. His parents had become his friends and he would miss flying with them, but being with Sillia was more important.

To Rigel's relief, Sillia loved the house and assured Rigel it was perfect. Funina and her husband were affluent and Sillia had grown up in comfort. Rigel talked to his employer and was told that he could fly domestically and the longest he would be gone was three days. There was no other route other than Arrynia where pilots were needed for the time being. He discussed it with Sillia and she favored continuing the Arrynia route to gain experience and then, if he still wanted to, transfer to domestic flying. Rigel accepted her advice and Sillia told him that she would study the Frejjan language while he was away and then start learning English, so she would be plenty busy. She would look for employment when she felt more proficient in the Frejjan language.

To ensure their Arrynian marriage would be recognized as legal on Frejja, they had to go through a quick ceremony at a government office. As they were traveling to the office, Rigel asked Sillia how long Arrynians usually lived and when she responded that most lived to one hundred and ten years, Rigel sighed and said humans like himself only lived to one hundred years on average.

Just as Thole had experienced, Sillia never encountered any discrimination on Frejja. It was actually the opposite - she had celebrity status and Rigel's friends enjoyed meeting her. Part of the reason was Sillia's personality. She was charming.

When Rigel returned to work, Sillia spent several hours daily studying the Frejjan language and learning how to read and write. The written Arrynian language used pictorial characters and she had to learn the Frejjan alphabet, which she found rather confusing. She had discovered a good Internet course she followed and with her hard work, she was advancing quickly. Reading and especially writing was a tough challenge, but she was alone in the house and had the time to dedicate solely to her studies. Her plan was to also learn English once she had mastered Frejjan so she would be able to speak English with Rigel's relatives. She had a few friends in the neighborhood and did not feel lonely and with her airmobile she could explore the countryside and just enjoy the vista of farm animals and lakes.

Rigel had told her that Frejjans did not have pets, but many Arrynians did keep a pet. It was usually a 'rollo', a highly intelligent animal resembling a small woodchuck without the large teeth. A rollo could understand at least forty commands and was totally devoted to its master. With a life span of fifty years, an Arrynian looking for a pet would carefully select the animal as it would be part of that Arrynian's life for a long time. Sillia planned to ask Rigel to buy her a baby rollo on his next trip to Arrynia.

Sillia was a materialist and did not have any spiritual beliefs. Organized religion did not exist on Arrynia, but spiritualism was common. Sillia only believed in things that had been proven and since no one had seen God she did not recognize there was a God. Rigel on the contrary had strong spiritual beliefs, but kept them to himself. He felt no need to talk about them. Eventually, Sillia figured out her husband believed in the afterlife and reincarnation and they agreed it was fine to disagree on matters of faith. They never allowed it to become an issue.

******

Clarence had recently retired and his thirteen years working on Frejja had been rewarding. Now at eighty-two years old, he just wanted to be home and enjoy retirement. He loved Frejja and wanted to explore the countryside, do some fishing and just think back on his life. There was one problem though and that was his heart. He suspected it would have to be replaced and his doctor confirmed his suspicion. Some of his stem cells were removed and a new heart would be grown from these cells and transplanted into Clarence in six weeks. The heart would actually be ready in five weeks, but the doctors wanted to watch the heart beat for a full week before implanting it.

Clarence spent the time while his heart was growing resting and enjoying sitting outside in his nicely landscaped yard. Once the new heart was implanted, he did not have to be so careful and he looked forward to it.

Lotte took Clarence to the hospital and neither of them felt concern. Medical care on Frejja was more advanced than on Earth and the surgery would be performed by an experienced android with his own doctor assisting. Lotte waited anxiously until the surgery was over and then saw Clarence wheeled out. The android came out and told her all had gone perfectly well and that his new heart was strong and beating without any problems. He advised Lotte to go home and return the next day as she could not yet visit with Clarence.

She was allowed a short visit when she returned and Clarence was awake and smiled at her.

"I'll heal soon, Lotte. I have no pain," he said and his voice was strong and vigorous. He had received pain medication so he would be able to rest and sleep.

After a week Lotte was allowed to bring Clarence home and he lay down in the airmobile. He was weak, but in good spirits and Lotte and Eva nursed him back to health. After a month, he was fully recovered and felt invigorated and strong.

The year before, Lotte had had both her knees replaced, but other than that she was in good health.

CHAPTER 27

Emrak was very proud of his family. Karol had given him another beautiful son, Rey, who was now two years old. Leo was already seven and Alison a young lady at fourteen years old. He enjoyed his work as flight instructor and to be able to come home every evening. Karol and his family meant everything to Emrak. In addition to his work as flight instructor, he was senior advisor to the president in all matters of space. He was considered the most experienced space person on Frejja. Mr. Parker had only one year left of his second presidential term, but Emrak's work as advisor would most likely continue with the next president. Karol's work as advisor to Mr. Parker would terminate when his presidency was over.

Elliot had married a Frejjan girl, Ultora, and lived a short distance away. He still worked at the same hospital and found his work interesting and challenging.

Mr. Taylor's second term as president of Mars was over. He was only forty-three years old and had never been married. Although he was plain looking, he had a winning personality and a heart of gold. True to his nature, he had stood up for the people of Bantizza and Martia had paid the whole cost of liberating them. Mr. Taylor mulled over what to do with the rest of his life. He did not feel like returning to Earth. Deep inside he wanted to find a wife and settle down and the best place to find a wife was Frejja. The recruiting android was still on Mars and Mr. Taylor walked over to his office and applied for residency on Frejja. The android instantly recognized Mr. Taylor as the former president and told him he would easily find a well-paying job within the Frejjan government as soon as he could speak the language. In one month the Frejjan ship would arrive to pick up new immigrants and Mr. Taylor did not waste any time starting his language lessons. The android had given him the software so he could learn by himself and his self-taught lessons worked out better than he had expected. A few times he dropped in to chat with the android in Frejjan just to check if he was understood and the android had no problem understanding him.

Mr. Taylor spent the first month as usual at the hotel on Frejja and at the end of the month he spoke broken Frejjan. To his surprise, Mr. Parker offered him a job as his assistant, but told him that he had only a year left in office and the new president may not keep him on. Anyway, he would have a full year to work on his language skills and then apply for the same job with the new president. Mr. Taylor was grateful for the opportunity. He and Mr. Parker had never met in person, but had interacted many times over the Internet discussing governmental affairs so they knew each other rather well anyway.

He found a small house not too far from his workplace and started his new job. Mr. Parker gave him all the details how the Frejjan government functioned and it did not take Mr. Taylor long to pick up all the intricacies of the economy, infrastructure and defense system. He was experienced after all and an intelligent man. He and Mr. Parker worked well together and liked each other. When they were alone, they spoke English so Mr. Parker could explain government affairs more efficiently. As he settled in and became used to Frejjan ways he knew he had made the right move. He felt peace within and liked his new job. Best of all, he was dating a Frejjan woman and hoped she would marry him.

******

The work day was over on Earth2 and many sat outside as darkness fell. The birds sat quietly in the trees and it was pleasantly warm outside, a peaceful summer evening. Then, all of a sudden, a greenish light appeared at the horizon and then slowly traveled across the sky. More colors appeared and the light moved in waves and covered the whole sky. It was an awesome sight of incredible beauty and lasted about an hour. People realized they were watching an aurora and enjoyed the display. When they hooked up their communication system the next day to contact Frejja it was dead. The person using the machine realized they had been hit with a solar flare that had fried the electronic device and it could probably not be repaired. They did have a spare, but the machine was very costly and to lose it was troublesome. The fried unit had not been covered and had been left out in the open, but the spare was stored underground and when they uncovered it, it worked. They checked the black boxes and found they were heavily insulated and had survived. Some of their other electronic equipment had also been fried, but anything that had been stored underground had survived the solar flare.

They had no knowledge of their sun's 'history' and sunspot pattern and how often they could be hit with solar flares, so from that day on they insulated all their electronic equipment. There was no damage to anything else and to their great relief the two airmobiles had survived without harm as they were always stored inside a metal building. They realized the solar flare had not been severe but a modest one. A severe flare may have damaged even protected equipment.

The population had increased to one hundred sixty people and the 3D printers were steadily building more houses. The last supply ship had brought four meat animals and two had survived the trip, luckily one male and one female. They were kept for breeding and the colonists had asked for another shipment of meat animals and egg laying chickens. The cost of the supply ship was an enormous expense for the colonists and without their gold deposit in the cave they could not have afforded to order supplies from Frejja. They all knew, however, that once their community was fully established, they probably would be self-sufficient or close to it, but building a modern community from scratch required lots of supplies.

The geologist, Ijakull, was looking for additional natural minerals on the planet. Using the airmobile and the most knowledgeable of the worker robots, the two explored a large area around the community and one day they lucked out. They had stopped at a wide, but shallow riverbed to rest for a few minutes when the robot called out -

"Platinum, look!"

Ijakull quickly climbed out of the airmobile and waded out into the knee-deep water holding a gold pan in his hand. It was a placer deposit and the geologist scooped up some of the sand from the river into his pan and shook it. He saw it was indeed what looked like a mix of platinum and iridium referred to as platiniridium. The robot recognized that the sand and gravel had a certain look that only platinum has and he had in the past helped mining it. The method was almost the same as gold panning. They carefully checked the riverbed and found that the deposit was large stretching for many miles and most of it was platiniridium and here and there a nugget of pure platinum.

Ijakull laughed out loud and wildly shook hands with the robot in his excitement. What a find! It was worth a fortune and both platinum and iridium were highly sought after in manufacturing of electronics, medical equipment and many other items. All they needed to do was to dredge out the sand from the riverbed and do the initial washing and processing of the minerals. The refining of the minerals would be done on Frejja.

The riverbed was not far from the community and the following day the robot that had found the deposit and ten men from the community started dredging manually. They carefully worked their way down the river and extracted the platiniridium and returned the plain sand to the riverbed. There was minimal disturbance to the river itself and they left no unsightly mess.

The colonists were hoping they could soon afford to buy the machinery needed to refine the minerals themselves, but the expense was too high right now. Perhaps in a year or so, they said to each other. They also needed a dredging machine, but it was unaffordable at the present time.

The platiniridium was refined on Frejja and found to be of high quality and together with the gold, the minerals generated a good income for the colonists. Their debt to Frejja was high though and it would take them a decade at least to become debt free.

There had been an accident in the cave with the gold deposit. The colonist, Oleon, had slipped with his chopping tool and with full force he had cut his thigh instead. A deep gash appeared and the blood was running fast out of his leg. It looked horrific. He was rushed to the clinic in town and the doctor saw right away that this may be beyond his capability to repair. Oleon had cut his artery and needed surgery. The doctor made an emergency call over the Interstellar Internet to Frejja asking for advice and one of the android surgeons, Atlas, appeared holographically and was able to see the wound through the communication device the doctor had. It was the latest model and the doctor was thankful the device had full camera capabilities and could receive and transmit images instantly. Atlas gave rapid orders to the doctor and Oleon was prepared for surgery. It was now life and death as he had lost a lot of blood. The doctor had no nurse, but he had trained one of the women to help him during surgeries and she had acquired enough skill to be able to assist him. They sedated Oleon and step by step the android took the doctor through the delicate surgery, first repairing the artery and then carefully sealing the deep wound. Atlas was highly accomplished and without him the doctor would have lost Oleon. He could not have handled the surgery alone.

Oleon recovered and was able to walk with a slight limp after six weeks and a few weeks later he was back in the mine. He was much more careful now and did not allow himself to get distracted. He sent a message to Atlas thanking him for saving his life and Atlas replied that every life he saved made his existence more meaningful.

The two female goats were milked daily and the does gave a gallon each, which was shared by the colonists on a rotating schedule. Meat and eggs were needed and they hoped the next shipment from Frejja would have live chickens. The female of the meat animals was pregnant, but to build a herd they needed many more. For the time being, they relied on freeze dried meat from Frejja. The fields around the community were well suited as pasture and if they only could get more animals, they knew they would have a herd rather quickly. Building a modern society from scratch was no easy task and so many things they had taken for granted when they lived on Frejja seemed unsurmountable on Earth2.

******

Rigel had brought back a baby rollo from Arrynia and Sillia was thrilled. It was a female, a furry bundle they named 'Rollo' and Rigel had visited with the little animal several times every day on the ship to ensure it would not die. He was relieved it had survived as Funina had been very particular when she selected the animal. It was an adorable little thing and so affectionate. Sillia had Rollo house trained within a week and Rollo's favorite time was when she sat in Sillia's lap. She understood several commands already. As a vegetarian, she ate a mix of vegetables, fruits, grain and alfalfa pellets. She grew rapidly and her adult weight would be about twenty pounds. Having a pet was a novelty and Sillia's friends were amused and curious. Some of them were openminded to having a pet themselves, but there were no pets to buy on Frejja. Sillia thought to herself that perhaps some more rollos could be imported from Arrynia and be offered as gifts.

Sillia was pregnant and the doctor told her fraternal twins were on the way, a boy and a girl. The doctor found the babies of great interest as they were the first offspring he had seen from a Frejjan and an Arrynian. The babies were transferred to the artificial womb and thriving. Both Sillia and Rigel were excited and looked forward to the day they could bring the twins home. Every week they visited the babies to watch them mature.

Rigel and Sillia were now proud parents of a boy, Ran, and a girl, Asta. Both had hair on their heads and they looked like a pleasant mix of their parents. They resembled Rigel more than Sillia and were good looking babies. The doctor examined them carefully and reported they were perfectly healthy. Sillia nursed them herself even though formula was more commonly used by mothers. Rollo was almost grownup and gently sniffed on the babies. She understood they were little ones and seemed to genuinely love them. Sillia enjoyed being a mother and to stay home with the babies. Rigel bought an android, Dotty, and she did all the household chores freeing Sillia from tedious housework. Sillia was small, but she was far from a weakling. Growing up on Arrynia with heavier gravity than Earth, her bones and muscles were very strong. She had adapted to the lighter gravity on Frejja, but exercised every day to maintain as much of her bone and muscle strength as possible.

Rigel brought back six more rollos from Arrynia and Sillia gave them as gifts to her friends. They were very appreciated and this started a trend, where Frejjans understood the value of a pet and its devotion to its master.

✳✳✳✳✳✳

Tothellim was the most experienced of Peturun's pilots and he was on his way to Peturun's trading partner, a planet in the Pleiades area. He knew of an area with unusual vibration that he must pass to reach his destination and he always passed with lots of room to spare. The vibration was strong enough to slightly shake his ship and he suspected it was a tunnel of more power than the shortcut tunnel to Mars. When he returned to Peturun, he asked his supervisor if he had their permission to fly through the tunnel. He had decided to take the risk and find out once and for all where the tunnel ended. Tothellim was unmarried and had no children and he knew he risked his life, but he was also curious and willing to accept the challenge. His supervisor was hesitant to let him embark on such a dangerous expedition and risk both his own life and the destruction of the ship with its high price tag. Tothellim was the best pilot they had and the supervisor felt he must consult with the president before giving his permission to Tothellim. As the president listened and thought about it, he replied -

"It could open up new opportunities for our planet and make new areas available to us. The furthest we have been is planet Mars." He fell silent and scratched his head while thinking and then made up his mind -

"It's worth it, let's explore this tunnel," he said. "If Tothellim is willing, this government is willing to support him. Give him our most advanced ship with the latest communication system. To be on the safe side, load the ship with food and equipment for several years. Give him my best wishes and when he returns, I want to meet with him in my office."

Tothellim was enthusiastic and notified Emrak. The two of them had been in contact over the Internet several times while Brandon and Brianna were training to learn how to fly through the shortcut tunnel and Emrak knew Tothellim was the best pilot he had ever encountered. Emrak was excited and asked Tothellim to record the tunnel as a holographic image and to stay in contact with him during the trip, if it was possible. The two men respected each other and Tothellim valued Emrak's opinion.

The ship was ready and fully packed. Only one copilot had volunteered to come along and four android crew members were onboard to oversee the mechanical systems of the ship. They had years of experience and were fully capable of both repairs and running the ship, but had only flown the ship through short tunnels, never longer ones.

It took a month to reach the tunnel and as they neared the entry of the tunnel, Tothellim and his copilot Rheo, who was very competent, switched to manual control, each of them manning one of the dual stations. The ship was literally sucked into the tunnel with incredible force and the vibration was enormous. Tothellim had the controls the first hour and they switched back and forth while traveling through the tunnel, which appeared to be waving back and forth the whole time. It was wide enough for the ship to pass through and it had enough room to safely accommodate a much larger ship. The ship was increasing in speed and the vibration increased with the acceleration. Tothellim was hoping the terrynium would hold up and not crack. It was exceptionally strong, but it did have its limits. The two men had no idea how long the tunnel was and started to feel fatigued and stressed. They had been flying fifteen hours and the speed of the ship was the fastest Tothellim had ever experienced. At eighteen hours the tunnel ended and they catapulted out of the tunnel at a fantastic speed. Now, nothing was in front of them and they engaged the autopilot and collapsed.

What an experience! Where were they? After a while Tothellim pulled himself together and checked the instruments. Everything had been recorded and to his astonishment he realized they were not in the Milky Way galaxy. The instruments showed a location in the Andromeda galaxy and they had traveled *two and a half million light years* from their starting point in the Pleiades! How was it possible? Both Tothellim and Rheo felt the instruments were wrong and called in two of the androids to double check their location. After an hour of carefully running tests on the computer system the androids confirmed their location. It was correct. They were indeed in the Andromeda galaxy.

"Every tunnel is very different," one of the androids reminded Tothellim and Rheo. "This tunnel is apparently a mega portal, perhaps even a black hole. It's impossible for us to know exactly how it functions. We just have to accept it's the biggest shortcut we have ever encountered as pilots."

There was a planetary body far away and they realized it must be a planet and if they continued, they would eventually see its star. As this trip was an exploratory trip, Tothellim decided it was worth it to investigate the planet. After a month they were nearing the planet and entered its obit. It was a large planet, twice the size of Earth, no moons and it was occupied. As night fell over the new planet, large areas were lit and they realized they were watching cities. The ship had a shuttle onboard as well as a drone equipped with advanced camera and recording capabilities and the next day Tothellim decided to launch the drone and watch from the safety of the ship as the drone flew above the planet's surface. They programmed the drone to stay at an elevation of two thousand feet and travel at only fifty miles per hour and launched it from cargo bay.

What they saw on their screen on the Bridge was an ultra-modern city with humans walking around. People looking exactly like Earth people and Frejjans. There were no vehicles on the surface, but a lot of traffic above ground at different altitudes. As the drone slowly flew over the city, Tothellim and Rheo watched mesmerized the images the drone transmitted. Neither of them had been to Earth and Frejja, but they had seen many holograms of both planets and this planet looked like Earth. Tothellim had only been to Mars and had never visited the other planets in the solar system. He had wanted to go to Earth, but Peturun had no trade with Earth and his supervisor had never suggested that Tothellim should go there.

The drone continued into the countryside and farm fields with crops appeared as well as herds with farm animals. There were homes here and there, but not many, indicating that most people lived in the cities. The drone continued and reached what looked like an ocean with ships tied up at the dock. Right next to the dock was an airfield with spaceships parked one next to the other. Some were extremely large and some were small and the men figured the small ones were for domestic travel and the larger ships for space travel.

Tothellim transmitted a command to the drone to return and it was soon back in cargo bay. He and Rheo agreed that the next day they should turn the ship over to the androids and descend to the surface with the shuttle. They concluded that the humans had seen aliens from different planets before and would not freak out when they saw the Peturuns. The size of their spaceships clearly told them that the humans were used to space travel. Tothellim and Rheo decided to land the shuttle on the airfield next to the port.

When the shuttle was close to the air field, Tothellim transmitted a message in English that they came in peace and only wanted to talk. He gave the frequency of his transmission. Tothellim spoke broken English, well enough to converse without a translation device. He had decided to learn English so he could speak with the Martians more freely as he routinely visited Mars to buy terrynium. The response was loud and clear -

"Go ahead and land. You are welcome here," the voice replied in English.

They landed softly and climbed out. A group of three women and five men dressed in uniforms, all humans, walked out to greet them and they all shook hands with Tothellim and Rheo. The air was fresh and it was warm with beautiful sunshine. The gravity was slightly heavier than on Peturun, but not a problem. The humans invited Tothellim and Reo inside and they sat down in the lobby.

"I am Rear Admiral Peter Harris and I am the commanding officer here. Please tell us where you come from and why."

Tothellim and Rheo introduced themselves. Rheo had to use his translation device, but Tothellim's English was well understood and he did most of the talking. He started by telling them about his home planet and its location, then the tunnel and his knowledge of Mars, Earth and Frejja as well as the planets around Peturun. It took him a few hours to explain everything and that their ship was now in orbit around their planet and tended by androids. The people listened with great interest to Tothellim's long story. They were especially captivated when Tothellim told them about Earth and Frejja populated with humans just like them.

"We know this corner of our galaxy rather well, but we didn't know about your tunnel," the Rear Admiral said. "It's unbelievable that you have traveled two and a half million light years. We have never visited the Milky Way and the furthest our ships can travel is about fifteen light years and of course we do use the tunnels we know about in our area." The Rear Admiral continued -

"The name of our planet is Veehnia and it orbits our star Vakria. There are four planets in our solar system and the other three planets are unoccupied. They're not habitable for human life. There are four billion people on this planet and we're all the same race, one country and one government. This is a peaceful planet and we don't have wars, at least not the last hundred years. There used to be very bloody domestic wars on Veehnia, but people realized wars don't solve problems. It took hundreds of years and millions of lost lives until people finally realized this fact. The quality of life is good on our planet and all citizens have their basic needs taken care of by our government. The people have full freedom and our government is not oppressive. Veehnia is rich in minerals and we export precious metals and other minerals to several planets and that's what we use our spaceships for. The tunnels we use are standard tunnels and none of them can compare with the two tunnels you use - the tunnel to Mars and the tunnel to our galaxy. We have never heard of terrynium before, but our ships are made with another alloy that is strong enough to cope with the vibration in the tunnels we do use. There are a few inhabited planets in our area and they are friendly. The people are humanoids like you are, but look a little different than us. We trade with them."

It was getting dark and they all went to the dining room in the building. The waiters were all human and they saw no androids. Tothellim tried to figure out if Veehnia was more or less advanced than Peturun, but he had not seen enough of the planet to know the answer. They were served beef with mashed vegetables and Tothellim had had similar food on Mars and liked it. It was obvious that Rheo also enjoyed the meal as he looked pleased while he rapidly gobbled up the food on his plate. After dinner they were taken to a hotel and it was decided they would exchange more information the following day. The androids onboard the ship knew that Tothellim and Rheo would probably not return for several days and with the ship in orbit, there was little for them to do but wait for the return of the pilots.

The following two weeks were very hectic and Tothellim asked the androids to transmit loads of information from the ship to the planet including the full recording of their travel through the tunnel. Holograms from Peturun, Martia, Frejja and Earth were also sent as well as information about all the planets and tunnels Tothellim knew about in the Milky Way. In return, the Admiral and his team transmitted straight to the ship's computers the locations of all the tunnels they were familiar with, the planets they traded with and customs on those planets and also a lot of information about their own planet Veehnia, its history, government, financial system and life in general. The Admiral did not know if their spaceships needed to be reinforced to travel through the tunnel to the Milky Way, but he would check with the engineers in charge of building the ships.

"We'll definitely visit your planet and will start training our best pilots to negotiate the tunnel," he said. "Eighteen hours with manual control, goodness, that's quite an accomplishment. We would make an initial trip landing on Peturun first, then Mars and finally our sister planet Earth. I will personally be onboard and I look forward to it. I hope we can be ready to leave in a year. I need to have our engineers analyze the strength of the alloy that our ships are made of to make sure they hold up to the vibration in the tunnel. Later on, we'll also visit Frejja."

"The trip from Veehnia to Peturun will take two months," Tothellim remarked. "From Peturun to Mars takes six months and you'll go through the second tunnel, which takes twelve hours. From Mars to Earth will take three weeks and you'll travel through one tunnel. Almost nine months of travel time in total. Add to that the time you'll stay on each of the planets. You may be away from home close to two years if we figure roundtrip."

"That is indeed a long trip," the Admiral replied slowly. "The ship will be manned only by people volunteering for the trip. I will go, that's for sure. I wouldn't miss it for anything."

Tothellim and Rheo spent another two weeks traveling around Veehnia by airmobile. The planet was beautiful and it appeared to Tothellim that Veehnia was slightly less advanced than Peturun, but ahead of Mars and Earth. Services such as education and medical care seemed excellent and they were told the crime rate was low. The people were friendly and curious to meet them. No one was put off by their appearance. Tothellim was well aware the Peturuns were not the best-looking people in the universe and, personally, he admired the looks of humans the most. Some of the women on Mars were stunning and being single he would love to marry a human woman. The Veehnians were also good looking.

After staying a month on Veehnia, Tothellim and Rheo returned to the ship with the shuttle and briefed the androids about the most important things they had experienced. In case something would happen to them, it was important that the androids would be able to report the details of the trip to the president of Peturun.

The return trip went well and the travel through the tunnel was strenuous, but this time Tothellim and Rheo knew beforehand that it would take eighteen long hours and that the ship would not break apart from the vibration, so there was nothing to fear. They landed on Peturun and even though they had only been gone five months, it felt to both of them as if a year had passed.

The president and his top advisors were eager to hear the news about the tunnel and Veehnia and its people. Tothellim showed all the holographic images from the planet and informed the president that in about a year Peturun would be visited by a ship from Veehnia. The president welcomed the news and said he looked forward very much to meeting them.

Tothellim had a month off before he had to report back for duty and after a few days he contacted Emrak and gave him a full report. He also transmitted loads of holographic pictures to Emrak and full details of the tunnel with visual images that could be entered into their flight simulator as well as the exact location of the tunnel. Emrak was flabbergasted when he heard that eighteen hours of travel time through the tunnel amounted to moving a distance of two and a half million light years. Emrak had never met Tothellim in person, but emphasized that he would be honored if they could meet. Tothellim replied that he would try to arrange a trip to Frejja, but it all depended on if his supervisor would approve the cost of the trip. Each space trip was hugely costly and there had to be some benefit to the trip to justify the expense. Emrak naturally understood this and he thanked Tothellim several times for all the information he had sent him.

CHAPTER 28

Emrak informed Mr. Parker about Tothellim's trip to Veehnia and then met with him in his office. There were only a few months left of Mr. Parker's presidency. Mr. Taylor was also present and all eager to hear the incredible news about Veehnia. He knew Tothellim rather well from all the trips he had made to Mars when Mr. Taylor lived there and he had great admiration for the man, his courage and abilities. Emrak showed all the images he had and some of them were put on the Frejjan Internet for the citizens to see. Tothellim's trip had truly been remarkable and it was the talk of the day for weeks on Frejja. People could not have enough of it and many expressed interest to go there and see the planet for themselves.

Karol was also fascinated to hear about the trip and she and Emrak spent hours discussing it. Emrak programmed the flight simulator with all the information and visual input about the tunnel to the Andromeda galaxy and invited Brandon and Brianna to try it. The next time they returned from Arrynia, they accepted the challenge and tried it. The simulator had dual controls and Brandon and Brianna were at each control knowing they could only leave for a few minutes for bathroom breaks and had to stay for the full eighteen hours. It was grueling. By fourteen hours they were both exhausted, but they held out and passed the test. They had held the ship perfectly centered and endured the incredible vibration without giving up. Emrak stayed the whole time and quietly watched in the back of the simulator. He was impressed. Brandon and Brianna were the most experienced pilots Frejja had and they were an asset to Frejja. When the test was finally over, Emrak asked them if they would be willing to fly to Veehnia. The travel time from Frejja to Veehnia would be about seven months. The whole trip could take fifteen months, if they stayed on the planet a month. Brandon and Brianna replied they would give their answer in about a week. They needed to think about it.

They were all together in Clarence and Lotte's house: Brandon, Brianna, Rigel, Sillia and Orion and the topic was a family decision whether it was too risky for Brandon and Brianna to travel to Veehnia. They spoke English and Sillia used her translation device so she could follow the conversation. Brandon and Brianna knew, of course, the decision was theirs to make, but wanted to hear what the family thought. Rigel and Sillia both voted yes while Orion was dead set against it and felt it was too dangerous. Clarence, always adventurous, voted yes and Lotte against. Three yes and two no. They had all seen the images on the Internet and found the project exciting, but the distance was mind-boggling and hard to fathom.

"Thank you all for your input," Brianna said. "We'll need to think about it further before we decide."

"I want to go and if we do, it should be our last long trip," Brandon said when they were alone. "Do you agree?"

"'I'll tell you tomorrow when I have slept on it," Brianna responded.

The next day she told Brandon she would go and that she agreed it should be their last long-distance trip. They notified Emrak and he was glad to hear they were willing to go and told them he would organize everything and have a ship packed and ready within one month. The decision was now made and there was no going back. Emrak selected a late model ship made with terrynium and equipped with the very latest electronics and full backup system should anything fail. Four experienced androids and two extra pilots would also be onboard and the two pilots had already volunteered to go. They also had years of experience. Four people had asked if they could go along as paying passengers at their own risk and Emrak gave his approval after mulling over it for a while. He had great trust in Brandon and Brianna and even though the trip was long, he felt they were so experienced by now that the risk was actually not as high as he had originally thought.

Family members as well as Emrak and Karol saw them off and the ship departed. They had seven months of travel ahead of them with two complicated tunnels to cross and would cover over two and a half million light years in distance. The ship felt rock solid and just knowing it had full backup systems gave them a sense of security. The engines they used had never failed and seemed to go on forever and two of the androids were engine specialists and had the expertise to repair all the common engine failures should anything go wrong. One of the androids was a medic.

They crossed the twelve-hour tunnel without problems and within two months they would enter the monster tunnel that would catapult them into the Andromeda galaxy. The speed of the ship had doubled when they came out of the first tunnel. They had entered the coordinates into the computers and traveled at enormous speed towards the tunnel. The androids and copilots were used to space travel and had no fear of anything, but strangely enough the four passengers kept their composure and never showed any sign of distress.

Just as Tothellim had experienced, Brandon and Brianna felt how the ship was literally sucked into the monster tunnel and the vibration started full force. The two copilots were ready to jump in and take over if they were needed and Brandon and Brianna were thankful to have them on the Bridge. The copilots had trained in the flight simulator and were capable of flying the ship through the tunnel. In an absolute emergency two of the androids would probably be able to fly the ship. They had in the past worked as copilots for years.

Now followed eighteen hours of hellish travel through the monster tunnel and the whole time the speed accelerated. The tunnel was moving and Brandon and Brianna had to work hard to keep the ship centered in the tunnel and prevent it from weaving from side to side in the tunnel. They took turns manning the controls with the person off the controls working almost as hard as the person in control. They took fifteen minutes off every three hours to catch their breath and a copilot stepped in. The vibration was beyond anything they had experienced and the ship shook violently. The passengers were in another part of the ship strapped into their seats and only their pale faces revealed their apprehension. None of them complained. One of the androids was sitting with them in case they would panic. Overall, the passengers were showing great courage, which was remarkable since none of them had ever been in space before. It was a married couple and two single men, all of them in their late twenties. They knew each other and had decided to join the spaceship as passengers as soon as they heard about the plans. What they had not revealed to anyone was that the four had no intention to return to Frejja and would ask Veehnia if they could stay. This would be an adventure of a lifetime, if they were allowed to remain on the planet.

They made it! The ship blasted out of the tunnel at a speed that Brandon and Brianna had never been faced with before. They checked all their instruments and could not find any damage from the vibration and the computers confirmed they had indeed traveled two and a half million light years. All that was left of the trip was one month of easy travel and they would be in orbit around Veehnia. The month felt like vacation. They spent time with the passengers and copilots going through the stored information about Veehnia to learn as much as possible about the planet before they entered orbit. They were now close enough to Veehnia to send messages and transmitted communication they were on their way and would soon be in orbit. Within an hour they received a reply they were welcome and to just go ahead and land with their shuttle.

Brandon slowed down the ship and they entered orbit. The shuttle seated ten people and all eight of them took off leaving the ship in the care of the androids. Brianna entered the location of the air field into the computer and off they went. The air was filled with excitement and as the shuttle descended to an elevation of five hundred feet they all looked out the windows. They landed on the same air field where Tothellim had landed and climbed out. Brandon, Brianna and the copilots wore their uniforms and the passengers were dressed in civilian clothes.

Rear Admiral Harris and the president of Veehnia were among a group of people greeting them when they climbed out of the shuttle. A year had passed since Tothellim landed.

"Welcome to Veehnia, my friends!" The president was all smiles and shook hands with all of them. "I'm President Curtis. Let's go in and talk."

They went inside and a lively conversation followed that lasted several hours. The passengers did not say much, but listened intently waiting for the right moment to ask if they could stay. Towards the end, before they went to dinner, one of them found the courage to gently ask the question -

"Is there any chance the four of us can stay here on Veehnia permanently?" He spoke in broken English.

The Veehnians were as surprised as Brandon and Brianna to hear the request and President Curtis chuckled and said -

"I guess you planned this all along, didn't you?"

"I'm afraid so. We couldn't resist the adventure."

"Of course, you can stay. It would be informative for us to learn from your culture. I will arrange with the right people in our government to find housing and work for you. I assume Frejja is a free planet and no complications will arise if you stay."

Brandon and Brianna nodded and assured the president the passengers had total free will to stay. It was their decision to make. The president made a quick call using his communicator.

After a pleasant dinner a vehicle arrived and the passengers were invited to come along. They waved goodbye to the crew and entered the vehicle that took them to a hotel. The following day they would be questioned about their work experience and offered permanent housing and employment. An android would deliver their luggage from the ship using the shuttle when the crew was back again on the ship.

The crew stayed on Veehnia a full month and communicated daily with the androids onboard to make sure all was well on the ship. They stayed in an elegant hotel on the top floor with a brilliant view of the city. The month they spent on Veehnia was the highlight of Brandon's and Brianna's career and a memory for life. They had two meetings with President Curtis and lots of information was exchanged and comparisons made between Veehnia and Frejja. Veehnia was not that different from Frejja with a fully democratic government and free elections. They were told by private citizens that the government was free of corruption and so was the media.

They learned also that religion was important and many people attended church services. The people believed in the Creator and there was only one faith on Veehnia. Some people had faith but did not feel the need to go to church, but the churchgoers and the non-churchgoers had the same beliefs. God was usually referred to as *Nature's God* or *The Natural God* meaning the Creator has no connection to any religion or government anywhere in the universe. God is a Spirit and beyond the material universe.

The guide told Brandon and Brianna that the horrible wars that had plagued Veehnia in the past were portrayed to be about religion. The true reason for the wars was to gain power and full control over the people and religion was used as a tool to accomplish the mission. Thousands of people died in the wars until peace was finally restored. The religion that survived was the current one with belief in the Creator and reincarnation. The people who had believed in the opposite religion had either died in the wars or converted to believing in the Creator. Brianna revealed how similar wars over religion had occurred on Earth in the past, but the religions were still in existence. The difference between then and now was tolerance for other people's beliefs and to allow people to believe whatever they wanted without starting a war over it. Brianna explained to the guide that at the present time organized religion on Earth did exist, but the number of people attending religious services was only a fraction of what it had been in the years past. People with faith preferred to interact with their God in private, in their hearts and minds. Many people on both Earth and Veehnia had no religious beliefs. Brianna concluded -

"Religion is not the problem. Fanaticism, caused by the human ego, is the true problem."

Education was advanced and free for all and higher education, also free, was encouraged. A mix of human teachers and androids taught the children and Internet discourses were part of the curriculum. Math and sciences were carefully taught and the graduating students had an advanced understanding and knowledge of the sciences. Brandon and Brianna visited several schools as well as a university and admired the Veehnians' dedication to education. There were also trade schools for people preferring to learn a trade. They would work with the robots and supervise them.

Veehnia's medical care was excellent, they heard, and the average lifespan was about one hundred and fifty years. Brianna asked whether drugs were legal and was told yes. Their guide explained that when drugs were legalized, almost a whole generation was lost and died from overdoses, but eventually the lesson sank in and young people wanted nothing to do with drugs. Now it was no longer a problem. It had been hard to see young people die by the thousands, but unless a drug addict asked for help, no help was offered. When drugs were legalized and addiction faded away crime plummeted, less police force was needed, prisons emptied and an enormous amount of money was saved. Brandon explained that both Earth and Frejja had experienced almost identical conditions with drugs.

They were also told that there was still some crime on the planet, but it was not severe and the police force had the situation mostly under control.

There was only one language, English, and one race on the planet and, because of it, no diversity. Everyone was white. The guide told them immigration was open and aliens were welcome to move to the planet, but so far the long distances between planets had prevented any form of immigration. The four passengers would probably become novelties, the guide said with a smile, and then added that Veehnia was underpopulated and more people were needed. Veehnian women often had only one child so they could have a career and too few children were born. The government offered many incentives to women to encourage them to have more than one child, but only a few women were willing to have a large family. The artificial womb did not exist on the planet, but may be one solution to the problem.

"We'll forward the information to your planet about the artificial womb," Brianna said to the guide. She explained how it worked and that she had used it herself for her two boys. The guide said it would be a welcome invention and the medical society would be grateful to receive the design of the womb.

After they had toured the city, they traveled around the countryside and the two copilots came along. Veehnia was very similar to Earth with rolling hills, farms and sparsely populated. Farming was mechanized. There was one ocean on the planet about the size of the Atlantic Ocean and small lakes were common in the countryside. One mountain chain stretched from north to south and the mountains were very tall. Veehnia had four seasons with a mild winter.

"Do people have pets on Veehnia?" Brianna asked. "Do horses exist?"

"Yes, we have cats and dogs and even horses for horseback riding," the guide explained. "In the wild there are insects, of course, and reptiles, birds, wild pigs, deer and a few other herbivore animals. The only existing carnivores are wolves and bears."

"Are there fish in your ocean?" Brandon asked.

"Plenty, and fish is very popular as food," the guide responded. "There are no whales or seals in the ocean like they have on Earth."

"Do you monitor pollution?"

"Definitely! Our government has very strict rules and has managed to keep waste and all pollution to a minimum. Veehnia is a clean planet. Recycling is also mandatory."

"Pardon my silly question, but is Veehnia a paradise?" Brianna asked hesitatingly, trying not to offend.

The guide laughed and said -

"It may appear so from my description, but please note we do have our problems also. The population is going down, not good. It needs to almost double so the economy can grow. This is a large planet. There's no diversity here driving new inventions and you can say that, yes, we suffer from a degree of stagnation. It's so easy to live here and people tend to almost snooze their way through life and enjoy easy pickings. Hardships foster inventions and people dragging themselves up by their bootstraps often give back to society by showing what can be accomplished if there is a will. We need people who can shake up society from its cozy sleep, who can solve problems by looking at the situation from a different angle, actually, we need a blitz running through the monotony we now have. We hope your passengers will add a spark to our society and energize us."

Brandon mentioned the passengers were only in their twenties and the married couple and the two single men had worked together as a team since they graduated from school. They made holographic programs featuring different things in life, often with a humorous twist. Their programs were used both for information and entertainment and were always thought provoking. Brandon had seen several of the team's programs on Frejja and enjoyed them a lot.

"An interesting group of people," the guide remarked. "Just what we need."

The month on Veehnia came to an end and President Curtis and Rear Admiral Harris accompanied the crew as they returned to the ship with the shuttle. It felt strange to be back on the ship after a month on the new planet. Brandon showed the president and the rear admiral the ship and the Bridge and the rear admiral remarked there was not much difference between the Frejjan ship and their own ships. The next month the rear admiral would depart from Veehnia to the Milky Way and he looked forward to the trip. One of the androids returned the president and rear admiral to the planet and took along all the luggage from the passengers.

The return trip was long and tedious and they crossed the two tunnels without mishaps. They had been gone fifteen months and Brandon and Brianna as well as the copilots were looking forward to coming home and see their families. They had contacted Emrak from the ship and when they landed a group of people waited for them to welcome them home again and it was an emotional reunion. Even Mr. Parker and Mr. Taylor were there. Mr. Parker was no longer president, but he and Mr. Taylor had been offered good positions in the government by the new president, Mr. Emmett, who was also present. Mr. Taylor had recently married his girlfriend.

They all went inside and Brandon and Brianna took turns giving a quick rundown of the trip. They would submit a formal report later on with all the details listed. The highlights of the trip would be posted on the Internet together with holographic images. Emrak chuckled when he heard the passengers had jumped ship and said with a smile -

"I sensed they would do that. It's a loss for Frejja. They're so talented and always see things from a different perspective. I'm sure they'll be a hit on Veehnia."

The whole crew were told by Emrak to take three months off as vacation with full pay and all Brandon and Brianna had to do was to submit a full report about the trip to Emrak. Copies would be sent to the president's office and Emrak also sent copies to the members of the Alliance and Tothellim over the Interstellar Internet. Emrak did not receive a reply from Tothellim, which surprised him. He would know why soon enough.

Brandon and Brianna worked out in the gym to regain their muscles as fourteen months total in weightlessness had taken a toll on them. They felt they needed the three months off to get back in shape. As they were working out, they often discussed the trip.

"Isn't it strange that it was only one race on Veehnia and only English was spoken?" Brianna wondered aloud. "I also noticed they all had common English names. I think Veehnia is a sister planet to both Earth and Frejja."

"I thought of that also," Brandon said slowly, reflecting on Brianna's comment. "Earth evolved with several races, but Frejja and Veehnia did not. Why? Earth has several languages while Veehnia and Frejja only have one language. I think we need an anthropologist to help us answer those questions. I don't know the answers."

CHAPTER 29

Veehnia's largest and most modern ship departed one month after Brandon and Brianna left and Rear Admiral Harris was onboard as well as three copilots and six androids. No passengers were allowed. The androids were all specialists in their own field. Two were trained pilots, two were mechanics, one was a medic and the last one was a jack of all trades, knowing a little about everything on a ship. The rear admiral and the copilots had spent many hours in the flight simulator training to negotiate the monster tunnel and felt ready for the task. They were prepared for the violence of the tunnel, but reality was worse than they had expected. The rear admiral had years of flying experience and held the ship steady in the tunnel, but the acceleration of speed and unbelievable shaking were more severe than he had expected. His copilot struggled to center the ship, but he managed to do so and the rear admiral stayed in his seat ready to take over if it would be needed. Without Tothellim's instructions and recording of the tunnel, it may not have been possible for the crew to handle the job. They made it through and felt jubilant when it was over. They transmitted a message to Tothellim they were on the way and after a month of easy travel they landed on Peturun, their first stop in the Milky Way galaxy.

Tothellim, Rheo, the president, an admiral and a few other government officials greeted them and it was a joyous meeting. A hectic week followed and the Veehnians were introduced to the latest technology on Peturun and a tour of the terrynium plant. The Veehnian ship had not suffered any damage in the tunnel proving that their own alloy was as strong as terrynium. The Veehnians were also shown the countryside by airmobile and they liked what they saw.

After several days Tothellim and Rheo caught the rear admiral alone and Tothellim said -

"Rheo and I respectfully ask if we can join you on your ship and return to Veehnia and become permanent citizens of your planet. We have notified our supervisor and he has approved that we can leave even though we still work under a contract with the Peturun government as pilots. Rheo is an experienced pilot and would continue working as a pilot for your planet and I would be honored to work as a flight instructor on Veehnia. I've had enough of flying and would prefer to stay in one place from now on."

The question took the rear admiral by surprise, but he recovered quickly and he instantly saw the benefit of Tothellim's proposal. On Veehnia when he interacted with Tothellim he had realized he was a man of high intelligence and his knowledge of space surpassed the capabilities of the Veehnian pilots. He also knew that Rheo was a first-rate pilot. He stretched out both his hands and shook hands simultaneously with the two men and burst out -

"*The honor is ours!* If you have cleared this matter with your supervisor and your government and they agree that you can move, we'll be delighted to have you. The ship leaves tomorrow. Have your luggage ready."

Both Rheo and Tothellim had already packed and said goodbye to their friends. Neither of them was married and they were ready for a new life. Both men were in their early forties. Rheo was studying English and Tothellim was also improving on his language skills. They boarded the ship with no regrets.

Ahead of them was the six-month trip to Mars, which Tothellim had made so many times buying terrynium. It was a first for Rheo. He had never been to Mars and was excited to see how people lived in 'the bubble'. Tothellim found the Veehnian ship easy to control and took it through the second tunnel with ease. The rear admiral watched quietly and thought to himself that here was a real master at the controls. In truth, he was.

They landed on Mars and spent ten days listening, learning and interacting with the president and Martians. The Veehnians and Rheo were fascinated and it was the first time they had seen such a prosperous community totally enclosed in a bubble and with the citizens thriving and enjoying a very high standard of living. The Martians told them they were all from Earth and that they had built their city from scratch starting with a hundred people and now they numbered eighty thousand citizens. They also mentioned the Alliance they were a member of and how they had been invaded by terrorists and managed to fight them off. The Veehnians would have liked to stay longer, but the next stop was Earth and they were expected on a certain day. They left telling the Martians to try to visit Veehnia and how very welcome they would be.

The trip to Earth was a quick voyage of only three weeks using the tunnel and Tothellim took the controls. It was with great anticipation they landed on Veehnia's sister planet and they were greeted by the American, European, Russian and Chinese presidents and a group of other officials. They planned to stay on Earth a full month to learn and tour the planet. The Veehnians, Tothellim and Rheo were all captivated by what they saw; the different races on Earth; how the planet was divided into separate countries with different governments and customs; they learned about wars that had occurred in the past; the different religions; the collapse of society in the year 2035 and the slow rebuilding of Earth to what it was now; the emigration of people from Earth to Mars and how they built Martia. It was a lot to take in and record so they would be able to share all of it with the Veehnians when they returned home. The rear admiral noticed people were more energized than the people on his own planet and in an interview, he mentioned his planet was open for immigration and anyone willing to make the long trip to Veehnia was welcome to move there. The trip was free. Veehnia would benefit from new blood.

The original plan had been to return to Veehnia from Earth, but they had added Frejja to their itinerary and looked forward to land on their second sister planet. It was a three-month journey. They were expected and Emrak and Karol, the president, Brandon and Brianna and some other officials were waiting for them. Tothellim had sent Emrak a message from Mars that he would be onboard and that he was moving to Veehnia. Seven months after Brandon and Brianna had returned from Veehnia, the ship from Veehnia landed on Frejja and with great excitement the crew exited the ship. Emrak hugged Tothellim like a brother and felt they had so much in common and it was a joyful reunion for Brandon and Brianna to see the rear admiral. They were also excited to see Tothellim again and to meet Rheo. The four had a lot to talk about and Brandon and Brianna wished them happiness and luck on their new home planet.

The Veehnians stayed on Frejja a whole month and carefully studied life on the planet and compared the lifestyle on Frejja with what they had seen on Earth. Frejja was definitely more laid-back than Earth and resembled Veehnia more than Earth. The rear admiral liked both planets, but he had found the energy on Earth irresistible. That was lacking on Frejja. He knew Veehnia needed a jolt of energy to transcend its present relaxed lifestyle and immigrants may help to achieve this. The rear admiral and his copilots visited schools, hospitals, the plant that manufactured spaceships and also toured the countryside. They were shown the technology available and one of the hospital units that was equipped with the artificial wombs. A doctor explained carefully how the wombs worked and the benefits of the system. The Veehnians had never seen anything like it and were enthusiastic about the invention.

The visit came to an end and before the ship left, a large vehicle pulled up to the ship and unloaded box after box. Emrak explained it was six complete units of the artificial womb with full description of the design and how to use them. It was a gift from Frejja to the Veehnian people. Full details were included how to build their own units. The rear admiral was touched to receive such an impressive gift and he knew each unit was very costly. Brianna had organized this gift and she and Karol had explained the low birth rate on Veehnia to the Frejjan president and he had approved the gift without hesitation.

It was an emotional farewell when the ship departed and Brandon and Brianna would never make a long-distance trip again and Emrak would lose contact with Tothellim. The Interstellar Internet could not reach the next galaxy. Rheo would continue flying and perhaps he would revisit Frejja one day.

The ship returned safely to Veehnia and Tothellim and the rear admiral took turns steering the ship through the two tunnels. When they landed on Veehnia they had been gone twenty-one months and the rear admiral felt it had been the most interesting part of his life. The copilots agreed.

The artificial wombs were sent to the most advanced hospital and carefully studied. They would start a new epoch on Veehnia and become immensely popular among women and eventually lead to an increase in the birth rate.

Tothellim and Rheo automatically became citizens and Rheo was given a furnished apartment not too far from his future workplace, which would be the air field where he had landed on his first visit to the planet. His command of the English language had improved and he spoke well enough to start working any time he felt ready. Tothellim would be a flight instructor and teach as well as oversee the lessons in the flight simulator and his workplace was outside the city where the school was located. One of the benefits of his employment was free housing and it was a private residence a short distance from the school. A lovely house, not too big, but fully furnished and equipped with all the necessary household items. Tothellim thought to himself *I have it made here* when he checked out the house. From the Veehnians' point of view, Tothellim was a master who outperformed the domestic pilots and they had a lot to learn from him, so a good salary and nice housing was a small price to pay. Tothellim was now almost fluent in English and took only a week off before starting his new job. No one discriminated against his alien appearance. Instead, he was warmly welcomed. He got along well with his students and was an effective teacher. The students felt he was the most advanced teacher they had ever had and learned from his many years of flying.

Tothellim loved his new life and enjoyed coming home at night and he did not miss flying at all. He was ready to get married and have children, but he did not know if a Peturun man and a human female could produce a child. He was popular and often invited to social get-togethers and he never turned down an invitation. Both he and Rheo had had the growths on their cheeks surgically removed. It was a minor operation that healed without scars and gave them a more pleasant appearance. They had also cut off their ponytails.

The four passengers were hired by a film company and were given free rein to produce any type of program they wanted. They had sharp intellect and saw shortcomings in the society that they focused in on and then presented a better version of the topic, always humorous and entertaining. Their first program was a hit and made people laugh at themselves. Many other programs followed as the group learned how far they could go. Some topics were taboo, but mostly they were allowed to pick their own subjects. As a team they complemented each other and they had become wildly popular. Government officials quietly observed the work of the filmmaking group as well as Tothellim's and Rheo's work and realized the immigrants had added energy to the society that was badly needed. At the next meeting with the president, they suggested immigration should be high on the list and free so that anyone from Earth, Frejja or the other known planets in the Milky Way could come to Veehnia and become citizens. They all agreed and asked Rear Admiral

Harris to organize the trip. The largest ship they had could accommodate a hundred passengers and a crew of six and it was readied to fly to Earth and, hopefully, return fully loaded. Rheo was asked if he wanted to be part of the crew, but he politely declined. He was flying a cargo ship and each trip was only a few weeks long and that fit him fine as he had met a Veehnian girl and did not want to be away too long. Tothellim was asked to train the pilots so they would be able to manage the two tunnels and he had a good team ready within a month.

The ship took off and was expected to return after about a year and a half. The captain of the ship would contact Earth and give the details of their mission as soon as they were close enough to transmit to Earth. The people on Earth knew of Veehnia from the first visit and many people had said to each other that they would be willing to go there if the trip was free. Now it was and a ship was on its way. Would anyone sign up?

******

People worked hard on Earth2 and it was a simple, basic life that was rewarding in its simplicity. All the modern conveniences they had grown up with on Frejja were absent, or at least most of them, but the tranquility on the planet nourished their souls. The mining was profitable and the gold deposit in the cave was larger than they had anticipated and may last for years to come. The platiniridium dredging and mining was also successful, but hard work as it had to be done manually. Every time the supply ship arrived from Frejja, new people would be onboard and join them and the number of citizens on Earth2 was now three hundred. Six children had been born and the oldest was now seven years old. They wore no implants. The parents were wearing the implants they had received when living on Frejja, but there were no implants suitable for children on Earth2. Some parents suggested the children should be 'natural' while others felt without an implant the children would be left behind. It was decided that the parents of each child should decide and a few units were ordered through the doctor from Frejja. The doctor was trained to install the implants. One of the units was for Nasha's daughter, now six years old.

A school had been established and four children were attending. One of the settlers was a teacher and had volunteered to become the first teacher of the school.

******

It was an ordinary day and the people were working. A full-size spaceship appeared on the sky and at first the settlers thought it was a Frejjan ship, but as it descended it was obvious it was a different design. It was similar to the saucer type ship Frejjans used, but not the same. There was no way of knowing if they were friends or enemies and the settlers decided it was safest just to wait and see. Since it was just one large passenger type ship, the Earth2 people sensed there was no danger.

The ship landed and one man and one woman climbed out of the ship waving to the group of people who had assembled. Most of the people were working at the mine and the few who were home were now outside watching the ship. The couple walked to the group of people and they were unarmed. They were humans with distinct oriental features but with light brown skin. The Frejjans were familiar with the different races on Earth and had seen images of oriental people, but these people had darker skin than oriental people on Earth. The man used a translation device and said -

"Don't be afraid, we're peaceful. We come from planet Etteron, which orbits the star Allinun. I'm Telly and this is my wife Ellala. We were hoping to settle here, with your permission of course. The rumor is out that a new planet is being settled and that immigrants are welcome. Our planet is so overcrowded that many want to leave. Is there any chance we can stay? There are a hundred people onboard willing to settle here."

"Wait until we get the people in charge. They're all in the mine."

One of the settlers ran to the mine and all the workers came running. The government members were soon present and tried to size up the situation. One of them asked -

"You say one hundred people are onboard. How many more will come?"

"Several million, if you would allow it. Our planet is very advanced technologically, but it's small and there are too many of us on Etteron. We all long for space and we don't know of any habitable planet other than yours that is mostly empty. In exchange, you would receive this spaceship when we all have settled here and we would transfer all the technology and machinery you need free of charge. We would bring everything we own over here and share it with you. It takes us only five months to reach you and our star Allinun is part of the Pleiades group of stars. We're a peaceful people and will work with you to advance your planet. Our government is willing to help move our people using their ships. This ship is privately owned and doesn't belong to the government. We're willing to learn your language and abide by your rules."

The government people circled together and quickly talked back and forth with each other. There were benefits, it was obvious. They needed people to advance their society and these immigrants offered more favorable conditions than they had ever imagined. They all agreed.

"Yes, we agree. The limit of people is one million with the terms you mentioned. We expect you make a detailed contract and specify exactly what will be transferred to us and we expect the technology and machinery to be sent to us before the people arrive so we can be sure you'll keep your word. We'll also continue to invite people from Frejja to our planet so we won't become a minority on our own planet. We intend to write a constitution that you will have to accept. There will be no such thing as an elite or dictatorship on this planet. Every citizen is free."

Telly stretched out his hand and shook hands with all the six government members.

"You have my word; we'll make a list of what will be transferred and we will naturally accept your constitution. Allow me to tell my people to come out of the ship. We have temporary housing with us that they will live in and we have ten worker robots and four 3D house printers that will start building houses."

A hundred people climbed out of the ship. They were nice looking people with kind faces and intelligent eyes. Last to exit the ship were the worker robots and they started immediately to unload all the cargo, which was substantial in volume. The robots and some of the men started to erect large tents on the field next to the community and as soon as they were raised, the people moved their luggage inside and put up cots for sleeping. There were some families with small children and the rest of them appeared to be single. All of them were young. Every person's name and personal information was entered into the computers.

The ship departed the following day and Telly was onboard. He would organize the whole move and coordinate with his government the best way to move the people out and also all the equipment that had been promised. Some of the people leaving Etteron were the most affluent on the planet and they and Telly would just pay their government to move the people using the government ships. The Etterons did not consider the monetary price they would pay for the move to Earth2 to be too high. Here was a pristine planet with ideal conditions for humans to live on and there was no other planet close enough that was empty and habitable. Telly's wife Ellala stayed on Earth2 to help install some of the electronics they had brought with them. She was technically very competent.

Ássurt was selected to write a constitution for Earth2 and he was the right man for the job. When the Frejjans first learned about Mars and then Earth, Ássurt, a history expert, read everything he could find about Earth's history from the stone age to present time. He found the latest American constitution and carefully modified it to fit the lifestyle on Earth2. Ássurt struggled with the word 'equal' and its true meaning. Obviously, all citizens have equal rights in the Court of Law, but are all citizens equal in capabilities? No, they are not. Job opportunities should be based on a person's merits and nothing else. A democracy must respect every person equally. In the Earth2 constitution, Ássurt clarified the word 'equal' and its definition in the Court of Law as well as in a workplace or similar situation. He also added all people were equal according to our Creator. When he was finished, he presented it to the Earth2 settlers for approval. It was well written and the modifications well thought out and the people approved it. It was now law. A copy of the finished constitution was then given to Ellala to share with her people. The translation device was used for audio translation and the constitution would have to be translated to their language in written form. Ássurt slowly read the constitution to Ellala in Frejjan and the translation device converted it to her language. As she listened, she nodded in approval and smiled.

"It's beautifully written and so fair," she said. "I can't think of anything that needs to be added. Please come with me and read it to my people."

When Ássurt had read the constitution to the Etterons there was applause and it was accepted by all. Several copies of it were framed and hung on the walls in various buildings.

The school teacher started right away giving Frejjan language lessons to the new people and with the help of the translation device it was successful. They were quick learners. Ellala set up the electronics they had brought along and the equipment was even more sophisticated than the Frejjan devices. Ellala knew how to use the electronics and demonstrated their use to the other people.

The Etterons had brought along enough food and personal belongings to be self-sufficient for a whole year, which was lucky since there was not enough food on the planet for an additional hundred people. The men tapped into the Zero Point Field for electricity and water was diverted from the stream into their tents. Bathroom facilities were a variation of incinerator toilets, more advanced than what the settlers had, and there was no pollution from the immigrants, a fact the settlers noticed. No one wanted to degrade the planet and the serene beauty of Earth2.

Within a few days they all asked for work and many willingly worked all day in the mine. Some of the men worked with the robots overlooking the house building. When the fall harvest was ready to cut, men and women chipped in and many of the Etterons had never done any kind of manual work before. Regardless, without complaining they worked hard and the harvest was processed in record time.

The ship returned from Etteron loaded with equipment. Telly was onboard. There was no room for passengers on the ship and as the robots unloaded the ship the settlers were in awe over the number of tools, appliances and instruments that was transferred over to their storage building. Everything brand new and more advanced than they were used to seeing. It was obvious Telly had kept his word. The most impressive item was a large autonomous tractor with implements and one dredging machine, also autonomous.

Earth2 was prospering. The ships from Etteron kept coming once a month unloading people and various equipment, foods and even one load of farm animals. The animals were for food production and had been put into hibernation for the space trip. When the ship arrived on Earth2 they were awakened without any visible harm. They looked like a mix of small cows and donkeys and were highly prized for their meat. The animals recovered within a few days and were put out to pasture.

In the meantime, the Frejjan supply ship arrived to pick up ore and unload passengers and the pilots were quite surprised to see all the changes. They toured the new houses and admired all the new equipment. One of the pilots asked -

"Do you need us anymore?"

"Oh, yes, we do. We do need more Frejjans to balance the population and we plan to pay off our debt to Frejja with ore. From now on, we'll be more specific what we order from you as the new people have brought so much from Etteron to us."

"Your gold and platiniridium have been of great quality and I heard you'll be debt free sooner than you think. Yes, we'll continue bringing people and the equipment you ask for," the pilot said.

Frejja still imported single men from Earth, but the people leaving Frejja to settle on Earth2 were mostly families and a small amount of single Frejjan women.

When Emrak heard of the new immigrants to Earth2 he felt a little uneasy at first, but he was able to contact Rasufilus for more information. Rasufilus had not personally been to Etteron, but he knew of the planet and its people and assured Emrak they were good people and not warriors and the planet had never been involved in a war. He also told Emrak that the planet was very advanced and affluent but seriously overcrowded. The citizens were oriental in appearance and one million of them would most likely be an asset to Earth2, especially since they had transferred so much equipment and wealth to Earth2 already and would probably continue doing so until all of them were relocated to Earth2. Emrak felt better after he had discussed the situation with Rasufilus, who he trusted completely as a man of integrity. Karol felt the Frejjans on Earth2 had struck a bargain and she knew from her days as president on Mars that no community can survive if the population is too small. It takes a certain amount of people to advance a society.

The Earth2 government had explained to Telly that one of the most important goals they had was to refine their own ore and Telly promised that before the immigration was over, they would supply the machinery needed to build a refining plant to process gold and platiniridium. Telly understood right away the benefit of refining the ore on the home planet and that the machines would eventually pay for themselves. The equipment brought from Etteron to Earth2 belonged to all citizens and profits from the mining were spent on infrastructure and equipment. All the foods from Frejja were equally shared with the Etterons. The present system was temporary and they all knew later on when the population had grown, people would receive salaries and commerce could then begin. Right now, the population was still too small with only three hundred Frejjans and one thousand Etterons. The cargo ships from Etteron were huge and could seat three hundred people, but it would still take decades to move the one million people that was agreed upon.

Telly was now permanently living on Earth2 and a natural leader. He was full of ideas, but never pushy and had never imposed his ideas on the Frejjans. A highly intelligent man, he would suggest improvements and explain pros and cons of what he said and then step back and let the Frejjans decide. On Etteron, he had run a business empire and he had used his wealth to pay for most of the equipment transferred to Earth2 as well as the fee for the government ships used to transfer cargo and people to Earth2. The Etteron people knew this, but the Frejjans still had not been told where the funding came from to pay for the move of the immigrants and all the equipment. Telly had become bored with his life on Etteron and had been looking for a new adventure in his life and being a pioneer and start over again was thrilling to him. He was a humble man and did not miss being the boss. To use his wealth to start a new life on a new planet was a productive way to use his money, he felt. Some of the affluent Etteron immigrants had also helped pay for the transport of the people to Earth2, but Telly had paid the most.

The Etterons were religious and built a church. They believed in one Creator, the afterlife and respect for every person's free will. The Creator they believed in existed all around them in a higher vibration and could be experienced with their hearts, not with their minds. It was never a punishing Creator. Some Frejjans liked the message of the Etterons' religion and started to attend the church meetings listening through the translation device.

CHAPTER 30

The Veehnian ship landed on Earth outside the capital and the people on Earth were informed of their mission. Within one week a hundred people had signed up and that was the capacity of the ship. All were young. Six families with children, some married couples without children and the rest were single people. They were all told about the two monster tunnels, twelve hours and eighteen hours respectively, and they took the news in stride. After a week, the ship took off and the passengers were a mix of people from the Far East, Africa and North America. Only a few from Europe had signed up. The trip from Earth to Veehnia would take nine months.

Going through the first tunnel caused a mild panic among the children, but the adults were remarkably brave and by the time they entered the second tunnel, even the children understood it would be uncomfortable but safe. The trip went well and the passengers kept themselves busy with exercising, looking at programs about Veehnia and listening to lectures about the history of their new planet and the Andromeda galaxy. Among the passengers were several professionals, a few artists, one musician, a female opera singer and a few who had done manual work. All of them spoke English well.

The ship landed on Veehnia and after each of them had been interviewed and their personal data recorded, they were offered housing and employment. After a few months they were all settled down and started to adapt to the ways of Veehnia. The newcomers had one thing in common and that was energy and their enthusiasm was invigorating for the Veehnians around them.

The Veehnian ship went through an overhaul and then took off again to Earth for another load of people.

Rheo had married his Veehnian girlfriend, who was not taken aback by his alien features and Tothellim was seeing a cute Veehnian girl, Anna, who he was very much in love with. They had met at the flight school and she worked in the office. She was ten years younger than Tothellim, but Peturun people had long lifespans and vigorous health. Tothellim was hesitant to pop the question, afraid she had not fully accepted how he looked, but his worries were unfounded. Anna knew already he wanted to propose but was afraid to, so she helped him along and said gently -

"It's OK if you ask me…"

Tothellim could not help but laugh and said -

"Am I that obvious?"

"My answer is yes!" Anna said firmly. She took his hand and looked into his eyes.

"Are you sure you can accept my looks?"

"In my eyes you're the best-looking guy I have ever met," Anna assured him. "I never get tired of your company, never." Tothellim was an impressive looking man, tall and muscular with a beautiful deep voice.

A month later they were married and it was a happy marriage. Rheo's wife was pregnant so Tothellim knew Peturun and Veehnian people were able to have children, which was very important for Tothellim. He wanted a family more than anything. He loved children. After a few months of marriage Anna was expecting and she carried the baby the natural way. The artificial wombs were now in use and several units had been built, but there were still too few units available so Anna decided to just let her pregnancy proceed naturally. She delivered a girl who looked mostly like Anna, but had Tothellim's hair at the center of her head and no hair on the sides. She lacked the growths on her cheeks and the ridged eyebrows of her father. Except for her hair pattern she looked mostly like a human baby girl, which was a relief for Tothellim. He was still a little self-conscious about his looks even though he had never encountered any discrimination of any sort. It was with awe he held his daughter and Anna stayed home to care for her. They named her Heidi.

Rheo had also become a father of a son and the baby had human hair growth, no ridged eyebrows but he did have the growths on his cheeks, which would be surgically removed. Rheo had asked for a transfer to the flight school as instructor and it was approved. He now worked together with Tothellim at the school. They were great friends. Rheo did not want to be away from his wife and son and even though he loved space travel his family was more important. He bought a house not too far from Tothellim and the two families were close.

******

The musician from Earth was a well-known pianist and soon after he arrived on Veehnia he started building a piano. There were wind instruments on Veehnia, but pianos were unheard of. With the help of two Veehnian musicians, the three of them built a grand piano that was close in quality to what he had used on Earth. He fine-tuned it and started practicing. At his first concert, the performance started with Beethoven's famous sonatas as well as the best of Chopin's nocturnes and the audience went wild. Applause and whistling filled the concert hall and the musician's future looked promising.

The musician also started a prosperous business building pianos. Sheet music was made available and recordings of his playing was featured on the Internet. When Tothellim listened to the recordings on the Internet he was fascinated and he told Anna that music of this quality did not exist on his planet. There was a waiting list to buy a piano and Tothellim put his name on the list right away. Hopefully, one of his children would be musical.

Among the newly arrived immigrants was a female opera singer and she found work with a Veehnian performance group. She had a powerful voice and adapted to Veehnian opera, which was written by composers from Veehnia and rather different from the classics she had performed on Earth. She also went on to have a successful career.

******

Sillia and Rigel's twins, Asta and Ran, were now five years old and a handful to control. They were full of energy and romped around the yard with Rollo taking part in the playing. Sillia and Rigel had a third child, a boy looking mostly like Sillia with no hair. When the third baby was born, Rigel switched career and stopped flying to Arrynia. He had tried to find a route closer to home, but there was none so he had continued flying with Brandon and Brianna to Arrynia. His new job was domestic flying and it was not as exciting as space travel, but he wanted more home life and to see his children grow up. Brandon and

Brianna had been almost strangers to him when he grew up and he was determined not to do the same to his own children. Funina and her husband had recently been visiting and liked Frejja.

Rigel's copilot was Thole, also a full captain, and they got along well. Rigel had an alien wife and Thole was an alien with a Frejjan wife and they often compared their views. Thole's son Ranus was fourteen years old and he and Terrin also had a second son five years old. Thole had fully adjusted to Frejja and had never gone back to Morekia, not even for a visit. He saw no point to it. His life was here on Frejja.

Rigel and Thole were on their way home with the autopilot engaged. Their saucer type ship with a high dome was full of cargo and heavily loaded. Booom! The sound startled them and they realized one of the engines had stopped working with a bang. The remaining engine struggled with the heavy load and they were slowly descending from an altitude of eighty thousand feet. Rigel quickly took the controls and tried to restart the engine to no avail. The ship slowly lost altitude and they realized there was no choice but to land. The engine sputtered but kept running. Thole was more of an expert at gliding than Rigel and asked for permission to take the controls. Rigel agreed. They were now at an altitude of thirty thousand feet and quickly dropping and the engine kept sputtering in a threatening way. When they were at five thousand feet it stopped and Thole was desperately looking for a field to land the ship. They were flying over the countryside and no homes were in the area, only farm fields. Thole focused in on a pasture and holding his breath managed to glide the silent ship and landed in between a herd of meat animals. They ran in a panic and five of them were killed by the ship. Even without the engines the ship landed at a high-speed plowing through the field stirring up huge clouds of dust and sand. Thole managed to maintain a horizontal position of the ship as it was moving forward on its belly. The vibration was seriously shaking the ship and Thole worried they would tip over. After a mile the ship finally came to a stop and Rigel and Thole sank down in their seats shaken to the core. They were alive. The ship was badly damaged and probably beyond repair.

Their landing had been seen on the screens at their home destination and help was on the way. Accidents like this were highly unusual and had not happened for many years. Rigel and Thole were stuck inside the ship as the exit door was against the ground. They waited an hour and then saw the rescue vehicles approaching and within an hour the workmen had cut an opening for them with a laser cutter so they could climb out. Both of them had shaky legs and were grateful to be alive.

They refused a medical examination and were taken home with an airmobile. What a story they had to tell their families. After two days both of them went back to work.

******

Telly asked the government on Earth2 about the first planet orbiting their sun and was told no one had ever gone there and conditions were unknown. They knew from Brandon and Brianna that the third planet was gaseous and uninhabitable. Telly calculated the distance to be two months' travel time with his space ship and decided to make an exploratory journey to the first planet. The Etteron government was diligently moving people to Earth2 and Telly felt there was no harm in taking his ship out of service for a few months.

The ship took off with four pilots, Telly, Ássurt and the six government members. Ássurt was known as a scholar and was invited to help interpret whatever conditions they would find. The trip went well and soon they were in orbit around the first planet. The planet was just a little smaller than Earth2 and had an oxygen atmosphere and the whole planet was a tropical jungle. Telly, Ássurt and the government members descended to the surface using their shuttle and left the pilots onboard. They flew a distance over the tree tops to get a quick look at the planet. Their instruments showed a tropical climate with a temperature of one hundred- and five-degrees Fahrenheit and ninety two percent humidity, almost sauna conditions. Here and there were thirty, forty primitive huts grouped together and they saw human beings walking around, but they were not modern human beings, they were prehistoric. Ássurt recognized them from his readings as Neanderthals and gave a brief explanation to the rest of the team. They all knew there was a risk to land and approach them, but decided to take the chance. Telly had a stun gun that would stop but not kill a person.

They landed about a hundred feet from the huts and opened the hatch. The heat almost knocked them out. On Earth2 the temperature never exceeded eighty degrees and was always pleasant. They stepped out of the shuttle and the gravity was about the same as on Earth2. The natives cautiously inched their way towards the shuttle and the men held spears in their hands and some of the women had slingshots as weapons. A few children were at the back of the group. The men wore loincloths and the women skirts to their knees and it looked like their clothing was made of huge leaves and stitched together. Their facial features were rough looking and had no resemblance to the more refined features of modern man and their brown colored hair was a wild mess.

Telly waved and smiled and showed his hands to let them see he was unarmed. His stun gun was hidden in his pocket. The natives now communicated with each other with single words and did not seem to have a structured language. The bravest one slowly walked to Telly and touched his face to perhaps check if he was real. Telly patted him on his shoulder and said hallo in Frejjan. This put the man at ease and he stared at them and the shuttle. His bewilderment was obvious and they had seen the shuttle come in for landing, just like a bird. Telly and the men started to walk towards the huts and the natives followed. At the huts the men sat down and after a few minutes the natives decided to join them, but they looked afraid and still held on to their spears. Telly put his hand on one of the spears and pushed it to the ground and shook his head. Somehow this gesture was understood and the rest of the men laid down their weapons. It was incredibly hot and nasty, but the natives seemed totally comfortable.

"Telly," Telly said and pointed at himself.

"Sidji," the native responded. He then pointed at a woman and said "Vuula". She was his woman.

What followed was a laborious attempt at conversation and the team pieced together that the natives were hunter-gatherers living mostly on a deer type animal and whatever roots and plants they could find in the jungle. Telly tried to find out why there were so few children in the village and he pointed at the children, then looked inside one of the huts as if to see if they were hidden inside and looked at Sidji with a questioning face expression. It took a while, but then Sidji caught on and started sketching in the sand with his finger. He drew a giant snake in the sand with an open mouth. Telly and the men were shocked when they understood that the children were eaten by the snakes. Telly pointed at Sidji's spear trying to ask if they could not kill the snakes. Sidji lay down and closed his eyes. Now the men understood. The snakes entered the huts at night and the sleeping children were easy prey.

Telly sketched in the sand a hut built on stilts, but Sidji gestured that the snakes were able to climb up on the stilts and enter the hut. The huts were flimsy with no doors and Telly made another sketch in the sand of a hut with a door so no snakes could enter at night. This simple solution seemed to have eluded them and they exchanged words with each other, perhaps agreeing they should try it.

Finally, Telly pointed at the snake Sidji had drawn in the sand and pointed to the jungle. He took a few steps and waved at the natives to follow him. They seemed to understand Telly wanted to see the snakes himself and they walked into the dense jungle. The men almost passed out from the heat, but quietly followed the natives about a mile into the forest. There they were, hanging in the trees above them resembling boa constrictors. Telly took out his stun gun and hit one of them. It came down with a thump. Telly quickly took Sidji's spear and killed the snake in the neck. The spear had a sharp point and easily penetrated the neck. The natives looked dumbfounded. Telly continued and every snake they could find they killed. The natives dragged the dead snakes back to their village to be used as food.

It would be dark in an hour and the men preferred to spend the night on the ship, but they would return the next day. Before they left, Telly again pointed to the huts and reminded them that they needed to build solid doors to their huts.

They took off with the shuttle while the natives stared at the miracle 'bird' and were soon in the clouds and out of sight. Back on the ship they told the astonished pilots what they had seen and told them that two of them could come with them the following day and the day after the other two could come along. Two pilots must remain with the ship at all times for safety's sake.

They returned five more days and learned a lot about the natives. Ássurt recorded everything with his holographic equipment, but they decided not to show the images to the natives. It may be too overwhelming to see themselves as an image and frightening.

The natives tried to invite them to eat with them, but the men evaded the invitation and ate their freeze-dried foods on the shuttle. It would have been too risky to eat their foods and they knew that they were not immune to the bacteria that probably flourished in the heat and humidity.

Before they left, Telly assembled six stun guns loaded with one hundred shots each and gave to Sidji. He slowly and carefully showed Sidji how to fire it. Since the guns were loaded already, all he had to do was pull the trigger. One stun lasted about an hour and this was not easy to explain to someone who had no idea what time was, but Telly managed to tell Sidji that the snake had to be killed quickly after it was stunned and with lots of gestures the message sank in.

All of the natives waved when they left for good. It was unclear to the men if the natives understood they would not come back. On the return trip back to Earth2 they all discussed whether or not they should release their discovery about the first planet. The natives were totally vulnerable and if hostile aliens were to invade the planet to exploit its resources, the natives would probably be killed off. They decided to release the news only to Earth2 citizens and no one else and if anyone asked if the first planet was habitable, they should all say no. It was also decided to allow the natives to evolve at their own rate.

The citizens of Earth2 were fascinated to watch the images of the natives and they all understood the importance of not revealing the truth about the first planet and that's how it remained for many years to come.

There was one nasty consequence of the trip. The whole team had picked up a fungus from the jungle and it resisted any modern treatment the doctor tried. It was growing in their sinuses and the doctor scoured medical literature for old remedies. He knew from former research that fungi had been a big problem in the past on Earth and that the remedy that worked - and worked better than the modern medicines of that time - was simple. He found it. It was old-fashioned, inexpensive baking soda, sodium bicarbonate, and by raising the pH in the body to highly alkaline, the fungus could not survive. Fungi thrive in acidic environments. There was an ample supply of baking soda on Earth2, which they used as a supplement for the ruminant animals. The doctor administered anti-fungal drugs together with oral intake of baking soda carefully checking their pH to ensure they tested alkaline. The baking soda was easy to drink mixed with water. For one week he kept his patients highly alkaline and then slowly lowered their pH to normal levels. It worked. All of them made a full recovery and the fungus just died.

******

Karol and Emrak had already been married fourteen years and were still very much in love. Alison was now a young woman of twenty-two years and Leo was thirteen and Rey eight years old. Alison loved her dad and wanted to be like him. She had decided to become an astronaut. She had also met Brianna and was influenced by her as well. Karol and Emrak told her the choice was hers to make and whatever she decided they would support her choice. Alison applied to the most prestigious flight school and was accepted, so it appeared she would not waver from her plan to spend her life in space like Emrak had done.

Emrak was still the senior flight instructor at the school working four days a week. He enjoyed spending as much time as possible with Karol and his sons. Karol worked part time as a teacher at the local school teaching several courses in political science and economics. She had fun doing so and she was well qualified.

Brandon and Brianna often came for a visit and the four of them always had so much to talk about. Brandon was sixty-four years and Brianna sixty, but they intended to work another ten years before they retired. For a while they had toyed with the idea of retiring on Earth2, but the thought of never seeing their grandchildren made them decide against it. Emrak was now sixty-nine years old, but looked years younger. He loved his job and was not ready to retire. Besides, he had a growing family to support and to have a steady income was necessary. In addition to his day job, he was also working as senior advisor to the Frejjan space program and hence earned two incomes. He had offered Karol a life in comfort and he had kept his promise. Their android Tyra did all the heavy housework, which enabled Karol to spend time with her children and any hobby she enjoyed. One of her hobbies was writing and she had written many articles that appeared on the Internet and her topics varied from politics, economics, psychology - based on her own childhood suffering - to descriptions of life on Mars, all of them written with flair.

******

Martia was doing exceptionally well. The asteroid mining was prosperous with many valuable minerals found. The mining was done by government owned equipment and all profits benefited the citizens.

A nice nest egg in the form of gold was buried underground to be used in emergencies. The Martians enjoyed the highest standard of living of any planet known and paid no tax. The population had now reached a hefty one hundred thousand citizens. All the housing was connected and 'the bubble' was huge. Immigration was free to anyone moving to Mars. It was well known that Martia was rich and the government had bought additional fighter spaceships from Frejja made with terrynium alloy and equipped with the latest weapons. Their total fleet of fighter ships numbered twenty-five and the pilots were well trained. All the pilots had regular jobs, but if they were needed, they were ready to report for duty in less than an hour.

The government was small and worked diligently for the people and knew the importance of being fully accountable to the citizens. The city/country was only fifty-eight years old and had developed into a modern nation in record time. The government had announced once the population reached one million, they would have to assess whether more people were needed and possibly stop immigration.

Mars had endured some bad weather events such as two marsquakes that were severe, but did not destroy the housing. Several damaging sand storms had taken place and required weeks of work to clear the sand from the buildings. The fresh water supply was still plentiful and new deposits of water ice had been found. The population was healthy and the community had been spared harmful diseases and dangerous microorganisms. The Martians were generally happy and the rate of sanity high. Everything was available to buy and there were many shops open for business. The population was mostly young, but there was a small number of retirees that found retirement on Mars pleasant and free of complications. Androids could be bought or rented if seniors needed help.

With government money available to fund new inventions, Mars had developed several important items and people with ideas tended to move to Mars hoping to turn their visions into finished products. Science was encouraged and several labs were working on improving the design of existing gadgets.

Crime did occur, but it was uncommon. Four murders had taken place the last ten years, but the perpetrators had been caught and brought to justice. A prison had been built far away from the community and when the prisoner had served his sentence, he was deported to the planet he came from. No woman had ever committed a crime. There had been no rapes, robberies or burglaries ever on Mars.

A group of ten Frejjan single women had moved to Mars, but only lasted one year. They found life in 'the bubble' suffocating and could not adjust to wearing spacesuits. They returned to Frejja and no other Frejjan women moved to the planet. There were still more men than women on Mars, but a handful of men did continue to leave Mars for Frejja every time the ship landed. Mars and Frejja were trading partners and the men moving to Frejja traveled on the cargo ships. The passenger ships had stopped since there were no longer enough men willing to move to fill such a large ship. Occasionally, a Martian woman would move to Frejja, but it was not that common. There were about a hundred immigrants from Peturun living on Mars, mostly families, who had traveled on the cargo ships from Peturun. Peturun was a steady buyer of terrynium and Mars had bought many technological inventions and specialized machinery from Peturun. The Peturun immigrants had adjusted to Martian life and intended to stay permanently.

The only thing the Martian government was concerned about was invasion of terrorist gangs, but with their fleet of fighter ships they were hoping their defense was adequate. The Alliance was still in effect and gave a feeling of added security to the citizens.

CHAPTER 31

On Earth2 the dredging machine was working all day long sifting out the minerals from the riverbed sand. Only two men and two robots were needed to supervise the operation. Care was taken not to disturb the natural flow of the river and not to leave any unsightly mess behind.

Equally efficient was the mining drill they had received from Etteron and even though it was a small model, it was efficient and fast. One of the men drove the vehicle with the drill attached and the robots collected the ore. With the drill in operation, twice as much ore was collected per day compared to using only manual labor.

Everything was going well, but then the peace on Earth2 was again disrupted. A group of five fighter ships landed early one morning. Twenty heavily armed aliens climbed out and they had their heads covered so there was no way to identify them. Telly ran out of his house and faced twenty guns pointed at him. He had brought eight very sophisticated, high-powered weapons from Etteron capable of blowing up all the fighter ships, but they were kept in the storage building and he did not know if any of the men had the composure to quietly get the weapons out. They did. A group of men were able to silently get the loaded weapons out and point them at the ships without the aliens seeing them. The men knew there were more aliens onboard the ships, but they had to be sacrificed. No person was in the way and they fired all eight weapons simultaneously. Kaboom! A shock wave went through the air. All five ships were hit and exploded in a ball of flames. It was so sudden and unexpected that the aliens turned around and started to run away from the area. They had no chance. Telly ran inside his house and got his high-powered stun gun out and fired in quick succession at them. They all dropped. Within minutes the men had the twenty aliens tied up and dragged them inside one of the buildings and removed their head covers. They were of the same race as the first plunderers seven years ago. Same flashlight eyes. It took an hour until the effect of the stun gun had worn off and they could talk.

"Where are you from?" Telly barked in Etteron using his translation device. He pointed his stun gun on the nose of the alien. To be stunned was a horrible experience and just to breathe was labor intensive.

"Humbrus," the alien mumbled.

"Humbrus is a peaceful planet. Where do you live now? Answer or I stun you again," Telly said in a threatening voice.

"Nowhere permanently. We land in deserted places and stay there until we run out of supplies. Then we get our supplies and move again. We move around all the time. We heard you have gold."

"Who told you we have gold?"

"Someone on the planet where Rasufilus found our brothers and destroyed their ships."

Telly had been told the whole story of the first plundering attack and how Rasufilus had found the location of the gangsters and eliminated all their ships. Someone must have seen when Rasufilus loaded the gold onto his ships and kept the secret to sell in the future.

The twenty aliens were locked inside the animal cages that had been used to transfer the meat animals from Etteron. The ship from Etteron was expected within a week and Telly advised the government members that the aliens should be loaded on the ship going back to Etteron. The ship could make a detour and drop the aliens off on Humbrus and let their government deal with the gangsters. It was the best way to leak the news that plundering Earth2 would not work. They all agreed.

The ship from Etteron arrived and the surprised crew saw what was left of the alien ships and went to see the aliens. They all thought it was a good idea to drop the aliens off on their home planet and let the Humbrus government deal with them. It took weeks to clean up the mess from the burned ships and bury the debris. Months later they heard that the Humbrus government had put the invaders to death and the citizens of Humbrus felt that the planet had been disgraced by the gangsters.

The Earth2 government sent an Interstellar message to Frejja telling them that they had been invaded for the second time, but had defeated the aliens. Frejja responded that they would post a message on the Internet and offer a reward for tips where the rest of the Humbrus gangsters could be found and caught. There were many more of these gangsters terrorizing peaceful planets.

Telly asked the government members for a meeting. All of them knew how efficient Rasufilus was and Telly suggested that they should invite Rasufilus and his three hundred pilots to reside on Earth2 and become citizens. They would be granted ten thousand acres wherever they wanted on Earth2 and be allowed to continue their work as mercenaries. Some of the pilots were married with families and Telly had heard that the total number of Rasufilus' team was about five hundred. If Rasufilus accepted, the citizens on Earth2 would never have to worry again about invasions. Earth2 was the size of Earth and at the present time the population was only one thousand three hundred people. The planet could easily support several billion people. Telly emphasized that the offer had to be too good to resist. Rasufilus and most of his pilots were Morekians, but some of his pilots were from other planets.

The government members were surprised to hear Telly's suggestion, but soon realized it was a clever idea and would enable the citizens to live in peace without the worry of being plundered. Rasufilus and his mercenary fleet were well known and feared. They all agreed and contacted Rasufilus over the Interstellar Internet. Without giving away all the details, they gave a brief message that they had an offer for him and would pay for his travel expenses. Rasufilus asked for the location of their planet and responded he and two other pilots would leave Bantizza the next day. It would take a little more than three months to reach Earth2 from Bantizza.

Rasufilus arrived and he and his pilots were warmly greeted by the government people and Telly. He looked around and exclaimed -

"This is truly a beautiful planet. And it's almost empty."

They went inside and using the translation device the Earth2 people told Rasufilus the whole story how the planet was discovered and settled and how they had been invaded twice. Rasufilus knew, of course, that they had been plundered in the past as he had caught the Humbrus gangsters, but he had only had a vague idea where Earth2 was located. Now that he saw the planet, he fell in love with it. The Frejjans conveyed that with the gold the planet had, they would be a target forever and then presented Rasufilus with their offer. He looked truly surprised, but understood that the people wanted to live in peace and his presence on the planet would ensure that. Ten thousand acres was a huge piece of land and the planet was the most attractive he had ever seen.

"Personally, I accept," he said. "I will send an encrypted message to my pilots on Bantizza giving them all the details and I hope to have a response tomorrow for you. I can't see how any of them would say no. This planet is heavenly. I would consider myself lucky to live here."

The following day the reply came in with an enthusiastic yes and the vote had been unanimous. Bantizza was not an attractive planet and there were no lakes or forests, mostly sand and open grass fields. Rasufilus chose the land beyond the nearby pastures and declared he and his men wanted to be part of the community and not too far away. They entered surveying information into the computer of one of the airmobiles and in half a day the job was done and property markers were in place. It was a lovely piece of land with two lakes, rolling hills, forest land and grass land mixed and a flat area where housing could be built.

Ássurt was asked to write a land grant document detailing the size and location of the land and the land was the legal property of Rasufilus and his men and their descendants and no future Earth2 government could reclaim the land. All government members signed the document and it was stamped with their new Earth2 embossed stamp. Rasufilus was emotional when he accepted the document and said in a firm voice that he and his men would do their part to defend their new home planet.

Rasufilus stayed a few more days and he and Telly discussed in detail what equipment they would need to start their community, such as temporary housing, food, 3D house printers, seed for crops and more. Rasufilus would hire a cargo ship to transport their equipment before they arrived and his ninety ships could transport five hundred and forty people, six per ship. They numbered five hundred and thirty people, so all of them would arrive at the same time. The move would be costly for Rasufilus and his men, but they were not poor and had been working steadily for years with well-paid assignments. All payments were distributed equally between the pilots and Rasufilus never paid himself more than his pilots. However, he was in charge and the leader.

Rasufilus left and four months later the supply ship arrived from Bantizza. Seven worker robots were onboard and ten of Rasufilus' men. They stayed on Earth2 and would start the house building together with the robots. Rasufilus and his people were expected in two weeks. The men from Bantizza loved what they saw and eagerly started preparing for house building. The flat area where their little town would be built was not visible from the Frejjan community and all the equipment was unloaded on their land close to where the town would be.

Rasufilus and his people arrived and all of them admired their new home planet. There were twenty-two children among them and most of the people were Morekians, but there were two Humbrus pilots, four Bantizza, four Kodetsian and six female Arrynian pilots.

A fast-paced period of activity followed and tents were raised to function as temporary housing, water was diverted to the tents, electricity hooked up through the black boxes and outside restrooms were also built until incinerator toilets would arrive. Everyone worked and Rasufilus was glad they had no job offers. In record time they had a functioning tent community and one more delivery would arrive from Bantizza with all sorts of equipment such as household items, appliances, tools and more.

One year passed and a neat and orderly small town had been built on Rasufilus' land. The land had been named Bavonilla, which meant 'beautiful land' in the Morekian language. The tents were gone and the most important infrastructure was in place. A road was being built between the Frejjan community and Bavonilla. Rasufilus and his people were now citizens of Earth2 with the same rights as the Etterons and Frejjans. The rest of the planet was owned by all citizens and could be used for recreational purposes. The population was now around ten thousand people.

The ship from Etteron came once a month and carried five hundred people. It would take a long time to move the one million people that had been decided on. Telly was running out of money and had spent his whole fortune buying equipment for Earth2 and moving his people. He had no regrets and felt peace within. In the future, the Etteron government would pay for half of the cost to move the people to Earth2 and the other half would be paid by the passengers themselves.

All people were required to speak, read and write Frejjan and it was voluntary but encouraged to also learn the English language. The school taught English as a second language and the children had no problem learning it.

The president now serving was Ássurt and the presidential term was one six-year term. The total number of the government team was ten people and Telly was Secretary of the Treasury. Rasufilus would have liked to join the government, but had too many assignments and could not afford to turn down a job offer. He and his pilots had families to support and Rasufilus had recently married an Etteron girl, Akinom, half his age and very pretty. When he left Earth2 to fulfill a military operation, he always left five ships and ten pilots behind to protect Earth2. The skill of the pilots and the weapons onboard the fighter ships were sufficient to fight off any gang of invaders.

The government people now earned salaries and so did all the working people. The gold from the mines paid for the salaries. No taxes were collected. All services were free such as doctor visits, schooling, transportation and so on. People now paid for their own food and several shops had opened. The food prices were very reasonable and there was no lack of basic foods. Specialty foods imported from Etteron and Frejja were expensive but sought after for special occasions. The mint produced silver and gold coins in small denominations and coins were the legal tender.

Houses could be built wherever the people wanted and everyone living in a house could buy the land the house was built on. The government sold the land inexpensively. The houses that had been given to the people for free in the beginning could be bought by the person living in it at a small cost and most people saved up to buy their houses from the government.

Earth2 experienced the very beginning of a functioning country with a constitution in place and a rising population. Industry was starting to grow and Telly had bought the machinery for processing ore with the last of his money. A plant had been built and all ore was now refined on Earth2. Everyone who wanted to work could find a job.

With all the gold and platiniridium they shipped to Frejja, their debt was steadily shrinking. The ship still brought thirty, forty Frejjans every time it arrived and Earth2 imported foods and many items they could not make themselves. They also imported goods from Etteron and paid with platiniridium, which was the payment preferred by the Etterons.

No invasion of terrorists had taken place since Rasufilus moved to Earth2 and not a single crime had been committed among the people. The future looked bright for Earth2.

******

Alison had just graduated from flight school and reported for duty on a cargo ship. She was now twenty-five years old and looked very pretty in her uniform and felt self-confident. Her cargo route was to Mars to pick up both passengers and terrynium sheets and it was an easy route as travel time was only two months and there were only four short tunnels to pass through. She had trained many hours to master the tunnels and she was ready. As junior pilot, she would be given a chance to take the controls in the tunnels, but one of the senior pilots would be ready to take over if she could not hold the ship steady.

Alison felt great excitement as the ship departed and Karol and Emrak were at the ship to wish her good luck on her first trip. Being on the Bridge was incredibly exciting and she loved it. She was allowed to fly the ship manually for hours at the time to gain experience and when they entered the first tunnel, she took the controls and held the ship steady in the center of the tunnel. Her captain saw she had the strength in her hands and the concentration needed to steer the ship and he let her take the ship all the way through to the other side.

This was the first of many trips she made to Mars and even though she had been only eight years old when she moved from Mars to Frejja, she remembered a lot of her Martian life and it was very exciting to return to Mars. When she compared Mars to Frejja, Frejja was the clear winner and she was glad she did not live in 'the bubble' anymore. It was fun to visit, but she felt Martia was too confined to live there permanently.

There was one thing missing in her life and that was a boyfriend. Boys felt intimidated by her and she talked to Karol about it. Her mother had to use all the tact she could muster to explain to her that she was in a masculine line of work, but that did not mean she had to lose her femininity. Karol had served four terms on two planets as president, but never lost her femininity and humbleness. Alison was the opposite by nature and her self-confidence had probably been interpreted as arrogance by the boys. They backed away from her. It was a hard blow to Alison's self-esteem to listen to her mother's words, but she thought about it and realized she was right. She had puffed herself up and she made a promise to herself to end it. After she adopted a less self-important demeanor, she felt better about herself.

Alison worked hard and had only two weeks off between flights. After one year, she took time off to master the fighter ships and it became obvious she had a special 'feel' for handling the ship. She was one with the ship. Emrak was with her when she was training and often accompanied her on her training flights and he told Karol that Alison was becoming a master. Her skill already matched a pilot with years of training. Emrak told Alison she had graduated to copilot. After her training as fighter ship pilot was finished, she returned to her cargo ship. Her duties as copilot were more demanding and she often piloted the ship the entire run from Frejja to Mars.

Alison had met a man on Frejja who she really liked. All was well and he patiently waited to see her between flights. Then one day he abruptly told her it was over and he did not have the patience to wait for months to see her for two weeks and then she would disappear for four months again. He needed a wife by his side, a mother to his children, not a space-trotting career woman.

Alison almost collapsed after the breakup. Was this her destiny? Must she choose between her dream job and being a wife? She went home to Emrak and Karol and told them she had been dumped as she cried her heart out. Her parents did not even try to talk to her the first day and just waited for Alison to approach them to ask for help. On the third day she did and Karol said gently -

"In your line of work, you have only two choices, either remain single and devote your life to your career or marry another pilot like Brianna did. Nothing else will work. No man will accept a wife who vanishes for months at the time. It will not, cannot work in the long run."

"I chose to remain single for that reason. I knew no woman would have the patience to wait for me alone at home with children while I was gone for months," Emrak added. "You will most likely meet another pilot so the two of you can work together just like Brandon and Brianna have done. They were lucky to have Brianna's parents offering to raise their children. By the way, your mother and I would be honored to raise your children."

Karol nodded and smiled. "Of course, we would," she said.

Alison was so surprised that she did not know what to say. She took their hands and said -

"What would I do without you? You're the best."

Alison had ten days left before she had to report back to her ship, but with the nurturance of her parents she found a new inner peace and the strength to face life alone.

Six months later she became captain of her ship, a dream come true, and she was more than qualified. She was the second female captain in the Frejjan fleet. Brianna was the first. She had been told there would be a new copilot onboard, but she knew nothing about him and looked forward to meeting him. On the Bridge was a tall man with a mop of dark blond hair and a welcoming smile.

"Good morning, Captain. I'm your new copilot Leif," he introduced himself in broken Frejjan.

"Well, hello and welcome," Alison said and shook hands with him. "I'm Alison. Where are you from? You have a slight accent."

"I grew up in northern Sweden, but when I was fourteen years old, my family moved to North America. I went to flight school and received my training in America and worked as a space pilot for two years flying between Earth and Mars. Then one day the Frejjan ship landed on Earth and invited men to emigrate to Frejja and I signed up. That was one year ago and that's why my Frejjan is so lousy. I'm working on it."

"I was born in America, but we moved to Mars when I was a baby," Alison explained. "My native language is English, so let's just speak English."

"When I arrived on Frejja, I had to pass a flight test and the instructor passed me right away, but I had to learn to speak at least some Frejjan before the government hired me. This is my first job as a Frejjan pilot."

"What's the name of the instructor who tested you?"

"Emrak, a hell of a nice guy."

"That's my dad. Yes, he is a nice guy and I love him."

Alison told Leif how she had lost her biological father in an accident and her mother, the president of Mars, had married Emrak and moved to Frejja when she was eight years old. She had never been back to Earth, but hoped to visit one day.

"My parents were not pleased when I moved to Frejja, but I have a sister still on Earth, so they have at least one of us there. I wanted to explore space and a free move to an advanced planet like Frejja was too tempting to pass up. My lifelong fascination is space exploration."

"Mine, too!" Alison exclaimed enthusiastically.

Alison asked Leif to take the controls and they took off for Mars. They had a full cargo bay with goods that the Martians had ordered and would return with terrynium sheets and, most likely, at least some Martian men willing to move to Frejja. Alison carefully watched Leif's skill as a pilot and how he controlled the ship through the first tunnel. There was no question he was fully competent and with a little more training he would easily make it as captain. She was pleased with him and liked him. He was easygoing and pleasant.

They spent ten days on Martia and enjoyed themselves. Martia had restaurants, many fun shops, holodecks, a concert hall and outdoor trips and they spent the whole time together. The two junior pilots went off by themselves. Leif had been there several times when he worked for Earth. He took Alison's hand and told her it was more fun to explore Martia with such nice company.

Alison laughed and said -

"Thank you. You're not so bad yourself."

On the return trip to Frejja, Alison let the junior pilots take the controls and she and Leif sat down and talked. He told her of his childhood in Sweden in the far north called Lapland, how he at first rejected the idea to move to America and disliked his new life in the Washington, D.C. area. Alison in turn told him about her life on Frejja, her mother's two presidencies, how Emrak had adopted her and that she also had two brothers.

When Alison was home again, she told Emrak and Karol about Leif and Emrak looked pleased. He had been the matchmaker, but did not say so. Only Karol knew.

They worked together four more months and Leif became full captain. The only difference in competence between Alison and Leif was that he had not yet trained to master the fighter ships, but he planned to do so in the near future.

When they landed on Frejja Leif asked her to stay on the ship so they could talk and when they were alone on the Bridge, Leif asked -

"Would you consider marrying me? I love you and always will".

Alison had not expected he would propose and was surprised, but happily so.

"Of course, I will. I love you, too."

During their two weeks off, they got married with Alison's family the only guests and Alison moved into Leif's little apartment near the air field. They were well suited for each other with the same goals and mostly the same outlook on life. Emrak and Karol were delighted to see Alison married to such a solid person. They were the same age, twenty-seven years old.

When they boarded their ship again it was as husband and wife and they shared the position as captain. They worked well together as a team.

On their return trip from Mars to Frejja twelve passengers were onboard and Alison felt uneasy around two of the men. They had only lived on Mars for a year and came from a Middle East country on Earth. The captain of the ship often mingled with the passengers and Alison had developed a feel for the mindset of the men eager to move to Frejja. These men had no such attitude. When Alison tried to converse with them, they gave short answers and never smiled. Alison told Leif about the two men and suggested they lock the entry to the Bridge. Leif agreed. They had four powerful stun guns and two laser guns on board and both Alison and Leif carried a stun gun concealed under their jackets. The Bridge was locked and the junior pilots also carried stun guns. The laser guns were on the Bridge ready to use. All of them were on the Bridge when they heard a tumult from the passenger lounge. Leif quickly put a bulletproof vest on and grabbed the laser gun.

"Stay here, all of you, to protect the Bridge," he said quickly. "I can take care of myself." Leif was a strong guy with nerves of steel and not easily intimidated. He locked the door to the Bridge.

Without being seen, he floated to the lounge and saw the two men both holding laser guns and staying down by having one foot under the bolted-down chairs. The passengers had been ordered to sit down on the floor along the wall and hold on to the handrails to prevent them from floating up and the guns were pointed at them. Leif did not hesitate. This was life and death and he realized it was a hijacking attempt. Should he stun them or use the laser gun and shoot to kill? He could not risk the passengers' lives and there had been incidents where a person was resistant to the stun gun and had managed to fire a shot after being stunned. Holding on to the rail with one hand he fired his stun gun. Both men fell. Leif could not get himself to kill the men with his laser gun.

The passengers and Leif moved the two limp bodies to cargo bay and all of them felt relief. The men were locked inside two cages and would be released to the police force on Frejja. Several of the passengers vented feelings of distress they had felt around the two men and all of them shook hands with Leif and thanked him for saving their lives.

Leif unlocked the Bridge and told the crew it was over and what had happened. From that day on, all passengers were checked for weapons and all luggage screened. This was the first time a hijacking attempt had ever taken place on a Frejjan ship.

CHAPTER 32

Alison's brother Leo was eighteen years old and considered an oddball by his friends. Most of his time was spent inventing. He had declared to his parents he had no time to attend higher education and he would educate himself. Leo was by no means an oddball; he just saw life from a different angle than so called 'normal' people. Since he was a kid, he had taken apart electronics and put them back together again. His goal was to create artificial gravity on spaceships to prevent loss of bones and muscles from months of weightlessness. His sister Alison worked out very hard after every trip to restore her physical strength. If he could invent gravity all the space pilots would return to their planet in better shape. Alison exercised daily when she was on her ship, but the weightlessness still took a toll on her body.

His first invention that became a success was to design a velcro floor with large loops. The people onboard would wear special boots with hooks attached to the soles and when walking across the loops, the hooks would catch preventing the person from floating away. It was so simple, but ingenious. Obviously, it was not artificial gravity, but it made walking upright easy and since the loops and hooks were large, walking on the velcro floor did not create much noise and the floor was easy to clean with a special vacuum cleaner.

Leo showed Emrak his invention and he loved it. Emrak presented the idea to his supervisors at the space program and they bought the invention from Leo. The payment was large and Leo was on top of the world for a while. In the future, Leo received a commission every time his velcro sold. Patents did not exist on Frejja.

A special velcro was created of extreme toughness with matching boots and the first ship was fitted with the novelty. It worked great and the crew and passengers walked around the ship and only needed to hold on to the rail lightly and some learned to walk without holding on to anything. It was also rather inexpensive to install the velcro floors.

The velcro was a temporary convenience until all ships had artificial gravity that worked.

Alison and Leif's ship was furnished with the velcro floors and they marveled at the simple but useful idea. It was fun to walk on the floor, sort of like playing with a toy.

Leo continued experimenting and his self-education exceeded what he would have learned had he attended a university. He spoke fluent English in addition to Frejjan. A loner by nature, he was totally self-sufficient with a mind that relied on his own instincts rather than listening to the mindset that was in vogue. Emrak and Karol recognized his inner strength and never interfered with his decisions. They both knew creativity is often misunderstood as odd behavior.

******

Brandon and Brianna decided to retire from space travel and at sixty-nine and sixty-five years respectively, they had had a long career. Their grandchildren, the twins, were now ten years old and the youngest grandson five years. They wanted to spend time with them and bought a house not far from Rigel and Sillia. They had enough money saved so they did not have to work anymore, but both of them wanted to do some kind of work to remain active. They just did not know what so they concentrated on furnishing their new house and figured they would eventually know what comes next.

Funina and her husband had recently moved to Frejja to be close to their only daughter and also lived in the neighborhood. Brianna was very fond of Funina and they visited often. Funina had learned to speak a little Frejjan so it became easier for them to talk to each other. Funina was happy when Brianna retired and she considered Brianna her best friend. The two women often picked up their grandchildren and went for picnics in the countryside and were gone all day. Brianna had never seen her own children grow up, so spending time with her grandchildren was cherished by her. Funina felt the same and was showering the children with attention. There was never any rivalry between the two of them; they were more like sisters. Rollo always came along and swimming in the lake was the best she knew.

Brandon often went to visit Leo and enjoyed hearing about his inventions. Leo wanted to hear everything about space travel from a practical point of view and to get ideas for inventions. Emrak would join them if he was home and their discussions were fast and touched on many facets of life in space and how to solve problems related only to life in space. Leo did not want to travel in space himself and found it too confined.

Funina had easily integrated into Frejjan society, but her husband Omunon struggled. Growing up in a matriarchy and accepting to be held back by women had shaped his personality. Funina had been the driving force in their marriage and she had made all the decisions. Her salary working for the government in a prominent position was much higher than his school teacher salary and living on Arrynia, where all men faced the same destiny, Omunon had never questioned his second-rate status. To retire and live on Frejja was of course Funina's decision and it did not even dawn on him he could refuse. They had had a happy marriage, but his 'doormat' standing in the marriage was a fact.

Now living on Frejja, he quietly noticed the men and compared their self-confident personalities with his own. He had no self-esteem, no drive to pursue new ideas, no ability to lead and take initiative. He asked himself if his life had been a total waste of time. Omunon was intelligent, but had never used his intelligence. His son-in-law Rigel and Brandon were strong men and he had recently met Emrak and Leo at a get-together and found them impressive. He did not fit in anywhere, he felt.

No one noticed his emotional pain except Karol. She picked up on it right away and her childhood neglect and being kicked aside had made her very sensitive to other people's suffering. Her opportunity to talk to Omunon came one day when he asked to see her garden and she decided to gently find out what was going on in his mind. Funina was inside talking to Emrak and Sillia and did not notice that they disappeared outside. They sat down in Karol's garden and with her gentle and tactful ways she got him to talk. His Frejjan was too poor to understand so they used the translation device. He slowly and with some embarrassment confided in Karol his lifelong hardship to subdue his personality and become an obedient follower. Karol understood. That had once been her own life. She told him about her childhood and how she had learned to overcome her lack of self-esteem with the help of her first husband. It can be done, she assured him. Karol advised him to decide exactly what goal he wanted to achieve and then take one step at the time towards his goal. Funina was a kind woman and not his enemy. What he needed to do was to tell her everything he had just told Karol and together they could change the situation so there was more equal status in the marriage.

Omunon followed Karol's advice and Funina finally understood his emotional suffering and they were able to work out the problems together. Funina loved her husband, but had never really understood the hardships the Arrynian women inflicted on their men by forcing them into obedience. She realized it was time to end the matriarchy on Arrynia and grant equal rights for men and also give them voting rights.

Funina started to write articles and posted them on the Arrynian Internet using the Interstellar system. The articles were shocking to the Arrynian women, but the men saw them as the light at the end of the tunnel and freedom at last. A one-person army, Funina continued writing and her articles started to have an impact on the female mindset. Perhaps it was time to end matriarchy, they thought. Then Omunon wrote an article and posted it and it was praised by the men. He gave an accurate description of the opportunities men had on Frejja compared to the lack thereof for the Arrynian men. No society could prosper if there was discrimination against half the population, he wrote. The change started on Arrynia with men's suffrage, then slowly one small change after another became law and within a few years men were allowed to run for government office. It would take a decade, but equal rights for men and women became law on Arrynia and the matriarchy was officially over. Funina had started the snowballing and Sillia applauded her mother. She had never approved of the system on Arrynia.

The five million Kodetsian population had obeyed the laws of Arrynia and accepted Kodetsian men had no voting rights, but within their own community there were equal rights between men and women. After the matriarchy ended, some Kodetsian men ran for office and won. There was no discrimination.

Omunon started to assert himself and gained more confidence. He was happier with life and himself and Funina treated him with utmost respect.

******

A colossal sand storm hit Martia and disturbed the peace and quiet. The storm moved walls of sand over the enclosed domes and darkened the outside. For two weeks the storm raged. The Martians were used to sand storms and calmly waited for it to end. The domes had never yet been seriously damaged by sand and the robots were impressive to watch as they methodically and quickly removed all sand from the domes. When the storm ended, they found one wing of living quarters had disappeared and the people were dead inside. Fourteen people had perished when the dome above their heads was swept away by the sand. Between each section of enclosed domes were emergency closures that could be shut and the residents in the adjacent wing had had no choice but to quickly close the wall knowing that the people in the next wing probably were dead.

As a result of this tragedy, the Martian government reinforced the entire dome structure at a very high cost, but the president and his advisors reasoned that if the domes would fail, there would be no country left. Martia had a substantial gold reserve for emergencies and gratefully used the gold to pay for the project. It took a year to finish the huge task, but the strength of the domes withstood any sand storm that occurred for many years to come.

******

Alison was pregnant and when the embryo was transferred to the artificial womb, they found out it was a girl. Alison and Leif were elated as were Emrak and Karol. They named the girl Solveiga, an old Norse name, after Leif's mother. All four of them were eagerly awaiting the birth and when the time came and they brought Solveiga to Alison and Leif's home it was such an exciting and loving moment. Alison and Leif had parental leave for three months and bonded with the baby. Both of them felt slight anxiety to leave their baby and go back to work, but after their leave of absence was over and they turned the baby over to Karol and Emrak they knew they could visit with the baby over the Internet every day and it made the parting easier to take. Karol and Emrak's youngest son Rey was now fourteen years old and both Karol and Emrak thought it was fun to have a baby in the house again. Their android Tyra did all the housework and Karol had lots of time to spend with her little granddaughter. Emrak was also pleased to have his granddaughter living with them and he often carried her around for hours when he was home. Leo and Rey loved the baby, their niece, but they were teenagers and busy with their friends and hobbies and Rey had a demanding school program and spent most of his time studying.

Alison asked Leif when they were back at work if they had made a mistake to have a child and not be able to raise the baby themselves.

"Absolutely not," Leif said firmly. "We'll spend all our off-time with Solveiga and when she gets older and we visit over the Internet, she will understand we're working and haven't abandoned her. Your parents are the best grandparents a child could ever have and Solveiga is lucky to have them. Could you imagine life without motherhood? I wouldn't miss being a dad for anything."

Leif's answer reassured Alison and she stopped worrying whether her decision to have a child had been right or wrong. She was just grateful to have a daughter.

******

Earth2 was thriving and the population was now twelve thousand citizens. In honor of Rasufilus, their town on the Bavonilla land was named Rasunom by combining 'Rasu' and 'nom' from his wife's name Akinom. The pilots had great respect and affection for their leader and knew that without him there would be no mercenary fleet. The town had one home for each family, two stores, several storage buildings and a brand-new road connecting their community to the Frejjan town. The Frejjan community was spread out over a large piece of land, but the town where the government buildings and the stores were located had been named Bliss.

The dredging machine gently scooped up sand and minerals and as the men collected the platiniridium, they made a startling discovery. Among the sand was a skeleton of a human baby! It was intact and had been perfectly preserved under the sand of the river and it appeared to be a homo sapient. The men took great care not to damage the skeleton and gently put it in the airmobile and rushed back to town. They called out for Ássurt, who was the most knowledgeable in history and anthropology and he came running out.

"Look, look, a skeleton under the river bed," shouted one of the men.

Ássurt took a good look and said -

"It's for sure a homo sapient and not a prehistoric species as we found on the first planet. We don't have the instruments to carbon-date the bones, but I'm guessing it's very old," he said and gently touched the bone. "Let's put the skeleton back into water to preserve it and when the Frejjan ship returns, we can ask them to take the bones and date them on Frejja."

The news spread among the people and they all realized they were not the first people on Earth2. A former civilization had lived on the planet and for some reason perished. Why? Was something wrong with the planet? Were they invaded or was it a natural disaster that had occurred? Was it a disease?

After the initial shock was over, the people came to the conclusion that whatever took the lives of the former population there was nothing they could do and the carbon dating from Frejja would give them the first clue what may have happened.

Several months later the report came from Frejja that the skeleton was around one thousand years old and a homo sapient. They could not identify any injuries to the skeleton and why the baby had died. The baby had been normal and healthy when it died. The mystery remained.

Over the years, several more skeletons were found and they were all carbon-dated to be of the same age as the baby. The Frejjans believed a disease killed them off. Hopefully, the present population was immune to it. The news about a former population reached Brandon and Brianna and they discussed it with Emrak and Karol. They all hoped the cause of death would not return and affect the Earth2 people now living on the planet.

Standard of living on Earth2 was good, not excellent, but slowly improving all the time. There was enough food to buy; education was good with the arrival of several experienced teachers from Frejja; medical care was sufficient with three doctors now living in the community and a dentist had recently arrived and opened a dentist's office. He was popular as people had not seen a dentist since they moved to Earth2. He also had his own lab and his android assistant made any dental implement the dentist needed. The dentist lacked the equipment to cryogenically freeze stem cells from baby teeth, but when President Ássurt heard about the problem, he immediately offered to fund the equipment. Earth2 made enough money from mining and the health of the people was of paramount importance. The next supply ship from Frejja brought the equipment and the dentist was grateful. His android assembled the machine and all children had the stem cells from their baby teeth frozen. If they lost a tooth the stem cells would be implanted in the tooth socket and regrow the missing tooth.

Ijakull, the geologist, and his robotic assistant continued searching the planet for minerals. Earth2 was the same size as Earth and it was a slow and tedious task to look for any kind of natural resources. They had found another cave with at least some gold and at other locations osmium and palladium. The palladium discovery appeared to be large and palladium was highly priced. Earth2 had enough minerals to pay its bills for many years.

Using the airmobile, Ijakull and three other men decided to thoroughly explore the rest of the planet. This had not been done before and the spaceship had only flown briefly above the planet at high elevation and the pilots had not noticed anything unusual. Ijakull had toured large areas of the planet, but never the opposite side of Earth2. Food to last several months and some scientific instruments for testing were loaded onto the airmobile.

Ijakull, the three men and the robot assistant flew at low altitude covering north and south and found that the scenery looked the same as their own area. When they reached the far side of the planet the landscape changed and vegetation became sparser with fewer trees. Large grasslands replaced the forests and stretched for hundreds of miles. No animals were seen. Then, at the opposite side of the planet, they found several volcanoes that no one had noticed before. They were rather small and appeared to be inactive. As they continued flying, they discovered what looked like a crater and landed to examine the cavity. They realized it must have been caused by the crash of a meteorite or a small asteroid. The diameter was about half a mile and the depth one hundred and fifty feet. Sand and gravel covered the pit. The crater looked old and the geologist reasoned that the crash may have been the reason the former population died. The impact must have sent dust high up into the atmosphere and probably blocked sunlight for several years. Without the sun, no crops would survive and the people starved to death. The climate may also have undergone a cooling period without direct sun.

While they traveled back to their community, they discussed their findings. Half the planet was lovely and very scenic and the rest was livable, but not as attractive. There were no deserts anywhere, so rain did fall on the whole planet. The grasslands were rather monotonous and dull, but fully livable and there were some clusters of trees here and there. People settling in that area could plant trees to break up the monotony. Several rivers ran through the area, but there were no lakes. In their own area, the number of lakes was plentiful. Earth2 had no ocean.

Ijakull reported their findings to the government and then posted a full summary of their expedition on the Internet for the Earth2 citizens to view with holographic images. Ijakull concluded that the most likely reason why the former population on Earth2 died was from the impact of the meteorite and its effect on the climate. The report was also sent to Frejja and the people read it with great interest.

Now that most of Earth2 had been investigated, the government realized that the planet could easily support several billion people, but nobody wanted such a large population. The citizens had all declared they preferred a sparse population and open, unoccupied lands. They wanted the planet to remain pristine.

******

Tothellim and Rheo enjoyed their new lives on Veehnia. Neither of them missed space travel and for both of them family life was the most important. Tothellim's daughter Heidi was now six years old and he and Anna had a newborn son as well. Life on Veehnia was easy with a high standard of living. He felt fortunate to have Anna as his wife and he adored her.

Heidi came home from school and looked sad, not her usual bubbly self.

"What's wrong, Heidi?" Anna asked.

"Vera said I look silly," Heidi said and started to cry.

Anna consoled her and assured Heidi she would contact Vera's mother, but Tothellim stepped in and said -

"Invite Vera to the house tomorrow and I'll be home. Looking different doesn't mean being different."

The following day the two little girls came walking to the house and Tothellim welcomed them. He bent down and shook hands with Vera and said -

"I'm Tothellim, Heidi's dad. I look a little different from your dad, but that's because I'm from another planet. Let's go inside and I'll show you a few pictures."

Tothellim had prepared some holographic pictures of Peturun and showed them to the girls. Vera gazed at the images in amazement and Tothellim showed various pictures from his planet, its people and then the Milky Way Galaxy. Both girls wore implants boosting their cognition and Vera had no trouble understanding everything Tothellim explained. She was listening in wonder and burst out -

"I can't believe you lived in another galaxy. It's awesome! Thank you for showing me these images." Then she turned to Heidi and said -

"Heidi, forgive me for what I said. I am so sorry."

"Of course, I do. Let's forget it."

That was the beginning of a long friendship between the girls and the only time Heidi experienced any discrimination. Heidi was a pretty girl and except for her Peturun hair growth, she looked like her mother. Her baby brother looked more like Tothellim and had the growths on his cheeks and mildly ridged eyebrows, but normal hair growth. The growths on his cheeks would be removed soon.

"Tothellim, you're quite a diplomat. You handled it so well," Anna said when they were alone and hugged him.

"Thank you, Anna. Lack of knowledge often makes people say the wrong things, even kids are guilty of it. The girls get along fine now."

Tothellim was a success at work. He had mapped all the tunnels used by Veehnia and sent out some ships on exploratory missions to find more tunnels. Each tunnel had high vibration at its entry and the instruments on the ships could easily detect the increased vibration from a far-off point. Closer to the tunnel's entry the vibration was powerful enough to shake the ship considerably. Of the ships Tothellim had sent out, one came back and reported they had stumbled upon an area with a huge vibration located at the end of the known area of the galaxy where Veehnian ships traveled. The pilots stated it must be a tunnel of sizable length as the vibration was strong enough to shake their ship from a long distance away.

Tothellim asked four of his most experienced pilots if they were willing to investigate the tunnel and all of them responded with an enthusiastic yes. They were willing to take the risk. Tothellim requested that one of the newest and most updated ships should be prepared for the trip. Food to last a year, water, tools, instruments and maps of the galaxy were loaded onto the ship and after a month it was ready for takeoff. Three of his most advanced android pilots would also be onboard as back-ups. A late model shuttle was stowed away in the cargo bay.

The two pilots in charge, Tyler and Jayce, were both unmarried and in their early thirties. All four of the pilots were adventurous adrenaline junkies ready to explore the unknown. The ship traveled two months to reach the tunnel and the vibration of the tunnel could be felt a long distance from the actual entry to the tunnel. Tyler and Jayce were at the controls and the other pilots ready to take over right behind them.

As they neared the entry, the ship vibrated enormously and they were sucked into the tunnel with a force that was hard to describe. All four of them had practiced flying through the eighteen-hour tunnel that connected the Milky Way to the Andromeda galaxy and this tunnel was wider in comparison, but it did float and swayed back and forth making it necessary to constantly adjust the steering of the ship. One mistake and the ship would touch the sides of the tunnel. After six hours Tyler and Jayce let the other pilots take the controls and they did a good job. The ship accelerated in speed the whole time and became harder to control and the vibration shook the ship violently. After another six hours Tyler and Jayce took over again and by this time it had become increasingly difficult to line up the ship in the center of the tunnel. Three more hours and they saw light. It was over! They blasted out of the tunnel at the highest speed they had ever encountered and with nothing but empty space in front of them they engaged the autopilot and checked the instruments. The tunnel had taken fifteen hours. Where were they?

The instruments showed that the distance of the tunnel had propelled the ship *thirty thousand light years* into the galaxy. They checked the holographic maps and found they were rather close to a star with two orbiting planets and they decided to continue traveling until they saw the star and could locate the planets. The androids ran tests on the computer system to ensure the distance they had traveled was correct. It was. The fifteen-hour tunnel was another mega portal, not to be compared with the eighteen-hour tunnel, but still a mega portal.

It took two more months until they spotted the star and one of the planets. It had no moons. They carefully slowed down the ship and entered orbit. The distance between the star and the planet was about right to support life, they estimated. The planet was a beauty and about the same size as Veehnia. Mountain chains, two large oceans and clouds here and there indicating an oxygen atmosphere. As night fell, the planet was illuminated and they realized it was inhabited.

The following day, the four pilots turned the ship over to the androids and boarded the shuttle. They slowly descended and found the planet had large cities with high-rise buildings and the skies had several layers of space vehicles dashing back and forth. The space vehicles were more sleek and faster than anything they had seen on Veehnia and the streets below were crowded with humanoids. They kept the shuttle above the traffic at a safe distance. Tyler focused their instruments to get a closer look at the people and saw they did not look exactly like humans, but close.

The pilots were so focused on looking at the streets they did not notice they were escorted by two space vehicles. One of the vehicles blasted a horn at them and gestured to follow them. Tyler waved and nodded. They were unarmed and felt they had nothing to fear.

The space vehicles flew outside the city and landed on a field where other vehicles were parked in neat rows. Tyler landed the shuttle next to the two space vehicles and the four pilots climbed out. The air was fresh and the gravity about the same as on Veehnia. It was sunny and warm. Tyler grabbed the translation device and the alien pilot entered his language into it.

"I'm Tyler and this is Jayce and we are from the planet Veehnia. We are unarmed and on an exploratory mission to find new planets," he said. He felt no fear and trusted his instincts that these people were not hostile.

The alien pilots were close to six feet tall and had human bodies with light brown skin. Their facial features were delicate and fully human and their dark brown eyes were rather large. They had thin necks and the size of their heads was larger compared to humans and they had no hair. Their eyes radiated extreme kindness and Tyler felt as if he was drowning in a wave of warmth. He thought to himself *how beautiful they are*. The aliens wore grey uniforms.

"Welcome to all of you. I'm Lorre and our planet is called Ljeviina and our star is Stellinus. We know of your planet Veehnia and I take it you traveled through the tunnel to find us." Lorre's voice was pleasant and his language melodious without harsh sounds.

"Yes, this was the first time we traveled through the tunnel. How do you know of our planet?"

"I mean no offense, but our civilization is more advanced than yours on Veehnia and we have flown our ships several times above your planet to study you. Our ships were cloaked and you never detected us. We were able to enter your computer system and found all the information we needed. We know, for example, you have been importing people from Earth and you have two citizens from Peturun. Our government prefers not to make our existence known to civilizations who are not as advanced as us. We find it is better to allow people on less advanced planets to develop at their own rate, but now that you have found us, we truly welcome you."

Lorre suggested they meet with his supervisor. They walked inside a very modern building in stone with large windows and Tyler noticed that Lorre and his co-pilot moved with graceful, fluid movements similar to a cat. Inside the supervisor smiled at them and said -

"I hear you risked traveling through the tunnel to reach us. Welcome, I'm Flar. It's not every day we have the honor of welcoming people from another planet to Ljeviina. I take it your ship is in orbit."

Flar explained that their planet had a population of three billion people. The people of Ljeviina were highly evolved and communicated as easily telepathically as verbally. Each person's goal was a lifestyle in full harmony with their mind and soul. Wars did not exist on the planet and the citizens were granted total individual freedom, which included speech, lifestyle, to work or not to work, choice of location to live and more. Labor work was done by robots and androids and the people had ample time for individual goals. Most people chose to work, but there was no stigma attached to those who preferred a lifetime to pursue meditation and soul searching. The government worked hard for the people and had earned their trust. The economy on the planet was good and there was no poverty. Anyone choosing not to work could apply for government assistance.

The Veehnians listened with great interest and Tyler thought to himself that he would not mind living on Ljeviina.

"How far behind you are we Veehnians in evolvement?"

"It's hard to say. Technologically, you are not far behind. Mentally and spiritually, you are at least two hundred years behind us. I mean no offense, of course, but our people have achieved a refinement of their psyche that you are still unaware of exists. You haven't started to search for it yet. That's why we never made contact with you and felt you should just evolve at your own rate. We never allow ourselves to quarrel over unimportant things and prefer to settle disagreements with diplomacy instead."

"I apologize for my naive question, but sometimes a dispute can clean the air, so to say, and result in improvements," Jayce said. "Are your people lacking adrenaline?"

All the Ljeviinans burst out laughing.

"That's a good one and fully legitimate," Lorre said when he recovered. "Of course, you have a good point. No, we're certainly no angels here and occasionally people do lose their temper. What I meant to say is that the most evolved people among us do resolve arguments with diplomacy, but not all have reached that point. We're constantly trying to transcend and some are better at it than others."

"Do you allow competition between companies?"

"Definitively, or we would risk total stagnation. Monetary reward does drive our economy even though no one is what you would call money hungry. We do have an affluent class here, but I have to say that the generosity of our affluent citizens is impressive. Large donations are common."

"Do you have different races?"

"No, just one race and you're looking at it," Lorre said with a big smile.

"Do you have crime?"

"We used to, but not anymore."

They continued talking for a while and then Lorre took them to a guest house where they could stay for the duration of their visit. It was a beautiful house and each of them had a private bedroom. Lorre told them he would pick them up the next morning and show them around. At dinnertime a woman showed up with a precooked dinner and served them. It was a vegetarian dinner, but very tasty and they liked it. The pilots assumed the people were vegetarians.

The next day was hectic and they enjoyed meeting the people. The women were almost as tall as the men and everyone they talked to had very kind eyes. Most men were dressed in pants and shirts, no suits, and the women wore dresses only. There were no foreigners on the planet and the Veehnians arose curiosity. Many came over to them and shook hands with them and wished them welcome. The city was ultramodern and some of the high-rise buildings were office buildings and some were apartments. The traffic was all above the city streets, but some of the space vehicles would land on the street to discharge passengers and pick up new ones. They toured one of the apartments that was empty and it was spacious and comfortable. Lorre stayed with them and was their guide.

The following day they toured the countryside and saw little towns here and there, but the landscape was not crowded by any means.

"Does your planet have wild animals?" Jayce asked.

"Yes, in the mountains," Lorre replied. "We have herds of hoof animals similar to deer, but also predators. Our oceans have plenty of fish, but no aquatic animals. People eat fish, but many are vegetarians. We do not eat meat. We keep cows for the milk only."

The Veehnians had noticed herds of dairy cows that were no larger than ponies. It started to rain and they returned to home base. They were told Ljeviina had four seasons and the winters were very mild with little or no snow.

The day after they toured the countryside again and here and there were totally isolated single homes. Lorre explained that those were the homes belonging to hermits and they required solitude. The hermit had chosen a life in total isolation to explore his mind and distractions from the outside world would interfere too much. They had highly developed psyches and were good at telepathic communication. Some of them wrote commentaries and posted them on the Internet for free. When Tyler asked if they were lonely, Lorre explained -

"You can't be lonely if you're friends with yourself. They communicate easily with their Higher Self or you can call it their spirit. They're totally free of ego and self-pride and have reached a refinement that is above what we so called normal people have. Their wisdom is impressive and once in a while they release a report and post it on the Internet for free so all citizens can share in their findings of the mind."

"How do they support themselves?"

"They grow most of their foods themselves and they can apply for government assistance. Some beings need a lifetime of meditation without keeping a job. We believe in reincarnation and the hermit may have worked hard in former lifetimes."

Tyler knew he could not handle life as a hermit, but he did grasp the idea and understood the motivation behind it.

In the foothills of the mountains were deep forests stretching for miles and they saw herds of grazing animals similar to deer. It was a tranquil setting. They camped overnight and returned to the city the following evening.

The highlight was a daylong boat trip on one of the two oceans and two fishlines trolling for fish were behind the boat. They were lucky and each line had a sizable fish that they cooked in the boat's galley. After dinner Jayce asked -

"Are there any problems or hardships on your planet?"

"At the present time, no, we have overcome all our problems," Lorre said. "In the past, a very long time ago, we had huge problems with a government that was dictatorial and suppressed the people. People lived in fear of the government and there were few jobs available and high taxes to pay for people who worked. Spy cameras were everywhere and privacy didn't exist even in people's homes. Add to that gangs of criminals trying to make a living any way they could. Finally, the government was overthrown in an army coup, but the damage the government had done to society was huge and people were apathetic and suicidal. When they regained their freedom, they didn't know how to act and it took a generation for people to start trusting themselves and their abilities. People are emotionally healed now and the present government works for the people, not for themselves. Many planets have gone through similar experiences. Perhaps hardships are necessary for growth."

"Would you call your present society a Golden Age?"

"Yes, that's a good way of putting it."

"Are there any hostile planets close to Ljeviina that could invade you?" Tyler asked.

"Yes, one, a planet called Ziggellus and its people are savages. They're advanced enough to have spaceships, but their demeanor is brutal. They totally lack sophistication and will kill others and not blink an eye. They're not capable of empathy. If they would invade us, we can probably fight them off, but there's no guarantee we'll succeed. They have ransacked several planets, stealing, raping women and destroying infrastructure just for the fun of it. They're unpleasant to look at also and have tails."

"I've heard of a famous mercenary called Rasufilus in the Milky Way. He never fails. Have you heard of him?"

"Actually, I have. You're right, he is well known for his competence. I'll remind our government about him when I return to work. Ziggellus is located close to the exit of the tunnel on our side of the tunnel."

"There's a new planet called Earth2 where he lives. The distance from Earth2 to Ziggellus is about four months. It's doable," Tyler said.

Before Tyler and Jayce left Ljeviina they gave the location of Earth2 to Lorre and asked him to pass it on to his supervisor in case they would need the services of Rasufilus in the future.

The visit came to an end and they had spent three weeks on Ljeviina. After thanking all the people who had been their guides, they boarded the shuttle and returned to the orbiting ship. Lorre said he was hoping to visit Veehnia, but there was no way of knowing if his government would allow a visit. The androids were eager to hear the news and watched all the holographic images from the planet.

The return trip was uneventful and they passed through the tunnel without incidents. All four pilots had a feeling of accomplishment as they landed on Veehnia and Tothellim and Rheo greeted them when they climbed out of the spaceship. They had been gone almost nine months without ability to transmit messages from Ljeviina and only when they exited the tunnel were they within transmission distance to Veehnia and notified them they were on their way home.

Tothellim and Rheo gave a bear hug to the four pilots and the following two days were spent reporting everything about the new planet and watch all the holographic images. A full report was also prepared for president Curtis, who was always enthusiastic about news from other planets. Since Tothellim was responsible for the trip and the safety of the pilots, he was truly relieved the trip had ended safely without perils.

Tothellim prepared a full report for Emrak with images of the tunnel and Ljeviina and since the Veehnian ships now went to Earth several times a year to invite immigrants, the crew could transmit the report over the Interstellar Internet to Emrak as soon as the ship was within transmission distance. He emphasized to Emrak he could share the report with other planets as he saw fit.

All four pilots were told to take two months off with full pay to rest up after the trip, which was accepted with gratitude. Any long space trip took a lot out of the pilots physically and they needed to exercise and rebuild their muscles after being weightless for several months. Leo's velcro flooring had not reached Veehnia yet, but Frejja, Earth and Mars had implemented the idea and as other planets noticed the flooring and inquired about it, they bought the velcro flooring from Frejja and installed it on their ships. It was a temporary solution until full gravity was available on the ships. Scientists were working on artificial gravity, but no workable and cost-efficient solution had been found. The velcro invention had made Leo a rich man and he received a commission every time the velcro was sold. He had bought his own house not too far from his parents. Leo and two hired engineers were involved in creating various items for space travel and their workshop was often busy until midnight.

Emrak received the report from Tothellim and was filled with awe as he read it. He immediately sent a message back to the Veehnian ship thanking Tothellim for his thoughtfulness and kindness to share the report. Emrak had often wished Tothellim would have settled on Frejja and he felt great affection for the man. It was mutual. Tothellim reported all space news to Emrak. Emrak shared the report with Earth, Mars and the member planets of the Alliance and received excited messages from all the planets thanking him for the information. Emrak sent copies to Brandon, Brianna and the president as well as Leif and Alison. One copy was also sent to Rasufilus.

At home, Karol and Emrak's granddaughter Solveiga was a lively toddler and at two years old a handful to control. Emrak and Solveiga loved to frolic in the yard. Alison was pregnant again and would soon make the transfer of the embryo to the artificial womb. Both Karol and Emrak were excited to have another baby to look after.

A year passed and Alison and Leif were now parents of a son, Sven, looking like his dad. Leif and Alison had wanted to name the baby Emrak, but Emrak convinced them it would be too confusing to have two people under the same roof with the same name, so they named the baby after Leif's father. Leif had completed his training as pilot for the fighter ships and in case their service was needed, both of them could still work together. They enjoyed each other's company and worked well as a team.

Karol and Emrak took custody of Sven and Alison and Leif went back to work. It was hard for them to leave the baby, but once they were back on the ship and involved with their daily routine, it became easier.

CHAPTER 33

Rasufilus was working on his house and his toddler son was playing next to him. He heard engine noises and looked up and saw a large shuttle coming in for a landing. No ship was expected at this time and Rasufilus felt unease. A teenage boy came running on the road from Bliss shouting -

"Rasufilus, a shuttle has landed with people from the Andromeda galaxy. They are asking for you!"

Rasufilus and the teenager jumped into Rasufilus' groundmobile and within a few minutes they arrived in Bliss. Two pilots, Lorre and Flar, waved at him, but they had stern faces. Flar spoke through the translation device -

"We are from the planet Ljeviina in the Andromeda galaxy. I'm Flar and this is my copilot Lorre. Our planet has suffered a horrible attack from people living on the planet Ziggellus. We need your help."

Rasufilus showed Flar and Lorre into the town offices and asked for tea to be served. As they sipped their tea, Flar described what had happened -

"It took us six months to reach you and we went through the fifteen hour and eighteen-hour tunnels to get to your planet. By the way, congratulations, this planet is awesome, what a beauty. Anyway, a week before we departed for Earth2, Ljeviina's capital was bombed and the whole city was demolished. *It's gone! Flattened. One million people died.* The criminals came from planet Ziggellus, two months' travel time from us, and they attacked late at night when people were asleep and couldn't get out of their apartments fast enough to rescue themselves. They raided our treasury and stole everything that was in there, all the gold that the capital city needs to function. Luckily, we have a few more locations they didn't find where we also store our money. They arrived with about a hundred ships and fired their weapons with huge explosive power and the whole city was an inferno. Then they raided the treasury and, in a blink, they were gone. Several survivors saw them and identified them as Ziggellus people. Why they felt they had to murder one million innocent people is a mystery to us. These are the worst savages in the universe with no feelings for humanity at all."

"I know of them and I agree, they are the scum of the universe. I also know of your planet and the fifteen-hour tunnel," Rasufilus said and his face showed the empathy he felt for the people who had died. "Do you have a plan?"

"We would like to hire you and your fleet and together with our fleet, which is one hundred and fifty fighter ships, we hope that our combined forces can wipe out the people on Ziggellus. The women are no better and appear to be as cruel as the men."

Rasufilus looked increasingly disturbed when he listened to the plan and said slowly -

"What you are suggesting is genocide and extermination of the whole population of Ziggellus. I know you're driven by anger and I fully understand your feelings. The loss you have suffered is horrific. May I suggest an alternative plan?"

"Please do."

"I will use eighty-five of my ships and they're equipped with the most powerful weaponry you can find in the universe. You have one hundred fifty ships and together we have two hundred thirty-five ships. That's a formidable force and more than we need to get the job done. If we surprise them and attack early morning at sunrise, we can blow up every single spaceship they have, their hangars, their plants manufacturing weapons and airmobiles and any other manufacturing plant they have that tie into fighting a war and raiding other planets. If we succeed, we'll totally cripple them and they won't be able to leave their planet. In addition, I'll send reports to the neighboring planets not to trade with them or resupply them and that will further cripple them. They will survive as we won't touch their factories that make everyday supplies and we won't touch their food industry, only factories and supplies that deal with space travel and war. Before they can rebuild and enter space again it will take a generation. Any calls for help from them should be answered with demands for a peace agreement first and then only humanitarian help should be offered. Second, we will force them to return the gold they stole from your planet and we will not leave until they supply the gold."

"We agree with your plan. What's your fee?"

Rasufilus mentioned his fee in gold and Flar accepted with a handshake. He had strict orders from his president not to haggle over the fee as the future of Ljeviina was at stake and there was no fleet known in the universe that could match the skill and competence of Rasufilus' fleet. Rasufilus was also well known for his fairness when conducting his military operations and how he went out of his way never to hurt civilians. Flar told Rasufilus that his fee would be paid from the gold they would retrieve from the people of Ziggellus. The fee was high but fair considering the high cost of paying three hundred pilots and maintaining all his ships as well as supplying food for the pilots during the long travel times in space.

"When I work with another planet's fighter ships, I'm in charge and run the operation," Rasufilus explained. "Your pilots will have to take their orders from me. We leave in two days from today and we'll stop at a supply place first to get all the foods and whatever we are low on. As soon as we're through the fifteen-hour tunnel we'll be within transmission distance and will notify you of our location. We'll meet up with you at a safe distance from Ziggellus and then we proceed according to my plan. All the details of the military operation will be sent to your ships when we're out of the tunnel. In the meantime, on your way back I ask that you use your cloaking ability and fly over Ziggellus so you can map the planet for us. The more details the better. Try to find the location of any plant they have where weapons and ships are manufactured as well as the plants we should not touch such as food production, factories for clothing and so on."

"We agree to all your terms and our pilots will work under your command. Our ship has cloaking ability and we'll do our best to map Ziggellus on our way back to Ljeviina."

"Be ready and wait for us outside the tunnel in four months. You will still not be back on your planet in four months, but just send all your information and the mapping of Ziggellus to your home base and the commander of your fighter ships and they can in turn forward the information to me. We'll slowly circle in space until we meet up with you. I'll send our ships through the tunnel at the rate of one ship every twenty minutes and that will delay us a little, but that's the only safe way of doing it. I'll give you the channel we use for communication and it's an encrypted and safe channel."

Rasufilus now conveyed the tactics he planned to use and Flar and Lorre knew they were listening to a military genius. The whole plan was quick and efficient using the element of surprise to get the job done without spilling blood needlessly. They recorded the plan and would send it to their home base when they were close enough to transmit.

Flar and Lorre said goodbye to Rasufilus and left the same day. They were in a hurry to return and wanted to be through the tunnel as soon as possible so they could start sending all the information to their supervisors. The mapping of Ziggellus would take two days and it was a dangerous process. If they were detected they would for sure be shot out of the sky. The cloaking of the ship had never failed, but if it would they would be in deep trouble.

Rasufilus informed his wife Akinom that he must leave in two days and would be gone about eight months. She was used to it, but she missed him terribly every time he left. Rasufilus was sometimes home for six months between jobs and he would not accept any job offer that involved shady deals. Most of his work came from governments that needed reinforcements and all his work was fully legitimate. He called his pilots to assemble in the town hall they had built in Rasunom and gave them the details of the assignment. Five ships and ten pilots would be left behind to protect Earth2 as usual and the pilots left behind were selected on a rotational basis. All the pilots were fully skilled to travel through the various tunnels and all were combat ready. The female pilots were as competent as the male pilots.

They left Earth2 and first stop was a workstation orbiting a planet at the edge of the Pleiades group of stars to pick up supplies. It was a small detour, but the only place that always had huge supplies in stock for the spaceships. They carried foods, water, fuel, weapons and almost everything the pilots were looking for when they stocked up. The only accepted payment was gold and there was a shuttle service to the surface of the planet they orbited. The gold payments were never stored on the workstation for security reasons. Rasufilus and his fleet left fully stocked.

******

The Ljeviina ship had entered orbit around Ziggellus and the ship was fully cloaked. All their lights were turned off and they were waiting for daylight. They could not use a shuttle as it had no cloaking ability.

Ziggellus was a rather big planet with an oxygen atmosphere and a population of about two billion people. They descended and stayed at an altitude of ten thousand feet and used minimal engine power to reduce noise. Flar assured Lorre they could not be heard on the surface. Their instruments were sensitive and would be able to discern enough details to make a workable map for Rasufilus. All day they flew over the various cities and there were no spaceships in the air. The regular airmobile traffic was far below them. When dusk arrived, they reentered orbit and turned the ship over to the androids so they could sleep. All the humans onboard were exhausted, mostly from the tension. The ship was still cloaked and the lights off. The following day they finished the job and with a sigh of relief they left the planet and restarted the full engine power at a safe distance from Ziggellus.

They were within transmission distance and prepared a very detailed report of Rasufilus' plan as well as all the mapping they had done of Ziggellus. Flar sent it to the generals who were waiting to hear from them and asked them to send the maps to Rasufilus' ship after they had organized all the images and identified the buildings to be taken out. The ships from Ljeviina were ready to leave and the generals only needed a day to get the maps ready and distribute all the details of the operation to the Ljeviina pilots. The full fleet left the following day and the timing was just right so they would arrive at the meeting place when Rasufilus arrived.

Rasufilus arrived first and the following day the Ljeviina fleet arrived. All of Rasufilus ships had built-in translation devices covering all the languages, but the Ljeviina ships had the portable devices. Rasufilus and his pilots spoke Morekian. Rasufilus made sure all the pilots had been issued correct orders and knew what buildings they were to take out. He himself and thirty other ships from his own fleet would take out the largest and most dangerous of the targets, the main plant manufacturing weaponry. The plant was huge. In a few hours it would be dawn on the planet and Rasufilus instructed the pilots to slowly circle until it was time to move forward on his command.

It was time! All the ships organized themselves into groups and each group would cover a specific area of the planet. The sight of all the ships entering the atmosphere of the planet must have been overwhelming for anyone watching on the surface. The different groups of ships took off to their assigned targets. Some had short distances to travel and a few groups had to fly a long distance to reach their location.

It was barely daylight and the early attacks were totally unexpected by the Ziggellus people. Chaos erupted as building after building in the industrial areas exploded with large bangs and went up in flames. The attacks came too fast for the soldiers on the ground to react. They could not even reach their supply of weapons before they were blown up. Everywhere was an inferno and people running to safety.

Rasufilus and his ships neared their target at low altitude and all the ships lined up.

"FIRE!" Rasufilus barked. The ships fired their high-power weapons and the whole plant literally exploded with an ear-splitting racket and huge flames shot up from the building.

"FIRE!" A second round of firing made sure the building and its contents turned to rubble.

"RETREAT!" Rasufilus shouted. As fast as they had arrived, they were gone and out of sight. They reassembled at high altitude and listened for any radio transmission.

"Mayday!" The call came in from a Ljeviina ship.

"We must have missed one building. It's not on our map, but it's a weapons storage building," shouted the pilot in a tense voice. "Two of your ships and five of ours have been shot down and we can't get close enough to take them out. It's nonstop firing from the ground. We need help!"

"We see your location on our screen. Wait for us. We'll be there in only a few minutes," Rasufilus yelled trying to sound reassuring. *Seven ships shot down,* he thought to himself. *Will this end in disaster?* Rasufilus had not lost a single ship of his fleet in years and now two had been downed and the pilots probably killed.

Within minutes Rasufilus and his ships arrived at the storage building. Rasufilus directed the ships to encircle the building at a high enough altitude so any direct hit from the ground would not inflict serious damage.

"FIRE! FIRE! FIRE!" Rasufilus' voice roared and the building was engulfed in flames and explosions were set off every few seconds.

Then one shot from the ground sideswiped Rasufilus' ship. Someone was still alive down there and had managed to fire a long-distance weapon and slightly hit Rasufilus' ship. There was no serious damage and the ship was in no danger, but Rasufilus knew what he must do.

"Wait here," he instructed the other pilots. "I'll dive-bomb to put an end to this mess." Rasufilus was a man of faith and close to his Creator and he silently asked for assistance. A dive-bombing was dangerous and only a last resort, but this was one of those occasions when it had to be done. He looked at his two copilots if they agreed and they showed thumbs up and nodded. They were fighter pilots and this was war. Rasufilus revved up his engines to maximum and took off like a bat out of hell. At low altitude right over the building he fired with maximum power and hit the target right on. As fast as he had swooped down, he was up in the air again and the whole maneuver was executed so fast and with such expertise that no one had time to react. He was safely back with his fleet again. The pilots waiting for him watched in awe from the sky. Anyone daring such an exercise had to have nerves of steel.

Rasufilus called all the ships to assemble at high altitude and report to him. It was a good report.   All the ships had hit their targets with no fatalities. It was too early in the morning and people were still in bed. The only thing that had gone wrong was the weapons storage building that Rasufilus had just eliminated.   So far, only the person shooting from the storage building had been killed.

"Regroup and we fly in formation to the government buildings at five thousand feet," Rasufilus instructed the pilots. "I'll be in the lead."

It was a formidable sight. The sky was covered with ships. Half an hour later they reached the government buildings and Rasufilus ordered his pilots to remain in the air and he would descend and initiate talks with the president and his advisors. The ships had hovering abilities and could remain in the same space as long as needed. The pilots would be able to hear the conversation between Rasufilus and the president.

Rasufilus landed his ship outside the president's office and waited. His engines were on and he could take off in a few seconds if he had to. The president and a group of ten people rushed outside towards the ship with angry faces. Rasufilus had heard of the Ziggellus people, but never seen one. The men were average height but muscular humanoids and they had long hairless tails. Their faces were human looking with small noses, flat ears and the corners of their mouths were pulled downwards giving them a brutal look. They had white skin that was unusually wrinkly and no hair.

"Who the hell are you and what do you want, you scum?" the president screamed furiously into his translation device set at maximum volume. His tail was swishing wildly back and forth. Rasufilus stayed in his ship and using his loudspeaker and translation device he responded calmly -

"We are from the planet Ljeviina and I and my fleet are mercenaries working with the Ljeviina pilots. My name is Rasufilus. All your ships, all your factories making weapons and spaceships have been eliminated and there is no way you can get off this planet now. We demand that you return all the gold you stole from Ljeviina and double the amount to compensate for the enormous cost to rebuild their capital that you destroyed."

"No way, are you crazy. We'll end up broke! I know who you are, Rasufilus."

"There is no discussion. Those are our demands. If you don't retrieve the gold right now, we'll open fire and destroy your planet. Look up in the sky. My ships are ready to fire." This was a bluff and the pilots listening in were smiling. Rasufilus was a man of high integrity and had respect for all lives, including the Ziggellus people.

The president was screaming in an agitated voice into his communicator and apparently received the bad news that everything was gone - all spaceships, all airmobiles, all factories manufacturing ships and weapons, all plants that made parts and engines for the ships, all was gone, nothing left. He apparently also heard that no factories dealing with foods, clothing and items needed for survival had been touched. The president looked as if he was going to pass out, but managed to calm himself enough to start talking to his advisors and generals. They talked among themselves for a short time and the president finally announced -

"We will meet your demands. I have ordered the gold to be sent over here right away. It will take a couple of hours."

"My ships will land on the field outside your capital," Rasufilus said. "If you fire on us we'll return fire using the firepower of our ships."

"There will be no firing," the president responded. He looked worn out, beaten, a shadow of himself. The news that his people were now stuck on the planet with no way to leave had shocked him. To rebuild everything would take a generation. Later on, he would also discover that Rasufilus had arranged with the planets they traded with that no ships or weaponry should be sold to Ziggellus. The trading partners had agreed to this arrangement. They were fully aware of the raiding the Ziggellus people had done and were disgusted with them.

Rasufilus lifted off ground and instructed the ships to follow him and land on the field. It was a large field, but the ships barely fit. The pilots did not exit the ships for security reasons. After three hours a caravan of vehicles arrived with the president in a groundmobile leading the convoy. Rasufilus and his two copilots climbed out of their ship. They were unarmed. Rasufilus' experience told him no shots would be fired by the Ziggellus people. It was over.

Rasufilus called the top commander of the Ljeviinan fleet using his communicator and had him verify the correct amount of gold. What was delivered was exactly twice the amount that had been stolen. It was correct.

"Mr. President," Rasufilus said. "The people of the planets that you have raided hope that this lesson will forever change your behavior and that your raiding will end right now, right here and never start again once you have rebuilt your factories. You have conducted yourself as savages not befitting civilized people."

It took a while for the president to find his presence of mind and he responded in a beaten voice -

"I will think about what you say, Rasufilus. We are no longer a threat to anyone. It will take us a whole generation to rebuild, perhaps longer, and when we have rebuilt our spaceships again, the people will have a changed mindset and probably not want to return to raiding other planets."

Then he surprised Rasufilus by stretching out his hand and said -

"Maybe you did us a favor."

Rasufilus shook hands with the president and said -

"I will contact you in one year to see how you survived and if your people need help, I will arrange that you get help."

The president and all the vehicles left and the top commanders from Ljeviina separated out Rasufilus' part of the gold, his fee. They all knew that without him, there would have been no happy ending to the mission. Then the commander asked Rasufilus how much it would cost to replace the two spaceships that had been shot down and when he was told, without hesitation he added enough gold to the pile to pay for the two lost ships. The last thing the commander did was taking one gold bar and placing it separately and he said -

"This is for the widows of the six pilots that gave their lives for our planet. It's a small token, but if they have children, it will help the widows support their families. Please give this gold to them with our deepest condolences for their loss."

Rasufilus was moved by the commander's thoughtfulness and assured him he would deliver the gold bar to the widows. He also thanked the commander for paying for his lost ships. The pile of gold that was left to return to the Ljeviina treasury was substantial and would help pay for rebuilding the bombed-out capital. The damage on Ljeviina was much worse than what had been inflicted on Ziggellus and one million people had been killed versus one or perhaps a few more on Ziggellus.

Rasufilus packed his part of the gold into several spaceships and said goodbye and shook hands with all the lead commanders from Ljeviina. None of them knew if they would ever meet again, but the rescue mission traveled around the Interstellar Internet and Rasufilus' fame just kept growing.

True to his word, one year later Rasufilus heard of a ship that would travel to Ljeviina and the pilots gladly delivered his message to the president of Ziggellus when they were within transmission distance. In response to Rasufilus' inquiry if they were in need of help of any kind, the president sent his regards to Rasufilus and reported that the whole population had come together and they were hard at work rebuilding all the factories and were hoping to be back to normal within fifteen years. The president added that their raiding days were over and they would never again be a threat to another planet. They had all the food and everyday supplies they needed. The Ziggellus people had sent apologies to Ljeviina offering their deep regrets for what they had done. The last thing the president said was -

"My people and I hold no grudge against you, Rasufilus. You did what was right and I respect you for it".

The message was touching but also surprising to Rasufilus. He had not expected that these formerly so cruel people had found the inner strength to recognize how wrong they had been. They had taken the first steps toward civilized behavior.

President Ássurt sent the report about Rasufilus' successful mission to Emrak and he read the report with great interest. Emrak had heard about Ziggellus and he was glad to hear their raiding days were over. He wished he would meet Rasufilus in person.

******

Work had begun on Ljeviina to rebuild the destroyed capital. The people were grieving the loss of one million citizens. Rasufilus' clever idea to double the amount of gold Ziggellus should return to Ljeviina had resulted in a net gain of gold returned to the treasury even after paying Rasufilus' fee and reimbursing him for his destroyed ships. Still, the cost of rebuilding a whole city was enormously expensive and the gold was not sufficient to pay all the costs.

At first, most of the citizens had demanded the whole population of Ziggellus should be eliminated, but later on as they heard how the mission had played out, they agreed Rasufilus' plan was the better way to end the raiding. The people felt indebted to Rasufilus and a message was sent to him from the people of Ljeviina with heartfelt thanks for his assistance. When Rasufilus received the message, he was touched and news of that sort made his dangerous work worthwhile.

Rasufilus told the widows of the downed pilots as gently as he could about the death of their husbands. All the wives of the pilots knew that every mission was dangerous, but it was rare that Rasufilus lost a ship and this was a sad reminder that his work was indeed very dangerous. The women were courageous and between them they had eight children to support. The gold bar they received was a welcome help to put food on the table, but if they would ever run into hard times, Rasufilus would not hesitate to pay for their living expenses.

He planned to stay home with his family for six months and not accept another job offer during that time. Akinom was pregnant and he wanted to be home when she delivered their second baby. There was plenty to do around the house and he enjoyed improving his home. His little son Vitzoll carried his tools around and Rasufilus was a proud father.

Rasunom was attractive and mostly finished and the people took good care of their properties. The infrastructure was not fully finished and it was a work in progress. If Rasufilus had worked on Earth2, he would have run for president, but being away so much made that dream of his impossible. The children in his town went to school in Bliss and they reached Bliss the old-fashioned way by using their feet. All the services and stores were in Bliss. Rasufilus taught math and physics in the school when he was home and there were now over a thousand students attending the school system, the oldest students were twenty years old. Some were from planet Frejja, some from Etteron and some were born on Earth2. The present population was fifteen thousand and growing.

Bliss now had suburbs and people commuted into town using groundmobiles. Some people had bought bicycles from Frejja and swore by them. People were still arriving from Etteron and every supply ship from Frejja had at least thirty Frejjans asking to immigrate. No one was denied to stay. There were enough jobs available so anyone who wanted to work could easily find a job. The citizens paid no taxes as the income from the mines generated big profits for Earth2 and the debt to Frejja was half paid off. Payments to Frejja had been larger than expected by the Frejjan government and in a few years the whole debt would be paid off and Earth2 could start saving. Building the infrastructure was an ongoing process and had taken a big bite out of the Earth2 budget, but roads, services such as water supply and safe processing of waste water had been costly projects and so far, the income from the mining had been used up and very little money was saved.

Telly's privately owned passenger spaceship was no longer used to ship people from Etteron to Earth2 and had been turned over as a gift to the people of Earth2. Everyone celebrated when Telly officially handed over the ship. It was a solid ship with many useful years left and the four pilots that had manned the ship were happy to finally settle down. The ship was used to train new pilots as well as for day trips around the planet at low altitude to show all the citizens how the rest of the planet looked. Each passenger paid a small fee to pay for the fuel of the ship, but it was inexpensive and everyone could afford it. The seating capacity was one hundred people. The ship was immensely popular and considered a national pet and was named the Tellyship. The people from Etteron now arrived on Etteron government ships.

Telly had spent his whole fortune helping Earth2 get established and was a folk hero. By now, all of them knew what he had done for the planet and he was revered by all the people. Telly intended to run for president when President Ássurt's term was finished in two years and no one doubted he would win by a landslide. Telly and his wife Ellala had no regrets that they had given away all their money to establish a modern, new country on a new planet. They now had no more money than the average citizen. The combined income from Telly's employment as Secretary of the Treasury and Ellala's job as a nurse at the hospital was more than enough to live on. Ellala had been a nurse before she married Telly and she enjoyed working as a nurse again. She was good and often assisted the doctors during surgeries. Telly and Ellala had no children.

Quality of life was good on Earth2 and the citizens were pleased with life. No one was rich and they did not have the luxuries that the people on Mars enjoyed, but they lived on a serene planet that was totally unpolluted and with huge open spaces for everyone to enjoy. Rasufilus supplied peace of mind for the citizens and no one had any desire to leave the planet.

Akinom gave birth to a girl and the birth went well. She spoke broken Frejjan and had trouble with the pronunciation so she spoke Etteron with her son Vitzoll. Rasufilus was almost fluent in Frejjan and also spoke English rather well and he spoke Frejjan with his son. The children became bilingual and fluent in both Etteron and Frejjan. English names had become popular among the people and Akinom and Rasufilus chose the name Grace for their daughter.

English as a second language was taught in school and all students were proficient in English by the time they graduated.

CHAPTER 34

Brandon and Brianna had been retired five years and wanted to visit Earth one more time before they became too old. They asked Funina and Omunon if they wanted to come along, but they felt it was too much for them and Cellie and Gordon said the same. Cellie had just turned eighty years old. Arvin and Maija heard about the trip and eagerly asked if they could come along. Brandon and Brianna often visited with Cellie and Gordon and Arvin and Maija were present most of the time, so they all knew each other well. Arvin was born on Mars and had never seen Earth. Maija spoke fluent English so there was no language barrier. Fenul and Rhea were now adults and wished their parents a fun trip. Arvin was only fifty-two years old and still working full time, but his employer allowed him time off so he could make the trip. Brandon was eager to see his mother Tina and brother James. Tina was still active at one hundred years old and her android took good care of her. Brianna had a sister and brother on Earth who she had not seen since she moved to Frejja.

The trip from Frejja to Earth took three months and all four of them had to prepare themselves for Earth's heavy gravity and much of the time was spent exercising. Brandon and Brianna were welcome on the Bridge and enjoyed visiting with the pilots a few times, but they were passengers and felt they should not interfere with the pilots' work. Maija had never been on a spaceship and was fascinated with the whole experience. Arvin had moved to Frejja thirty years ago and had not been in space since then and he also found the trip fun.

They landed outside San Francisco and James and his wife and Brianna's brother and sister were there to greet them. The gravity was fierce and they struggled to walk. Just to drag themselves to the airmobile was an effort and they had to laugh. They knew they made a spectacle of themselves.

James had a big, old-fashioned house not far from the harbor and several guest rooms. Brandon and Brianna and Arvin and Maija dragged their feet inside and sank down on the sofa. They knew they had work to do getting in shape for Earth's gravity. In three months, when the visit was over, they would probably be able to run and jump, but right now they were glad if they could pull themselves upstairs to their rooms. James' wife Beth served a lovely fish dinner and soon after Brandon and Brianna and Arvin and Maija felt they had to lie down. They collapsed in bed and fell into a deep sleep.

The first week in James' house were spent doing resistance training and weight lifting and at the end of the week they started to feel more at ease. Brandon and Brianna knew from experience it usually took them a month to adjust to heavy gravity, but they were older now and not as flexible as they had once been.

All four of them went to visit Tina. Tina's android Lily opened and was thrilled to see Brandon and Brianna again. Tina came out walking slowly and leaning on a cane. She did not look a hundred years old and was of clear mind. It was a happy reunion and Brianna explained who Arvin and Maija were. Drew and Cellie were distant relatives and Tina remembered Cellie clearly and was excited to meet Cellie's son and Frejjan wife. She had a rough idea how far away Frejja was and Brandon had holographic images along and showed his mother and Lily many pictures from Frejja and left the pictures with them to watch when they had returned. Tina had lived a quiet life since Drew died and she and Lily had become very close. She had made arrangements with her son James to take in Lily when she passed on and Lily understood that she could be a great help to James and Beth as they aged. They had no android.

They spent all day with Tina and Lily and went back twice to visit before they returned to Frejja. It was hard to say goodbye, but Tina was at peace and made it easier for them.

Brianna's brother and sister were all excited to meet them and they had great fun together even though they were very different from Brianna. They had lived a traditional lifestyle while Brianna had spent her life in space seeking adventure. Brianna told them about life on different planets and they enjoyed hearing all the stories and watching all the pictures, but to actually travel into space themselves was out of the question. They had no desire to do so.

After a month they were able to move around more easily and they had booked a month-long trip around the world. Domestic travel was fast with the supersonic planes and they visited China, Australia, the Middle East, Europe and Africa. All countries were safe to visit. Maija knew from reading that Earth had different countries with different ethnic people. On the planets Brandon and Brianna had visited, there had been only one country and one ethnic population. The trip around the world was the highlight of their visit and an incredible adventure for Arvin and Maija. They loved Earth and the diversity.

"There is an energy here on Earth that is electrifying and doesn't exist on Frejja," Maija remarked.

"I feel it, too," Arvin said and nodded in agreement.

Perhaps the most exciting adventure was a safari in Africa to watch the wildlife and the herds of wild elephants. They were awestruck. Lions, zebras, herds of buffalo, giraffes were in full view and they also made a trip to central Africa to watch gorillas. Brandon and Brianna had never traveled to Africa and found the wildlife just as exciting as Arvin and Maija. Both Arvin and Maija announced that they would not mind living on Earth. Both of them knew the history of Earth and the collapse, but life on Earth at the present time was invigorating, they felt. They took lots of holographic pictures to bring back to Frejja.

The last month they spent many days on James' fishing boat just enjoying the ocean and watching the seabirds. Brandon and Brianna remembered when they were kids and had spent weekends on Drew's boat fantasizing about space. Now, at the end of their lives, they knew they had realized their dream. Frejja had no oceans and Arvin and Maija were impressed by its vast size and the tides created by the Moon.

"Instead of going straight back to Frejja, can we make a detour and see Martia?" Maija asked.

"I'm sure we can. Give me a day to check it out," Brandon responded.

They were lucky and the launch window to Mars was open. Brandon booked seats on the spaceship to Mars and also seats on a Frejjan ship expected to land on Mars about a week after they had reached Mars.

Their departure from Earth was emotional and they all knew they would probably never meet again. Even Tina was there to see them off and she leaned on Lily for support.

The three weeks of travel to Mars went fast and they landed safely. The sight of Martia from space was truly impressive and the domes stretched for miles. With a population of one hundred thousand citizens and growing, the size of Martia was immense.

Arvin had not seen Martia since he left thirty years ago and viewed it with a newcomer's eyes. He felt right away he had made the right decision to leave Mars and the indoor living Martia offered was suffocating. Maija was all eyes and totally astonished by life in 'the bubble'. The standard of living on Mars was the highest of all planets and people lived a pampered lifestyle, but they had to wear a spacesuit when they went outside, not a fun thing. They stayed in a comfortable hotel and explored many of the domes and saw the terrynium factory and several other plants that now were in operation on Mars. There were no relatives to visit as they all had moved to Frejja. They toured the schools and medical facilities and all were equipped with the latest technology. The highlight was a two-day trip away from Martia by bus and they stayed overnight in a hotel quite a distance from Martia. There was no need to wear a spacesuit as the bus was pressurized and hooked up to the hotel. Maija wanted to experience wearing a spacesuit and she and Arvin walked around outside the hotel for an hour wearing spacesuits just for the fun of it. The outdoors on Mars was boring with endless sand and dust and there was really not much one could do for fun on the Martian surface. Still, the trip was enjoyable as everything was new to Maija. Brandon, Brianna and Arvin had seen the area outside Martia before and knew it was not to compare with Frejja.

"It's been interesting to see Mars, but I couldn't live here. It's too confined," Maija told Arvin.

"That's how I felt when I left," Arvin responded. "I was sick of wearing a spacesuit and I felt literally suffocating. I wanted fresh air and the outdoors."

After two weeks on Mars, they boarded a Frejjan passenger ship and started the return trip home. In two months, they would be back on Frejja. The whole trip had taken over nine months and the price tag had been high, but all of them felt it had been worth it and money well spent.

Fenul, Rhea, Emrak and Karol as well as Rigel and Sillia waited for them when they landed. Emrak had seen many planets, but never Earth and he was eager to hear about the trip. Karol's android had prepared dinner for them and after dinner they stayed up half the night talking. All of them stayed overnight and the following day they spent hours watching the holographic pictures. The safari pictures were a hit and the sight of wild animals roaming free was a wonder. Everyone was mesmerized when they watched the pictures. Emrak felt he was too old to make a trip to Earth, but Rigel and Sillia expressed interest and Fenul and Rhea agreed. They could not afford such an expensive trip now, but perhaps later in life they would be able to.

The adventure was over and after two weeks of exercising, they were back to normal. The effect of weightlessness had worn off and they felt strong again.

******

On Earth2 Telly was running for president and he ran unopposed. Every citizen voted for him. President Ássurt turned over the office to President Telly and wished him success. Ássurt had been a first-rate president and advanced the planet a great deal. His intelligence and leadership had been admirable and he had worked hard for six years for the people not sparing himself. Now it was Telly's turn and he was highly popular and loved by the people. All wished him well. With over fifteen thousand citizens and growing all the time, the work of the government had become more involved and complicated. The people on Earth2 were no longer a little colony. Rather, Earth2 functioned as a small size country and the economy, school system, medical care and manufacturing required experienced leaders. Earth2 still had a small debt to pay off to Frejja and President Telly was determined not to add to the debt. The mining was profitable and every payment to Frejja had been substantial. If things went well, President Telly hoped Earth2 would be debt free when he left office. He had no intention to tax the citizens and they all had to live within the budget.

President Telly carefully picked his cabinet. Six government offices needed to be filled and he chose Ássurt as his Secretary of the Treasury and Rasufilus as his Secretary of Defense. President Telly made special provisions for Rasufilus so he could assume his government office and still continue his mercenary work. It was not a full-time job and only required a few hours a week and as long as he was within transmission distance, he could fulfill his duties over the Interstellar Internet when he was away on assignment. Rasufilus gladly accepted the offer.

The first teacher on Earth2, a woman, became Secretary of Education and another woman was asked to serve as Secretary of Planning, an important department organizing the future of Earth2. There were many talented people among the citizens and all the people asked to serve accepted their cabinet positions. The members of the new government started working and the total size of the government was twenty-two people.

There were no lawyers on Earth2, but basic, common-sense laws were in effect and easy to understand. No crime had ever been committed and no police force was needed. Perpetrators of serious crimes faced deportation and people guilty of minor crimes had to pay money in restitution to their victims. In addition, they could never apply for a government job.

The mint had improved their skills and the new coins were flawless and elegant looking. There was no excess of coins, but to expand the economy and to have more money in circulation more coins were needed. The mint worked two shifts a day to keep up with demand. There was no bank yet in Bliss and people kept their money at home.

All news was posted on the government website so it was easy to access any information. All images were holographic.

******

The android that had assisted the Earth2 doctor in the repair of Oleon's leg, Atlas, had asked his superiors at the Frejja hospital where he worked if he could move to Earth2. The hospital owned him and he had been created on Earth, then sold to Mars, then bought by Frejja. His surgical skills were extraordinary and his personality kind and pleasant. He was truly popular among the doctors at the hospital. Atlas' programming was the latest available and he was equipped with a full package of human feelings. He spoke English and Frejjan fluently and enjoyed telling jokes. When Atlas' superior asked why he wanted to move to Earth2, he responded -

"I feel I'm needed there and I would enjoy training the local doctors. It's a new planet and I would enjoy being part of its development."

The hospital was hesitant to release him, but Earth2 was considered Frejja's pet project and after discussing the matter with the board of directors, it was agreed to allow Atlas to move to Earth2. Atlas was thankful when he heard the ruling. On Earth2 he would be free. No one would own him.

The three doctors on Earth2 were delighted to welcome Atlas and he was offered a small, but cozy wooden house close to the hospital to live in. It was fully furnished and Atlas loved it. He was only thirty-five years old and had many years ahead of him until he expired. Atlas received the same salary as the other doctors. Occasional updating of his programming or repair work was done for free. Atlas started working right away and he took over the patients that were in need of serious care. Oleon came to see him just to shake his hand.

One of the immigrants to Earth2 was a woman from Earth, Viola, a young, adventurous lady who had first moved to Mars, then Frejja and finally to Earth2, where she decided to settle down. Her command of the Frejjan language was passable. Viola was a musician and became a music teacher at the school in Bliss. There were only wind instruments on the planet and Viola ordered five digital pianos and five violins from Frejja and the purchase was approved by the school. She selected the most musical students and her goal was to build an orchestra that was capable of giving performances. Viola set out to train the students and she knew it would take several years until they were ready to perform in front of an audience.

Viola was totally unconventional and at the age of twenty-nine, she had had few boyfriends. Her free spirit scared the men away. She was pretty and funny with a beautiful figure, but her bohemian lifestyle did not appeal to men who were looking for a wife. She moved to Mars from Earth when she was twenty-two years old and soon realized Mars was too cramped for her, so she moved on to Frejja. At first, she really liked her new planet, but after five years she became bored again and moved to Earth2. Finally, she felt at home. She could breathe here. Viola was a talented musician and an accomplished piano player as well as a good violinist.

Viola had lived on Earth2 one year and felt contented. Every day she practiced playing and wished she had a full piano instead of her digital version, but that was all she could find. She had posted on the Internet that she would perform for free at the school auditorium and she had chosen to play the best of Chopin's nocturnes and etudes and a few other famous pieces. Perhaps no one would show up, she thought to herself.

She was shocked to find a packed auditorium and as she sat down, she felt totally calm. Her music was a gift to the people and she played with a sensitivity that moved the audience and it was obvious her heart and soul were involved. When she had finished the applause was long and some shouted "more". As an encore, Viola played Chopin's Fantasy Impromptu and the audience loved it.

When the auditorium was empty and she was ready to leave, she looked up and saw a man. It was Atlas. Viola knew who he was. He had been featured on the government website and she was glad such a skilled doctor was living in Bliss.

"I'm Atlas, the new doctor from Frejja," he introduced himself. "I wanted to tell you in person how much I enjoyed your playing. I'm able to appreciate all the things you humans enjoy and I truly loved your performance."

"Atlas, thank you, your kindness warms my heart. I'm grateful when my playing is appreciated. Do you play any instrument?"

"I'm afraid not. I spent all my time studying to become the best doctor and surgeon. Can we sit down and talk for a while?"

"Sure, I'd love to."

Atlas noticed her command of the Frejjan language was not the best and suggested they speak English. They found they had so much in common that time flew and Viola thought Atlas was the most interesting being she had ever met. He could discuss everything and his sensitivity was amazing considering he was a machine.

"I know you're a machine, but you come across to me as more human than some of the men I have met," Viola blurted out.

Atlas smiled and said -

"Actually, I feel more human than machine. I'm able to learn on my own and my feelings are evolving all the time."

When they said goodbye, Atlas asked if she would want to go for a drive in the countryside with him the next weekend and she said 'yes' without second thoughts. She liked him, machine or not. How easy he was to be with, how kind he was and for the first time in her life she had found someone who understood her and her different way of looking at life. Moreover, he was awfully handsome to look at.

He picked her up in a rented groundmobile and they drove far out into the countryside where no people lived. It was the only road out of Bliss and stretched about two hundred miles. The government intended to add on to it, but there was no money available at present. Viola had packed a small lunch for herself and hoped he would not mind watching her eat. She knew, of course, androids did not eat. A small lake right next to the road looked inviting and they stopped to enjoy the scenery.

"This planet is so beautiful. Let's go and sit by the lake," Atlas suggested.

Viola put a blanket down and they sat down at the water's edge.

"Eat your lunch, Viola. You must be hungry. I don't mind, you know that."

They stayed all day by the lake and walked along the shore. Viola confided in him her parents' disapproval of her desire to live free as a bird and how she at age twenty-two left Earth to get away from them and their criticizing. How she had never had a real boyfriend, but had substituted her music for married life and resigned herself to spending her life alone.

"Would you let me into your life as a friend? Even an android needs someone to talk to," Atlas said with a chuckle.

Viola was so smitten with his charm that she spontaneously gave him a hug.

"I would love to have you in my life," she said.

Atlas told her that he knew, of course, he was a machine, but he lived his life as a human among humans and felt more at ease with humans than with androids. He was often lonely and would love to have a companion. At first his programming of human feelings had been basic, but he was evolving all the time and now his feelings were as strong as any human's. He loved his work and healing sick people, but he knew he wanted more in his life than only work.

"Would another android be the answer?" Viola asked.

"Perhaps, but a girl like you would be better," Atlas said with a smile.

They started spending time together and Viola taught Atlas how to play the violin. He learned fast and was able to accompany her when she played the piano. They had fun together and laughed together. Viola was head over heels in love with Atlas and after they had been dating four months, he got up the nerve to ask Viola to marry him. He loved her.

"Yes, I will marry you, Atlas, I can't wait to be your wife." Viola put her arms around his neck and whispered into his ear "Are you functional?"

"Fully functional, all recent androids are," Atlas whispered back and smiled at her. Her shy question did not surprise him and he thought it was just common sense and natural.

"I think we should talk to the president if there are any laws or rules against a marriage between a human and an android," Viola said.

Atlas agreed and they went to see President Telly. He was not surprised when he heard why they had come to seek his advice and he understood Viola's affection for Atlas.

"There is no law on the books forbidding a marriage between an android and a human," Telly said. "When I look at Atlas, I don't see an android, but a being that has evolved into a variation of a humanoid, a new species perhaps. Marriage doesn't have to be between two identical beings. Look at Rasufilus. He is a Morekian and his wife is from Etteron and they look very different. One of Rasufilus' female Arrynian pilots is married to an Etteron man and they also look very dissimilar. You're two beings who want to share your lives together out of your own free will. There is nothing sinful here. Faith should not be a determining factor either. Personally, I can't see how any divine being would object to a happy union of two beings and I see no problem from an ethics point of view."

Viola took Atlas' hand and said -

"Thank you, President Telly, for telling us your viewpoint in such clear language. We love each other and will get married."

The following week they were married by a government official authorized to perform the ceremony and they were officially a married couple. Viola moved into Atlas' house. They announced their marriage on the Internet and hundreds of people posted messages wishing them well and happiness. There were no comments of disapproval.

During their long, happy marriage Viola never regretted her decision to marry Atlas. His understanding of her complex personality gave her the belief in herself that she had lacked before. She felt whole. Atlas, for his part, told Viola that without her his life would have been only work without the spark of life that comes from sharing one's life with a loved person. The quality of their love life surpassed Viola's expectations.

Atlas noticed Viola's lack of enthusiasm for cooking and decided to learn how to cook. He quickly scanned the Internet and entered all the facts into his memory and surprised Viola with a home cooked meal.

"It's out of this world!" Viola expressed with approval. "Thank you, honey."

Atlas took over all the cooking and found he truly enjoyed this new hobby. He became very good at it and Viola's appreciation every time he served her dinner gave him a warm feeling. When Viola ate, he always sat down and firmly believed dinner was a family event and all members should be present.

A year later one of the nurses, a Frejjan woman, came into his office and asked to talk to him. She asked if she could speak freely and the matter was sensitive. Atlas nodded and told her no topic was off limits.

"Atlas, my daughter Reata is sixteen years old and pregnant. I know you and your wife can't have children and my family doesn't approve of abortions. The father of the child is Frejjan and he is also just sixteen years old. Is there any chance you and your wife would want to adopt this child?"

"Yes, of course we would," Atlas exclaimed with great interest. "It would be a gift from heaven and my wife would love to become a mother. I would also be happy to have a child. When can I see Reata? I need to examine her and, if you don't mind, I would prefer to care for her during her pregnancy myself."

"She is waiting outside," the nurse said.

Reata came in and shook hands with Atlas. She was very pretty and about five months pregnant. Atlas carefully examined her and took some lab tests.

"Everything is normal and the baby is as healthy as can be," Atlas announced. "Reata, my wife and I would be most grateful to adopt your baby, but you must realize that once you have signed the adoption papers it's final. You can't have the baby back. If you want, you can visit us and see your baby. Are you sure this is what you want?"

"I'm totally sure and I don't want to see the baby after birth or later on either. That way I won't bond with it. I know you'll give the baby a good home and that's all I care about. I will not change my mind. The baby is yours. I'm only a kid myself and I'm not ready to be a mother. My boyfriend feels the same."

Atlas rushed home to tell Viola the news and she was overwhelmed with happiness. The baby was due in only four months and Viola started to plan a nursery. The house was small and their guest room would have to be converted into the baby's room. Viola's work as a music teacher was only part time and she planned to stay home with the baby the first months and then look for a reliable baby-sitter when she returned to work.

Reata gave birth to a blond baby girl and Atlas delivered the baby. The birth went well and was pain free thanks to the new medications that were now available. Viola was allowed to watch the birth and it was an emotional moment when Atlas placed the newborn baby in Viola's arms. Reata was half asleep and not aware of the birth and Viola and the nurse quickly moved the baby to the recovery room. The nurse cleaned the baby and dressed her and then gave her back to Viola to hold. Reata had agreed to use a breast pump and pump out her colostrum the first few days and then she wanted all ties between them to end. She felt that was the best way to heal and get over the loss of the baby so she could return to her regular life again. She never saw the baby.

Two days later Viola and Atlas brought their little daughter home. They named her Melody. Atlas was the most attentive father and adored his little girl and Viola told him that being a mother was one of the best things that had happened to her.

After asking around, Viola found an Etteron woman in her fifties, Bellinnia, who was perfect as a babysitter for Melody. Bellinnia had no children and was glad to take care of the baby. She would help raise the baby and became almost like a grandmother to Melody.

One evening when they were talking, Atlas asked Viola if she missed her parents. Melody was sleeping in Atlas' arms and he watched her with a smile.

"No, never," Viola replied. "When I left Earth to go to Mars, they didn't even see me off. I think they didn't care that I left. I'm the only child so they have no other grownup children and now they're alone. Maybe they thought I would come back. I'm sure they have no idea where I am and where I live."

"Living on Earth2 so far away from Earth, there is almost no chance you will ever see each other again," Atlas said slowly. "Have you forgiven them?"

"No, I haven't. I don't owe them anything. They didn't want me. Love can't be forced. Parents can't demand that their children should love them; they must earn it."

"I understand now how you feel, but if you would be able to forgive them you would find peace and be free. My love for this little girl is endless and I know you feel the same. Let's honor her free will and support her in her choices and never force our will upon her."

Viola put her arms around him and said -

"You're a great dad and husband. The best."

CHAPTER 35

President Telly had been thinking about the enormous grasslands on the far side of Earth2 and felt it was a resource that should be utilized. In his mind he pictured herds of meat animals. Grass and water were plentiful and could support thousands of grazing animals and as the population continued to grow, they needed more meat. There was always a shortage of meat on Earth2. He discussed it with Rasufilus as he knew he had seen most of the planets within travel distance and knew which planet had herds of animals.

"The obvious planet is Bantizza, where we came from," Rasufilus said. "Bantizza has large grass fields and there are herds of beef animals there, top quality meat. I miss those steaks we had on Bantizza and that's all I miss from that planet. If the animals will survive three months of travel is the question."

"We know how to safely put the animals into hibernation," Telly explained. "We moved about one hundred meat animals from Etteron to Earth2. They lost a lot of weight during travel, but they all survived and have increased in numbers. The supply of meat on this planet is far below what will be needed in the future. If we can import five hundred animals and just drop them on our grasslands, we'll have sufficient meat supply in the future. The grasslands can support thousands of animals and there are no predators to worry about."

Rasufilus loved the idea and promised to contact Bantizza right away and inquire how many animals they would be prepared to sell. Bantizza replied they would be willing to sell one thousand animals with the right number of males to females. The price was high though and they asked to be paid in gold. All the animals would fit into two of their largest cargo ships and would be delivered in one shipment. They asked for exact instructions how to put the animals into hibernation and their veterinarians would take care of it. Two Bantizza veterinarians would travel along on the spaceships and bring them out of hibernation after landing.

President Telly agreed to the price and he knew it would put a dent in the Earth2 budget, but they had the gold and they needed the meat. They also needed more goats for milk. At least a hundred female goats were needed and part of the grasslands could be used for breeding more goats. Chickens for egg production had survived on a ship from Frejja and they were pampered to ensure their survival. Slowly, the food supply increased with more foods to choose from. A slaughter house would have to be built next to the grasslands and a cargo ship of some sort for transport of the meat to the stores in Bliss.

President Telly and the Secretary of Planning met several times a week to organize the future of Earth2. Everything had to be planned from scratch. A road would be needed to connect Bliss with the grasslands area and a small town with the necessary infrastructure would have to be built for the families working in the slaughterhouse and tending to the farm business. The government was still in debt to Frejja and money was tight. The only way Earth2 could meet all the new expenses was to lower the payments to Frejja and just stretch the installments over a longer period of time. The population kept growing steadily and had now reached seventeen thousand.

It was a big occasion when the two spaceships arrived from Bantizza and they landed next to a river. The grasslands stretched as far as the eye could see with rolling hills and a few trees here and there. President Telly and his cabinet members arrived with the Tellyship and watched the unloading of the animals. They were half the size of standard cattle found on Earth. The vets had woken them up from hibernation on the ship and as they were unloaded, they swayed, but managed to walk down the ramp and onto the grass. All of them were skinny, but with the endless grass supply they would soon regain the lost weight.

The ships would stay two days to ensure the animals survived and then return to Bantizza. Ássurt handed the gold to the captain in charge as payment for the animals. It was early summer and by the time winter arrived, the animals would be strong enough to scrape the snow aside and reach the grass. The winters were mild with moderate snow and the river would most likely not freeze. One family had already volunteered to move to the area and would report to the government over the Internet how the animals fared over the winter. Their 3D printed house would be transported on the Tellyship unassembled together with all necessary household items and foods the family needed and the government would pick up the tab for the entire move as well as the cost of their house. They had only a baby so there was no concern about schooling of the child. Eventually, this outpost would grow into a town of more than a thousand people, but that was many years away.

The veterinarians and the crew from the two ships slept outside and swam in the river during their stay on Earth2. They enjoyed the scenery and to feel land under their feet and would have liked to stay at least another week, but they had orders to return after two days and did not want to defy instructions. All of them loved Earth2 and they had flown at a low altitude and noticed the beauty of Bliss.

The young family settled down knowing they were the only humans on that side of Earth2. Both the husband, Pollox, and his wife Lyra were independent and self-sufficient and had true pioneer blood in their veins. They had grown up on Frejja in a farming area and were excited to become the caretakers of the new herd. Pollox had a small salary as caretaker, enough to live on. To finish their house, start a garden and build a barn for future chickens and goats would keep him busy. In an emergency, they could be reached with the Tellyship in twenty minutes and the airmobile took about fourteen hours to travel to their homestead.

They enjoyed sitting outside their home in the evening watching the wind move the grass back and forth. The river was a hundred feet away and the only sound came from the wind and the water moving peacefully downriver. To catch fish was easy and they usually caught one for dinner within ten minutes of lowering a baited hook. Neither of them was lonely and they felt one with nature.

Pollox inspected the herd every day and towards the end of summer they all had regained their lost weight. As the herd moved it became harder to find them and he wished he had some kind of transportation. At sunrise, he set out on foot and even at a brisk walk it took him often two hours to find the herd. He realized that the only way to keep up with them was to have a vehicle. He took a chance and sent a message to the president asking if he possibly could get an airmobile. To his surprise, President Telly responded the government realized the distances involved and agreed with Pollox' request. The Tellyship would deliver an airmobile free of charge to be used by Pollox and other future farmers. It was electric and the black box supplied electricity. Pollox had also ordered building materials for a barn and he asked the government to remove the cost from his salary.

Two days later the ship arrived and dropped the vehicle and building materials off. The pilot stayed and visited with them until the evening and then took off. Pollox was allowed to slaughter whatever meat they needed from the herd and he kept their large freezer well stocked. Lyra had served thick steaks which the pilot truly enjoyed.

"How can you stand it out here in the wilderness all by yourself?" he wondered. "I would go nuts."

"We love it. We don't feel lonely at all," Lyra replied. "We have each other, the baby, Nature and heavenly peace and quiet. What more do you want?"

"Someone to talk to," the pilot said. "It's too quiet here."

"Only a certain type of personality can live like this," Pollox interjected. "You have to trust your own abilities and be a leader rather than a follower. You can't be afraid to make decisions and if your decisions are wrong, well, you accept the unintended consequences and learn from them. Then you go on from there. On the plus side, we have total freedom, we make our own schedule and both Lyra and I are sort of hermits. By the time the baby is ready to start school, there will probably be another family or two living out here. That's just fine. Until then we don't mind our solitude."

The pilot thought about what Pollox had said and remarked -

"I think I understand how you feel. This is not a lifestyle for me, but I get what you say."

The visit was a nice break for Pollox and Lyra and winter was around the corner, so they did not expect company again until the next spring. No one knew for sure how severe the winter would be on the grasslands.

Fall arrived, the nights became colder and the grass turned yellow and dry. The herd was eating all day long as if they knew they needed to gain a fat layer for the winter. Snow blanketed the ground as the first few inches fell and winter had arrived. Pollox and Lyra enjoyed the change in season. The temperature dropped and the wind was strong most days and they realized the grasslands had more severe winters than the mild winters in Bliss. When it snowed, only a few inches came down, but it was rather cold and windy the whole winter.

Pollox was busy building his barn and Lyra often helped him. It was a 3D printed barn and not difficult to assemble. They were hoping to afford to buy a few animals the next summer.

The herd did well and continued eating the grass under the snow. The river did not freeze so they had access to water. The first calves were born at the end of winter and Pollox checked on them every day. He was grateful to have the airmobile as the herd was living a hundred miles away. All the calves survived and so did their mothers.

The wind stopped when spring arrived with heavy rains filling the river to capacity and drenching the ground. No wonder the summer grass was so thick and lush with so much rain coming down in the spring. In between the rain they enjoyed warm, lovely spring weather and wild flowers were growing on the fields. Insects were buzzing all over the flowers and the spring grass started growing. Pollox had managed to herd the cattle towards their homestead using the airmobile as they were entirely too far away. It worked and they ended up just a few miles from their house. The rains ended when full summer arrived and it only rained a few times during the summer. Pollox kept careful records of the weather.

Pollox and Lyra had now lived a full year at the outpost and experienced all four seasons. The climate was harsher than in Bliss, but they loved the grasslands and had no intention to ever leave the area. They had put down roots and felt they were in the right place. Lyra was expecting her second baby soon and they were planning to go back to Bliss with the airmobile so Lyra could safely have her baby at the hospital.

They returned to Bliss and stayed at the guesthouse in town until Lyra went into labor. A healthy boy was born, their second son, and all went well. Pollox had several meetings with the government officials reporting the details of the climate on the grasslands, the condition of the herd and how many calves had been born. President Telly told him they could not afford to build a slaughterhouse at the outpost and move more families out there, so for the time being they would transport the number of cattle the town needed using the Tellyship and do the slaughtering in the small slaughterhouse in Bliss. Pollox was secretly glad to hear that as he and Lyra enjoyed being alone at the outpost.

The airmobile was packed to the gills when they took off from Bliss. Food supplies, tools, fencing and cages with four egg laying chickens and a rooster as well as one male and two female goats. To their relief, the airmobile lifted without complaints and the long journey back home went well. Pollox and Lyra liked Bliss and the beauty of the area, but the grasslands was home and they felt emotional and grateful to be back.

The barn was finished and the animals stayed inside until Pollox had the fencing in place. He worked fast and the corrals were soon fenced in and he let the goats out. The fencing was portable so he could rotate the corral space when the goats had eaten all the grass and the chickens had a separate area. The eggs were a luxury they thoroughly enjoyed and they had been lucky to find the chickens. One of the female goats was pregnant and the other was lactating, so they now had a gallon of milk per day. Lyra milked the goat by hand. Her days were very busy with two small children, the goats and her vegetable garden. She had a washing machine, but no dishwasher. They had run out of money. The government held Pollox' salary and when they returned to Bliss the next summer, they would buy a dishwasher. Earth2 ordered some of the needed goods from Frejja and some from Etteron. The Etteron appliances were very advanced and sturdy. Ships from both planets landed regularly on Earth2 delivering supplies and people. It was a prosperous time.

Pollox taught his older son, Janus, how to swim that summer. If he would ever fall into the river, he would at least be able to swim to shore. The little three-year-old was like a fish in the water and had no fear at all. Their drinking water was pumped from the river and they did their swimming downriver from the pump. The water was pure and good tasting. Janus did most of the fishing and would often return with several large fish for dinner. With his implant he had the comprehension of a six-year-old and mastered the fishing skill with ease. Lyra always kept a watchful eye on him from the house.

Their lives were true pioneer inspired and very safe. No dangerous animals or hostile people were around and Janus' playmates were the goats. He especially liked the buck and somehow the buck understood Janus was a child and never tried to head-butt with him, a favorite sport goats enjoy. When the buck lay down to chew the cud, Janus would lie down with his head on the buck's back and often fell asleep. The buck considered Janus his pet and would not move until Janus woke up. The does were very docile and would never hurt Janus.

******

Emrak was back from the hospital resting from a heart transplant. He was healing fast and at age eighty-two, he looked twenty years younger. Karol and their android Tyra looked after him and after a week he was out of bed and walking around already. Solveiga was at school, but Sven was only four years old and enjoyed playing with grandpa all day long.

Karol had never been sick and felt grateful over her good health. The grandchildren needed them. Karol and Emrak's two sons, Leo and Rey, were adults now and on their own. Other than his weak heart, Emrak was in good health and energetic and had recently retired from work. He looked forward to taking the grandchildren on fishing trips and to show them Frejja's countryside. Their airmobile was fast and they could cover long distances in one day.

Emrak was sitting in the sun reflecting on his life. The happiest years of his life had been with Karol and to be a father. To see Alison and his two sons grow up had been a rewarding experience. He often thought about how unspoiled and loving Karol was and with her sensitivity she always found the right solutions in touchy situations. How lucky he was to have her. His career as a starship captain had been full of adventures and even his work training young pilots had never been boring. Emrak felt at peace with life. If he would be lucky enough to live out his lifespan, he had many years left and he intended to make the best of his retirement years.

Brandon and Brianna would stop by often and Emrak and Karol always enjoyed their visits. The last time they visited, Brianna told them her father Clarence had died at the age of one hundred and one. Lotte was still alive.

******

Tothellim asked the same four pilots who had discovered Ljeviina if they were willing to undertake another exploratory trip in the Andromeda galaxy. They would travel through he fifteen-hour tunnel again and then continue in another direction to search for more planets. The area had more stars in addition to Stellinus, which was the star Ljeviina orbited. It would be a long trip, perhaps last two years, and was totally voluntary. Tothellim cautioned them the trip would take a lot out of them physically and they would have to spend several hours every day working out to keep themselves in shape to counteract the weightlessness.

Tyler and Jayce did not hesitate and both agreed to the trip. The other two pilots needed a day to think about it, but returned and said they were willing to go. All four were unmarried.

Tothellim selected the most powerful ship of the fleet and huge supplies were loaded onboard, everything they could possibly need for two years. The Veehnian government members were excited that Tothellim had arranged this trip and looked forward to hearing the news when the ship returned. Four androids would also be onboard, two as pilots, one as a medical doctor and the fourth was an experienced mechanical engineer.

They took off and in two months they would reach the tunnel. The fuel tanks were full with enough fuel to last several years. Once they were in space, the ship needed very little fuel and their speed would double or even triple going through the tunnel.

The pilots had been rather weak when they returned from Ljeviina six years earlier and did not want a repeat of that situation. This time all four of them exercised vigorously and they had plenty of time for it. All of them got along well and were great friends.

They were close to the tunnel and could feel the vibration already. Tyler and Jayce were at the controls and they were sucked into the tunnel with great force. Now started fifteen hours of agony and they all took turns controlling the ship. The acceleration of speed was enormous and fighting the controls took all the arm strength the pilots had. Finally, they blasted out of the tunnel and into open space. Tyler adjusted the course of the ship and they traveled in the opposite direction of planet Ljeviina. Their goal was a star called Arros with one orbiting planet. The pilots on Ljeviina had given them the location they believed was accurate, but they had not been there themselves and could not guarantee they would find it. Jayce entered the location into the computers and they just had to hope they would spot the star. Three months later they did and they now saw the planet. It was the size of Mars and they carefully slowed the ship down and entered a low orbit. It was daylight on the planet. Something was wrong, very wrong down there on the surface. Everywhere they looked they saw what looked like gigantic explosions. Tyler looked with their powerful telescope and gasped -

"There are beings down there and it looks like they are conducting warfare of some sorts. Take a look."

All of them, including the androids, took turns looking at the surface and came to the same conclusion. The planet was in the midst of a war and it looked serious. They could not risk being seen and to use the shuttle would be suicide. As they orbited, they saw one area of the planet that appeared to be intact and not involved in the war. The buildings were not demolished and beings of some sort were walking around. The telescope was extremely powerful, but they could not make out enough details.

"I volunteer to use the shuttle and land in the area that's not engaged in the war. I take my chances," Tyler declared. "Our mission is to explore and we can't do that by watching from orbit."

"I come along," Jayce said right away.

The other two pilots preferred to stay on the ship and said the landing was too risky.

"If we're not back in five days or if you don't hear from us on the communicator, just leave and return home," Tyler instructed the crew. "We take off tomorrow at sunrise."

The shuttle stayed at a high altitude until they reached the area where they intended to land and they found a large enough field next to what looked like an official building. The whole area was shabby and run-down. Old apartment buildings with peeling paint were all over the area and they saw no private homes anywhere. Garbage was strewn on the streets and small animals resembling dogs were wandering around. The noise of the shuttle landing was loud enough to draw the attention of a group of people a distance away and they came running. Another group of people came out of the buildings. They were humans, but with unrefined features similar to early man on planet Earth, but not as primitive as Neanderthals. They had white skin, shoulder length hair and were not particularly clean looking. All of them stared in amazement at the shuttle and when Tyler and Jayce climbed out, they seemed afraid. The pilots were dressed in neat uniforms and with their refined facial features of modern man they looked quite different from the people on the planet. Jayce carried a translation device. He realized right away that these people were hundreds of years behind them in evolvement and would not understand what a translation device was. He set the device on 'search' and then started talking –

"Do you understand us?"

The people were talking among themselves and the device started flashing. It had found their language.

"Don't be afraid. We're here on a peaceful mission. I'm Tyler and this is Jayce. We come from another planet called Veehnia. What's the name of your planet?"

None of them seemed capable of answering. They stared at the translation device unable to understand how it could produce their language.

"This machine will translate for us so we can understand each other," Jayce said.

"My name is Udde," one of them finally said in a language that sounded rather pleasant. This planet is called Sorenia. Is that a spaceship?"

"No, it's called a shuttle and we use it to travel from our spaceship to the surface of your planet. Our ship is in orbit around your planet," Tyler explained. He was unsure if the people understood what 'orbit' was and for sure they had no knowledge about their own galaxy and space in general.

"Take us to your leader, your president," Jayce said.

The shuttle door was locked just in case anyone would try to enter the ship and Udde started walking towards a building a few hundred feet away. It was a two-story wooden building with peeling paint and two men came out to meet them. They had short hair and beards and their appearance was more pleasing than the other people, but their facial features were unrefined like the others.

"Are you the leaders?" Tyler asked.

Both men jumped when the device spoke in their language.

"It's only a machine, don't be afraid. Can we go inside and talk?"

The men led them inside and they sat down in a small room with a creaky, wooden floor. A wooden table and chairs were the only furniture. Tobacco smell permeated the air and both men lit up pipes as soon as they sat down.

Tyler slowly explained who they were, where they came from and that they were on an exploratory mission from another planet. The shuttle was only a local vehicle and their spaceship was orbiting their planet. It was unclear how much they understood of what they were told as they listened without showing any emotions.

"We are Trury and Retken. I, Trury, are president of my country and Retken is my advisor. Our country is called Mulerna."

"Are there different countries on this planet?"

"Yes, two more countries, Rotsalio and Ziuglin. They are in war, but we are neutral and won't take part in the war. They're killing each other with explosives and the war have been going on for over ten years and not ended yet."

"What are the explosives made of?"

"We don't know for sure. They make'm themselves and it's easy to make."

"Why are the two countries at war?" Jayce asked.

"It's a religious war and both sides are crazy. They believe in two different gods and each side are trying to force their god on the other country. We have spied on them and over half of the people is dead in both countries. They don't care if all of them die. They hate each other."

Tyler and Jayce noticed the poor command the men had of their own language and suspected they were illiterate.

The shuttle was equipped with powerful weapons, but it would still not be enough to end the war. The spaceship, however, could easily put an end to the war by firing its weapons on the buildings where the explosives were made.

"You said the war has been going on for ten years. Where is the food coming from? Who grows the crops?"

"We do," Trury said. "That's the only reason they don't kill us. We send all the food to them so they can fight the war. At harvest we load our trucks full with grain and other food and drive it over there. They don't pay us and we're too afraid of them to ask for money. All we hope are they leave us alone."

"This is total lunacy," Tyler said to Jayce. "If we knew he exact location of all the buildings where they make the explosives, the shuttle could take them out. Without explosives the war may end. The metal framework of the shuttle is strong enough to take a hit from their explosives."

"Does anyone know the location of the buildings where they make the explosives?" Tyler asked.

"Retken does," Trury replied. "He's our spy. He grew up in the war area and knows the towns rather good."

"Listen carefully," Tyler said in a firm voice. "Tomorrow at sunrise Retken will accompany us in the shuttle and point out every building they use to make the explosives and we'll destroy those buildings. We must be there early, before they are out of bed. Will you come along, Retken?"

Retken nodded and promised to wait outside the shuttle before the sun rose. Tyler and Jayce returned to the shuttle and checked out the weapons onboard. They were impressive and designed to deliver enough firepower to enable the crew of the shuttle to escape in dangerous situations. Jayce sent a transmission to the ship that they were safe and gave a brief report of the planet and what their plans were. They received a reply that their message had been received.

Tyler and Jayce stayed onboard overnight and rose well before it was light. They looked outside and found Retken waiting in the dark. He entered the shuttle and looked fearful.

"There's nothing to fear. The shuttle is totally safe," Jayce reassured him.

They strapped him into his seat and Tyler started the engines. The shuttle lifted and rose to a thousand feet, then took off at tremendous speed towards the war zone. Retken trembled with fear and was white as a sheet in his face. He had never been off the ground and even airplanes did not exist on his planet. All he knew were the old-fashioned dilapidated trucks they used on the surface. He watched the instruments with awe and when he looked out the window he almost jumped out of his skin with fear when he realized he was way up in the sky. Jayce kept an eye on him to make sure he would not pass out. They quickly neared the war zone and all was quiet on the ground. Down on the surface was a horrendous mess of bombed out buildings, corpses lying dead on the ground and nothing but destruction everywhere they looked. Tyler descended to a lower altitude.

"Retken, pull yourself together now, *be alert*," Tyler told him in a strong voice. "Show us the buildings quickly. Look out the window and start working."

Tyler's authoritative voice brought Retken out of his fear and he quickly pointed out the buildings. He knew them all. They were small and easy to destroy. With Tyler running the shuttle and Jayce aiming and firing, they were an expert team. They had full training in warfare and knew their business. When the weapons fired at the building, it exploded from the explosives inside and was reduced to rubble within a few minutes. All together Jayce blew up thirty buildings. Retken was watching Jayce with his mouth open as Jayce aimed and fired. He had never seen anything like it. No one came out of the buildings and Tyler and Jayce realized the people on the ground must be terrified at the sight of the shuttle firing away up there in the sky. The people had never seen an airplane even and had no idea what that thing in the sky was. This made the whole operation easy and no one shot at them.

"Point out the building where the leaders are," Tyler shouted to Retken.

"There, the small house," Retken said in a weak voice, worn out from nerves.

"Give me the name of the commander," Tyler ordered.

"Keid is the leader for this country, Ziuglin, and Drako for the other country, Rotsalio."

"How far is it to Drako's building?"

"It's short distance with truck," Retken replied.

Tyler descended to only fifty feet above the ground and hovered in the air. Through the loudspeaker he barked into the translation device -

"Keid, go outside and listen carefully. *Go out now!*"

Nothing happened. Tyler fired a warning shot that sounded like a thunderclap next to the building.

"Get out now or I'll blow the building up with you in it," Tyler shouted.

Keid came out running in panic from the building.

"*Stop!* Get inside your truck and drive to Drako. We'll meet you there."

Tyler hovered above the building until he saw Keid climb into his old truck and start driving towards Drako's side. Tyler followed a distance away and when they reached Drako's side he waited until Keid arrived. He stayed inside his truck.

"Drako, come outside. You will not be hurt. *Now!*" Tyler's voice demanded obedience as he spoke into the translation device.

Drako came out, looked up at the shuttle and freaked out. He went down on his knees and started praying. Tyler landed the shuttle a short distance away and told Retken to come along. Tyler and Jayce wore powerful stun guns hoping they would be unnecessary.

"Retken, tell Keid to sit down with us and negotiate. Go quickly."

Retken ran over to Keid's truck and opened the door. He gestured wildly while he explained to Keid that he had no choice but to obey. Tyler and Jayce instructed Drako to get up and follow them. Drako managed to rise from his kneeling position, but he was shaking.

Tyler kicked the door open to Drako's building. Six men were hiding inside and they looked at Tyler and Jayce with fear.

"Out, get OUT!" Tyler barked.

The men took one look at Tyler and Jace and ran out. Both Tyler and Jayce were tall, muscular men and looked like soldiers. They sat down with Keid and Drako and Retken was also present to represent his country, Mulerna. The building was a ramshackle cabin and the only furniture inside was a table and eight chairs, all made of wood, and the air smelled of pipe smoke. Tyler switched off the translation device and told Jayce -

"Let's keep our language simple so they understand us. We're not dealing with high intellect here. They're way behind us in evolvement." Jayce nodded. Tyler switched on the device and started talking -

"Keid and Drako, I am Tyler and this is Jayce. We come from another planet very far from here and as you can see we're more advanced than you are. We come in peace and our mission is to explore other planets, not to conquer them, but to offer help and assistance to beings in need of help. It's obvious you need help. You've been at war for ten years and neither of you are willing to give in and ask for peace. Keid, explain what this war is about and why you still fight after ten years."

Both men were startled when the translation device spoke in their language. They were rough looking, dirty and radiated hate when they looked at each other.

"It's religious war and our god, the real god, has told us to fight in his name and kill them who will not stop believing the false god and accept our god as the only real god," Keid said. He fumbled for words and appeared unsure of himself.

"Drako, is your reason for fighting a ten-year war the same as Keid's?"

Drako nodded.

"Both of you are convinced that your god is the true god and both of you are trying to force the other side to abandon their beliefs and accept your beliefs. No god demands killing of any being in his name! I repeat, no god will ask beings on any planet to engage in war in order to force the losers of the war to submit to beliefs that are wrong for them. Religious beliefs must not be forced on anyone. This is pure tyranny. God does not ask anyone to believe in him. It is a free choice.   You are all individuals with free will and personal freedom. You are free to believe or not to believe. Neither of you has the right to kill anyone. The end result does not justify the means. With that I mean that the end result - one religion - does not justify the means, which in your case is mass murder. Am I making myself understood?"

There was no answer and both men looked bewildered. Jayce interjected -

"Look around you. This planet is a mess, dirty, poverty stricken and there is no prosperity anywhere. Is that what you want? A dead planet with no survivors? Your gods watching your warfare feel despair over your stupidity and lack of respect for each other's lives."

All of a sudden Drako broke down and started to cry. Tyler put his arm around his shoulder to comfort him.

"I'm finished, I want peace," he sobbed.

"Keid, do you feel the same?" Jayce asked.

He nodded, also ready to cry, but was able to contain himself.

"We need help, someone to lead us," Keid pleaded, his voice faltering from emotion.

Tyler switched off the device and turned to Jayce -

"Cooper, our android engineer, is a born leader. He would be the perfect choice to take over here and lead them. His programming covers the full spectrum of emotions and he has just the right sensitivity to deal with these people. In addition, his engineering skills would come in handy to rebuild their society from scratch. I know they'll accept him as their leader. I'm gonna contact him from the shuttle. I'll be right back."

Jayce smiled and did thumbs up.

Tyler returned after fifteen minutes and was all smiles.

"Listen guys, our ship is flying around your planet and we have an android called Cooper on the ship. An android is a very advanced machine that looks like a person. Cooper is an engineer and would be the best leader you could ever have. He has agreed to stay here with you and lead you back to prosperity and peace. His skills are phenomenal, truly remarkable, and he has agreed to staying here with you permanently. If you agree to let him take over and lead you, we will return tomorrow and bring him along."

"Yes, I agree, thank you," Keid said and hope lit up his face.

Drako had stopped crying and said -

"We can't do this alone. I can't wait to welcome him. I'm glad to take orders from him."

"Will the two of you shake hands as the first step towards peace?" Jayce suggested.

Keid, Drako and Retken all shook hands and their faces were relieved and full of hope for the future.

"Retken, do you want us to return you to Mulerna or will you stay?"

"I stay. I want to talk to Keid and Drako. We have much to plan now when we have peace."

Tyler and Jayce took off and returned to the ship. Cooper was anxious to hear all the details and assured them he had no regrets and would dedicate himself to lead the people and steer them in the right direction. Jayce downloaded the language into Cooper's memory bank so he would not need a translation device. He was eager to start and looked forward to his new life. Cooper loved space and exploring, but to guide these people into a new way of thinking, where respect for each individual is paramount and to make them understand that every person has free will, was a challenge he could not resist.

From the ship's computers, he downloaded as much information he could find about politics, economics, manufacturing and anything he guessed would be useful into a separate memory bank. Tyler and Jayce helped him pack the shuttle full with equipment. Six black boxes for electricity, a brand-new electronics communication system, two commercial size 3D printers, an airmobile and various tools they were sure did not exist on the planet. The shuttle was so full that there was only room for Tyler and Cooper and Jayce had to stay on the ship.

The next morning, they returned to the surface with the shuttle and a group of people, including women and children, awaited them. Cooper shook hands with all of them and everyone said 'welcome' to him. Cooper was very handsome, state of the art and looked exactly like a human being and the people were amazed when they heard he spoke their language. He was sophisticated, gentle and would lead them with fairness. Sorenia was too far from Veehnia to transmit messages and Tyler told Cooper it was only a slim chance they would ever return to Sorenia.

"I would be so happy to see you again, but right now I'll be very busy just restarting their society," Cooper said. "I did notice the mess, the state of the buildings and lack of supplies. It will be a challenge, but I have all sorts of ideas that I will implement. Sometime in the future I will be able to transmit a report to a Veehnian ship and tell you of our advancements. I also have to establish a government and write a constitution. I'm eager to start working."

Tyler hugged Cooper and wished him lots of luck.

The return trip went well and they landed on Veehnia. Tothellim, Rheo and the president were there to greet them. Ten months had passed since they left and they climbed out of the ship on wobbly legs. They knew it would be weeks until they regained their physical strength. After a short debriefing, Tyler and Jayce were taken to their homes to rest. It was agreed they would meet again the following day and Tyler and Jayce would give a full, detailed report of the mission with holographic images. Both of them slept like dead that night.

Tothellim and Rheo eagerly waited for them the next morning and the president was also present. It took Tyler and Jayce several hours to outline everything they had seen and experienced on Sorenia and how they had stopped the warfare. On exploratory trips the captain of the ship, which had been Tyler, had full authority to make decisions and give out equipment as he saw fit. There were no objections when the president heard they had loaded up the shuttle with all the items and an airmobile for the new planet. They all watched the images with great interest and studied the faces of the people.

"They must be at least three, perhaps four hundred years behind us," Tothellim remarked. "Cooper will have his hands full to organize and modernize their society. I'm glad he wanted to take on the challenge. Without him those people would struggle for years to rebuild their society."

They spent the rest of the day discussing the trip and after dinner, Tothellim told Tyler and Jayce they were allowed three months off with full pay to regain their strength.

Tothellim prepared a full report for Emrak and gave it to the captain of a Veehnian ship destined for Earth to pick up immigrants. The captain promised to send the report to Emrak from the ship as soon as they were within transmission distance. Tothellim received Emrak's greetings a few months later and he expressed his sincere gratitude for the report. Emrak shared the report with people he felt would benefit from the information.

Tothellim and Rheo enjoyed their work as flight instructors and part of Tothellim's work was to organize exploratory trips. He was well paid and very popular among his students. Both Tothellim and Rheo had good marriages and their children often visited with each other. Heidi was already fifteen years old, a cute teenager, and Tothellim's son Logan was eight years old. Rheo also had two children.

After being on the waiting list for ten years, Tothellim finally was able to buy a piano. Heidi was not interested in music, but Logan started playing when he was four years old and was musical. He was advancing rapidly and Tothellim had found an android music teacher that was really good. Logan loved playing and mastered rather difficult classical pieces. He had recently declared to his parents that he wanted to become a musician and they supported his choice fully. When Logan played, they all sat down to listen. Heidi was animal crazy and wanted to become a veterinarian. Pets were popular among the citizens and in the countryside, there was a shortage of large animal veterinarians. She had not decided what type of veterinarian she would be. Her dog was her best friend.

CHAPTER 36

Earth and Mars were in mourning. A passenger ship from Earth with one hundred people onboard had just entered the shortcut tunnel to Mars when the ship flew right into the side wall of the tunnel. The ground crew on Earth watched the ship on their screens and saw it enter the tunnel. Almost immediately, they saw what looked like an explosion. The ship vaporized and all onboard were killed. Since no one survived and the ship's recording log was lost, they could only guess what had happened. Perhaps the pilot had a seizure or was distracted for a second and lost control. The ship was almost new and it was unlikely the engines would have failed. This was the first fatal spaceship accident. The track record for flights between Earth and Mars had so far been flawless. No one feared space travel any more. After the accident many people expressed fear and announced they would never set foot on a ship. The company owning the ship had no explanation to give to the passengers' families and many bookings were canceled. The company survived, but just barely.

The news reached Emrak and Brandon and Brianna. They were sad to hear it and worried it may happen to Alison and Leif. If they had just known the reason why the accident happened, but it remained a mystery and would never be clarified. Most people were guessing the pilot had suffered a seizure or passed out for some reason. Alison and Leif were disturbed when they heard of the accident and decided that when they traveled through any tunnel from that day on, they would call in the backup androids to be ready to take over in case both the captain and the copilot would become incapacitated for some reason. They did not know the pilot by name.

******

Little Melody was her dad's delight and was running around the house like a whirlwind. She babbled endlessly and was growing fast. Atlas picked her up and threw her up in the air and both laughed. She was already two years old and had strong will.

"More, Dad, more, more," she giggled and Atlas kept tossing her up in the air. He adored his little girl and so did Viola.

Viola and Atlas hoped to adopt a second child, but very few children were available for adoption. They considered themselves fortunate to have Melody. It was known at the hospital that Atlas and his wife were willing to adopt another child and all they could do was hope.

Atlas had a difficult operation coming up and had prepared himself by looking at similar surgeries on the Internet special library for doctors. His patient had a tumor in the frontal lobe of the brain that had to be removed. He had performed several successful brain surgeries, but the location of the tumor was where language is produced and there was a chance the patient would lose his ability to speak.

On the day of the surgery Viola wished him success and Atlas and three doctors started the difficult operation. It took hours and Atlas carefully removed the tumor. It was not cancerous, but big. After the surgery, Atlas stayed at the hospital until the patient woke up and he spoke gently to him. To his big relief the patient understood his question and was able to respond in an intelligible way.

Most of Atlas' work consisted of ordinary medical procedures, but occasionally his skills were put to the test. He was the most competent doctor at the hospital and highly valued. In addition, everyone liked him and his gentle personality.

******

Cooper started his work by conducting a reconnaissance trip of Sorenia and he asked Keid, Drako, Trury and Retken to accompany him in the airmobile. The airmobile seated six people and the glass dome made for excellent visibility. Retken had lost his fear of flying, but the other three men were frightened. The planet was the size of Mars and had forests and grass fields and looked rather lush. Farm fields that had not been cultivated for years were overgrown with weeds. There were many rivers and lakes but no oceans. It was apparent the planet had sufficient rainfall.

"Do you have four seasons?" Cooper asked.

"Yes, and the winter are cold with snow," Trury replied.

"How many people live on the planet?"

"We don't know," Drako said.

Cooper looked at the surface and the damage from the war was evident all over the planet. Many towns and small cities were just heaps of rubble. They spent three days flying and slept under the open sky. It was late summer and warm. Keid and Drako were respectful to each other, but avoided talking. The shuttle flew over Mulerna and Cooper took a close look at the country of Mulerna. It was large and appeared fertile with many crops growing. Harvest time was close and the yield plentiful.

"How do you harvest your crops? Do you have tractors?"

"Yes, but some of the work are done by men," Retken said. "Our tractors are old and not good."

"Are there any mines on your planet?"

"Yes, silver mines," Keid said. "Nobody have looked for ore and there can be minerals on the planet we haven't found yet. There are not many people alive. If we find ore, there is not enough people to work in the mines."

Cooper noticed the men used simple language and wrong grammar and wondered to himself if any of them had any education at all. He deliberately chose simple words so they would understand him.

"Can you guys read and write?"

"No, we never been to school," Trury said. "There are some people who can read and write."

"Do you know how to tell time?"

"Some people understand it, but we don't."

"Do you have factories manufacturing goods and things for the people?"

"Before the war we had factories, but not now. Nothing are made anymore."

"Can you count numbers?"

"Only a bit."

Cooper realized it would be a true challenge to update the people. He was hundreds of years ahead of them and thoroughly educated. Communication skills had to be improved and that meant starting schools right away, for the children and grownups alike. The planet was beautiful and would regenerate with time, but education, medical care and just about everything related to modern life had to be created from scratch. There was no infrastructure, no functioning electric power, the roads were only dirt roads and the only vehicles he had seen were old worn-out trucks. Trash was everywhere, no one had running water and there was no sewage system. When they returned, Cooper instructed the men to appear in the government building the next morning at sunrise.

The next day they met again and Cooper started the meeting using as simple words as possible -

"Keid, Drako, Trury, you are the leaders of your countries. From now on you will become local leaders only and I will be the acting president over all three countries and my office will be right here in this building. The first thing you will do is to count how many people live in your country. Everyone must be counted and please report the numbers to me. Every former teacher you can find should report to me as well. I also want to talk to anyone with an education or skill of any kind. Can you do it?"

"There is one woman I know and she can count numbers. I'll ask her to help us," Trury said.

"We'll try to find all people with education," Retken added.

"Is there anyone right here in town who can read and write?"

"One person and he was a teacher here in Mulerna," Trury said.

"Retken, please find the teacher and send him to me today, if you can," Cooper asked. "For now, please return to your home area and start the counting of people. Try to locate any person, man or woman, with an education or skill or trade. I hope you can report back to me within a few days. I'll stay right here and do my work in this building."

After a few hours there was a knock on the door and a man in his early forties walked in.

"I am Reyya. You wanted to see me."

Cooper noticed right away that this man was alert and carried himself with more dignity than the others and he had refined facial features. It was a relief to finally interact with someone who was educated.

"Welcome Reyya," Cooper said and shook hands with the man. "I mean no offense, but tell me about your education first, so I know where we stand."

"There were schools around when I grew up and I attended school until I was twenty years old and after that I self-educated. Actually, I never stopped self-educating and I have lived with my books my whole life. I can read and write in my language and I can master more than basic math. I understand all the sciences and if I would have access to more books, I'm fully capable of learning new things. My mind is very active."

"What are you doing now? Are you working?"

"There is no work and especially not for a person like me. The war has destroyed everything and turned the people into morons, pardon my language, but it's true. The word has spread and we all know the war is over and that you are our new leader. I can't tell you how happy we all are to have you here."

"I offer you a job as my vice president. As soon as I know the legal tender you use here, I'll tell you what your salary will be. You'll have to work hard and it will be tough in the beginning for both of us until we have a functioning society. Do you accept?"

"With pleasure. Can I start now?"

With Reyya at his side, Cooper felt liberated. He was the perfect intermediary between himself and the people and he worked tirelessly, only taking one day off per week. He was married without children and his wife, Littiana, started working at the office also. She had more than basic education, could read and write, do basic math and was highly intelligent. Reyya had told Cooper she was a bookworm and loved reading, whatever books she could find. Her official title was 'advisor to the president'. She was an attractive woman, slim and with an alert mind, always willing to help.

Cooper lived in one of the rooms in the government building. There was nowhere else to stay. He had the 3D printers but lacked the aggregate for them and he was hoping to find someone among the population with knowledge of the minerals available on the planet so they could start making aggregate.

Reports trickled in to the president's office. The total population of the whole planet was only half a million people, a fraction of what the population had been before the war. The toll the war had taken was horrendous. Sorenia was the size of Mars, fertile and could easily support three billion people. Cooper also received a list of people with education and it was a paltry ten thousand people, but there were two thousand people with a skill or competence in a trade. Everyone else of the population had basic skills and no education. Even though schools had been available before the war, many children did not attend as it was not mandatory. The numbers were not encouraging, but Cooper was optimistic. Among the educated people were two geologists and Cooper asked Retken to find them and bring them to his office. Within a week they showed up. They were in their forties and had hidden from the war in the countryside.

"I'm Stimillo and this is Borvio. Welcome to our planet. We are both geologists and before the war we worked together for the government of the country that is now under the leadership of Drako. How can we help you?"

"I'm so happy to see you," Cooper said. He noticed that their facial features were more refined than the rest of the population and they were eloquent and sharp.

"I would like to hire you as geologists. There is no money to pay you a salary now, but when we have started the mining and manufacturing, you will receive back pay. None of us is paid now as there is no money available."

"We accept your job offer," Borvio exclaimed. "Thank you for offering us the opportunity. I take it you want us to find whatever ore is available for mining. There's plenty of silver around and other valuable minerals. An hour from here by truck is a large silver mine. It hasn't been worked since the war."

"Yes, I want you to find all available ore, but your first job is to make an aggregate for our 3D printers, so we can start building houses. The aggregate has to be strong enough to survive the winter cold."

"We have read about 3D printers. I'm sure we can find the right minerals to make the aggregate."

"What's your education?" Cooper asked.

"We are both licensed geologists and we were educated in the school system that existed before the war. It was a good system. The war ended all education unfortunately."

Retken drove the geologists to the building where the printers were stored and they inspected them carefully. They understood how they worked and the following day they would start making different mixes for testing.

Cooper asked Reyya why the geologists looked different than the rest of the people.

"We are all a mixed race. The geologists have less of the native blood. Long time ago there were two races and one of them looked like Tyler and Jayce and the other race, the native race, was more rough looking. Eventually they intermarried. Most people are of mixed race now. The people looking like Tyler arrived here after the native race was already living here. We don't know where they came from. That happened at least a thousand years ago."

Electricity was needed in Cooper's office and he hooked up one of the black boxes and had power. He powered the communication system with it and entered all the data he had downloaded from the ship's computers. It was convenient to have the information available in the office. There were no appliances available at present that needed electricity, so the rest of the black boxes remained in storage.

Cooper himself was equipped with a powerful lifetime bank of mini-sized batteries and a few hours of electricity every month was all that was needed to recharge his batteries. The black box supplied the electricity.

Cooper designed a sewage system for the town and sketched it on paper the old-fashioned way. There were eight plumbers on the list and he asked them to start working on it. He asked Retken to hire twenty men to remove all garbage from the streets and to create a landfill that could be filled in later on. He also asked Retken to start weekly garbage pickup from the houses and to get the details from Reyya. The two geologists and Cooper inspected the silver mine. It looked really promising with large silver deposits. He asked Trury and Retken to organize a team of mine workers to start working in the mine right away. On the list of people with a trade, there were several people listed as supervisors for mining with years of experience. They were glad to get a job and within a few weeks the mine was put into production. Some of the silver was so pure they used it to make coins and soon money was in circulation and salaries could be paid. The people working in the mint had previous experience in making coins and produced very nice-looking coinage. The silver mine had two daily shifts and employed two hundred people.

Cooper ordered full cleanup of Rotsalio and Ziuglin where the war had been fought and the debris was enormous requiring months to clear away. Several landfills had to be created and were later covered. There was nothing toxic in the landfills and eventually they became farm fields. Old construction vehicles were available for the cleanup.

On the list of educated people were several writers and Cooper asked them to start a newspaper. Computers and Internet did not exist and there was no postal service, so the papers would have to be sold in the towns only. Printing presses that had not been used for years were dusted off and put to use. Cooper had only known a world of high tech and electronics, so he had to search in his memory bank for information how life functioned hundreds of years ago. It was so inefficient and slow that he sometimes became frustrated.

After only a few months, many adults had a job and things started to move forward fast. Several teachers had visited Cooper and with the help of Reyya's wife Littiana schools started to open all over the planet. Adults were strongly encouraged to attend and learn how to read and write and do basic math. For children school was mandatory and starting at age five all children must attend school. The earliest a student was allowed to leave school was sixteen years old, but to graduate with a diploma or degree required several more years of study. Old textbooks that had survived the war were found, but there was a severe shortage of books and the printing presses were working around the clock printing books in addition to the newspaper.

The airmobile was necessary when looking for minerals around the planet and Cooper took the time to train Reyya, Stimillo and Borvio how to fly it. It was autonomous, but also had manual controls. All three men were intelligent and quick learners and after some training they understood the mechanics of it. They had some trouble understanding the computer system, but with Cooper's patient instructions they learned how to fly the airmobile safely. Cooper turned it over to the two geologists and asked them to find minerals for the aggregate as well as any minerals and ore that could be mined and generate income for the planet. The airmobile had a powerful communication system onboard and they would be able to communicate with Cooper through his office system.

Cooper gently fired Trury, Drako and Keid and replaced them with the most educated people on the list. To his relief, they took it well and they understood that the position of president required a literate person. Reyya became president of Mulerna in addition to being Cooper's vice president. A former owner of several manufacturing plants, Hovara, became president of Rotsalio and a former book publisher, Nerelum, was now president of Ziuglin. Both men had organizational skills and were competent leaders. When the war started, they lost their businesses and had to go into hiding.

Drako and Keid expressed fear that they would be assassinated. Cooper knew it was true. Reyya had heard rumors that there was a plot to kill the two men.

"The two of you are responsible for millions of deaths and almost destroyed your countries," Cooper said slowly. "Can you blame the people for despising you? You are now facing the unintended consequences of your actions. The government cannot protect you. There is one thing you can do and that is to agree that Reyya writes a formal apology from you to the people of your countries where you express sincere remorse for your actions. The first issue of the newspaper will come out next week. Do you agree?"

Both men nodded and looked relieved. Trury had nothing to fear. He was by nature a decent man and had never abused the people.

People looked forward to the first issue of the newspaper, Sorenia News, and on the front page the apology from Drako and Keid appeared. Reyya urged the people to look to the future and that nothing useful would be achieved by harming Drako and Keid. It worked. The plot against them was scrapped, but both of them were shunned for the rest of their lives and they ended up living hermit lives in their native countries.

Cooper wrote a column in the paper he called 'President's Corner' and in the first issue he wrote -

"Do not expect the government to take care of you. Rather, aim for self-sufficiency and independence. That is the only way our three countries will advance. Sorenia has free speech and never fear expressing a different point of view. Looking at a problem from a different angle may produce a solution."

Most people were illiterate, but there were always a few educated people around willing to read the whole newspaper aloud. Half of the adult population attended school and were eager to learn how to read and write. The other half felt they could not learn and were too old. No one was forced.

Cooper instructed Hovara and Nerelum to immediately start food production in their countries and ensure a sufficient amount of food was available. Many people had starved to death during the war and the surviving population was emaciated. Mulerna had large herds of meat animals and was willing to sell stock to the other two countries to start their herds. They also sold seed for grain production.

Food stores only existed in Mulerna and people in charge of food production sold all excess food supplies to Rotsalio and Ziuglin. Almost overnight, stores opened up and basic foods became available for the people to buy. Vegetable seeds were sold so people could start a garden.

Only Mulerna had a little hospital. Cooper called in six doctors from his list and asked them to start a hospital in Rotsalio and Ziuglin. There were no medical supplies, no medicines and no technical equipment for the hospitals and the doctors made long lists of what they needed and handed them to Cooper.

The geologists had been lucky and found the right materials to make inexpensive aggregate for the 3D printers and manufacturing of the aggregate started with both day and night shifts. The minerals had to be ground into a fine powder to be used in the printers. One of the black boxes supplied the electricity needed. The two printers were commercial grade and each printer produced a medium size building in twenty days. The first buildings became medical centers and the printers worked around the clock. They were portable and were moved to each area where a building was needed.

Cooper's next project was to start manufacturing. Supplies were desperately needed. Large factory buildings had to be built and fast. The printers were needed elsewhere and steel was not yet available. Mulerna had several sawmills and could supply framing and building materials. Cooper knew that these buildings were temporary and would be replaced with modern steel buildings in the future, but he had to work with the materials available at the present time and the buildings were needed now, not later. There was an old abandoned steel mill in Mulerna that he planned to revive and the planet had lots of iron and carbon for steel making. Cooper was an experienced mechanical engineer and knew he had to be involved in most facets of restarting production of goods.

The following year Sorenia went through a whirlwind of activity. Everyone looking for a job could find employment and sufficient food was now available. People started to gain weight and their health improved. Fertility rose and more children were born. All children attended school and night school was offered for adults who worked during the day. It had been a colossal effort, but Sorenia had risen from the ashes. Cooper was loved by all the people and worked seven days a week, never taking a day off. He was mulling over the possibility of introducing computers, but could not decide if it was premature. The people had just learned how to read and the concept of computers may be overload. Reyya and Littiana advised against it and said the people were not ready yet. Reyya and Littiana both mastered the communication system in the government building and knew it would be incomprehensible for the average person to master such a futuristic machine. Cooper understood and agreed.

A constitution was needed and Cooper found several versions from the files he had downloaded from the ship's computer. Veehnia's constitution was too advanced, but he felt a simplified version of People Democracy would be right for Sorenia. People Democracy was used on Earth, Mars and Earth2 and a variation of it was also used on Frejja. He wrote the constitution based on People Democracy with a few changes and thought to himself that amendments could be added later. A printed version of the document was hung in all stores and official buildings as well as printed in the newspaper. It was approved by the people.

A formal government was needed and Cooper had enough people to choose from to form a small cabinet. He needed more room and one of the printers was used to build a government office to house all the members in one building.

CHAPTER 37

Fifteen years had passed since Telly and his team visited the first planet in orbit around their sun and he decided to make a second trip to check on the people. Ássurt was invited to accompany him and accepted. Telly asked both Rasufilus and Atlas if they were able to take the time off and come along, but both declined and said they could not be away for that long. The journey to the first planet would take two months each way. Atlas was concerned a medical emergency might occur while he was away and Rasufilus felt he had to be home to be ready to take on a new assignment. He needed the money. Telly selected one of the doctors from the hospital and a biologist and both of them were excited to go. The four pilots who always flew the Tellyship were eager to return to the planet. Supplies were loaded on the ship for both the crew and the natives and they departed.

With the ship in orbit, Telly and his team descended to the surface using the shuttle. The pilots had to take turns as two of them had to stay on the ship at all times. Telly picked the same area to land as the last time and the hamlet was still there. The noise of the shuttle brought all the natives out and they recognized 'the bird' right away. They jumped up and down and waved in excitement. Telly spotted Sidji and his wife Vuula and they had aged considerably, but looked to be in reasonably good health.

They climbed out of the shuttle trying to ignore the wall of heat that hit them. The natives were truly happy they were back and Telly shook hands with Sidji and the other men. They all walked to the hamlet and Telly noticed every hut had a door. There were many more children around compared to last time and all of them looked rather healthy and well fed.

They sat down and Telly used a stick to draw in the sand to facilitate the conversation. He first drew a snake and Sidji smiled and shook his head. It was obvious they had the problem under control and his wife ran to their hut and returned with the stun guns showing Telly they had defeated the snakes. Telly checked the guns and most of them were almost empty. He would reload them before they left. Using gestures, he asked Sidji if they had enough to eat and Vuula pointed to her stomach and nodded. Telly also asked if they had been at war with their neighbors. He grabbed a spear and pointed it at Sidji and pointed to the jungle, but Sidji did not understand until he drew two people facing each other in the sand. Then he understood the question and shook his head. It was apparently peace on the planet.

The following day the doctor took blood samples of all the people using a high-tech instrument that resembled a gun. He ran the samples through the computer on the shuttle and found their DNA was too similar.

"They're all related, too much inbreeding," he remarked to the others. "They need new blood."

Nutritionally, they were slightly below average and all of them had worms. The doctor knew there was no point to worm them as they would get the worms right back. One of them had a tumor on his back that should be removed. A biopsy showed it was cancerous. Telly asked Sidji to ask the man if he would submit to surgery and somehow Sidji understood the question and convinced the man to consent. The shuttle had a tiny corner that functioned as emergency operating room and the doctor was able to sedate the man and safely remove the tumor. There was no way of knowing if the cancer would come back, but for the time being the patient was out of danger.

No one was very old and the doctor guessed their lifespan was probably no more than fifty years. The heat and bacteria took a heavy toll. One of the women was close to giving birth and the doctor decided to induce the baby and give her an easy childbirth. He gave her the medication and towards the evening she was in full labor and gave birth without pain to a healthy-looking baby.

A little girl and her parents approached the doctor and the parents lifted the girl's skirt revealing she had a tail. The doctor nodded and took the girl into the shuttle. To surgically remove the tail was easy and only required a local anesthetic. She trembled with fear, but after the doctor had sedated her the tail was cut off within minutes. The small incision would heal within a week.

Their teeth were brown from chewing on a root that was probably addictive. The doctor pointed to the root and shook his head. All of them understood the root was bad for them, but they were addicted and could not stop. Many of them had lost several of their molars and had trouble chewing. The doctor gave each person a combined vitamin and mineral injection using a pain free injection gun.

"How do you choose your wives?" Telly asked Sidji using drawings in the sand.

Sidji gestured to the jungle and Telly understood they came from the next hamlet. It took quite a while for Telly to make Sidji understand they must go further, far away, to find their wives. That part he understood, but not the reason for it, but he nodded and promised they would go further away from now on to find their women.

Telly and the crew ate their meals on the shuttle and returned to the ship every evening. The pilots took turns visiting the planet. All of them took anti-fungal medication hoping they would not pick up the fungus again.

The biologist asked Sidji to accompany him on several walks into the jungle so he could observe plants and animals alike. He decided not to collect samples to bring back to Earth2 as the risk for contamination was real, but he took many 3D pictures of plants, insects and animals wandering around in the forest.

Ássurt studied the natives from an anthropological point of view, their language, habits, what they ate, how they interacted with each other. He recorded his findings and intended to write a summary of his conclusions and post it on the local Internet. He also counted them and Sidji explained one person had died of old age. Apparently, the Earth2 people had not transmitted any disease to the natives, which was one of the concerns they had discussed before the trip. They knew the natives had no immunity to the illnesses and infections of the modern world.

The visit was over and they said goodbye to the natives. This time the natives understood they were leaving their planet and would not return the next day. They had spent two weeks together and learned a lot from each other. Telly had reloaded their stun guns and all the supplies had been unloaded for the natives to enjoy such as tools, simple clothing, freeze-dried food, toys and other items Telly knew from the last visit they could use. Telly and his men were ready to leave as the heat was unbearable. The return trip went well and they landed safely on Earth2.

The biologist, Ássurt and Telly all posted separate reports on the local Internet and the people dove into the articles with gusto. The 3D images of the natives were so different from their own world. Everyone felt they were looking back in time to the roots of their own beginning.

None of the team developed any fungal or other disease from the visit.

******

Atlas did not need to sleep, even though he often would lie down a few hours at night to rest. One night when lying down he heard a strange noise from the outside and it sounded as a baby crying. He opened the front door and there was a bundle on the front steps. It was totally dark outside and he saw no one but the baby. Atlas quickly picked the bundle up and it was a newborn baby boy. He was cold and must have spent several hours on the front steps until his crying alerted Atlas. He hurried inside the house and examined the baby. The baby had been washed and he could see from his umbilical cord that he had been born the day before. Atlas realized it was another teenage pregnancy and the mother did not want to be known. The staff at the hospital knew he and Viola wanted another baby and the mother of the baby must have heard it and decided to give the baby to them. She probably could not take care of the baby herself. Atlas carefully examined the little boy and found him in good health, but hungry and with a soiled diaper. It was an Etteron baby or perhaps a mix. He ran into the bedroom and woke Viola up and she was startled when she saw the baby, but so excited she could hardly speak. Viola put a clean diaper on the baby and she still had infant formula in the house. After the baby was dressed and warm, she gave him a bottle of formula that he drank without fuss.

Viola and Atlas registered the baby as their own and no one ever came forward to claim him. They never found out who the mother was and both of them felt it was better that way. It was obvious she wanted them to have her baby and knew they would give him a good life. They named him Paragonne from the word 'paragon'.

Viola took a month off from work to care for the baby and Bellinnia was as excited as Viola when she found out there was another baby in the family. The two women were close and really liked each other. Viola only worked part time, so Bellinnia only needed to spend half days with the children. She was fully reliable and had strong maternal feelings.

Atlas felt they needed a larger house, but Viola suggested they just add on to their existing house. She was fond of the house and liked the convenient location. A carpenter and a few helpers added three rooms to the house and that was all the space they needed.

Paragonne was healthy and grew fast. Melody adored him and was strong enough to hold him. She was now four years old and understood her new brother had been placed on their doorstep as a gift. He was a good-looking baby and they could see now that he was half Etteron and half Frejjan. Viola and Atlas were truly grateful for the baby and their love for each other was stronger than ever.

******

The population on the Moon had held steady at four thousand for years. People living there were used to the conditions and the standard contract was for two years and then return to Earth. The mining of terrynium was booming and half the profit went to the people on the Moon and half to Earth, where each country received some of the money according to an agreement. The Moon was not independent and preferred to be part of Earth. The government on the Moon handled only local matters and major issues were handled on Earth by the Advisory Board. Earth never interfered in the local affairs of the Moon colony and that's why the Moon citizens never demanded independence. The arrangement worked well without complications.

In addition to the terrynium mining, the Moon refined the minerals from the asteroids that were continuously dropped from the work station in orbit. The Moon enjoyed affluence and the colonists could afford to order high quality foods and goods from Earth. After the two-year contract expired and the people returned to Earth, many chose to go back to the Moon after a year. It was a quick way of saving money as the cost of living on the Moon was very low.

Life on the Moon was not risk free and a few years back a terrible moonquake had occurred. An entire wing of the housing had collapsed and the residents all died. Small moonquakes were common and of no consequence, but the quake that destroyed the housing had been major and the mines had also experienced damage.

A terrynium mine had suffered extensive damage when a tunnel caved in and twenty worker robots and three humans perished. When the engineers examined the tunnel, they suspected the many moonquakes had weakened the support structure of the tunnel and caused it to collapse. After that accident, all the mines were carefully inspected and the tunnels reinforced with extra supports.

The workstation orbiting the Moon had also been targeted by criminals. It was known that workstations processing minerals often had loads of gold and other precious metals onboard for short periods of time. Usually, the shuttle would transport the refined minerals on a daily basis from the workstation to the Moon's surface, but the shuttle was undergoing repair and a large supply of gold was held on the station until the shuttle was back in service.

Without warning, five fighter ships showed up and one docked with the station. The other four ships hovered nearby with weapons aimed at the workstation. With powerful weapons drawn, the gangsters were too dangerous to fight off and the crew had no choice but to hand over the whole supply of gold worth millions of dollars. That saved them from being shot. The invaders had worn masks and it was unclear what race they were, but they had used a translation device so they were not from Earth.

The only way the criminals could have known that the workstation had gold onboard was from an informer on the station. No one admitted to being a snitch and after a lengthy investigation, the robbery remained unsolved and active exploration of the crime ceased, but it was not abandoned. It was hoped that one day in the future the snitch would talk, perhaps brag about his or her role in the robbery, and then the person could be apprehended. Whoever it was, the person had nerves of steel and had passed a lie detector test. The crew onboard had been sixteen men and four women. The androids working on the station were not suspects.

All security was beefed up after the robbery and more shuttle vehicles were put into service to avoid another incident. Information between the workstation and the lunar government was encrypted using a more powerful encryption language than before and refined minerals were picked up within hours of finish by a shuttle. All precious metals were stored on the Moon in an undisclosed location only known to a small number of trustworthy employees and transport of the gold to Earth was highly confidential.

Living in 'the bubble' on the Moon was not as advanced as it was on Mars, but the people still enjoyed a rather high standard of living with quality food, entertainment and a workweek of thirty hours. No taxes were collected. All heavy work was done by worker robots. No children lived on the Moon. People paid for food and their apartments, but almost everything else was free such as transportation within 'the bubble', medical care, the two holodecks and tourist trips around the Moon. It was easy to save a substantial amount of money and then return to Earth and buy a house cash. There was no shortage of volunteers who wanted to try a stint as a worker on the Moon.

******

Ella, a young woman in her twenties, was glad to have her mother Rose back from the Moon workstation. Rose had worked as a cook for two years up in space and was finally back on Earth. She felt physically weak and knew she had hours of exercise to endure to regain her strength. The workstation had supplied light gravity from rotation, but two years up in space had still taken its toll on Rose. Her job as a cook for so many people had been laborious even though two androids had assisted her. Now she was back and had decided never to return to work in space again. Her pay had been above average and she had saved it all.

Rose bought a house and an airmobile and Ella never asked how she paid for it. She assumed her mother had been well paid as a cook. When Rose invited Ella to accompany her on a vacation trip to Europe she started to wonder to herself how her mother could afford it. They had a wonderful time in Europe and Rose paid for all the expenses. Now Ella was suspicious and added up the cost of everything her mother had bought.

"Mom, were you involved in the robbery on the workstation?" she asked point-blank.

"Yes, please don't give me away," Rose responded with a pleading voice.

Ella looked at her mother in horror and Rose started to shiver.

"How did you contact the robbers?" she asked.

"I was able to enter the communication room and sent a message to my brother with just one word "now". My brother lives with them and we had an agreement that if he ever would receive a message from me with that code word, it would mean gold was onboard and they could raid the station. I deleted the message right away and no one found out. My brother made a quick stop on Earth and hid my part of the gold in my apartment. I knew when I sent the message that they may not be close enough to act in time, but they were and as you know they succeeded."

Ella broke down crying and said -

"How could you?"

They returned from Europe and Ella knew what must be done. Rose trusted her daughter's loyalty and was not overly concerned. Ella barely talked to her mother on the trip home.

Within hours of landing at the airport, Ella reported her mother to the authorities and she felt no remorse for doing so. Rose was arrested and confessed. She understood the game was over and she was sentenced to fifteen years in jail without parole. Ella never visited her mother in prison and Rose died after serving eleven years. All the leftover gold in Rose's house was returned to the Moon. The money received from the sale of her house and airmobile was sent to the Moon as well.

******

On Earth2 President Telly had served his six-year term and the next president must be elected. The geologist, Ijakull, was running for the office of president and won easily. He was well liked by the people and his many postings on the Internet about the planet were highly popular. He kept the same cabinet as Telly had appointed and asked Telly to work as his all-around advisor. This was a new position and would not interfere with the work of the Secretary of Planning. Telly's new post was powerful and he attended all government meetings. With a population close to twenty-five thousand citizens, the work required by the government had increased. The debt to Frejja was now rather small and the government looked forward to being debt free. Roads were needed in addition to more infrastructure and once they were debt free, the government hoped to have the funds to pay for it.

Earth2 was a well-functioning country. Standard of living had slowly increased. Food supplies were adequate and the crops abundant. The rich grass on the far side of the planet was appreciated by the meat animals and their numbers had increased substantially. Egg laying chickens and the number of dairy goats for milk production were now sufficient for the citizens' needs.

Pollox and Lyra were still alone out on the grasslands and for five years they had taken care of the herd of meat animals. They lived a true pioneer life and were secretly glad that the government did not have the funds to start building a settlement in their area. They worked hard and also homeschooled their children. Janus was eight years old and the younger son four years. A baby girl had been born the year before.

The population was mostly young, but there were some retired people on Earth2. Telly had organized a pension system and anyone over seventy years could apply if there was a need. Of the retired people on the planet, only a few had applied for a pension and the others felt they had enough savings to support them. The pension was moderate, but sufficient to live on. A certain percentage of the income the government earned from mining was saved for pensions.

Rasufilus was responsible for domestic law and order as well as defense of Earth2 and since he settled on the planet, only one incident had taken place. One man had threatened another with a knife and the argument was over a girl they both wanted. Rasufilus quickly disarmed the man and made him understand that a stabbing would mean deportation at his own expense. No other crime had ever occurred.

Recreational drugs and alcohol were not available and no one had ever suggested to import them. The government was relieved there was no demand for them and did not bring up the subject on purpose. They preferred not to deal with it.

The town was very spread out and the preferred method of transportation was bicycles. Some people could afford to buy an airmobile and there were a few buses to transport people to work free of charge. The bicycles were inexpensive and imported from Etteron. Airmobiles could also be rented.

Paragonne had just started walking and was full of energy. Melody was protective of him and acted as his second mother. He was on a mission to explore his world and nothing was safe. When he found his dad's doctor's bag Atlas only laughed and quickly rescued his bag. Atlas had an angel's patience with his children and was totally devoted to them. So was Viola. On the weekends, if the weather permitted, the family rented an airmobile and went on day trips to the countryside and had picnics at the lake. Atlas' cooking skills were highly appreciated and his family could hardly wait until he unpacked their lunch. He always fed the baby himself.

"Dad, this is the best ever," Melody announced as she was digging in and Viola nodded and did thumbs up. To Atlas, his cooking was a treasured hobby and never a chore. He preferred to also do the food shopping so he could pick the best groceries he could find.

Atlas joined his family when they swam in the lake and he was a good swimmer. Viola never thought of Atlas as a machine. He was her precious husband and the only man she could imagine being married to. They had never argued and saw life from the same viewpoint. When she needed to talk, he was always there listening carefully to what she said. Atlas himself had no hang-ups and was a pillar of stability for his family.

******

Alison and Leif were now traveling between Frejja and Mars delivering cargo. It was an easy two months' travel time to Mars with three weeks off after each trip and they stayed with Emrak and Karol. While the children were at school, they worked out in the gym and then had time to spend with their children. Solveiga and Sven saw more of their parents than Brandon and Brianna's boys had seen of their parents. Solveiga and Sven loved their grandparents, but were equally devoted to their parents and every time Alison and Leif returned, they bonded with the children. Several times their supervisor had asked them if they wanted to make a trip to Veehnia or other far away planet, but they always responded that it would have to wait until their children were adults. Then they would accept the offer.

Alison and Leif were nearing Mars and Leif slowed down the engines. He fired the retro-propulsive thrusters to reduce the speed of the ship and make a soft landing. *The thrusters failed to ignite!* Leif tried desperately to start them and nothing happened. The ship was descending fast and they were now at an altitude of only two thousand feet and falling at a tremendous speed. Leif made a desperate attempt to ascend, but it did not work. He had lost control of the ship and they made a horrific crash landing right outside Martia. Within seconds the ship exploded and was on fire. Everyone onboard was dead.

Witnesses on the surface were in total shock. It was obvious to observers that the thrusters had failed to ignite. Frejjan ships had never had an accident and they were known for their high quality and their fighter ships were among the best on the market. Rescue workers were on the scene within minutes and sprayed flame retardant from their tankers until the fire was out. The ship's hull was intact and the terrynium had been strong enough so the ship had not broken apart. They braced themselves when they entered the ship. Alison, Leif and two copilots were strapped into their seats and all were dead. Three androids were still functioning, but just barely, and after being helped out of their seats and brought inside the government building, they gave a full account of what had happened and the failure of the thrusters to start. They described Leif's heroic attempts to ascend to avoid a crash landing, but to no avail. The androids explained that they had landed with enormous force and the impact had probably broken the backs of the humans onboard, possibly also their necks. Because of the quick response of the crew on Mars, the fire had not had time to destroy the ship and had not reached the interior. Alison and Leif were only thirty-nine years old.

All the humans were stored at the morgue. Frejja sent a ship to Mars to pick up the dead bodies and onboard was a team of experts to conduct a thorough examination of the ship. The ship had been towed inside a pressurized hangar and it would take months until the inspection of the engines and thrusters was complete.

Frejja and Mars were in mourning. Outside Emrak and Karol's home a government airmobile arrived and the president himself was part of the group of people delivering the sad news to Emrak and Karol. The children were at school and Emrak and Karol were grateful they were spared from hearing about their parents' death from government officials. They wanted to tell the grandchildren themselves as gently as possible when they were alone.

Emrak and Karol collapsed in their chairs too shocked to even speak. Emrak was white in the face and Karol was crying in her handkerchief. The president gave them all the details and assured them they would get whatever information was found as soon as it was available. The bodies would arrive from Mars in four months.

The officials left and Emrak and Karol had only a few hours until the children would be home. They managed to calm themselves somewhat and they knew they had to tell the children right away or they would hear about the accident on the Internet.

Emrak told the children to sit down and as gently as he could he told them what had happened and that their parents had died instantly without suffering. Both children cried violently. Karol had her arms around Solveiga and Emrak held Sven. It was the saddest day in their lives. The children did not go back to school for a week and Karol encouraged them to talk to her about their feelings. She knew they needed to talk about it and to receive emotional support. The four of them grieved together and slowly, very slowly, healed together. Alison and Leif would never be forgotten and months later they were able to watch all the holographic images they had of Alison and Leif without breaking down. The funeral was hard to get through and they supported each other emotionally.

Emrak and Karol were now legal parents of the children. They were in good health and Emrak was fully recovered from his heart transplant surgery. At age eighty-six he functioned and looked twenty years younger and Karol was in excellent health. The Frejjan life span was about one hundred and twenty years, longer than on Earth, and Emrak hoped he would live out his normal life and see the children grow up. Alison and Leif's life insurance would be deposited into an account for the children and be turned over to them as adults. Emrak was not a poor man and did not need any financial help to support the children.

The report from Mars came back and stated that the thrusters had failed from a malfunctioning fuel pump. Frejja had only experienced one other spaceship accident and that was seventeen years earlier when Rigel and Thole had their incident. Brandon and Brianna had also experienced a failed engine from a defective fuel pump early in their career when they flew between Earth and the Moon. That ship had been manufactured on Earth.

Everyone who had known Alison and Leif mourned their tragic death.

CHAPTER 38

On Earth, almost one hundred and fifty years had passed since the collapse and this event in history was no longer relevant in people's minds. The history books outlined the tragedy in detail and the school children were taught why it happened and the rebuilding of society, but most people felt it happened so long ago and it was not important any more. Perhaps this mindset was not such a good idea as history has a way of repeating itself.

Before the collapse, organized religion had been very important with strong belief in a traditional God, but at the present time church attendance was down and few people identified with those ideologies any more. Religion had shifted to spiritualism that was experienced on a more personal level. Many felt the answers came from within and to associate with the ascended masters was the only way to connect to a higher realm. The masters were divine beings vibrating at a higher frequency and offered advice through messengers with ability to connect with the masters. The guidance from the masters was posted on websites to aid the people and the advice was practical and up to date on all things happening on Earth and covered just about every topic people needed help with. The masters had lessened people's fear of death as it was now known death is only a passing into a different realm and by no means the end of life. People felt liberated.

Earth also had a fair amount of people who were atheists, or materialists, and their lack of faith was respected as well. The new society was tolerant and every person's free will was honored. To force one's opinions onto another person was considered rude, uncivilized and disrespectful.

Wars were also a thing of the past and competition between countries an outdated way of life. Cooperation was more common and ethnic differences were not important.

All the statutes of People Democracy were still in effect and the constitution had worked well for one hundred and twenty years. Several amendments had been added and the original text modernized, but most of the original statutes were in force and people liked the system and saw no reason to change it.

The economy on Earth was good and the banks had to abide by strict usury laws. Many loans were interest free enabling entrepreneurs to start new businesses with ease. Corporations were limited in size to prevent monopolies. The economy was free as no one was allowed to manipulate the system.

Women's equal rights were assured and since the artificial womb was introduced, most women who wanted children had them early in their career rather than delaying motherhood. Many hired an android to look after the children and some used daycare centers. Fertility was not as high as it had been in the past and every child was welcome. Adoptions were favored over abortions and society wanted more children to be born. The global population was four billion and had not increased for years.

The average lifespan was about a hundred years, but some hardy souls lived past a hundred years. Health, as well as mental health, was superior compared to the past and there were cures for cancer, diabetes and the common illnesses that had plagued people a hundred years ago. People enjoyed life and all its opportunities to grow, learn and improve themselves.

Men were masculine, women were feminine and the topic was not under debate. It seemed silly to question such a natural matter, but in the past before the collapse, it had been a big issue. Children were told they could choose if they wanted to be boy or girl leading to endless confusion, even mild insanity. Some men became feminized and there were women who were more like men than women. Thankfully, that sad chapter in history faded away and equilibrium returned. To people reading about it, it just confirmed that the time before the collapse deserved to be called the dark ages.

******

Eight years had passed and more than half of Ljeviina's capital had been rebuilt. Even though the people of Ziggellus had sent formal apologies, some of the Ljeviinans had a hard time to forgive. The president had posted numerous times on the Internet that to heal as a nation from the tragedy, the population had to forgive the Ziggellus people. To continue hating them would not benefit the people. It was time to move on.

On Ziggellus, the people were rebuilding as well. The standard of living was lower than before Rasufilus' strike against them, but the people knew they were now paying the price for their raiding. Only the most cruel among them wanted to continue their former lifestyle, but the majority of the people wanted no part of it. It would be years until the first space ships were built and they could leave their planet.

In the past on Ziggellus, children's minds were corrupted before they even started school by watching Internet holographic pictures and movies aimed at 'toughening up' the children. Nothing was off limits and cruelty and vulgarity were emphasized. Parents did not object as raiding and invading was normal behavior and the few people with sane minds were shoved aside and silenced. They actually risked their lives if they spoke up and most of them just gave up and disappeared from society. For them, the remote countryside became their refuge and they educated their children themselves. All of them lived in fear of the savages running the society and they knew the insanity rate was high among them, children included. The power elite had the whole population under their control and it seemed the degradation was in a down spiral with no end in sight.

After Rasufilus taught the leaders of Ziggellus a lesson everything changed. The people from the countryside came back to the cities and took over. The president managed to stay in office by expressing deep remorse, but his whole cabinet and all the top leaders were incarcerated for life. The education system, entertainment and Internet sites were literally scrubbed clean and all the vulgarity removed as unfit for children and adults alike. Civilized behavior was emphasized and a moral code created. Many were unsure how to react in the beginning, but slowly people turned around and embraced the new lifestyle and all the old ways were shunned. The most important change was that children were not exposed to brainwashing techniques at an early age and could enjoy a normal childhood, where children were allowed to be children and could grow up nurtured.

******

Cooper and Reyya were hard at work and the three countries of Sorenia had gone through a metamorphosis. The three years that Cooper had lived on the planet had been difficult and sometimes frustrating, but the fruit of his labor was now obvious everywhere. All three countries had been cleaned up and Rotsalio and Ziuglin had been swept clean. Crops were growing on the fields, no garbage was visible anywhere, each country had a medical center and several schools had been built in each country. Roads were being built to connect the three countries and the sewage system that Cooper had designed had been installed in many local towns. Running water was still unavailable in some areas because of a shortage of water pipes. The system had been designed and as soon as manufacturing of the pipes was finished, the project would start. It was expected that all homes would have running water within a year.

The biggest success was the large silver mine in Mulerna. The silver deposits were more plentiful than anyone had expected and would supply high quality silver for decades. Stimillo and Borvio had found several more silver mines with slightly less deposits than the Mulerna mine and they had been in production until the war started. There were many natural caves in Rotsalio and Stimillo and Borvio systematically explored every one of them. One of them was a gold mine, literally. Several veins of gold were found and the geologists were sure that what they saw was just a small part of what was available in the cave. Another cave had large deposits of copper as well as gold. It would take them several years to finish their work and many valuable minerals would be found. When Cooper heard their reports, he realized the supply of precious metals was more than the planet needed and they could sell the surplus, but how? They needed a trading partner and they needed to import many items that could not be manufactured on Sorenia at the present time, such as appliances, machinery, tools and electronics. The closest planet was Ziggellus, three months' travel time by spaceship, and the next planet was Ljeviina, five months away by ship.

Cooper decided to try to amplify the signal from the communication system. It was the best system Veehnia had and he felt lucky Tyler had given it to them. Cooper was able to make an amplifier and hooked it up to the system. From the memory bank he retrieved the code to Ziggellus and sent off a signal. To his surprise he received a response. He grabbed the translation device and explained who he was, what planet he lived on and that Sorenia was looking for a trading partner. The operator on Ziggellus knew of Sorenia and explained they would not be back in space for another ten years, but their neighbor planet Mineata, a former trading partner with Ziggellus, would be the best choice and they were closer to Sorenia than Ziggellus was. They were as advanced as Ljeviina and would most likely be willing to trade consumer goods for precious metals. The operator gave Cooper the code to Mineata.

Cooper sent a signal and after several tries, he heard a response from Mineata. The operator told Cooper he knew about the war on Sorenia and was glad to hear it was over. They had all the items Cooper asked about and would be willing to sell them for silver, gold, terrynium or any of the platinum group metals, which they needed for manufacturing of electronics and robots. Cooper replied they had some of the metals, but he would return when he had more exact information what Sorenia had.

Cooper transmitted the whole list of items they needed and the operator promised to contact him and give him the price they would ask for the items. The distance between their planets was only one month as there was a shortcut tunnel they would use to reach Sorenia.

A week later Cooper heard from Mineata and the same operator conveyed the cost of the items. Cooper knew they had enough silver available to pay for the whole shipment. Work in the gold mine had already started and by the time the Mineata ship arrived, some gold would be available and could be used as payment.

The ship arrived from Mineata five weeks later and six crew members exited the ship, two females and four males. They were humans with white skin, but their faces and bodies were covered with hair. They had no hair around their eyes and mouth, but it was obvious they had hair growth on their entire bodies. Two had blond hair and the others medium brown hair. The females had as much hair as the males. They were not bad looking, just unusual. The captain introduced himself as Volrex.

Cooper greeted them and explained he was an android and the acting president and originated from Veehnia. The crew members were quick to laugh, gregarious and very sociable. Cooper instantly liked them and they seemed to take a liking to Cooper in return. Volrex explained they knew of planet Veehnia and the fifteen-hour tunnel. A group of robots unloaded the ship and when finished a huge pile of merchandise was lined up on the ground: appliances; tools; computers; four airmobiles; communicators; medical equipment and more. Cooper looked at the items and saw right away that they were very advanced and high quality.

Cooper, Reyya and the crew went inside the government building and Cooper had a large number of crates loaded with mostly silver, but also unrefined gold nuggets that had been extracted just a few weeks ago. The crew accepted the unrefined gold and offered to deliver the equipment needed to process the raw gold into pure gold. Cooper accepted right away. He knew the equipment would pay for itself in the long run. The silver in the crates exceeded what was needed as payment and several crates were left in the government building after the robots had loaded the gold and silver onto the ship. Stimillo and Borvio joined them and explained they were systematically exploring the whole planet for precious metals and what they had found so far was amazing. Copper was abundant as was terrynium and they were also looking for the platinum group metals. Within a year they would know what was available on the planet.

Sorenia had no spaceships and Cooper asked if Mineata would be willing to sell a few in the future. The crew nodded and said of course they would, but they were very expensive. Cooper was a trained pilot and the only one on Sorenia who could fly a ship. He knew it would be a challenge to find people on Sorenia with the intelligence needed to learn how to fly a spaceship and to master all the electronics. In the present shipment were five thousand implants, but he knew all the citizens would need one to boost their cognition.

The new 3D printed government building was spacious with a conference room, large dining room and a well-equipped kitchen, at least by Sorenia standards. Three women had prepared dinner for them and it was obvious the crew approved of the food as they quickly emptied their plates. The only time Cooper felt awkward was when dinner was served and he was the only one who did not eat.

The crew stayed for a week and toured the three countries. Many things were discussed and the crew saw the huge need Sorenia had for modern consumer goods. Mineata had everything they needed and robots did most of the work in their factories. What Mineata lacked was precious metals which, of course, Sorenia had in abundance so it was a promising partnership. They also toured the cave with gold deposits and the crew realized that the minerals their planet so desperately needed were available right here on Sorenia and they understood that all the minerals had not been found yet. Sorenia had just pulled itself up by its bootstraps and was a work in progress.

"You probably need some sort of defense," Volrex said as he admired the gold in the cave. "If the word gets out that you have all these precious metals, you'll be invaded. There are gangs of criminals roaming the space. On the ship, we have an arsenal of weapons and portable high power laser weapons that we can sell to you right now. We will only keep what we need onboard to defend ourselves on our return trip, but we're willing to sell all the extra weapons we have on the ship."

Cooper had already thought about the possibility of criminals and quickly agreed. Before the crew left, they unloaded all the weapons and it was a sizable stack of very modern, powerful weaponry and Cooper paid with the extra silver that was still in crates in the conference room. Before the crew left, Cooper handed them another long list of items they needed and Volrex promised they would return in two months. On the list Cooper had entered ten thousand implants and Volrex hesitated when he saw the number, but promised they would deliver as many as they had in stock.

This was the beginning of a partnership that benefitted both planets. The factories on Mineata were swamped with orders from Sorenia and Sorenia's mines were working two shifts a day to extract as many minerals as fast as possible to foot the bill. Every two months the ship arrived from Mineata and slowly the standard of living improved on Sorenia. What Cooper had accomplished in four years was a miracle.

The steel mill in Mulerna had been updated and was in full production. The steel was needed to erect modern factory buildings and many other items. Several hundred people worked at the mill. In the future, Cooper had plans to buy robots to do the heavy work, but he had to make certain there were enough jobs available for the citizens without an education and working in the mines and factories ensured them a steady employment.

The first batch of microchips were implanted on government employees, doctors, teachers and various professionals. They were simple to place behind the ear and the doctors implanting them had no trouble with the procedure. Reyya and Littiana were stunned at the difference when they received their chips and the geologists could hardly believe how fast they could process incoming information and make quick decisions. The implants were a hit and everyone was looking forward to receiving one.

Cooper knew that he could not advance the citizens too fast and he had to watch carefully how the people adjusted to the modernization. For some people, like Reyya, there were no limits while other people of less sophistication were afraid and felt threatened from too fast advancement.

The people could benefit from better grooming and many of the people still looked untidy. Cooper asked Littiana to make sure there were barber shops open in all towns and if more barbers were needed, the existing barbers should train more. Some of the homes had running water and it was expected that everyone would have it within a few months.

"How often do people take a bath?" Cooper asked Littiana.

"Perhaps once a week. Some people hardly ever bathe," she replied. "There are people who only wash their hair a few times a year." Cooper had noticed that Littiana always had clean, shiny hair and was without fail nicely dressed. She was an attractive woman.

"Please start a campaign in the newspaper emphasizing a neat appearance and the importance of being clean," Cooper suggested. "Perhaps the women could benefit from a beauty salon in town."

Littiana laughed with an amused look on her face and agreed. She went to work right away and found just the right pictures in the office computer of well-groomed men and women and wrote a humorous article showing how not to look. It was a hit. People started to look at themselves and realized they could greatly improve how they looked and soon there were a barber shop and a beauty salon in most towns. Littiana wrote several more articles with suggestions and the latest trend became 'neat and clean'.

"Do you know of any historian who knows the true history of Sorenia?" Cooper asked Reyya.

"Only one, a very educated woman living here in Mulerna."

"Please find her and ask her to come to my office," Cooper said.

A few days later a woman in her early thirties knocked on Cooper's door and entered his office. She was very pretty with shoulder length dark blond hair, refined features and her dress revealed a beautiful figure.

Cooper felt like whistling, but reminded himself it was inappropriate behavior for a president.

"Mr. President, you wanted to see me. My name is Rosalie," she said with a low melodious voice.

"Rosalie, welcome. I'm looking for a well-read person who knows the true history of Sorenia and can write a book about it. May I ask about your qualifications?"

"I was educated before the war and continued my education until the war closed the schools. During the war, I kept studying and lived with my parents. I rescued as many of the original documents from my school's library as I could get my hands on. They are the original documents and I also rescued books going back hundreds of years in time. Sorenia was more sophisticated long time ago and the education system was good. I have all the documents and books safely stored in my house. It's a small house just fifteen minutes from here."

"I would like to hire you to write a history book covering as much as possible about Sorenia's history and going back as far as you can in time. It's of paramount importance that all facts can be authenticated. The book will become the new history book for our school system and will also be available for sale to anyone wanting to know our history."

"I'll be happy to write the book. Can I work from home?"

"Of course. You will need to use a computer and we just received a bunch of them from Mineata. Let me show you how they work."

Cooper spent the rest of the day training Rosalie how to use the computer. She was quick to learn and understood after a while how it worked. Cooper told her if she got stuck, he would come over to her house and help her. He also gave her an implant and asked her to have the local doctor attach it.

They sat down and talked for a while and Rosalie told Cooper she had never married as the men were too primitive and uneducated. During the war she had spent her time reading and educating herself in history, the arts and learning about astronomy and space travel.

Once a week Rosalie visited Cooper with a layout of her writing and Cooper found he looked forward to seeing her every week. Rosalie seemed fond of him in return. She knew of course he was an android, but she valued their discussions and Cooper was the only man she had met who appreciated her sharp mind. Rosalie was highly intelligent and she had asked Cooper to teach her English. Her computer had lots of material in English and she wanted to access it. Cooper was created on Veehnia and his native language was English. He agreed and started giving her lessons including how to read and write in English. With her new implant Rosalie was a quick learner.

Rosalie invited Cooper to her house. It was a small wooden cabin, but it was her own house that she owned and everything inside was orderly and functional. Her parents had contributed some of the money to pay for it. Their relationship turned to a deep friendship and Cooper started taking a day off a week from work so he could spend more time with Rosalie. He was totally fascinated with her and would like to marry her, but was afraid to ask her.

A nudge from Littiana did the trick. She had noticed Cooper's interest in Rosalie and told him with a smile on her face-

"If you don't ask, you'll never get an answer."

Cooper laughed and decided to give it a try. The next time he was in Rosalie's house he popped the question -

"Rosalie, I can't live without you. I adore you. Will you marry me? I know I'm an android, but I would do my best to be a good husband."

Rosalie laughed and gave Cooper a big hug and said -

"I love you, Cooper, and my answer is yes."

A week later Reyya married them as he was the official government person authorized to perform wedding ceremonies. Cooper moved into Rosalie's house and he had never been happier and she felt the same. They were best friends as well as lovers and they communicated mostly in English. Rosalie was learning fast and was able to speak English rather well. He taught her so many things about the universe and other topics and she soaked everything up like a sponge. Cooper's intellect was what she had yearned for and never found. She loved him dearly.

Cooper found Rosalie's parents pleasant and her mother had barely any native features. Her father was more of a mix, but pleasant to be with. Both were literate and dignified. Rosalie's father had run the printing press before the war and her mother had worked at the local hospital's lab as a technician. Her parents did not mind their son-in-law was an android as long as Rosalie was happy. She was their only child.

A few months later, Rosalie noticed Cooper was anxious to discuss something with her and said -

"What's on your mind?"

"Do you want children?" he asked slowly.

"Of course, but we can't have any, so I've pushed those thoughts out of my mind," Rosalie said. She was surprised he even asked.

"I have a suggestion and I ask you to be open-minded. To become a father would be a dream come true and I know you would be an excellent mother. If we use a donor, we would become parents."

"What the heck are you suggesting?" Rosalie was indignant. "Infidelity? Go to bed with another man? I want no part of it."

"Think of it from a different angle. This has nothing to do with being unfaithful. We love each other and nothing changes that. A donor will give us the gift of a child and the performance should be looked upon as a 'service' to get the job done and not as an act of infidelity. My feelings are as strong as any biological man would have, but I'm able to put jealousy aside and focus on the real issue and that is we both want a child."

"Who would this donor be?"

"A man I highly respect and like a lot and that is Reyya."

"They can't have children."

"The problem is with Littiana, not Reyya. He told me so."

Rosalie was not convinced and she felt confused. She had only been intimate with one man and that was Cooper.

"I would feel totally awkward," she said.

"So would Reyya. He is a man of strong morals. Littiana may not agree either. If you can get used to the thought, I think he would at least consider the idea. We are talking strictly of an act of service."

Rosalie mulled over the idea for the rest of the day and at night she had made her decision.

"I'll do it. I will just have to tell myself it's a necessary thing I'll have to endure to become a mother."

Cooper hugged her and asked her to show up in the conference room the following day and they would approach Reyya and Littiana.

Cooper conveyed his plan as gently as possible to Reyya and Littiana and both were taken aback by his suggestion. Finally, Littiana broke the silence and said -

"You have my blessing. I understand it's a gift that Reyya will give you and has nothing to do with infidelity. It will not hurt our marriage in any way."

Reyya looked at her with surprise.

"I've never been unfaithful to my wife, but I understand we have to look at it from a different point of view. The goal is a child and we all know there is only one way to accomplish procreation. My first thought was to say no, but now that Littiana approves of the idea, I'll change my mind and say yes. Will the child know who the father is?"

"As an adult, yes, we'll reveal who the father is and I'm sure he or she will understand," Cooper replied. "The two of you will be part of the child's life and perhaps act as the second set of grandparents. If someone would ask who the father is when Rosalie is pregnant, I suggest we just say it was a medical procedure using a donor. By the way, various methods are done on Veehnia all the time to help women conceive."

Rosalie was ready and Reyya came over. Cooper went for a walk to be out of the way. They kept their clothes on and the whole affair was over quickly. As Cooper had said, Reyya did them a favor as an act of kindness.

Unfortunately, Rosalie did not conceive and she admitted to Cooper she had been very tense. The second try worked and Rosalie was expecting. There were no odd feelings between Rosalie and Reyya and both put the incident behind them.

As Rosalie's tummy grew, Cooper would put his head against her abdomen and listen to the baby's heartbeat with a smile on his face. The baby captivated him. Both of them looked forward to the birth.

The hospital was well supplied with equipment and medications from Mineata and the doctor gave Rosalie a pain free delivery. She gave birth to a handsome boy with refined features and they named him Halcyon meaning happy and peaceful. Reyya and Littiana were as excited as Cooper and Rosalie and could hardly take their eyes off him.

Rosalie nursed the baby and preferred natural ways over bottle feeding. Reyya and Littiana usually came over on Sundays for a short visit to hold the baby and admire him. They felt like grandparents. Rosalie's parents were also excited over the baby and had accepted the explanation that the father was a donor. They suspected it was Reyya, but never asked and never pried into private matters.

Cooper was a very proud father and told Rosalie over and over how happy he was to be a father. As the baby grew, they started to look for a bigger house and found a large 3D printed house not too far from their own house. Cooper bought it and they sold their little cabin.

******

Tothellim and Anna docked their boat after a day of fishing in the ocean. Lately, they went alone on their boat trips as their daughter Heidi was away and studied to become a veterinarian. Logan had just given his first piano concert and it was well received. He wanted to become a professional piano player and his prospects for success were excellent - he made the piano sing. With school work and six hours of piano practice every day, he had barely any free time.

It had been a windy day on the water with four-foot waves and they were glad to be back at the dock. After they had covered the boat with its mooring cover, Tothellim carried the pail of fish and they walked to their airmobile. They were tired and looked forward to just rest as the airmobile transported them home. It was not there! It was gone!

"Someone stole it," Anna gasped.

Crime did exist on Veehnia, but it was not severe and most people ware law-abiding.

"I'll call the police and then we have no choice but to find an airmobile to rent so we can get home," Tothellim said.

He called on his communicator and within minutes the police arrived in an airmobile. Tothellim gave them all the details of the stolen vehicle and the police officers ordered a rental to pick them up. It arrived within a few minutes and they climbed aboard. Tothellim swiped his implant over the scanner to pay for the rental, entered the destination into the computer and they were on their way home. The airmobile was insured, but the inconvenience to live without it was troublesome. Tothellim could bicycle to work, but Anna needed a vehicle for shopping and to pick Logan up from school.

"I'll rent a vehicle for you, Anna, until our airmobile is returned," Tothellim reassured her.

The police found the vehicle a long distance away. It was a heap of metal and had apparently crash-landed. Inside was an android, barely functioning and unable to move and with a damaged motherboard. Its identification number had been filed off. The android was stored in a cage at the police station and a programmer replaced his motherboard and restored his speech.

"Did you steal the airmobile?" the police interrogator asked.

"Yes, I was ordered to do it."

"By whom?"

"My new owner, Owen. He's fifteen years old and he stole me off the street as I was doing errands by pretending he had a message for me from my real owner. Once we were in his house, he activated my kill switch and reprogrammed me making me into a criminal. I've been working for him for months now stealing in stores and taking the airmobile. Even though he reprogrammed me, he wasn't able to reprogram all my data and I understood what I was doing was illegal. That's why I crashed the airmobile to end it all. I'm not a criminal and all I want is to be returned to my owner."

The police searched their records and found that a person had reported a stolen android a few months earlier. The android gave the address to Owen's house and they picked him up, a snooty kid with an arrogant attitude. He confessed and was taken into custody and ended up in a juvenile prison for ten years without parole. The android went through repairs and was returned to his owner. Owen's parents were beside themselves with embarrassment over their son's behavior and offered to pay for a new airmobile, but Tothellim assured them the insurance company would pay for a replacement. Tothellim felt sorry for the parents and wondered to himself how he would feel if Logan had pulled a stunt like that. He was grateful his children were well-adjusted and had no mental hang-ups.

Androids in general were very safe and none of them had gone insane. All incidents that had occurred were due to human lawbreakers abusing them for their own benefit. Criminals convicted of reprogramming androids illegally could expect long prison terms without parole.

Tothellim was in his early sixties and had no plans to retire for at least ten years. He loved Veehnia and had never regretted moving there. Rheo and Tothellim worked closely together and the two of them took pride in every pilot who graduated. The training program the pilots went through was very thorough and covered any possible accident they could face in their career. Tothellim had heard of Alison and Leif's tragic crash-landing on Mars and had sent his condolences to Emrak and Karol. When a spaceship malfunctions, there is not much even the best pilot can do, but Tothellim always tried to find solutions that he could teach his students.

Life on Veehnia was pleasant and the immigrants from Earth had indeed added a spark to the laid-back lifestyle on the planet. The Veehnian ships still traveled a few times a year to Earth to pick up immigrants and always returned with all the seats taken. The people from Earth adjusted quickly to Veehnia and no one had ever returned to Earth. There was some trading between the two planets and the ship from Veehnia usually carried cargo that had been ordered by Earth. Likewise, Earth sold many items to Veehnia.

******

A year had passed and Emrak, Karol and the children were doing well. As a family, they had healed from the death of Alison and Leif. Emrak and Karol spent a lot of time with the children and they often made day trips with their airmobile. Neither of the children was interested in space as a career and were perfectly happy to live out their lives on Frejja. They would often look at the pictures of Alison and Leif to keep their memories alive and they were able to do so now without feeling devastated. Emrak and Karol were always willing to offer support.

CHAPTER 39

Twenty space fighter ships landed on Ziggellus outside the capital and a high-pitched voice called the president on the communicator. The president was the same person who had dealt with Rasufilus and he drove out to the ships with two of his assistants. The whole government on Ziggellus was made up of the people who had previously lived in the countryside and were now in charge.

Two men dressed in black leather climbed out of their ship and their laser guns showed they meant business. The president realized they were one of many criminal gangs famous for roaming the universe and making quick raids on unprotected planets. One of the men was from Humbrus and the other one appeared to be from Earth. Humbrus people were nasty looking, short humanoids with shiny eyes, no hair and faces with deep furrows. The president thought to himself that in the past his own people had behaved in the same manner and he was glad those days were behind them.

"I'm Keetoh, the leader of my fleet of ships, and this is Rob, my assistant. We need a place to live for a while and we know Rasufilus blew up your military equipment and ships. If you object, we'll just shoot you down."

The president knew they had no choice but to allow them to stay. They still had no weapons for defense and their priority had been to rebuild space ships, not weapons. Money was in short supply and they could not afford to manufacture everything they needed.

"How long will you stay?" the president asked trying not to sound intimidated.

"Maybe a year. We'll stay at one of your hotels. There are seventy-five of us and we prefer to stay in one building. We also need two groundmobiles to check on our ships every day. Show us your communication system, now."

The two men hopped into the president's groundmobile and they entered the government building.

"Here are our main computers and they run all our communications," the president said and pointed to the machines.

Keetoh pulled out his laser gun and shot ten shots into the machines. They disintegrated in a pile of fire and smoke.

"Now you can't call for help," he said with a grin. "Show us your hotel."

They drove back to the ships and Keetoh ordered his men to exit their ships and lock them up. They followed the groundmobile on foot to the hotel. Most of them were from Humbrus, some were from Morekia and the rest appeared to be from Bantizza. Rob was the only human from Earth and he was Rose's brother. His gang had been the criminals robbing the workstation orbiting the Moon. Rob did not know his sister was in prison.

The nightmare began. All communication systems on Ziggellus were shot and there was no way to call for help. The vulgarity and brutal manners of the invaders were horrific. Every day young girls would be kidnapped off the street and brought into the hotel as entertainment for the men. Some were killed when they tried to fight and some were dumped back on the street when the men were finished with the girls, all of them ruined for life with deep emotional scars. The police were helpless without weapons and the criminals were heavily armed.

The president and his cabinet discussed endlessly how to overpower them, but could not find any solution that would actually work. Ten of the criminals were on guard all the time outside the hotel and they were well armed. To enter their spaceships and use their communication system was also impossible as they had guards there, too.

After a month one of the doctors entered the president's office and suggested -

"There is a sedative that we can use. It takes effect two hours after you swallow it and has no odor and no taste. I suggest we put it in their dessert. They use food tasters to check for poison in the food, but the chefs at the hotel have noticed they don't check their dessert. Even if they do, nothing would happen to the food tasters for two hours anyway. Once they fall asleep, they will not wake up for ten hours and that's when we can put them into chains and drag them away. The guards always drink beer and we can put the sedative in the beer before bottling the beer. That way the guards will start to feel sleepy after two hours and then just fall asleep even if they try to stay awake."

"Do you prefer to sedate them rather than killing them?" the president asked.

"The citizens of Ziggellus are now civilized and it would ruin our new reputation to kill them. There are seventy-five of them and killing them would remind people of our past when we were fanatics and behaved in the same manner as they do now. Let's not sink to their level, but rather end this situation without loss of life. Killing is not the answer to atrocities, setting an example is. The way we handle this situation will be the legacy we leave behind and will determine how we are judged in the future."

"I agree with you," the president said after a moment's hesitation. "Let's plan it out right now."

Every detail was carefully planned and the chefs at the hotel had been notified by one of the delivery men, who was part of the police force. The beer had been bottled and was ready. The chefs put the proper doses of the sedative into the dessert and the waiters served the criminals dinner as usual. No one suspected anything. The beer was delivered to the hotel and the guards had no inkling anything was wrong. They all drank the beer. Several cases were delivered to the men guarding the ships.

The plan worked perfectly and after two hours all of them were fast asleep. The police force stormed into the hotel and dragged them out and transported them to the local jail. All of them were put into chains and locked up. No one woke up during the process.

All their guns were confiscated and the ships were now officially the property of Ziggellus. The ships looked new and were very advanced and the weapons onboard ultramodern. There were no serial numbers or company logos anywhere on the ships to indicate where the ships had been manufactured. They needed to find out so future sales of ships to criminals could be stopped.

The criminals were shocked when they woke up in jail. Keetoh was interrogated, but remained silent. Rob was not as stoic and broke down.

"Where did you get the money from to buy your ships?" the police officer asked.

"We robbed the workstation orbiting Earth's Moon. The gold was worth millions and before the robbery we only had five ships. Now we have twenty. Most of the gold was spent buying the ships."

"What company sold you the ships and what planet are they on?"

"A company on planet Sobovela. It's a tiny planet not far from Peturun and they sell anything you want, including weapons. They had the ships in stock and we paid for them with the gold from the workstation. Their government is corrupt and allows illegal sales if they get some of the money."

"Those ships have to be returned to Sobovela and the gold paid back. The gold is the property of the Moon and must be returned to them."

The distance from Ziggellus to the Moon was too far to transmit messages and four of the best pilots on Ziggellus familiarized themselves with the design of the fighter ships. They had traveled through the tunnels many times and could master it. To arrive within transmission distance, they would have to travel through both the fifteen hour and eighteen-hour tunnels and then they would be in the Milky Way Galaxy. The ships were made with terrynium and strong enough to go through the tunnels. After the ship was packed full with food and equipment it took off with four pilots. It would take a little less than four months to reach their destination.

Once they were through the second tunnel they started transmitting and hovered around the area waiting for a reply. They had sent a complete report of the invasion of their planet and the imprisonment of the gangsters. The ships belonged to the Moon and they needed a reply how they should proceed.

The reply came in after a few hours and was a total surprise. The reputation of Ziggellus had been known for years and most planets had heard of their raiding, but it was also known Rasufilus had taught them a lesson and hence the people of Ziggellus had abandoned their former ways.

"Your honesty is commendable and proves you have truly abandoned your criminal ways. The citizens of the Moon have decided to give you all the ships as a gift and we wish you luck in your new way of life. We will contact the authorities on Sobovela as we are closer to them than you are and can communicate with them from the Moon. The fact that you didn't kill the criminals indicates to us you are a civilized people now and that was part of the reason why we decided to give you the ships as a gift. We will deal with the government of Sobovela and there is nothing more we ask you to do. Our best wishes to the people of Ziggellus and good luck rebuilding your planet."

The pilots sent off a message with heartfelt thanks to the people on the Moon. All four pilots were touched and felt emotional when they heard the reply.

The return flight went well and they landed safely on Ziggellus. The president, the doctor and the whole cabinet were present and the pilots played back the recorded message from the Moon. Everyone was amazed and moved. The president turned to the doctor and said -

"We all thank you, doctor, for your words of wisdom about the criminals. If we had killed them, we would have ruined our reputation and still be shunned."

"I'm just happy it's over," the doctor said. "What will you do with the criminals?"

"They will be charged with illegal invasion of our planet, kidnapping and rape of young girls and murder. The judge will most likely sentence them to hard labor."

As the president had guessed, the criminals were sentenced to fifteen years of hard labor as a chain gang. Some of the men had never worked a day in their lives and for the first time they had to do manual labor. The judge ruled that after they had served their sentence, they must be deported to the different planets they came from.

The fleet of spaceships became the property of the government of Ziggellus and were used as mini 'cargo ships' until their full-size ships were ready. They traveled to Mineata and were able to reestablish good relations with them and were allowed to buy electronics to replace what the gangsters had destroyed. The Mineata people understood that everything had changed on Ziggellus and the people were no longer a threat to anyone. Many trips were made to Mineata and having the necessary tools and equipment speeded up the rebuilding of their society.

******

Halcyon was thriving and growing fast. At two years old, he was not still for a minute and everything had to be investigated. He kept Rosalie and Cooper on their toes and they had to laugh at his curiosity.

"Rosalie, would you agree to having another child?" Cooper asked with a hopeful voice.

"Yes, Halcyon needs a sibling," Rosalie responded smiling.

Reyya agreed to be a donor again and the first try worked. Rosalie was not as tense and perhaps that was the key it worked on the first try. It was obvious that both Reyya and Rosalie were very fertile, which was not the norm among the population. Many women on Sorenia had trouble conceiving. Rosalie was grateful she was pregnant and looked forward to her second child. She told Cooper two children were enough and she did not want a third child.

Her pregnancy was uneventful and she gave birth to a little girl. They named her Celeste, meaning heavenly. Little Celeste was not as big and sturdy as Halcyon had been at birth, but totally healthy. Cooper held her and looked at her with awe. His devotion as a father was no less than a biological father would feel and he loved his children.

Rosalie's mother came over and helped her with the children every day for a few hours and that was all the help Rosalie needed. Cooper was home earlier from work than he used to be and was willing to do any chore around the house. He was very handy and worked fast. Halcyon was already out of diapers and Cooper had toilet trained him. He had endless patience with the children and if they were crying or cranky, he carried them around for hours. Rosalie admired his parental skills and felt lucky to be his wife.

******

On Earth, in two of the Middle East countries there were grumbling men. Both countries had female presidents. There were other countries in the Middle East that were also run by female leaders and some of the men were agitated and felt pushed aside. The countries led by women all flourished with strong economies, equal rights both in the court of law and in society at large. Truth did not set these men free, rather, resentment and a desire to revert to the old male dominated culture drove them and they were increasing in numbers. They formed an underground movement continuously recruiting new members. The governments of the two countries were aware of them, but were biding their time hoping to avoid wars. The Middle East had been at peace for over sixty years and most citizens liked the new modern societies.

The underground had acquired nuclear bombs from a secret stockpile that only a few of the older government members were aware of existed. All nuclear weapons worldwide had been deactivated in 2062. Somehow the underground had found the secret stockpile and seized the bombs with the intention to use them to overthrow the government.

A one-half megaton bomb was set off in one of the two nations in the countryside. The impact on the population was horrible and many people died. The underground claimed responsibility and warned more bombs would be detonated unless the government resigned and turned over leadership to them. In the neighboring country, a bomb was detonated as well.

The governments of the two countries did not back down. Through the media they declared that no terrorist gang would ever succeed in seizing power. The underground replied with another bomb closer to the capital. Neither country had active armed forces, but they had a military reserve, fully trained but with no combat experience. The Reserve was called in and combed the area hoping to find the terrorists to no avail. They had simply vanished. The situation in both countries was the same. The cat and mouse game continued for close to a year and the government members moved to a secret location. The scenario was the same in both countries and the citizens were traumatized by never knowing if another bomb would be set off. The areas where the bombs had exploded were now empty and all the people had been forced to leave their homes and evacuate due to radiation.

The Advisory Board advocated restraint to avoid full scale civil war. The two countries had no intention to solicit military help from neighboring countries fully realizing it could escalate into a large war. The Venusians were involved and working closely with the Board. They knew from experience they were dealing with an elitist force, referred to as fallen beings in the universe, and there was no way to make peace with them. Many planets had been plagued by fallen beings and it had always been difficult to defeat them and return power to the people.

The citizens addressed the terrorists on the Internet and pleaded with them to give up.

"We will never accept you as our leaders no matter how many bombs you drop," a group of people posted.

Huge demonstrations were held outside the capital against the terrorists and the people held banners stating 'you will never rule us' and chanted 'give up and go home'. Perhaps it was the never-ending mass demonstrations by the citizens that finally convinced the terrorists that they would never succeed in taking over their governments and rule the people. After a year of protest from the people the deadlock ended and the extremists simply vanished. The two governments never found out who they were. To their relief, the terrorists had not taken the bombs and they were found in a basement outside the capital in one of the countries and another stash was found in the second country. They were all dismantled by experts from the Reserve and peace in the two countries was restored. The citizens, not the Reserve, had defeated the terrorists without firing a single shot.

The whole world had been watching the Middle East and globally the people were reminded that war was never the solution. Everywhere on Earth people were relieved peace had returned to the Middle East.

******

Atlas and Viola had already been married twelve years. The children were half grown and Melody was eleven years old and Paragonne seven. Melody was very pretty and looked mostly like her mother Reata. Paragonne looked Frejjan, but with some Etteron features. He had light brown hair and was nice looking. Melody did not live up to her name and was not musical, but Paragonne played the violin rather well.

Viola looked younger than her forty-one years, but she had asked Atlas how he would 'age' himself.

"When I'm fifty, you will still look thirty-five. We'll look lopsided, you and I," Viola exclaimed to Atlas.

Atlas laughed and responded -

"It's easy and any robotic mechanic can age me a little. I've seen it done in the workshops on Frejja. It's a minor cosmetic procedure. Nothing needs to be done for ten years, my dear. You don't look a day older than thirty-five."

Viola felt reassured and put her arms around Atlas.

"You're the best husband and father, a treasure. Without you, I would be lost."

"You and the children are the best part of my life, Viola," Atlas responded and held her tight.

The children were doing well in school and Melody had declared she would be 'a doctor like dad' and Paragonne was endlessly playing with various building sets. It was obvious he had mechanical abilities. Viola was still a part time music teacher and liked her job. Once a year she gave a free concert and it was always well attended.

Atlas had recently bought an airmobile and the family often made day trips to the countryside on weekends. Several trips had been to the grasslands and they stayed overnight sleeping under the open sky. They all found the area interesting, but preferred the lush nature around Bliss.

Earth2 was growing fast and the population was thirty thousand citizens. About a hundred people arrived annually from Frejja and immigrants from Etteron continued to arrive. The original agreement to allow one million people from Etteron to settle on Earth2 would take generations to achieve, but when one million Etterons had moved to Earth2, the government would not allow any more people from Etteron.

Several inquiries had been received from Bantizza if immigration was allowed and the government had replied that they would allow a maximum of one hundred thousand people to immigrate and then close immigration from Bantizza. The immigrants would be fully responsible for their own transportation cost and must bring enough funds with them to buy or rent their own housing on Earth2. These new, more harsh rules, had been implemented to prevent excessive immigration. Apparently, the veterinarians who had accompanied the meat animals from Bantizza had fallen in love with Earth2 and spread the word on their home planet and people had become interested in moving to Earth2. There was no limit yet to Frejjan immigration as the government considered Earth2 to be a sister planet to Frejja. Immigrants from Mars and Earth faced the same rules as Bantizza, but only a handful of inquiries had arrived from those two planets. People leaving Mars usually moved to Frejja as they still offered free tickets to immigrants. Veehnia also offered free tickets to immigrants from Earth. The ships continued to travel to Earth and always returned to Veehnia with every seat taken.

Life on Earth2 was simple and old-fashioned compared to Frejja and other advanced planets. People believed in family life and traditional values. Fast living and entertainment were not essential. Spending time in Nature was of great importance and Earth2 was such a beautiful planet and so sparsely populated that anyone could find untouched nature not too far from Bliss. Lakes were everywhere and people who owned an airmobile could easily make day trips to more distant locations. It was this laid-back lifestyle that attracted so many people to the planet in addition to the planet's beauty. No immigrant to Earth2 had regretted moving there and most people felt they had found their roots. The government on Earth2 would never allow unlimited immigration and carefully monitored the impact of the immigrants on quality of life on Earth2. So far, the population was so small that overpopulation would only affect future generations.

Earth2 had paid off the whole debt to Frejja and declared that day to be an annual holiday. More funds were now available and the government was carefully allotting money in order of importance to the project.

Pollox and Lyra had informed the government they could handle the herds of animals themselves and did not need another family to assist them. The oldest son Janus lived in Bliss during the school year as his parents were not able to teach him the more advanced subjects such as math and science, but they picked him up on holidays and in the spring when school was over. The government did not insist and just told Pollox if they needed help, they would get help.

Rasufilus and Akinom felt their children had grown up too fast. Vitzoll was now sixteen years and wanted to be part of his father's fleet. He looked more Morekian than Etteron and was close to his dad. Rasufilus had trained his son to fly his ship and Vitzoll had the same 'feel' for flying as his father had. He quickly mastered flying the ship and declared he wanted to be part of the fleet. Rasufilus knew it would be a hard life and he had hoped his son would choose an easier way to make a living, but Vitzoll could only envision his future life as a member of his father's fleet. Rasufilus had full respect for his son's free will to choose his own lifestyle and promised Vitzoll that once he had graduated from school, he would make him a junior pilot. The first year would have to be as Rasufilus' junior copilot, so he could observe how Vitzoll reacted under pressure and his ability to adapt to various war situations. Rasufilus cautioned him that if he did not live up to the high standards of his fleet, he would be fired. Vitzoll agreed and he knew his father always meant what he said. Rasufilus was now sixty-five years old, but looked younger and he had no intention to retire for at least ten years. He was in good health and full of energy.

Grace, a copy of her mother, was thirteen years old and horse crazy. She spent hours on the Internet watching holographic images of horseback riders and dreamed of having her own horse. She had no interest in competing. The equestrian competitions she had seen on the Internet were fun to watch, but Grace was a loner and wanted a horse for cross country riding and to be one with her horse.

Rasufilus noticed her longing for a horse and a plan took shape in his head. When he lived on Bantizza he had often watched the horses running free on the grass fields. The breed was native to Bantizza and the horses were rather small, only fourteen hands, but with strong legs and large feet and incredible endurance. The horses could carry a rider all day without tiring and were used to living outside all year round. Bantizza had winters and the horses were never stabled.

He requested a meeting with President Ijakull and Telly and made a proposal -

"My daughter is crazy about horses and I must agree it is a noble animal. If we take the seats out of the Tellyship, we could fit thirty horses. Three stallions and the rest mares and that should be enough breeding stock to start a herd. Half of them can be on our land and half on the grasslands. I would ask that one of the horses will be a trained horse for my daughter. Bantizza has the right kind of horse breed to fit here on Earth2, a short, sturdy horse with large feet that is perfect for country riders. They would have to be put into hibernation by the vets on Bantizza and we would wake them up here ourselves. I'm sure many here on Earth2 would love to own a horse."

Both Telly and the president were smiling and nodded as Rasufilus presented his case.

"I love the idea," the president said. "Earth2 is made for horses and the government will pay for them and the fuel for the ship. There are not enough animals on our planet and horses would be a welcome addition to Earth2. If you arrange the deal, we'll pay for it."

"I also like the idea," Telly said. "I have never seen a live horse, only on the Internet, but to have a herd of horses living on our planet would be just right. Inquire if they have a horse trainer willing to move here. He could train the horses as people are buying them and also teach a few of our people to train horses. It wouldn't be bad to have someone on the ship who knows horses to keep an eye on them during transit."

Rasufilus made all the arrangements and Bantizza asked a lower price than he had anticipated. They had a young trainer, Berrill, willing to move to Earth2 and he agreed to travel with the horses. Rasufilus bought one fully trained mare for Grace and also twenty saddles and bridles, halters and some other stable equipment. The trainer was guiding him and suggested the equipment he would need. Rasufilus hired him to teach Grace how to ride.

The four pilots who always flew the Tellyship took off for Bantizza with the money to pay for the horses and equipment. It was only a three months' travel time.

Six months later they returned. In the meantime, Rasufilus and Vitzoll had built a small barn and a corral for Grace's horse. The horse would live mostly outside, but to have a barn and be able to bring the horse in during the worst of the winter had been recommended by Berrill. Rasufilus and his men all had five acres of land and their little town was spread out. The rest of their land was open.

The ship landed on Rasufilus' land and Berrill came out. Bantizza people were fully human looking with the exception of their eyes, which were strangely shiny, almost looking like flashlights. Other than that, they looked exactly like Frejjans. Berrill turned out to be a happy-go-lucky guy with a quick laugh and a warm handshake, handsome and in his mid-twenties. He had lived around horses his whole life and could not imagine a life without them. To live on Earth2 had been a dream of his ever since he heard the vets, who delivered the meat animals, describe the beauty of the planet. With just enough money in his pocket to rent a room somewhere he felt he could get by until he had a steady job as a horse trainer.

"I'll wake up half the horses and your daughter's horse and unload them and then the ship will take the rest of the horses to your grasslands. I'll leave the grassland horses asleep until we get to that area," Berrill said to Rasufilus using a translation device. Rasufilus had lived on Bantizza, but never learned the language as he did not want to stay there permanently. Berrill could only speak the Bantizza language, but during the three months' travel time he had studied Frejjan for hours every day and hoped to speak the language within a few months. He also intended to learn how to read and write Frejjan as soon as possible.

One stallion and thirteen mares were unloaded and they were all very skinny from losing weight during transit, but they appeared otherwise to be in good health. Rasufilus and his men led one horse each down the ramp and walked them to the end of their town Rasunom. Rasufilus' land Bavonilla had several thousand acres for the horses to roam on with ample grass and water. The horses belonged to the government, but would eventually be sold and the money returned to the government.

Berrill had a big smile on his face and turned to Grace and said -

"This lady is yours, Grace. I selected her myself and she is only four years old, but fully trained and rock solid. She doesn't spook easy and she has a heart of gold. Her name is Ylja and she knows her name. I'll teach you how to ride her. We start tomorrow."

Grace was overwhelmed and just kept on patting Ylja. She and Vitzoll led the mare to the corral that had been prepared for her behind Rasufilus' house and the rest of the horses were turned free on the Bavonilla land. The beauty of the land was awesome with rolling hills, green grass and deciduous trees. A stream with crystal clear water ran through it.

"I have never seen a more beautiful piece of land. Wow, you sure are lucky," Berrill said as he looked around.

Rasufilus and his men boarded the Tellyship and the ship took off to the grasslands. They unloaded the horses a long distance away from the meat animals. Eventually they would probably run into each other, but the horses would most likely avoid the meat animals. The ship was barely soiled as the horses had been asleep the whole journey. The horse equipment was stored in a government warehouse in Bliss until it was needed.

Pollox had been informed that horses would be unloaded on the grasslands and asked to keep an eye on them.

The Tellyship returned to Bliss and Vitzoll waited for them with their groundmobile. Rasufilus had invited Berrill to stay with them until Grace could handle her horse alone and Berrill had gratefully accepted. Akinom greeted Berrill and wished him welcome. She had prepared their guest room for him and announced dinner would be ready in ten minutes.

The next month Berrill taught Grace horsemanship. He did not allow Grace to ride until the mare had recovered from the trip and gained a few pounds. After two weeks of almost nonstop eating, Ylja was ready and Berrill saddled her up. Grace had natural balance and learned fast. One of Ylja's gaits was a running walk in addition to a standard trot and she could 'run' for hours without tiring. Berrill brought one of the mares in from the field that he knew was trained and saddled her up. He knew Grace was ready for cross country riding and he wanted her to be able to handle Ylja all by herself before school started in the fall. The rest of the summer he worked hard to teach Grace how to handle her horse in all situations and after a month Berrill's work was done. He was confident Grace had learned enough and the rest she would learn just by riding Ylja and taking care of her. Berrill had refused payment for teaching Grace how to ride.

He had read about how Rasufilus liberated his people on Bantizza thirty years ago and saved them from a full dictatorship. It was taught in school. Now the planet was a democracy and the people were free. Berrill had great admiration for Rasufilus.

Rasufilus and his family had become very fond of Berrill and Rasufilus invited him to spend weekends with them any time he needed to get away from Bliss.

"You don't need a special invitation," Rasufilus said to Berrill. "Just show up, you're always welcome in our house."

Berrill was grateful and shook hands with them and gave Grace a hug. He had a job waiting for him in Bliss at the mint and he had rented a small apartment in town. His employer had agreed to give him time off any time he had to train a horse as long as he returned when the training was finished. Earth2 had granted Berrill citizenship.

Berrill gave his best at the mint and was appreciated by his employer. In the fall, the first horse was sold and he took the time he needed to train the horse and rider and then returned to work. He often worked overtime and never charged for it, a fact his employer noticed. The process of making coins fascinated him and he involved himself in all facets of the coin production, eventually becoming very good at his work. His employer told him he had employment for life, if he wanted to, and Berrill responded he loved his job. His dream was to have a horse ranch and breed and train horses, but with his limited funds he knew he would probably never be able to afford to realize his dream.

Berrill was artistic and while at home he sketched a new coin with a galloping horse on one side and the opposite side featured a horse head. The magnificence of the horse came through in both of the sketches and he made the two sketches also in a mini size for the engraver to copy. He showed it to his boss and asked if there was any interest to create a new coin celebrating the horses now living on Earth2. To his surprise his boss loved the sketches and bought them paying Berrill a hefty sum for them. The engraver would start right away working on the dies, he said. Berrill refused payment at first, but his employer knew he was strapped for cash and convinced him to accept the payment. Berrill gratefully shook hands with his boss. When the new coin was in circulation everyone admired it.

Grace lived for her horse. She raced out early in the morning to spend time with Ylja before school and after school she ran home to ride her. Ylja learned her routine after a while and would be waiting to see Grace come running full speed. Both of them loved their rides and Grace rode her horse with a simple rubber bit that Ylja seemed to like chewing on. Grace had featherlight hands and Ylja never feared the bit. They understood each other perfectly. When Ylja lay down in the grass, Grace would lie down with her head on the mare's neck and her arms around her. Her family would look from the house and they all laughed. The scene was endearing. Rasufilus was glad he had approached the government and suggested they introduce horses to the planet.

******

In the year of 2188, prosperity and peace were abundant on the known planets in the universe and the people on these planets lived without fear of their governments. Members of the government showed respect for the citizens and worked for the people, not for themselves, and they were all term limited. None of the known planets was controlled by a dictatorship.

The Moon colony was prosperous and Mars was known as the most affluent planet in the universe. Its citizens lived comfortable lives with short work weeks, no taxes and most services free. They had everything except the outdoors and an oxygen atmosphere, but most Martians did not consider the outdoors important. They loved their easy lives on Mars.

Frejja was a wonderful and easy planet to live on and very popular. Its pet planet Earth2 was considered the most beautiful planet known and attracted people looking for an old-fashioned lifestyle with traditional values.

Ljeviina and Ziggellus had almost finished rebuilding and Ziggellus was now a truly peaceful planet with a new mindset.

Sorenia had morphed into a modern planet under the leadership of Cooper and was on a fast track to becoming a great planet to live on with modern amenities increasing all the time. The planet still had a long way to go before it would reach the affluence of Earth, for example, and would have to endure growing pains to reach a high standard of living. Nevertheless, it was a planet with a great future.

All the other known planets were also doing well with no severe problems. Arrynia was no longer a matriarchy. Veehnia was thriving with people from Earth 'waking up' the laid-back citizens on the planet. Morekia, Kodetsia and Bantizza were now democracies with good economies and free citizens.

Peturun, Etteron and Mineata were prosperous and peaceful. Etteron was still slightly overpopulated, but with continued emigration to Earth2 the problem would eventually go away. Humbrus was a peaceful planet as well. Gangsters born on Humbrus and caught in the universe would face a firing squad if they were returned to their home planet. Humbrus showed no mercy whatsoever with any former citizens shaming their planet. They took pride in their civilized society with high morals and ethics.

The common denominator for these planets was that the citizens were free and had no fear of their governments. No planet can thrive under the yoke of tyranny and a planet run by a dictatorship has no innovations and no prosperity.

Earth had emerged from a full global collapse with tremendous loss of people to a peaceful planet without wars and with governments running their countries according to the wishes of the citizens. It had taken a long time for planet Earth to overcome all its problems, but it had now entered the Golden Era.